big
NATE
GREAT MINDS THINK ALIKE

More

big NATE

adventures from

LINCOLN PEIRCE

Novels:

Big Nate: In a Class by Himself

Big Nate Strikes Again

Big Nate On a Roll

Big Nate Goes for Broke

Big Nate Flips Out

Big Nate: In the Zone

Activity Books:

Big Nate Boredom Buster

Big Nate Fun Blaster

Big Nate Doodlepalooza

Comic Compilations:

Big Nate From the Top

Big Nate Out Loud

Big Nate and Friends

Big Nate: What Could Possibly Go Wrong?

Big Nate: Here Goes Nothing

Big Nate Makes the Grade

Big Nate All Work and No Play

Big Nate Game On!

Big Nate: Genius Mode

Big Nate: I Can't Take It!

Big Nate: Mr. Popularity

big NATE

GREAT MINDS THINK ALIKE

by LINCOLN PEIRCE

Andrews McMeel
Publishing®

Kansas City • Sydney • London

Big Nate is distributed internationally by Universal Uclick.

Big Nate: Great Minds Think Alike copyright © 2014 by United Feature Syndicate, Inc. All rights reserved. Printed in China. No part of this book may be used or reproduced in any manner whatsoever without written permission except in the case of reprints in the context of reviews.

Andrews McMeel Publishing, LLC
an Andrews McMeel Universal company
1130 Walnut Street, Kansas City, Missouri 64106

www.andrewsmcmeel.com

14 15 16 17 18 SDB 10 9 8 7 6 5 4 3 2 1

ISBN: 978-1-4494-3635-3

Library of Congress Control Number: 2013944315

Made by:
Shenzhen Donnelley Printing Company Ltd.
Address and place of production:
No.47, Wuhe Nan Road, Bantian Ind. Zone,
Shenzhen China, 518129
1st Printing - 1/13/14

Big Nate can be viewed on the Internet at
www.comics.com/big_nate

ATTENTION: SCHOOLS AND BUSINESSES
Andrews McMeel books are available at quantity discounts with bulk purchase for educational, business, or sales promotional use. For information, please e-mail the Andrews McMeel Publishing Special Sales Department:
specialsales@amuniversal.com

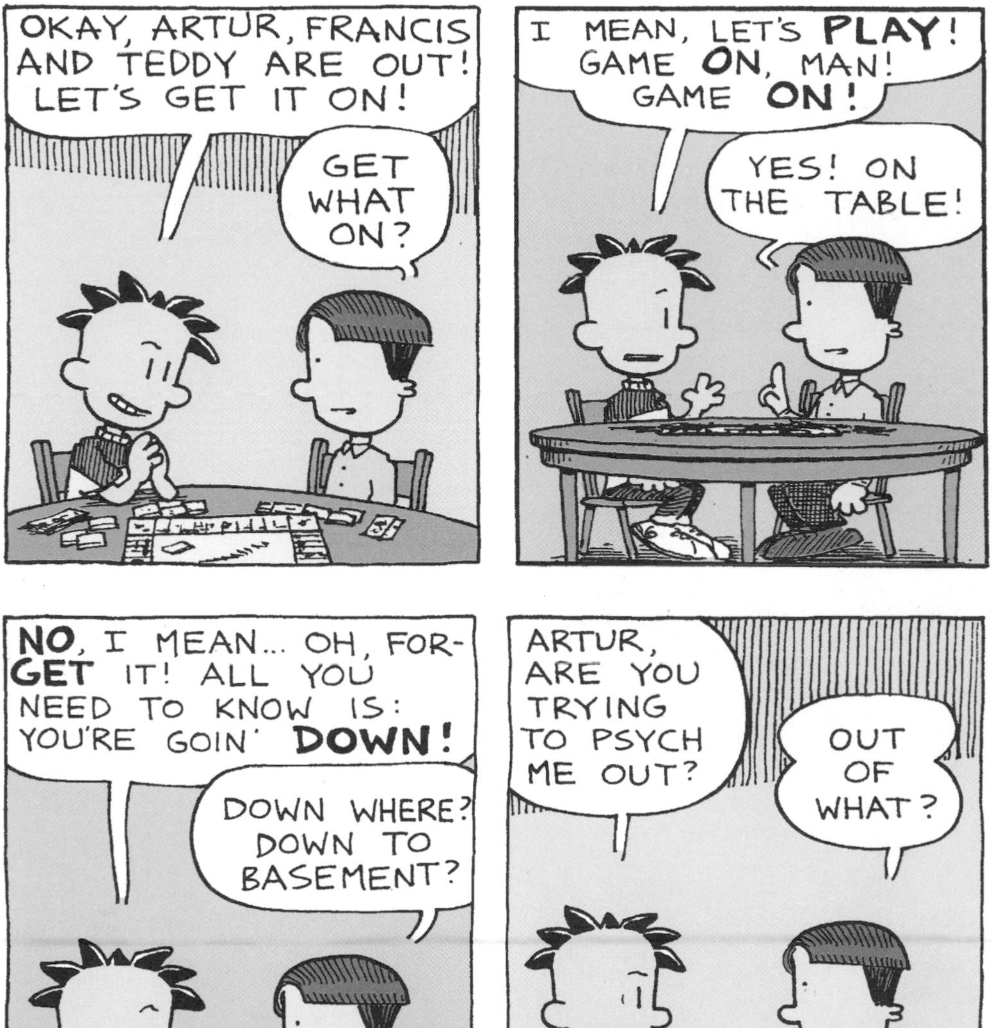
OKAY, ARTUR, FRANCIS AND TEDDY ARE OUT! LET'S GET IT ON!
GET WHAT ON?
I MEAN, LET'S PLAY! GAME ON, MAN! GAME ON!
YES! ON THE TABLE!
NO, I MEAN... OH, FOR-GET IT! ALL YOU NEED TO KNOW IS: YOU'RE GOIN' DOWN!
DOWN WHERE? DOWN TO BASEMENT?
ARTUR, ARE YOU TRYING TO PSYCH ME OUT?
OUT OF WHAT?
peirce

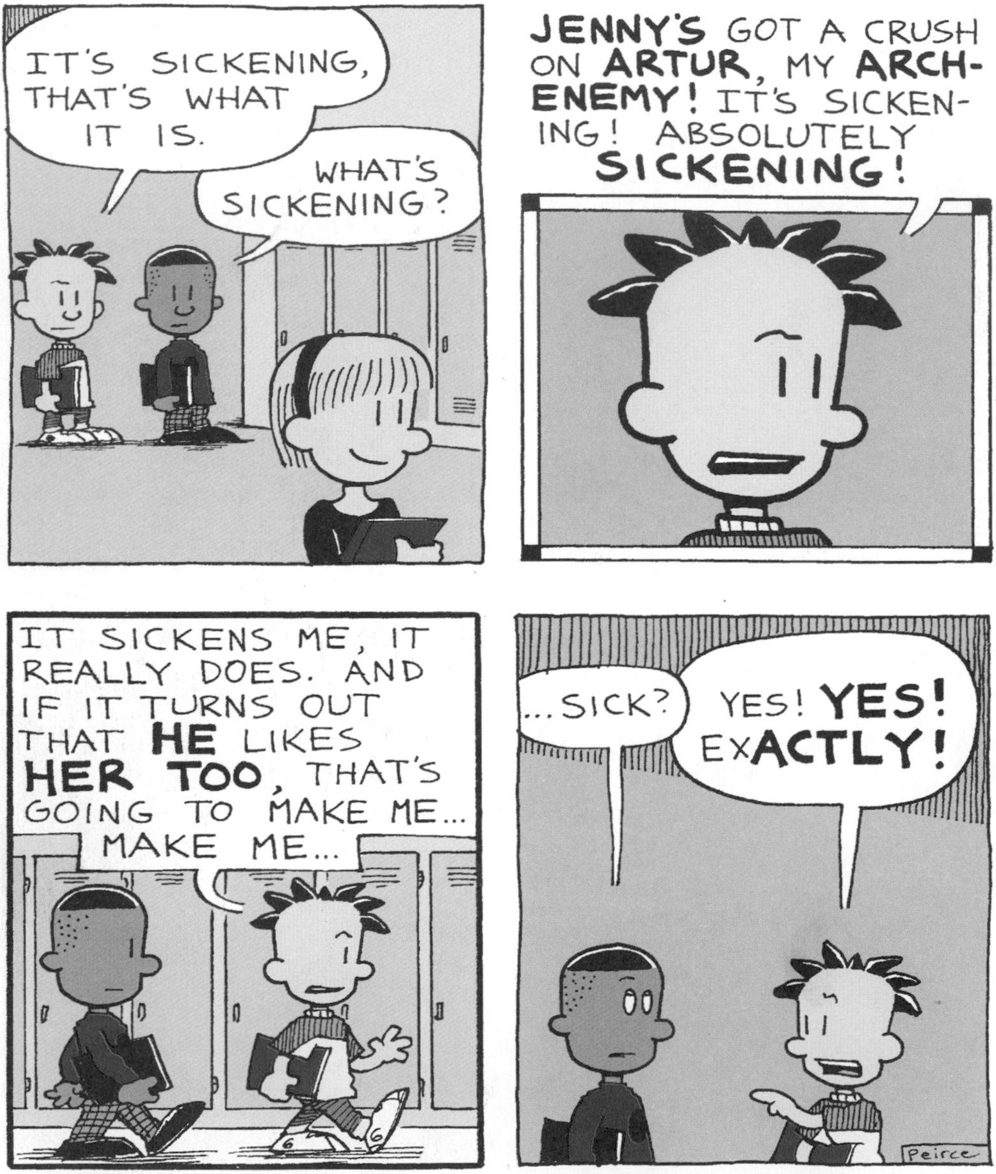
IT'S SICKENING, THAT'S WHAT IT IS.
WHAT'S SICKENING?
JENNY'S GOT A CRUSH ON ARTUR, MY ARCH-ENEMY! IT'S SICKENING! ABSOLUTELY SICKENING!
IT SICKENS ME, IT REALLY DOES. AND IF IT TURNS OUT THAT HE LIKES HER TOO, THAT'S GOING TO MAKE ME... MAKE ME...
...SICK?
YES! YES! EXACTLY!
Peirce

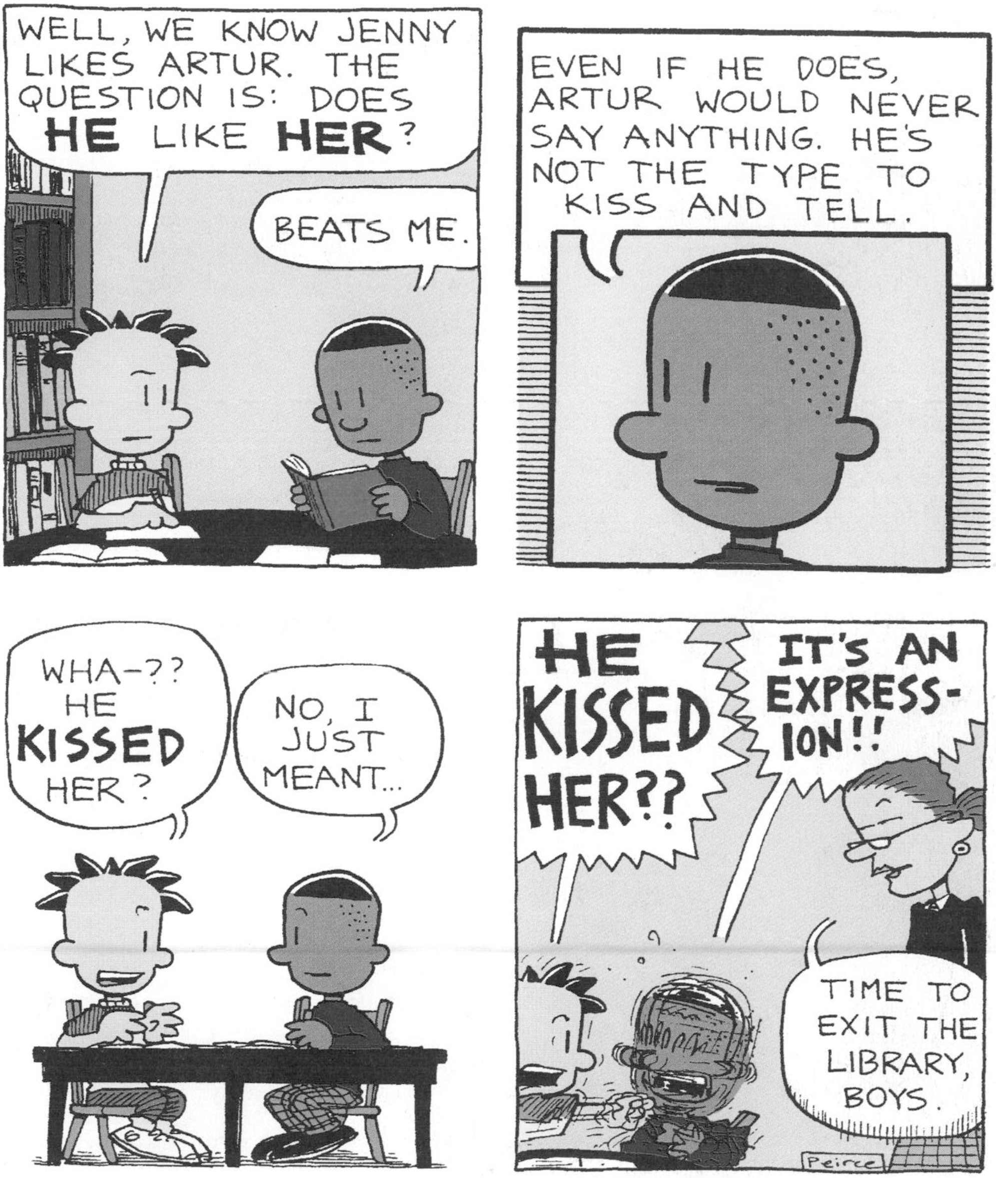

WELL, WE KNOW JENNY LIKES ARTUR. THE QUESTION IS: DOES **HE** LIKE **HER**?
BEATS ME.
EVEN IF HE DOES, ARTUR WOULD NEVER SAY ANYTHING. HE'S NOT THE TYPE TO KISS AND TELL.
WHA-?? HE **KISSED** HER?
NO, I JUST MEANT...
HE KISSED HER??
IT'S AN EXPRESS-ION!!
TIME TO EXIT THE LIBRARY, BOYS.
Peirce

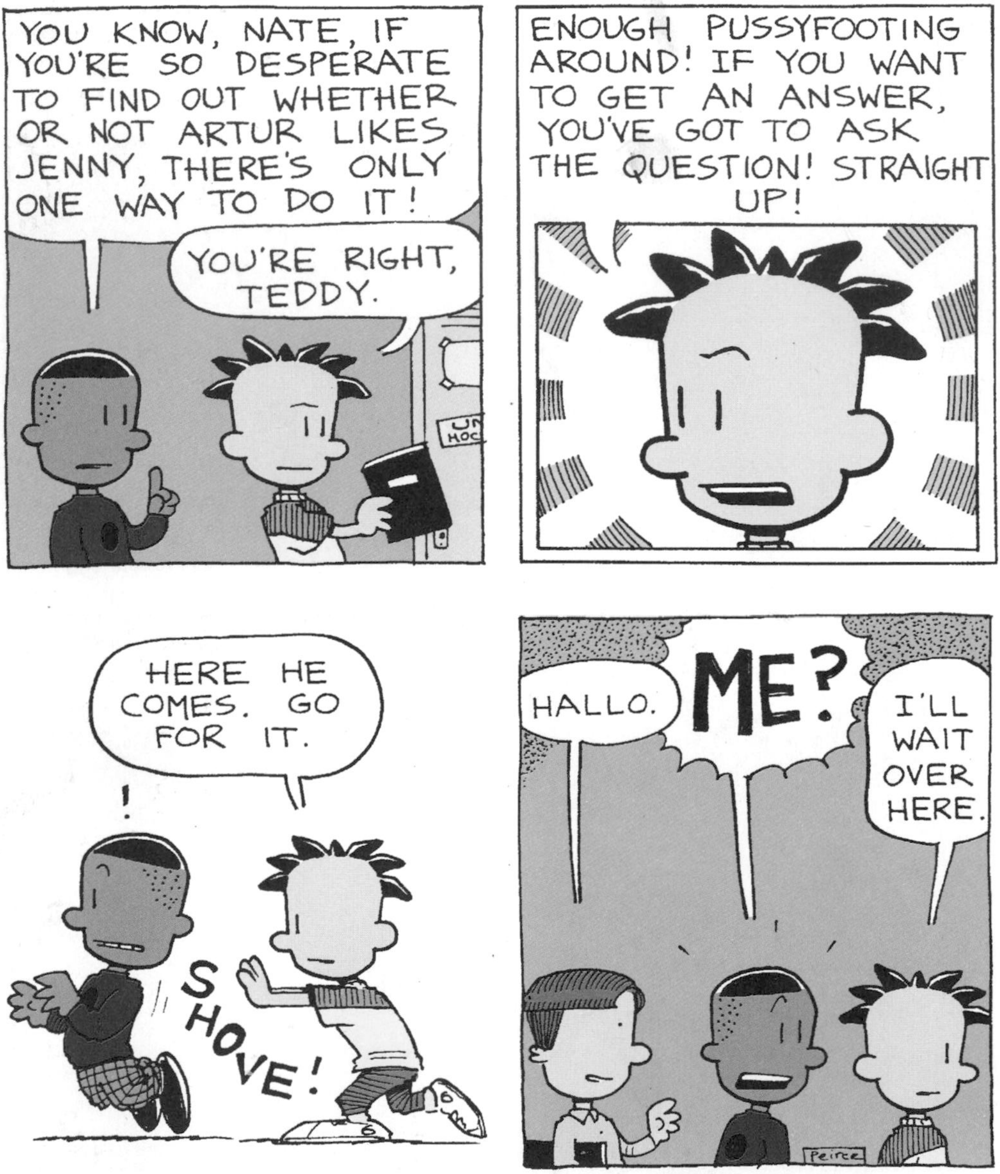
YOU KNOW, NATE, IF YOU'RE SO DESPERATE TO FIND OUT WHETHER OR NOT ARTUR LIKES JENNY, THERE'S ONLY ONE WAY TO DO IT!
YOU'RE RIGHT, TEDDY.
ENOUGH PUSSYFOOTING AROUND! IF YOU WANT TO GET AN ANSWER, YOU'VE GOT TO ASK THE QUESTION! STRAIGHT UP!
HERE HE COMES. GO FOR IT.
!
SHOVE!
HALLO.
ME?
I'LL WAIT OVER HERE.
Peirce

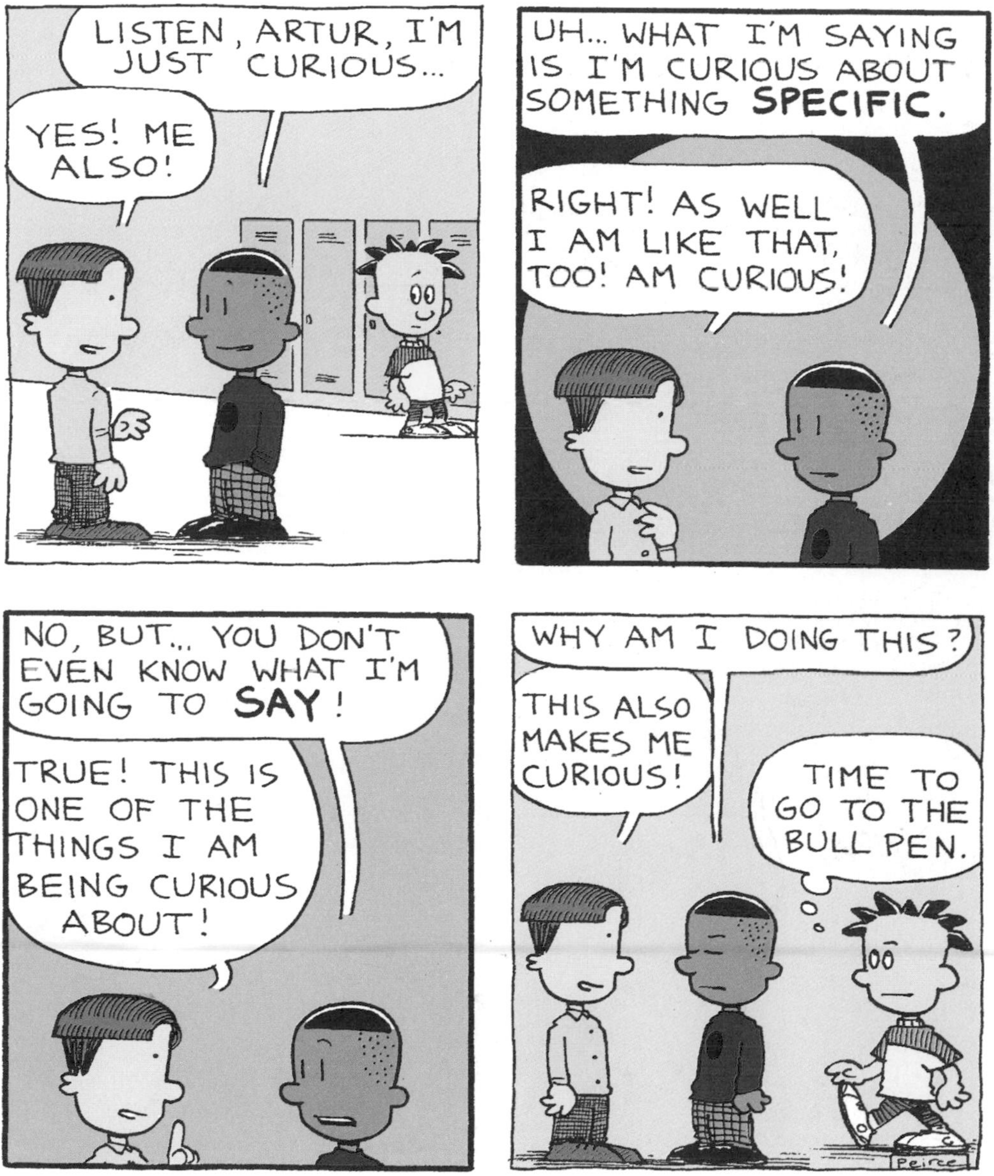
LISTEN, ARTUR, I'M JUST CURIOUS...
YES! ME ALSO!
UH... WHAT I'M SAYING IS I'M CURIOUS ABOUT SOMETHING **SPECIFIC**.
RIGHT! AS WELL I AM LIKE THAT, TOO! AM CURIOUS!
NO, BUT... YOU DON'T EVEN KNOW WHAT I'M GOING TO **SAY**!
TRUE! THIS IS ONE OF THE THINGS I AM BEING CURIOUS ABOUT!
WHY AM I DOING THIS?
THIS ALSO MAKES ME CURIOUS!
TIME TO GO TO THE BULL PEN.
Peirce

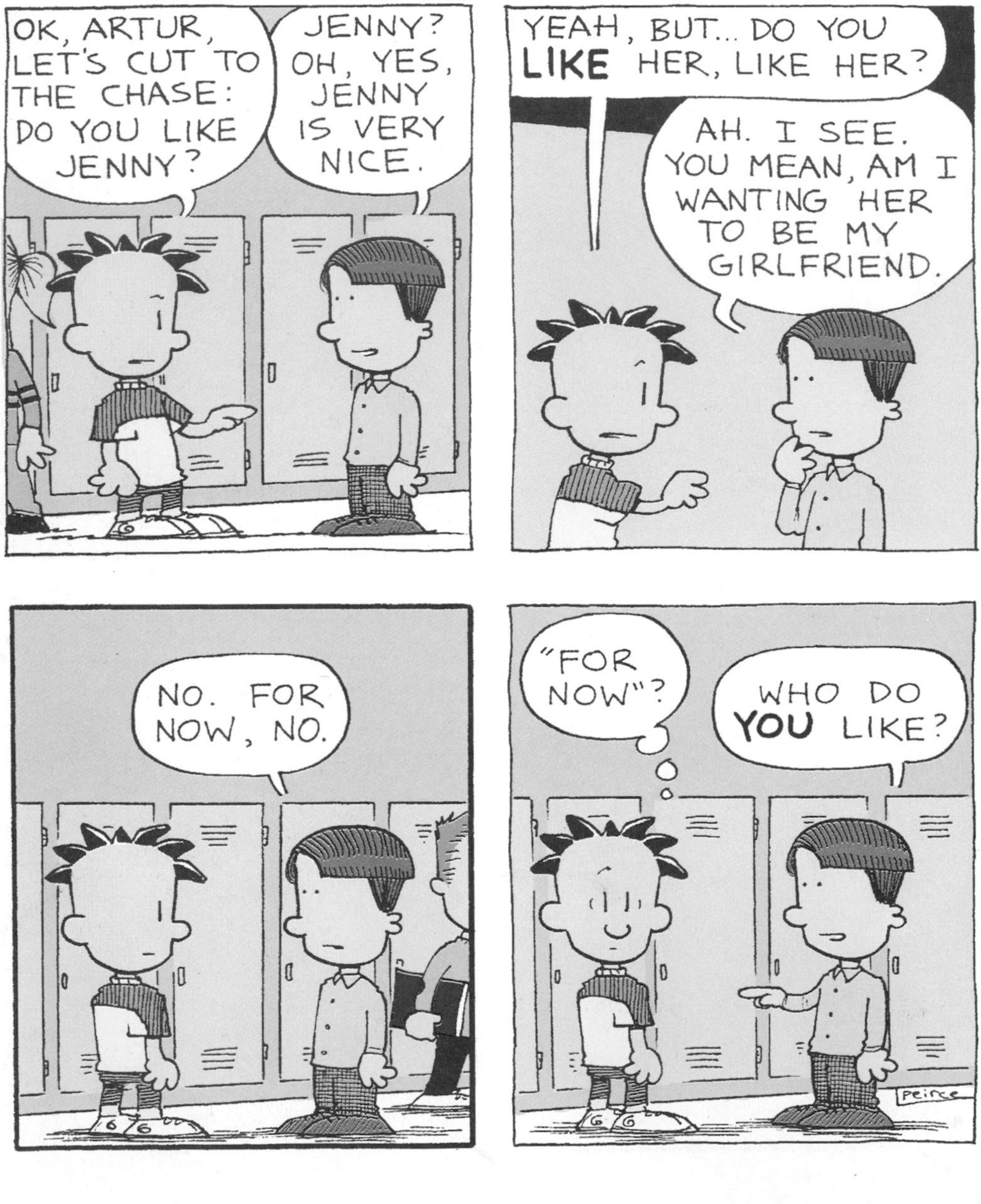
OK, ARTUR, LET'S CUT TO THE CHASE: DO YOU LIKE JENNY?
JENNY? OH, YES, JENNY IS VERY NICE.
YEAH, BUT... DO YOU **LIKE** HER, LIKE HER?
AH. I SEE. YOU MEAN, AM I WANTING HER TO BE MY GIRLFRIEND.
NO. FOR NOW, NO.
"FOR NOW"?
WHO DO **YOU** LIKE?
PEIRCE

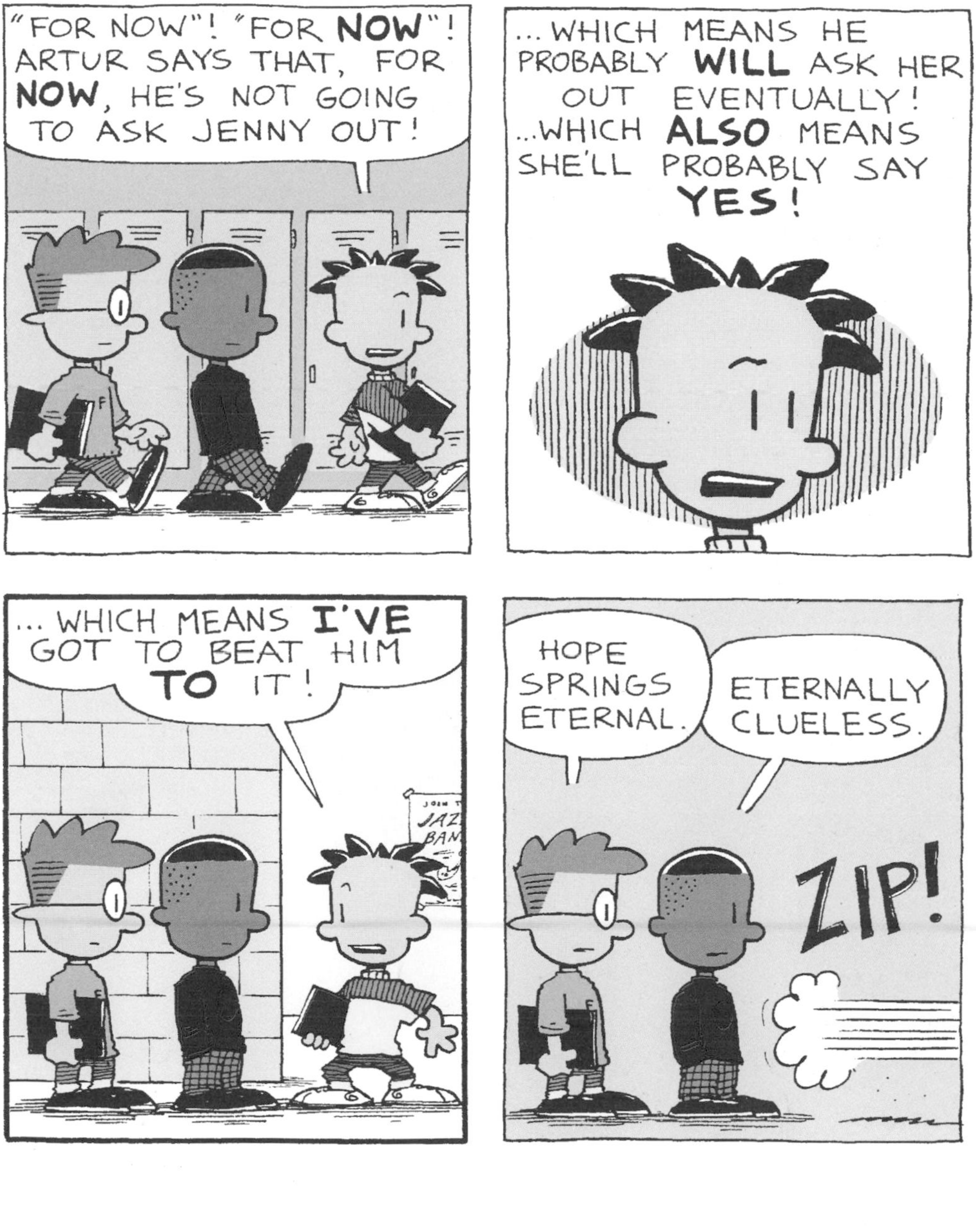
"FOR NOW"! "FOR NOW"! ARTUR SAYS THAT, FOR NOW, HE'S NOT GOING TO ASK JENNY OUT!
...WHICH MEANS HE PROBABLY WILL ASK HER OUT EVENTUALLY! ...WHICH ALSO MEANS SHE'LL PROBABLY SAY YES!
...WHICH MEANS I'VE GOT TO BEAT HIM TO IT!
HOPE SPRINGS ETERNAL.
ETERNALLY CLUELESS.
ZIP!

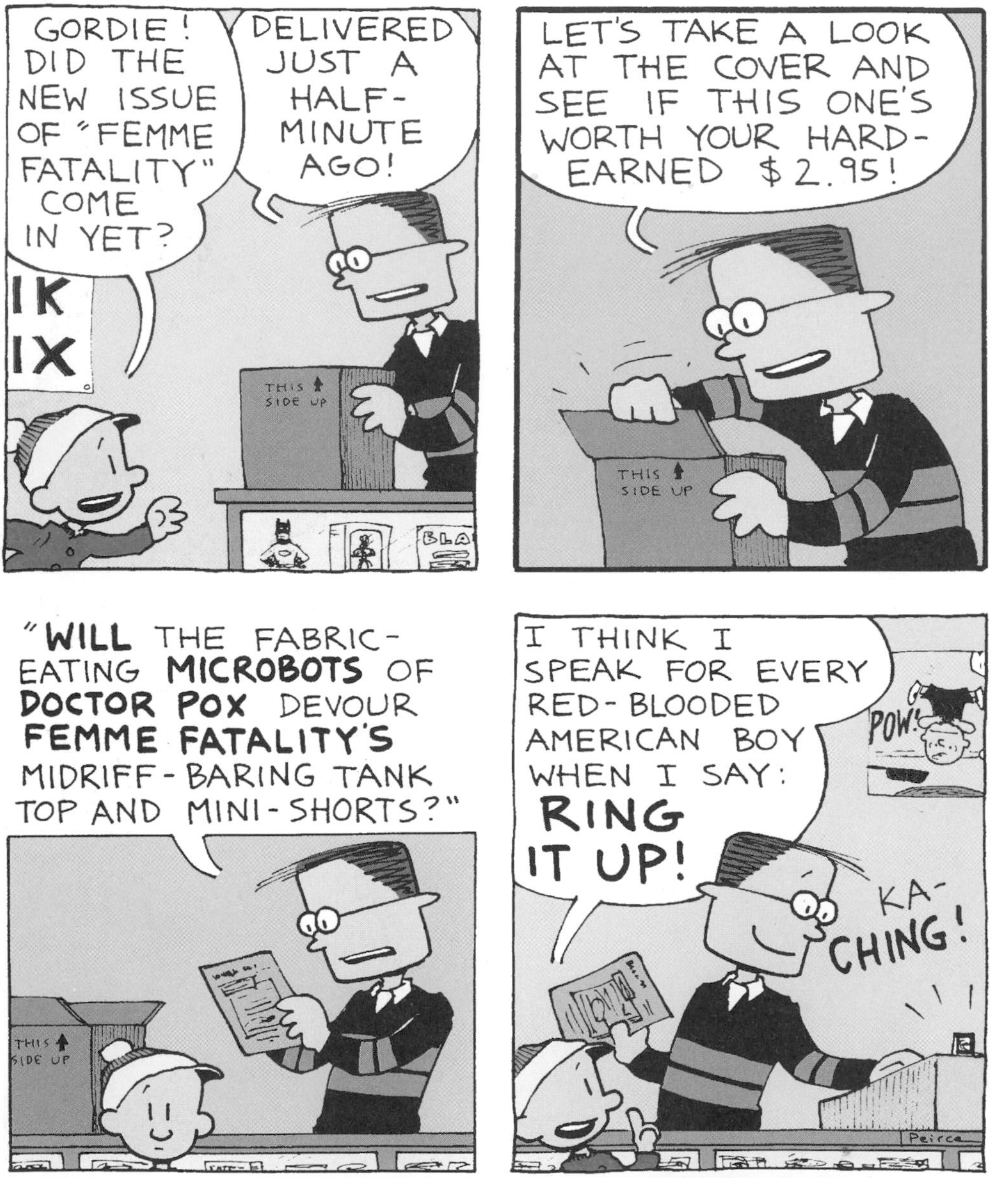
GORDIE! DID THE NEW ISSUE OF "FEMME FATALITY" COME IN YET?
DELIVERED JUST A HALF-MINUTE AGO!
IK
IX
THIS SIDE UP
LET'S TAKE A LOOK AT THE COVER AND SEE IF THIS ONE'S WORTH YOUR HARD-EARNED $2.95!
THIS SIDE UP
"**WILL** THE FABRIC-EATING **MICROBOTS** OF **DOCTOR POX** DEVOUR **FEMME FATALITY'S** MIDRIFF-BARING TANK TOP AND MINI-SHORTS?"
THIS SIDE UP
I THINK I SPEAK FOR EVERY RED-BLOODED AMERICAN BOY WHEN I SAY: **RING IT UP!**
POW!
KA-CHING!
Peirce

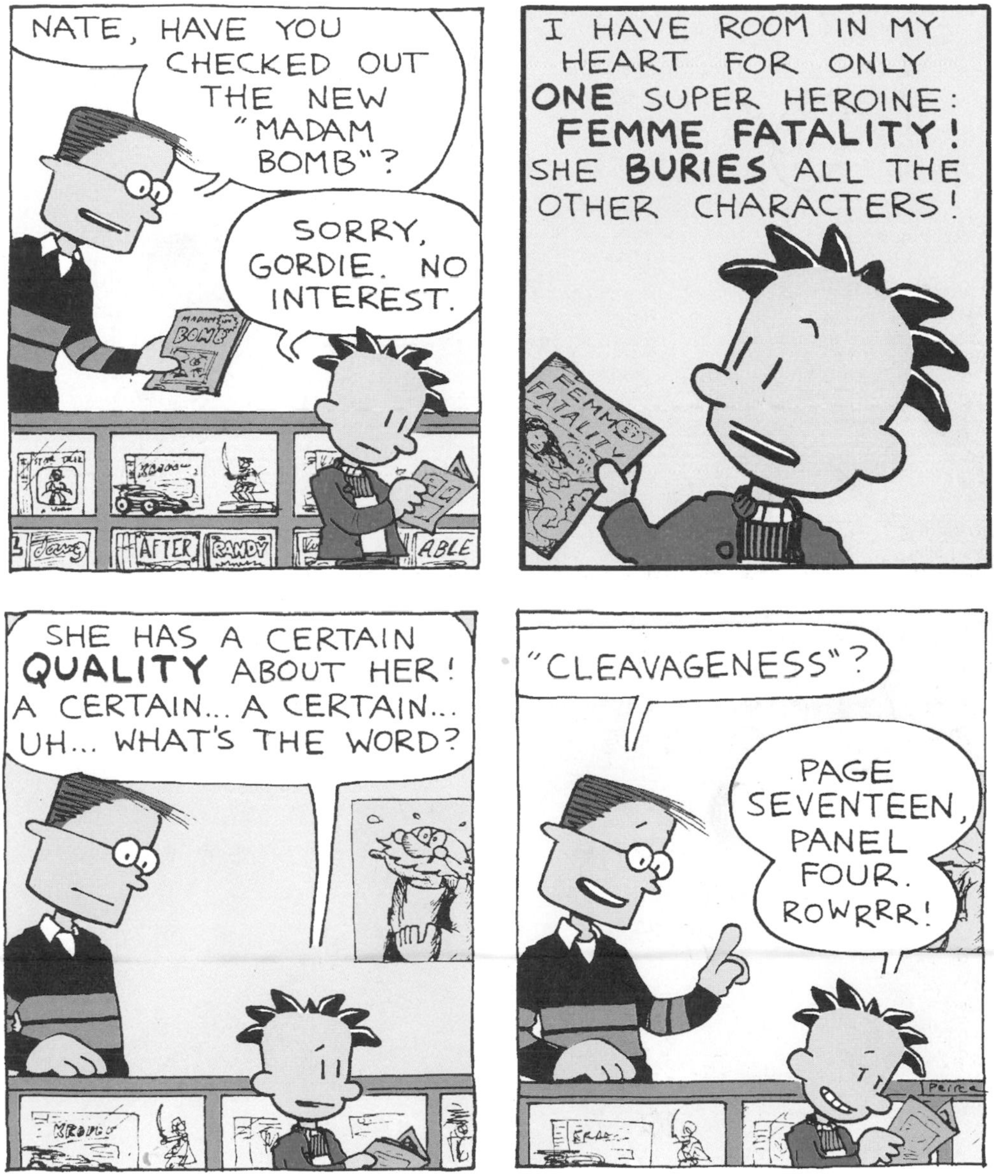
NATE, HAVE YOU CHECKED OUT THE NEW "MADAM BOMB"?
SORRY, GORDIE. NO INTEREST.
I HAVE ROOM IN MY HEART FOR ONLY ONE SUPER HEROINE: FEMME FATALITY! SHE BURIES ALL THE OTHER CHARACTERS!
SHE HAS A CERTAIN QUALITY ABOUT HER! A CERTAIN... A CERTAIN... UH... WHAT'S THE WORD?
"CLEAVAGENESS"?
PAGE SEVENTEEN, PANEL FOUR. ROWRRR!

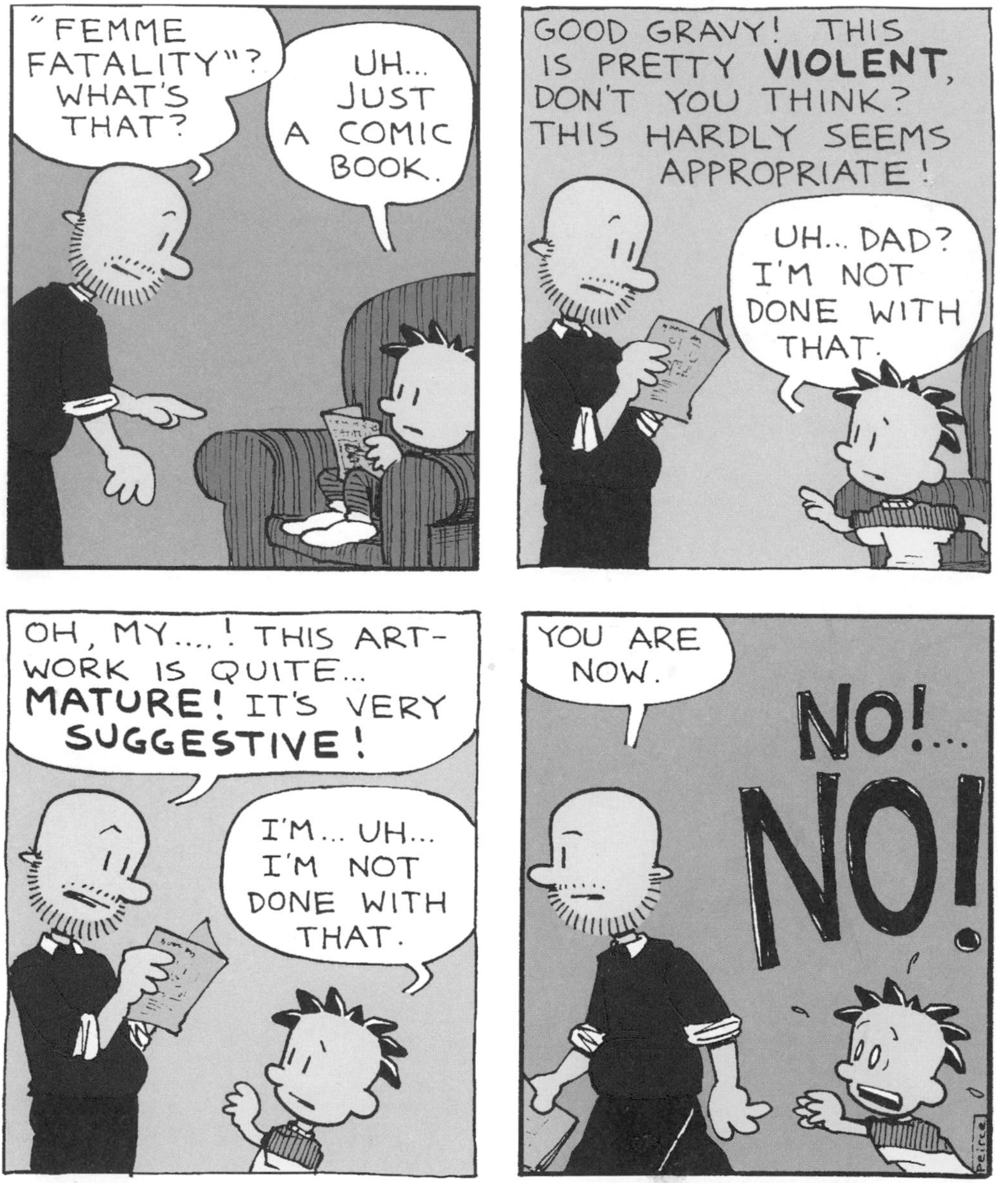
"FEMME FATALITY"? WHAT'S THAT?
UH... JUST A COMIC BOOK.
GOOD GRAVY! THIS IS PRETTY **VIOLENT**, DON'T YOU THINK? THIS HARDLY SEEMS APPROPRIATE!
UH... DAD? I'M NOT DONE WITH THAT.
OH, MY....! THIS ART-WORK IS QUITE... **MATURE!** IT'S VERY **SUGGESTIVE!**
I'M... UH... I'M NOT DONE WITH THAT.
YOU ARE NOW.
NO!... NO!
Peirce

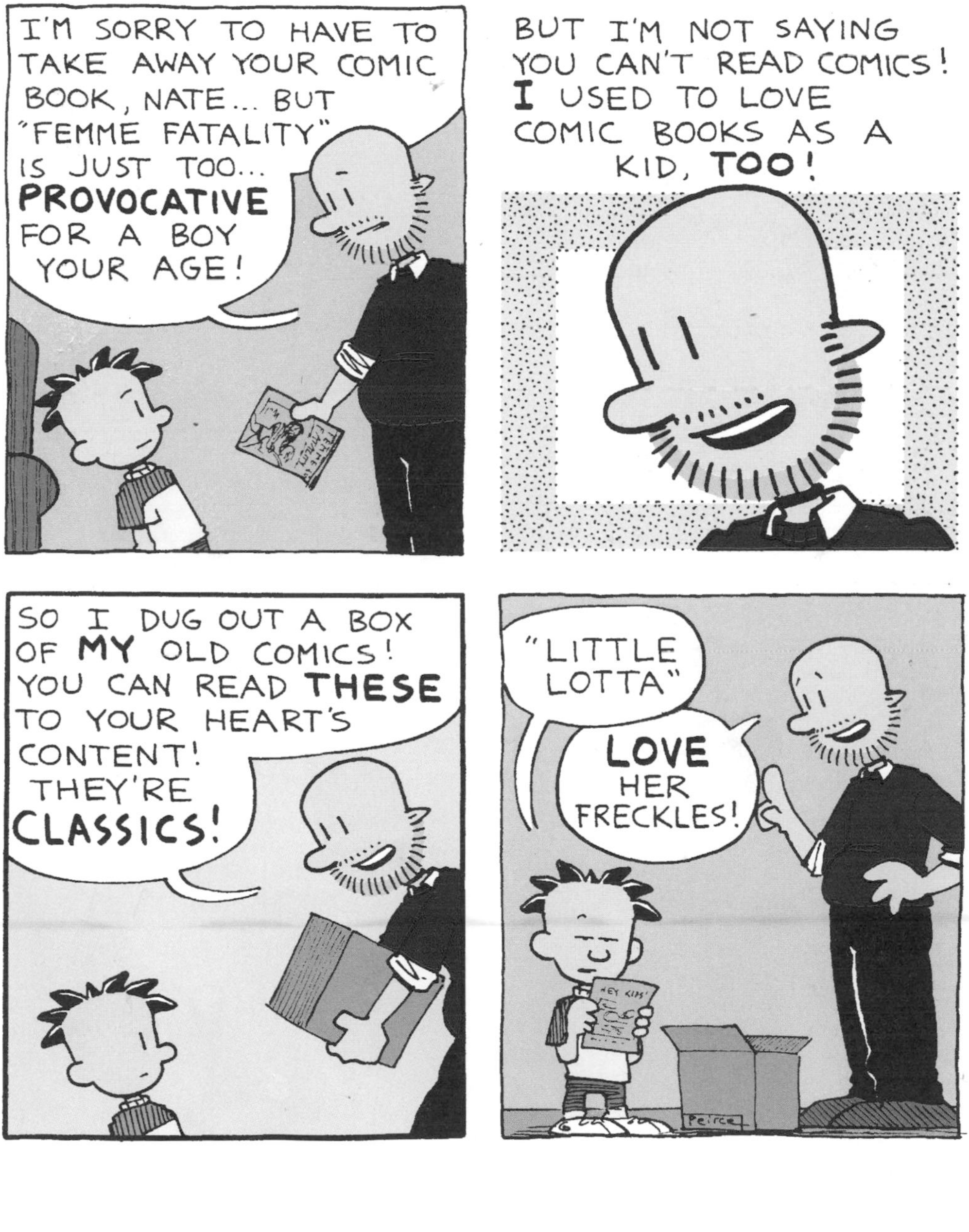
I'M SORRY TO HAVE TO TAKE AWAY YOUR COMIC BOOK, NATE... BUT "FEMME FATALITY" IS JUST TOO... PROVOCATIVE FOR A BOY YOUR AGE!
BUT I'M NOT SAYING YOU CAN'T READ COMICS! I USED TO LOVE COMIC BOOKS AS A KID, TOO!
SO I DUG OUT A BOX OF MY OLD COMICS! YOU CAN READ THESE TO YOUR HEART'S CONTENT! THEY'RE CLASSICS!
"LITTLE LOTTA"
LOVE HER FRECKLES!
Peirce

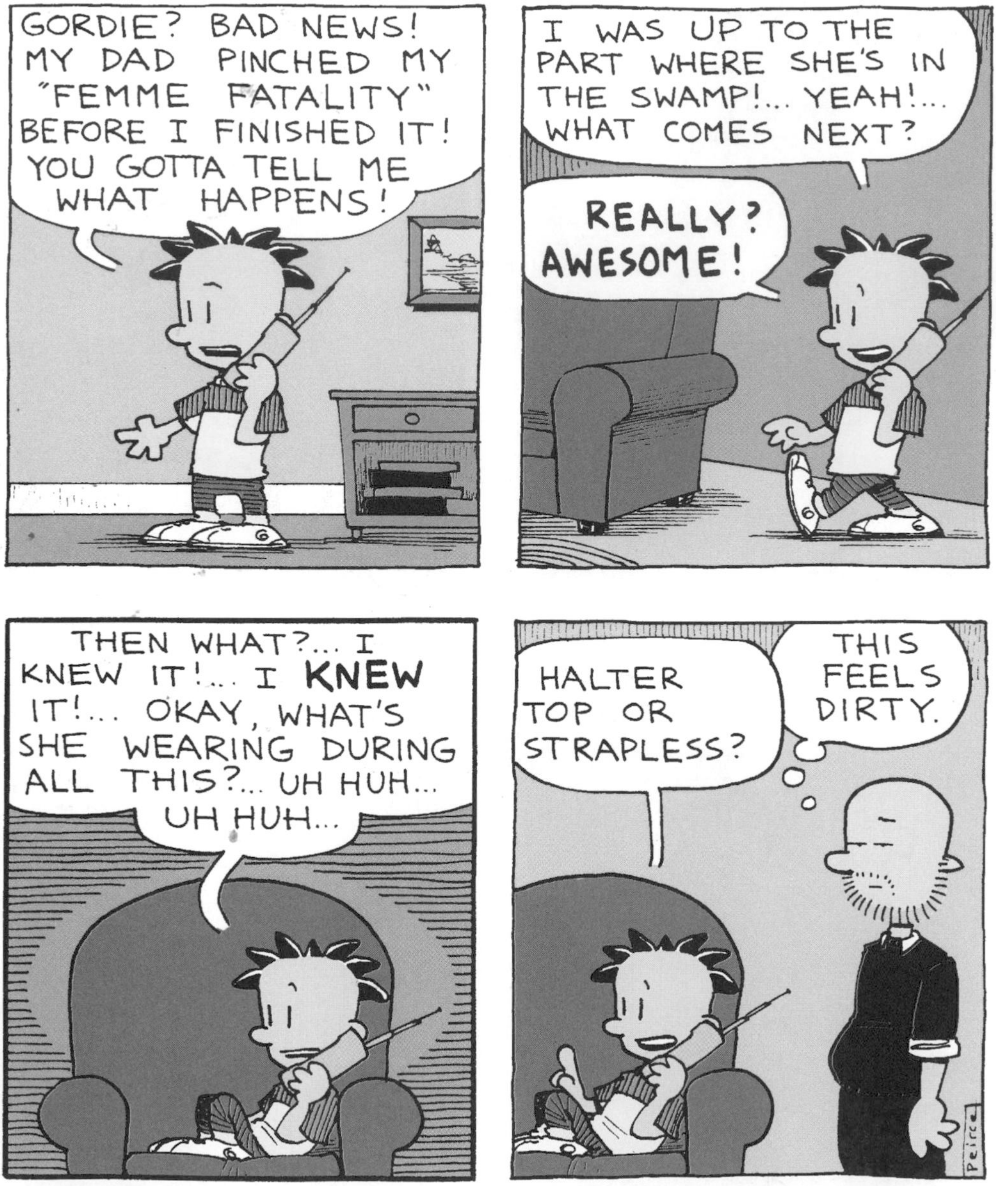
GORDIE? BAD NEWS! MY DAD PINCHED MY "FEMME FATALITY" BEFORE I FINISHED IT! YOU GOTTA TELL ME WHAT HAPPENS!
I WAS UP TO THE PART WHERE SHE'S IN THE SWAMP!... YEAH!... WHAT COMES NEXT?
REALLY? AWESOME!
THEN WHAT?... I KNEW IT!... I **KNEW** IT!... OKAY, WHAT'S SHE WEARING DURING ALL THIS?... UH HUH... UH HUH...
HALTER TOP OR STRAPLESS?
THIS FEELS DIRTY.
Peirce

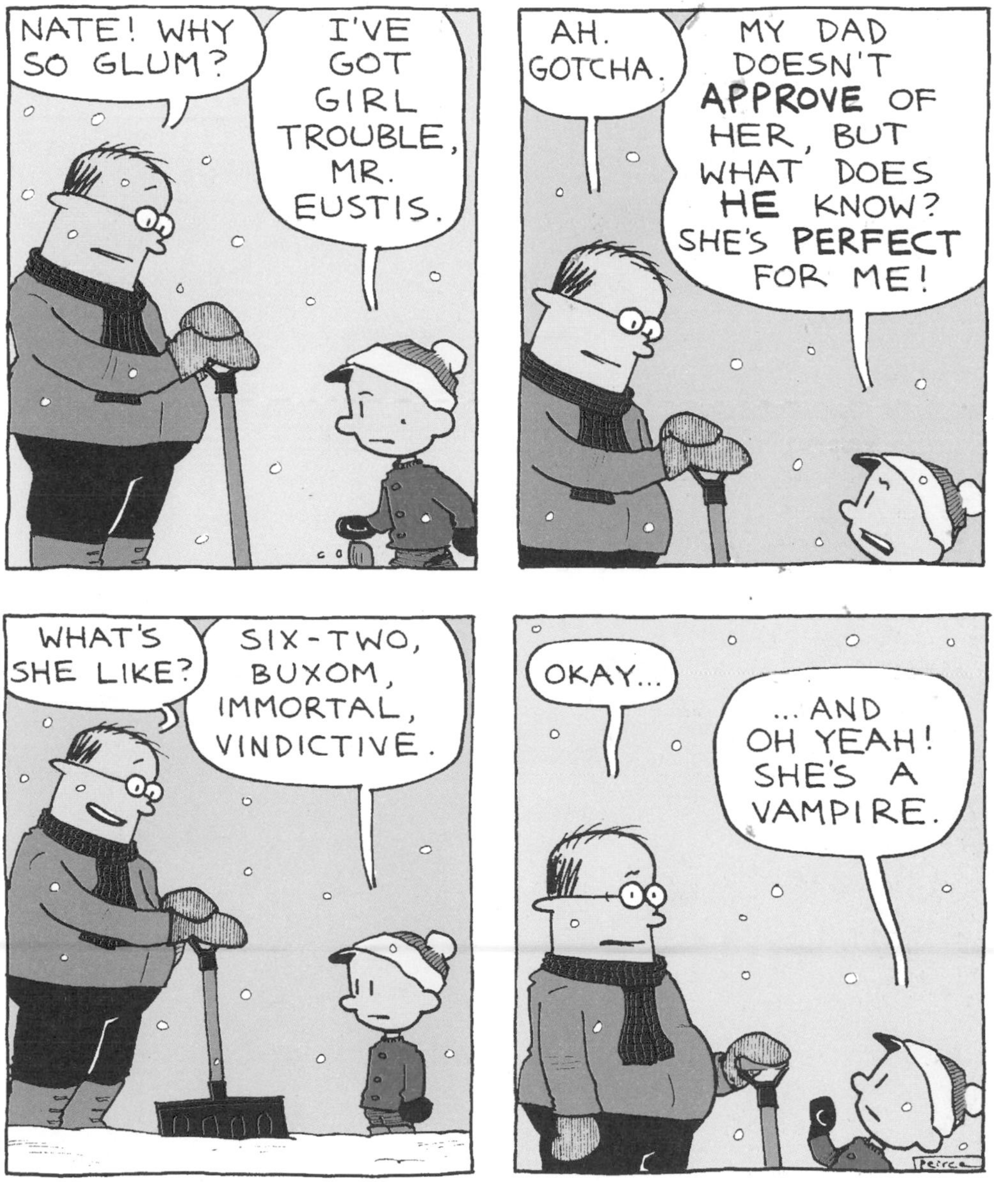
NATE! WHY SO GLUM?
I'VE GOT GIRL TROUBLE, MR. EUSTIS.
AH. GOTCHA.
MY DAD DOESN'T **APPROVE** OF HER, BUT WHAT DOES **HE** KNOW? SHE'S **PERFECT** FOR ME!
WHAT'S SHE LIKE?
SIX-TWO, BUXOM, IMMORTAL, VINDICTIVE.
OKAY...
...AND OH YEAH! SHE'S A VAMPIRE.
Peirce

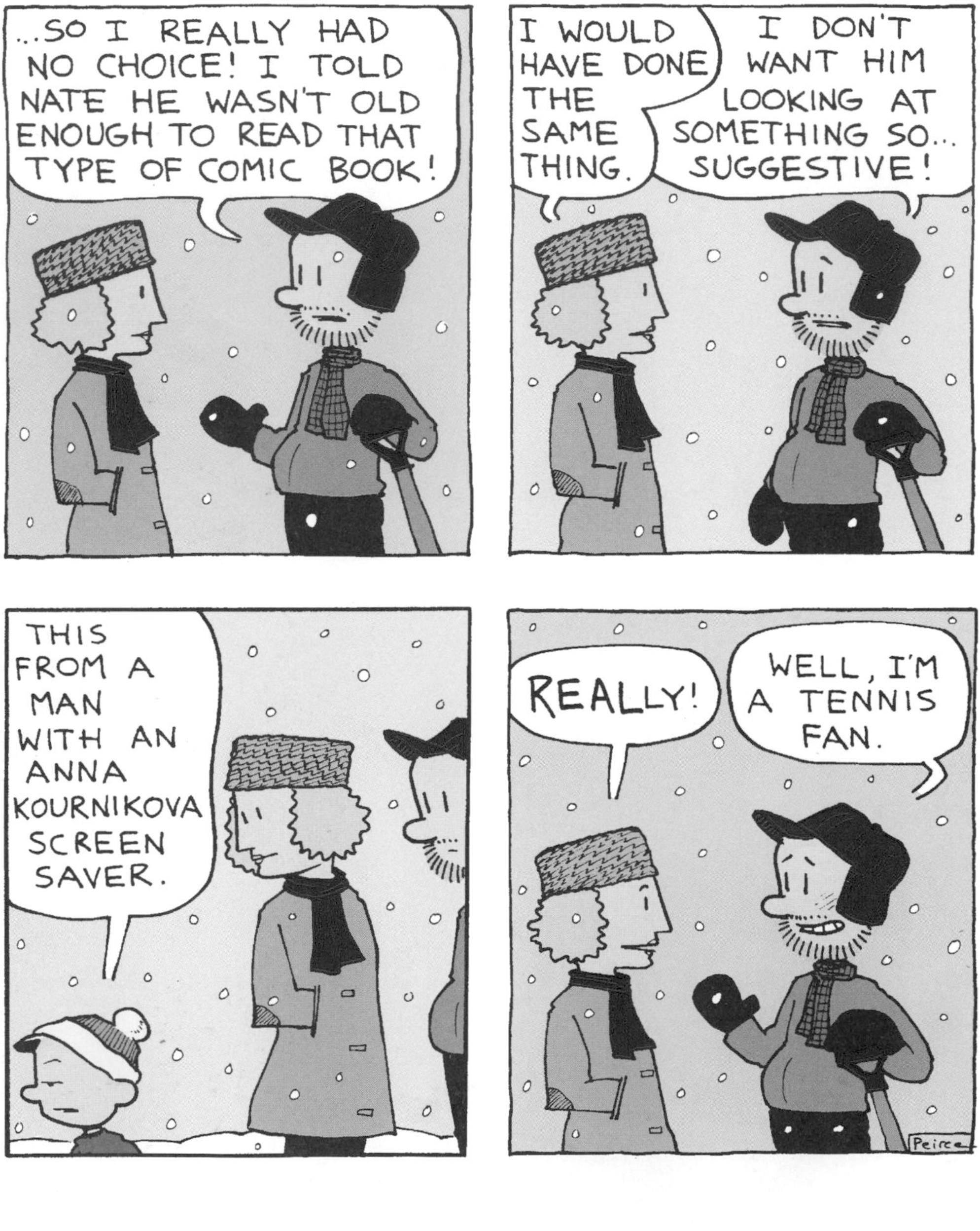
...SO I REALLY HAD NO CHOICE! I TOLD NATE HE WASN'T OLD ENOUGH TO READ THAT TYPE OF COMIC BOOK!
I WOULD HAVE DONE THE SAME THING.
I DON'T WANT HIM LOOKING AT SOMETHING SO... SUGGESTIVE!
THIS FROM A MAN WITH AN ANNA KOURNIKOVA SCREEN SAVER.
REALLY!
WELL, I'M A TENNIS FAN.
Peirce

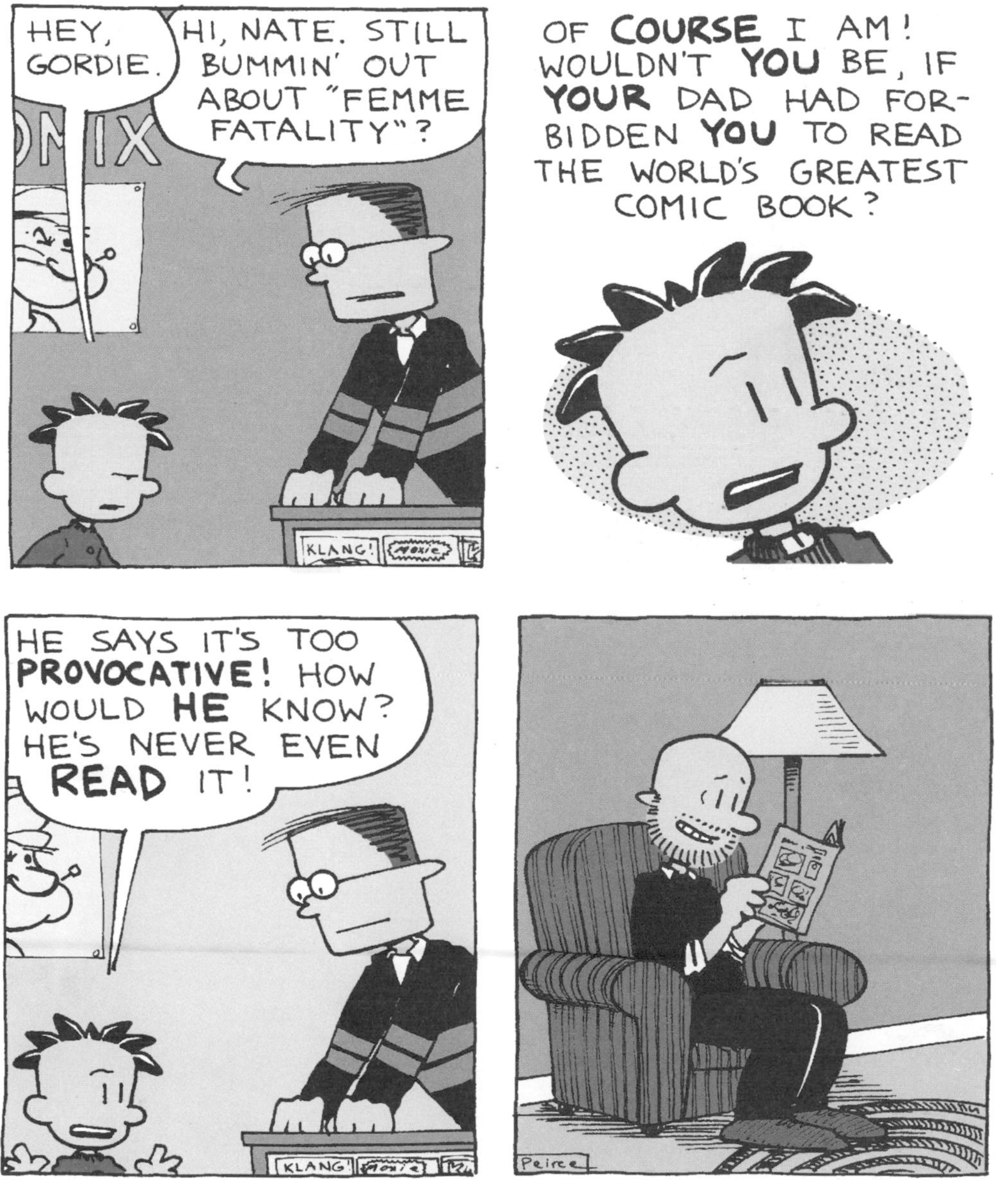
HEY, GORDIE.
HI, NATE. STILL BUMMIN' OUT ABOUT "FEMME FATALITY"?
OF COURSE I AM! WOULDN'T YOU BE, IF YOUR DAD HAD FORBIDDEN YOU TO READ THE WORLD'S GREATEST COMIC BOOK?
HE SAYS IT'S TOO PROVOCATIVE! HOW WOULD HE KNOW? HE'S NEVER EVEN READ IT!
Peirce

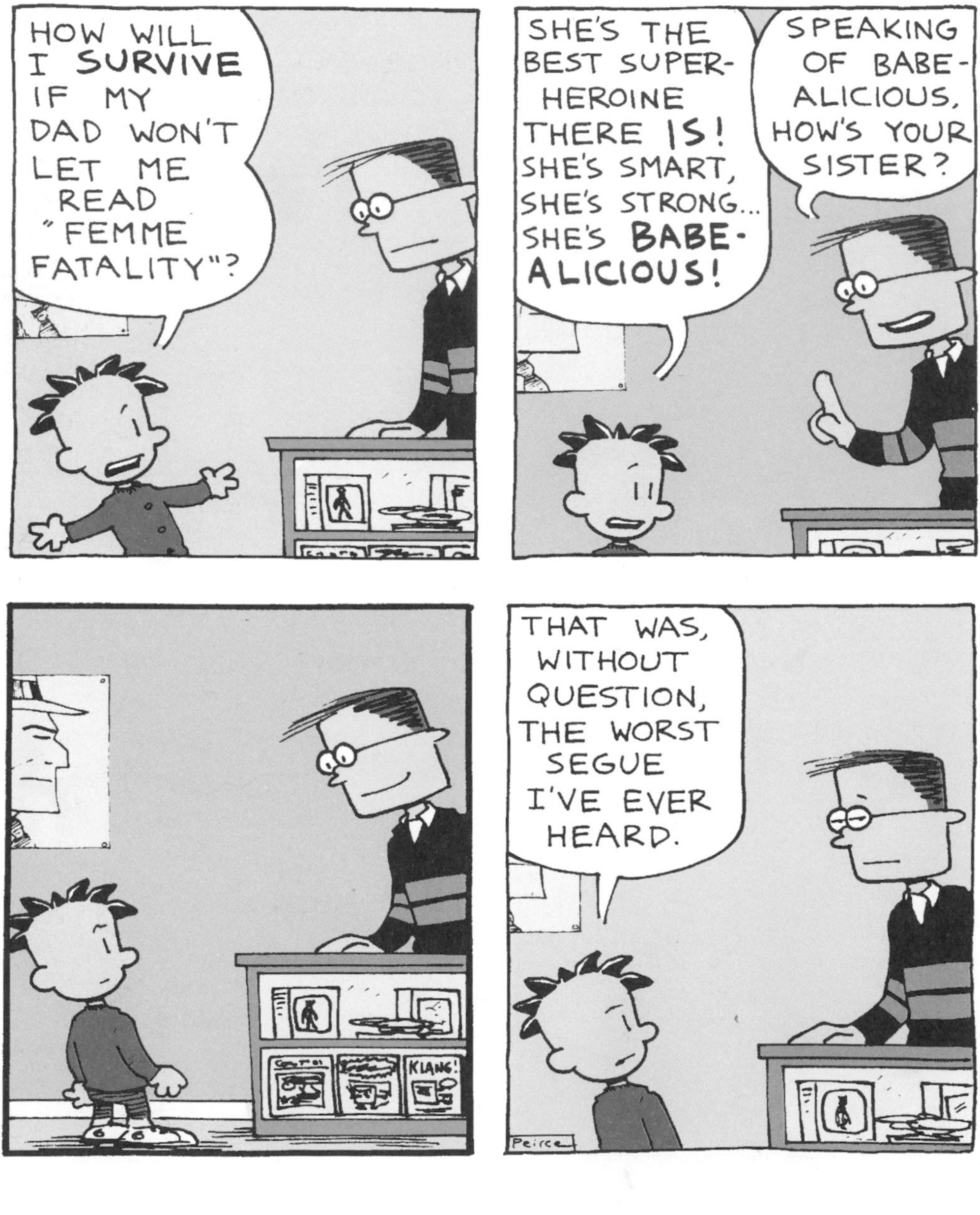
HOW WILL I SURVIVE IF MY DAD WON'T LET ME READ "FEMME FATALITY"?
SHE'S THE BEST SUPER-HEROINE THERE IS! SHE'S SMART, SHE'S STRONG... SHE'S BABE-ALICIOUS!
SPEAKING OF BABE-ALICIOUS, HOW'S YOUR SISTER?
KLANG!
THAT WAS, WITHOUT QUESTION, THE WORST SEGUE I'VE EVER HEARD.
Peirce

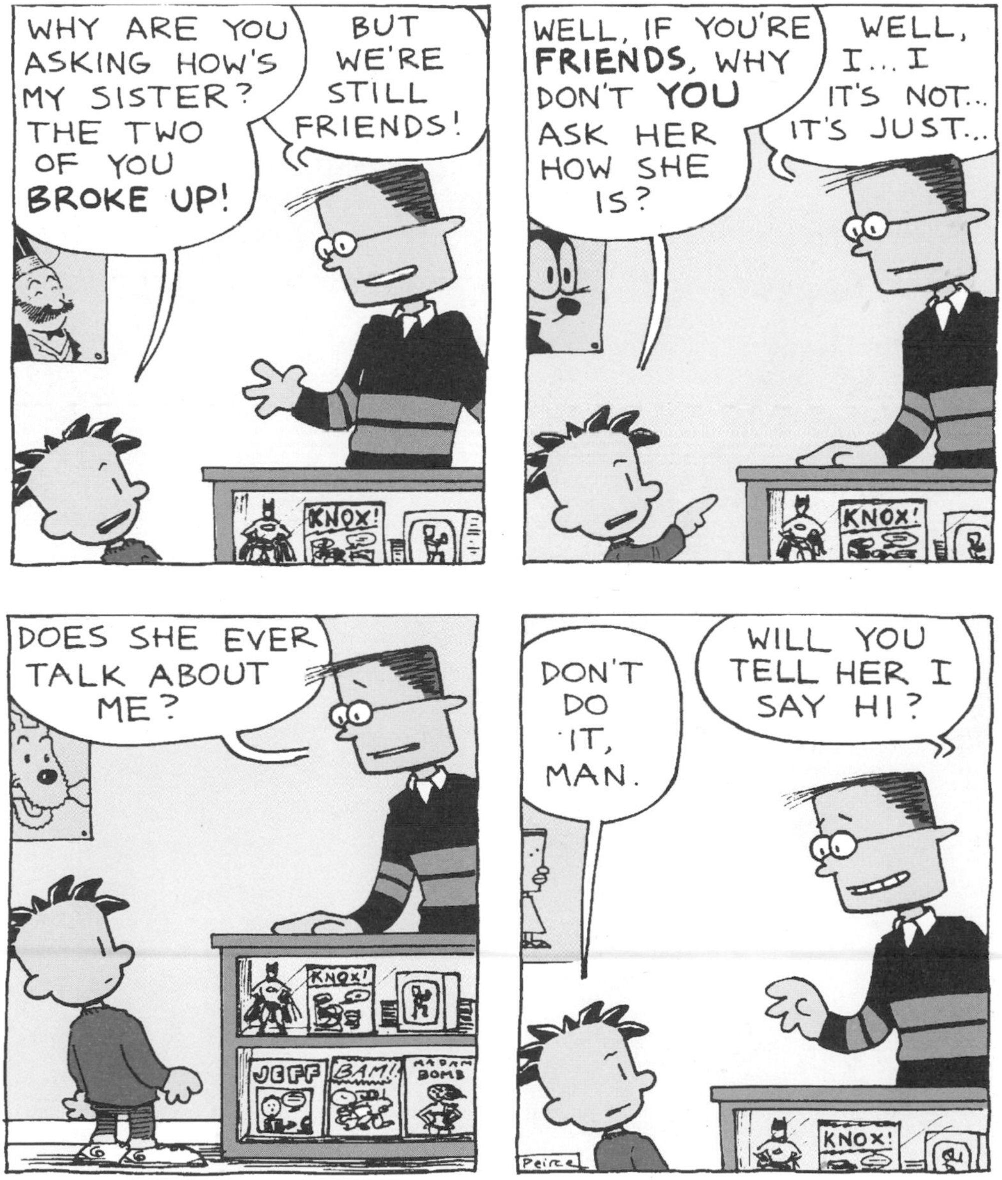
WHY ARE YOU ASKING HOW'S MY SISTER? THE TWO OF YOU **BROKE UP**!
BUT WE'RE STILL FRIENDS!
KNOX!
WELL, IF YOU'RE **FRIENDS**, WHY DON'T **YOU** ASK HER HOW SHE IS?
WELL, I... I IT'S NOT... IT'S JUST...
KNOX!
DOES SHE EVER TALK ABOUT ME?
KNOX!
JEFF
BAM!
MADAM BOMB
DON'T DO IT, MAN.
WILL YOU TELL HER I SAY HI?
KNOX!
Peirce

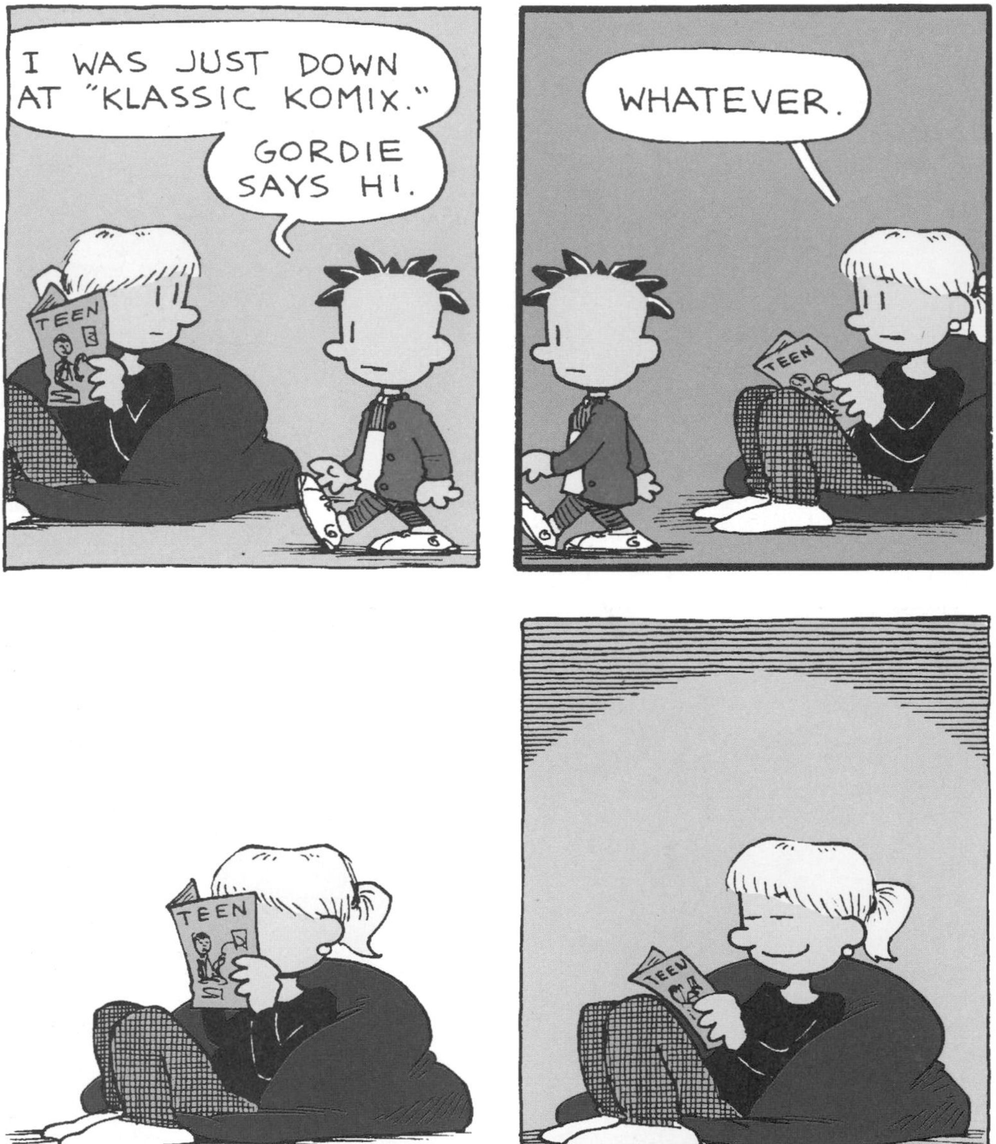
I WAS JUST DOWN AT "KLASSIC KOMIX."
GORDIE SAYS HI.
WHATEVER.
TEEN
TEEN
TEEN
TEEN
Peirce

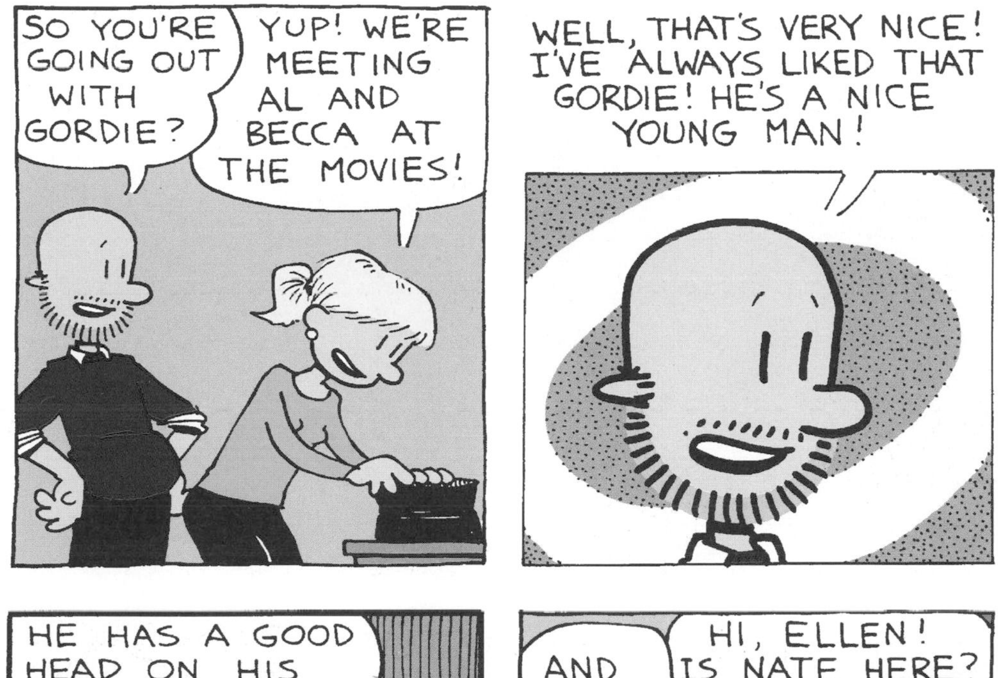
SO YOU'RE GOING OUT WITH GORDIE?
YUP! WE'RE MEETING AL AND BECCA AT THE MOVIES!
WELL, THAT'S VERY NICE! I'VE ALWAYS LIKED THAT GORDIE! HE'S A NICE YOUNG MAN!
HE HAS A GOOD HEAD ON HIS SHOULDERS!
DING DONG
AND YET...
HI, ELLEN! IS NATE HERE?

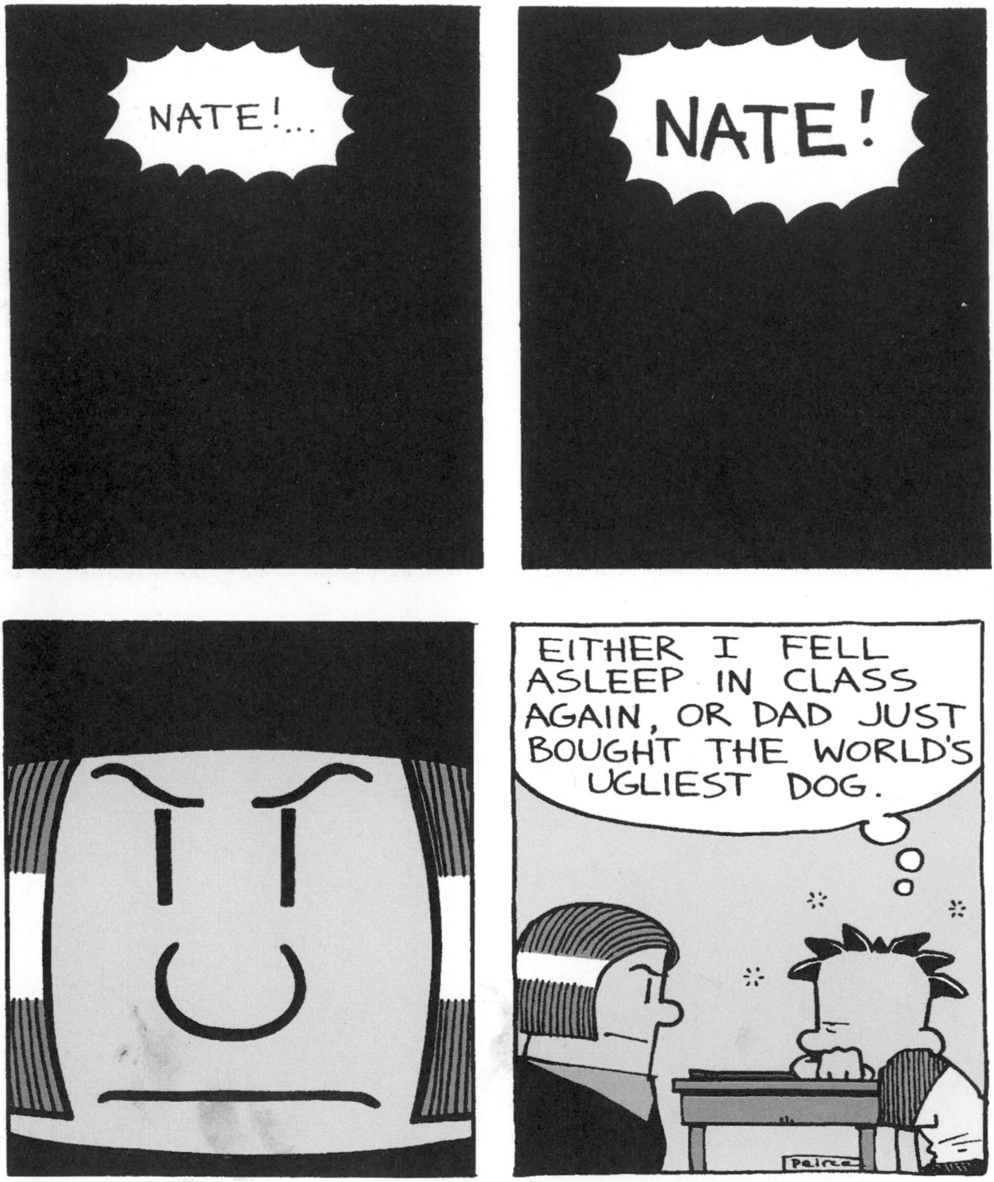
NATE!...
NATE!
EITHER I FELL ASLEEP IN CLASS AGAIN, OR DAD JUST BOUGHT THE WORLD'S UGLIEST DOG.
PEIRCE

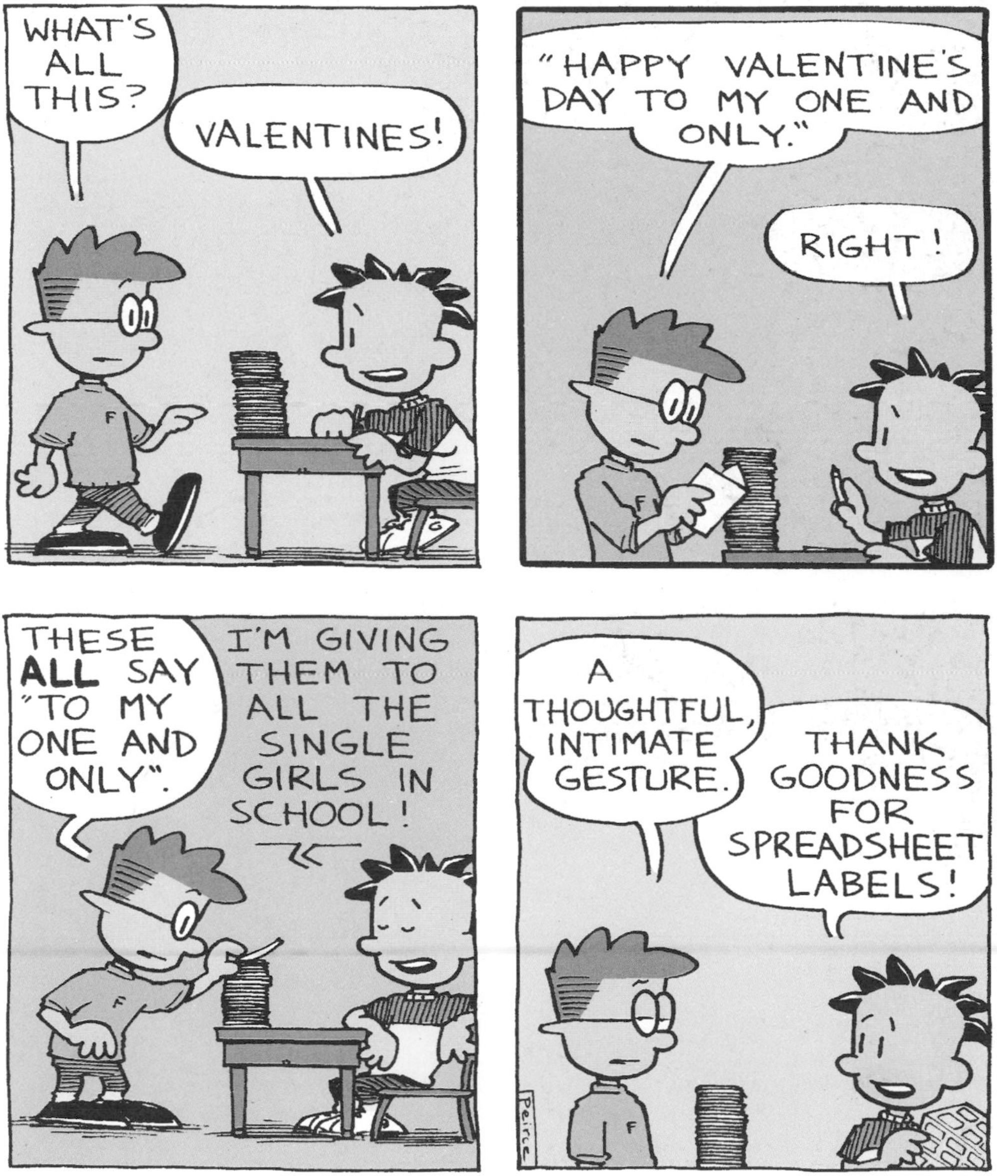
WHAT'S ALL THIS?
VALENTINES!
"HAPPY VALENTINE'S DAY TO MY ONE AND ONLY."
RIGHT!
THESE **ALL** SAY "TO MY ONE AND ONLY".
I'M GIVING THEM TO ALL THE SINGLE GIRLS IN SCHOOL!
A THOUGHTFUL, INTIMATE GESTURE.
THANK GOODNESS FOR SPREADSHEET LABELS!
Peirce

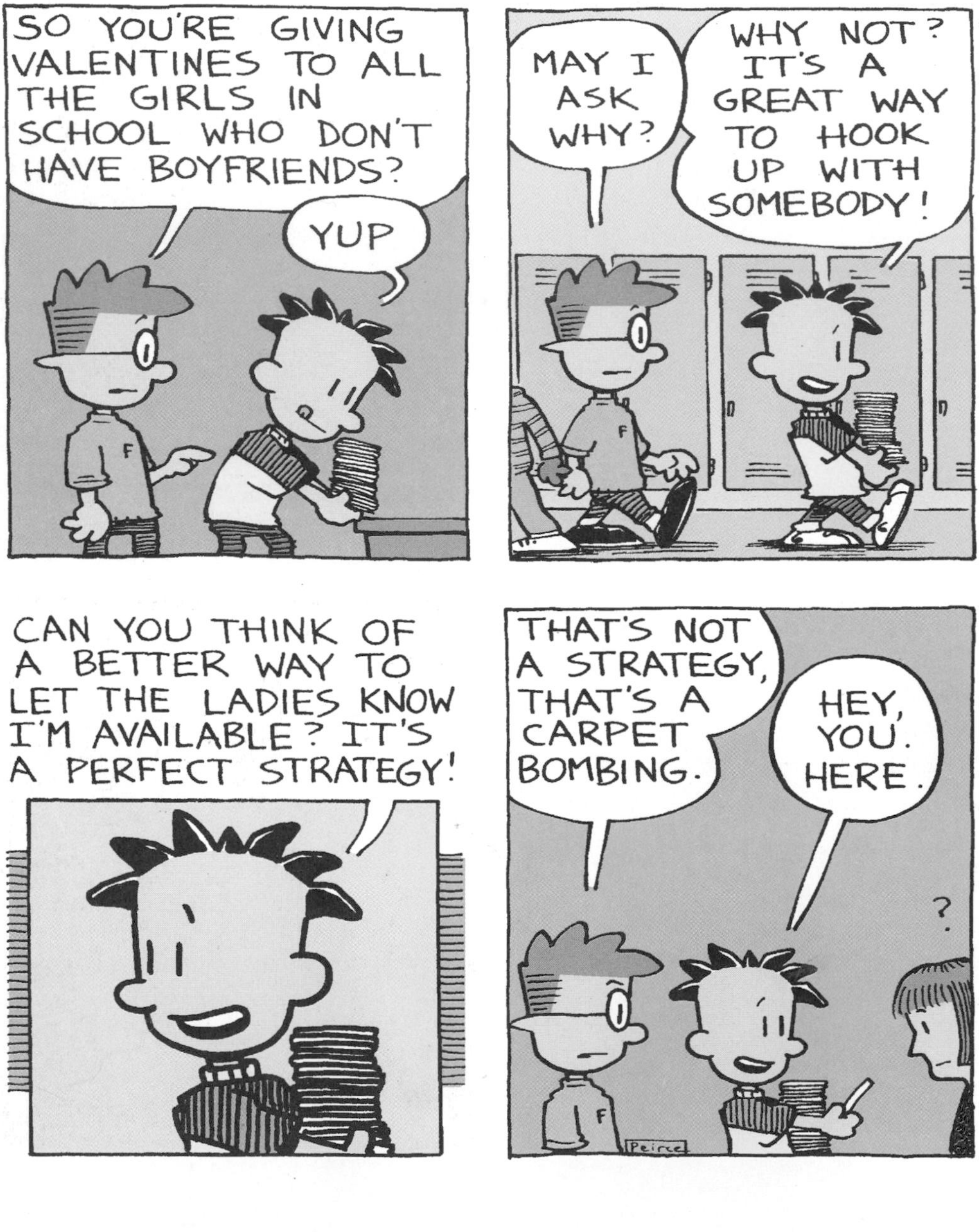
SO YOU'RE GIVING VALENTINES TO ALL THE GIRLS IN SCHOOL WHO DON'T HAVE BOYFRIENDS?
YUP
MAY I ASK WHY?
WHY NOT? IT'S A GREAT WAY TO HOOK UP WITH SOMEBODY!
CAN YOU THINK OF A BETTER WAY TO LET THE LADIES KNOW I'M AVAILABLE? IT'S A PERFECT STRATEGY!
THAT'S NOT A STRATEGY, THAT'S A CARPET BOMBING.
HEY, YOU. HERE.
?
Peirce

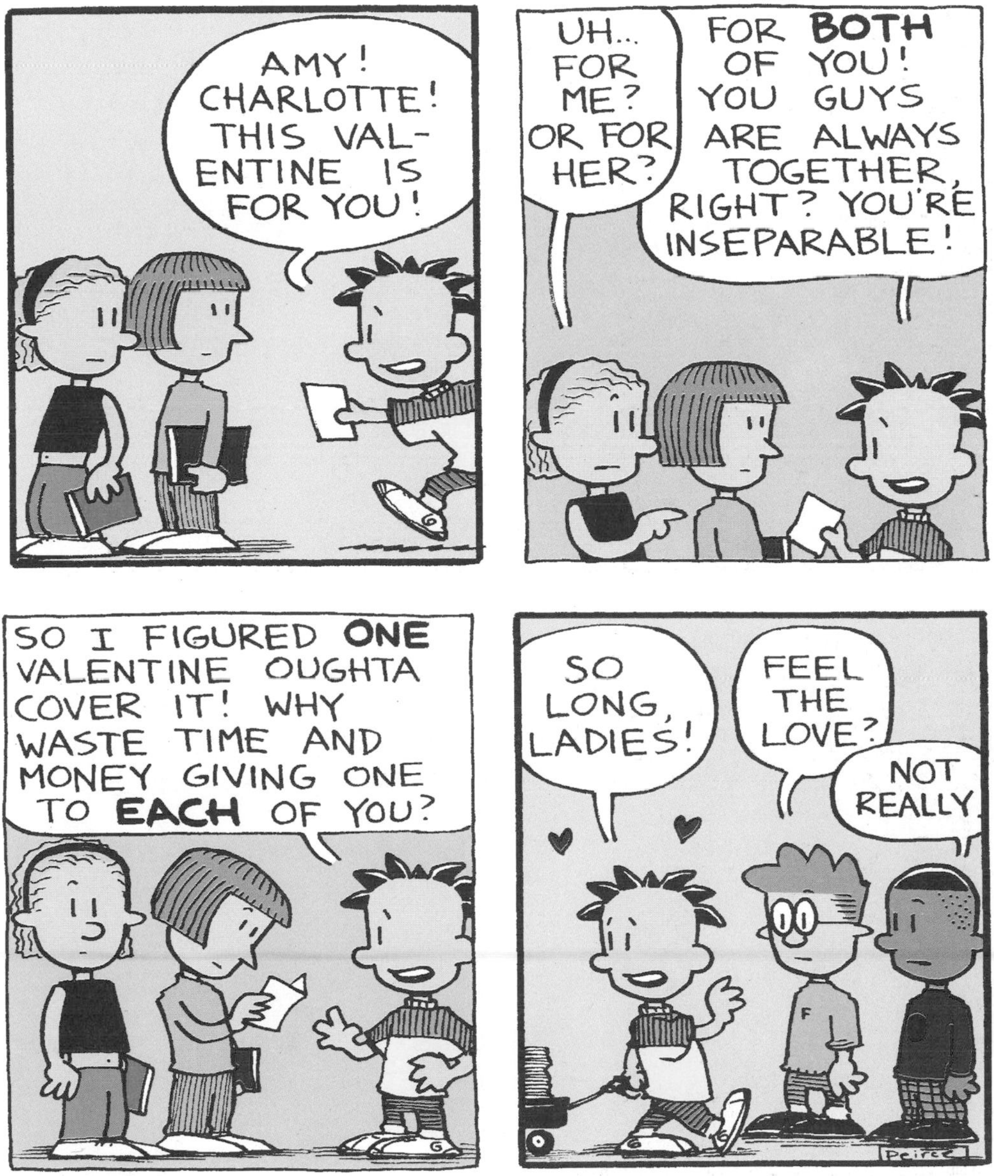
AMY! CHARLOTTE! THIS VALENTINE IS FOR YOU!
UH... FOR ME? OR FOR HER?
FOR BOTH OF YOU! YOU GUYS ARE ALWAYS TOGETHER, RIGHT? YOU'RE INSEPARABLE!
SO I FIGURED ONE VALENTINE OUGHTA COVER IT! WHY WASTE TIME AND MONEY GIVING ONE TO EACH OF YOU?
SO LONG, LADIES!
FEEL THE LOVE?
NOT REALLY.
Peirce

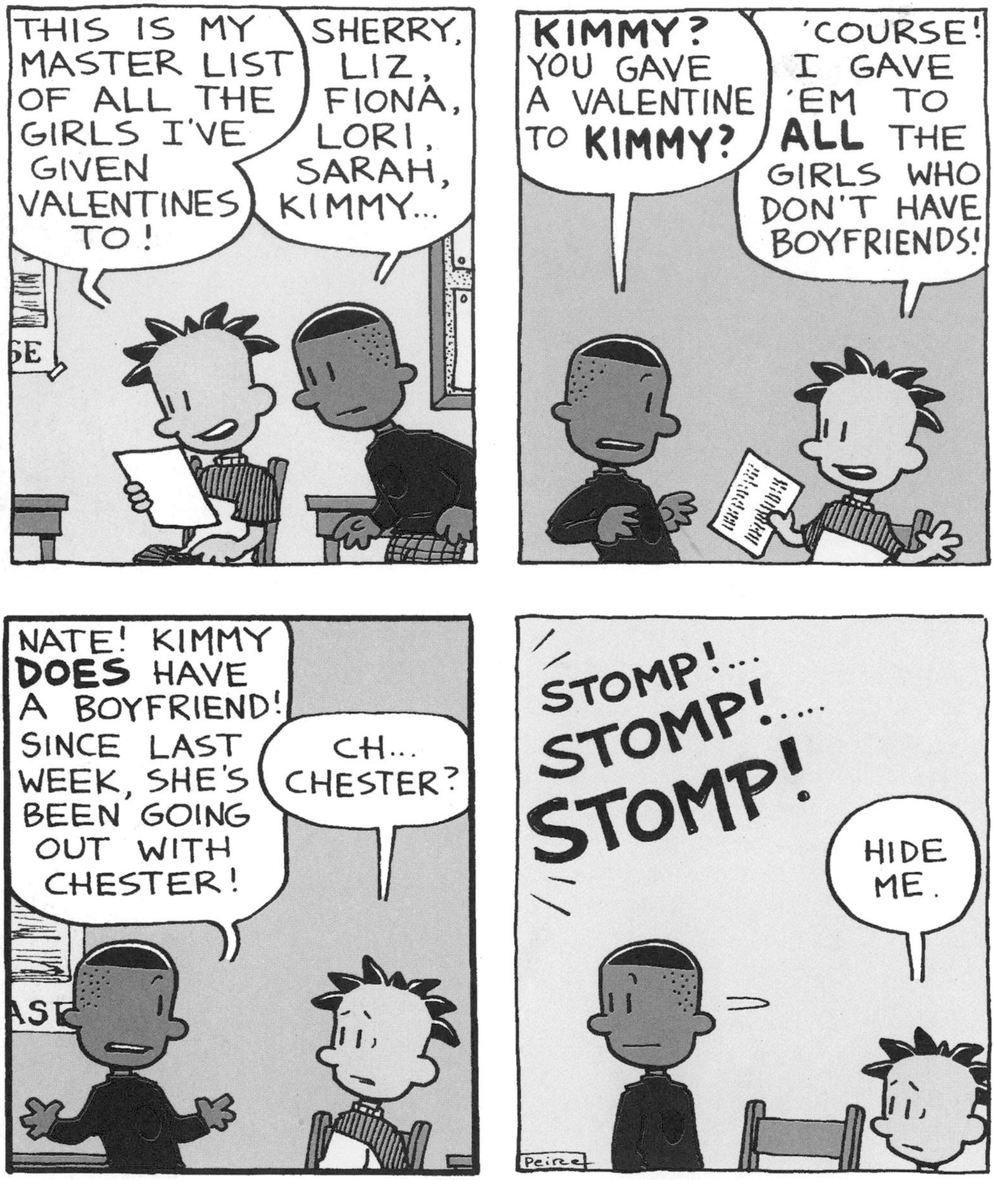
THIS IS MY MASTER LIST OF ALL THE GIRLS I'VE GIVEN VALENTINES TO!
SHERRY, LIZ, FIONA, LORI, SARAH, KIMMY...
KIMMY? YOU GAVE A VALENTINE TO KIMMY?
'COURSE! I GAVE 'EM TO ALL THE GIRLS WHO DON'T HAVE BOYFRIENDS!
NATE! KIMMY DOES HAVE A BOYFRIEND! SINCE LAST WEEK, SHE'S BEEN GOING OUT WITH CHESTER!
CH... CHESTER?
STOMP!...
STOMP!.....
STOMP!
HIDE ME.
Peirce

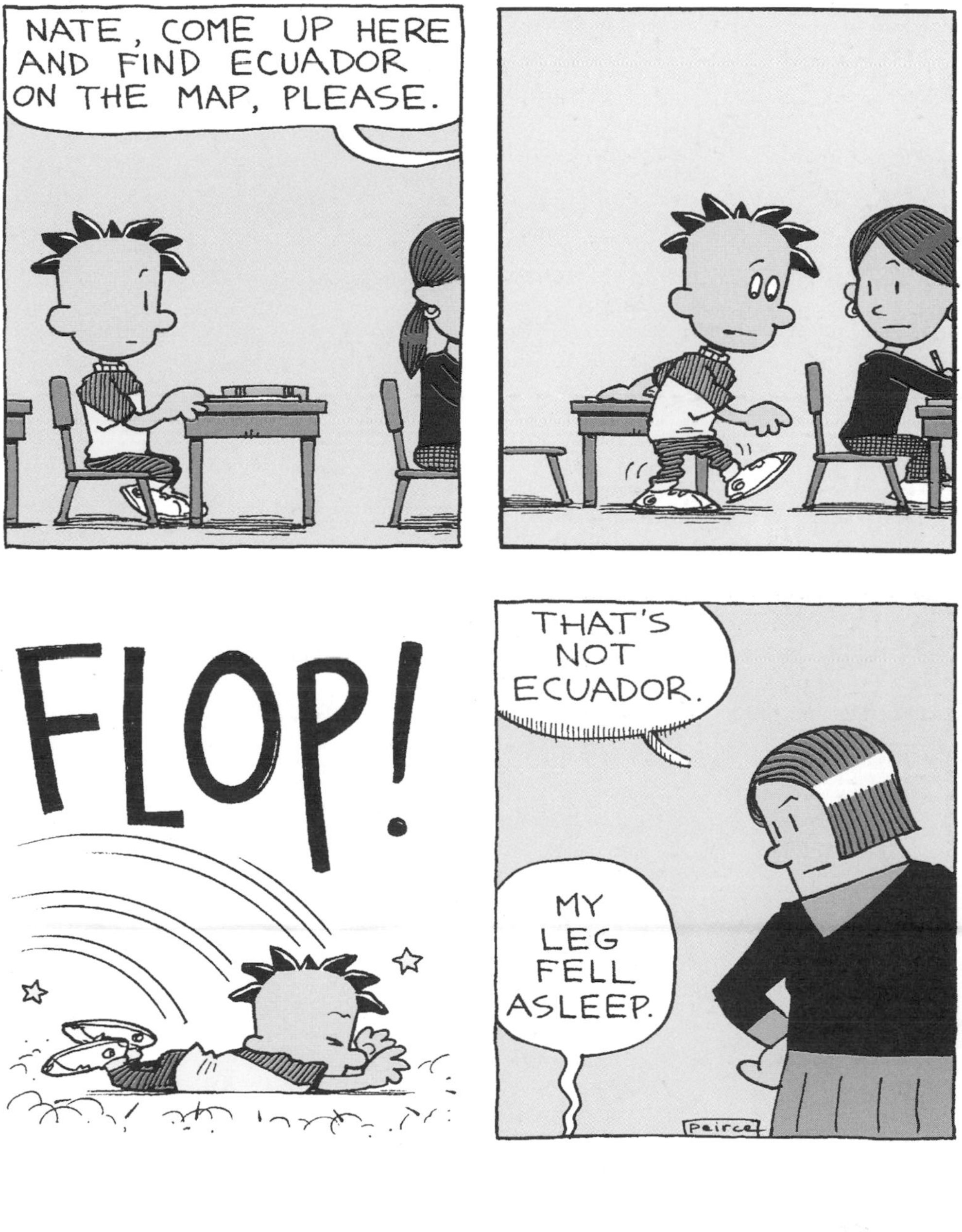
NATE, COME UP HERE AND FIND ECUADOR ON THE MAP, PLEASE.
FLOP!
THAT'S NOT ECUADOR.
MY LEG FELL ASLEEP.
peirce

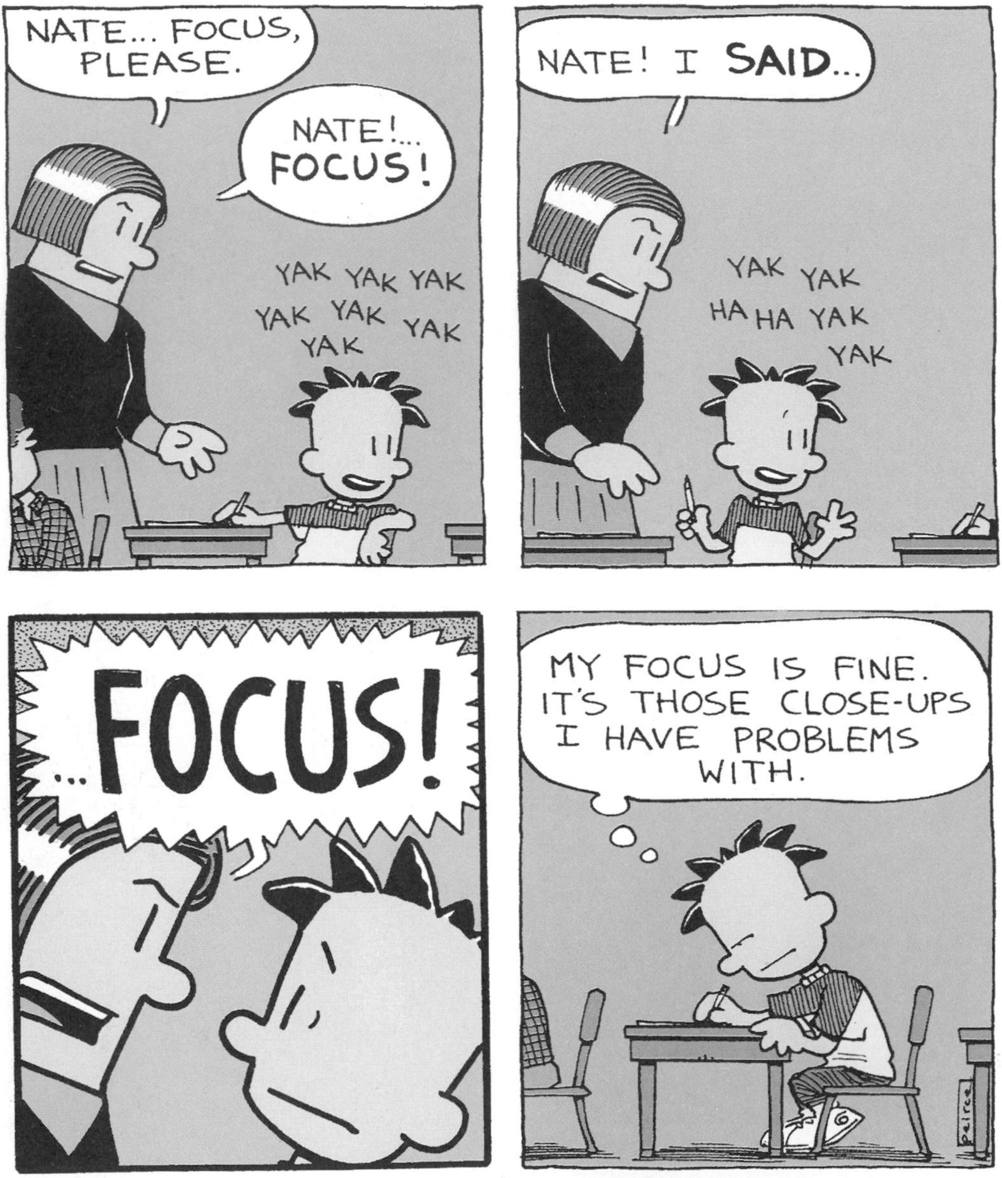
NATE... FOCUS, PLEASE.
NATE!... FOCUS!
YAK YAK YAK YAK YAK YAK YAK
NATE! I SAID...
YAK YAK HA HA YAK YAK
...FOCUS!
MY FOCUS IS FINE. IT'S THOSE CLOSE-UPS I HAVE PROBLEMS WITH.
peirce

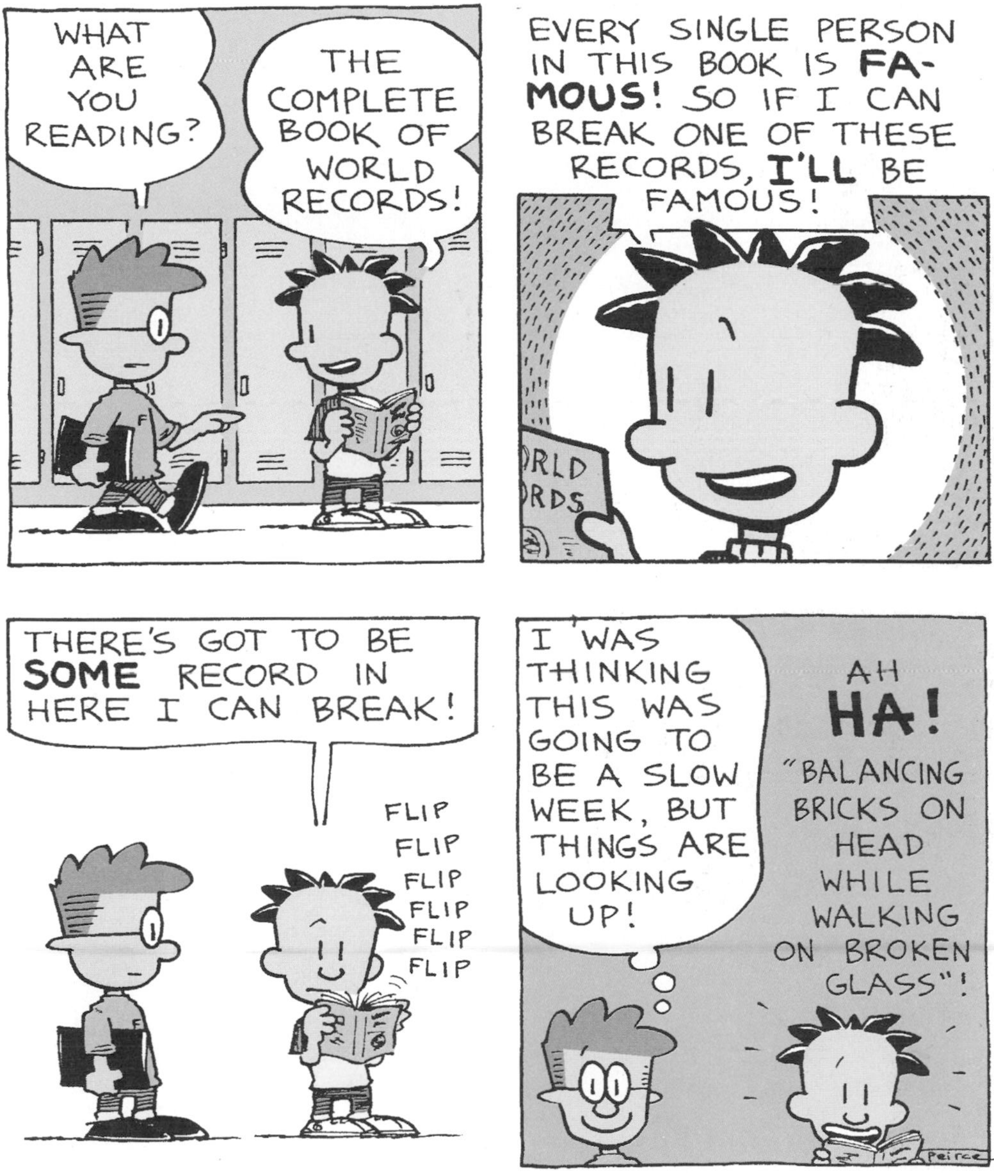
WHAT ARE YOU READING?
THE COMPLETE BOOK OF WORLD RECORDS!
EVERY SINGLE PERSON IN THIS BOOK IS FAMOUS! SO IF I CAN BREAK ONE OF THESE RECORDS, I'LL BE FAMOUS!
THERE'S GOT TO BE SOME RECORD IN HERE I CAN BREAK!
FLIP FLIP FLIP FLIP FLIP FLIP
I WAS THINKING THIS WAS GOING TO BE A SLOW WEEK, BUT THINGS ARE LOOKING UP!
AH HA! "BALANCING BRICKS ON HEAD WHILE WALKING ON BROKEN GLASS"!
peirce

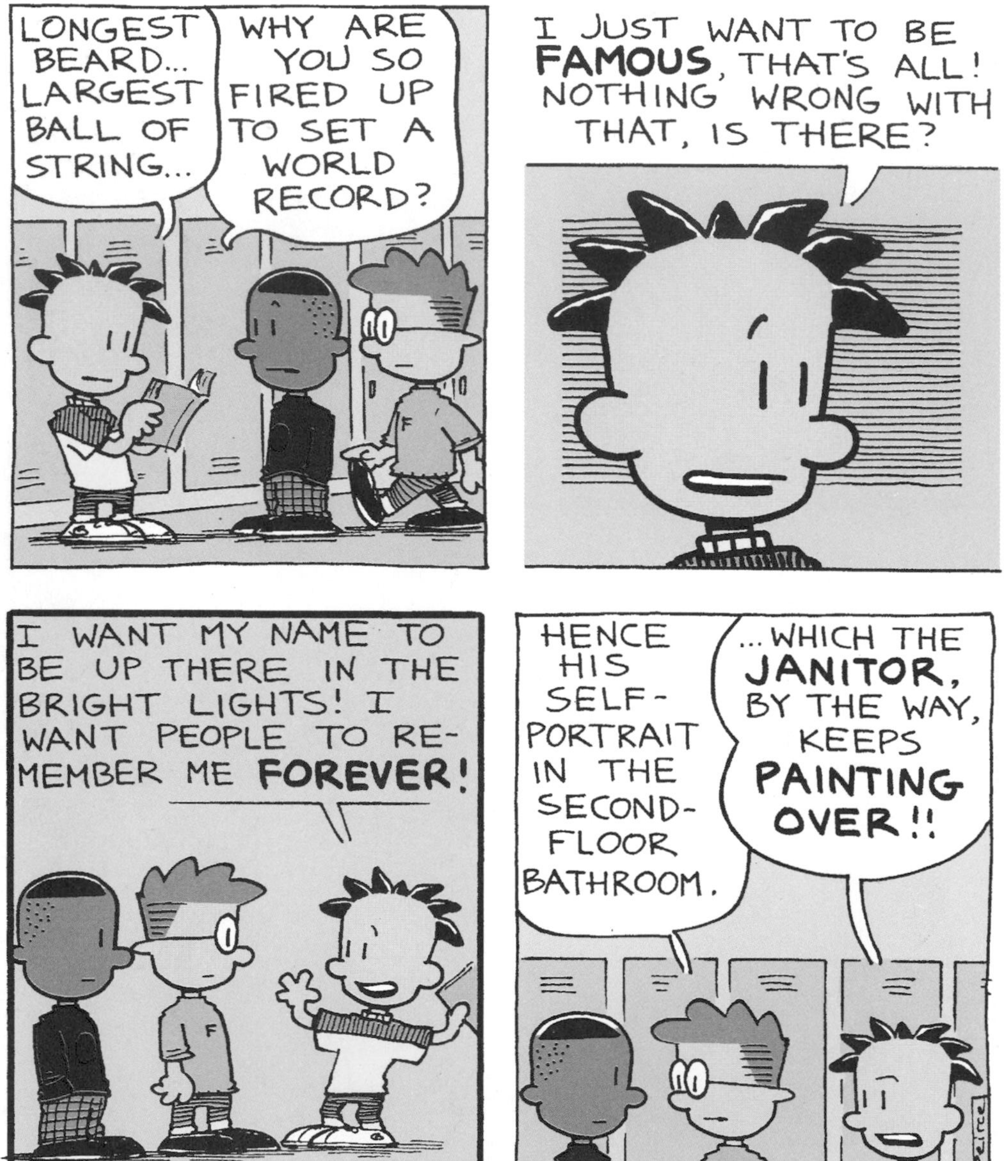
LONGEST BEARD... LARGEST BALL OF STRING...
WHY ARE YOU SO FIRED UP TO SET A WORLD RECORD?
I JUST WANT TO BE **FAMOUS**, THAT'S ALL! NOTHING WRONG WITH THAT, IS THERE?
I WANT MY NAME TO BE UP THERE IN THE BRIGHT LIGHTS! I WANT PEOPLE TO RE-MEMBER ME **FOREVER**!
HENCE HIS SELF-PORTRAIT IN THE SECOND-FLOOR BATHROOM.
...WHICH THE **JANITOR**, BY THE WAY, KEEPS **PAINTING OVER**!!
Peirce

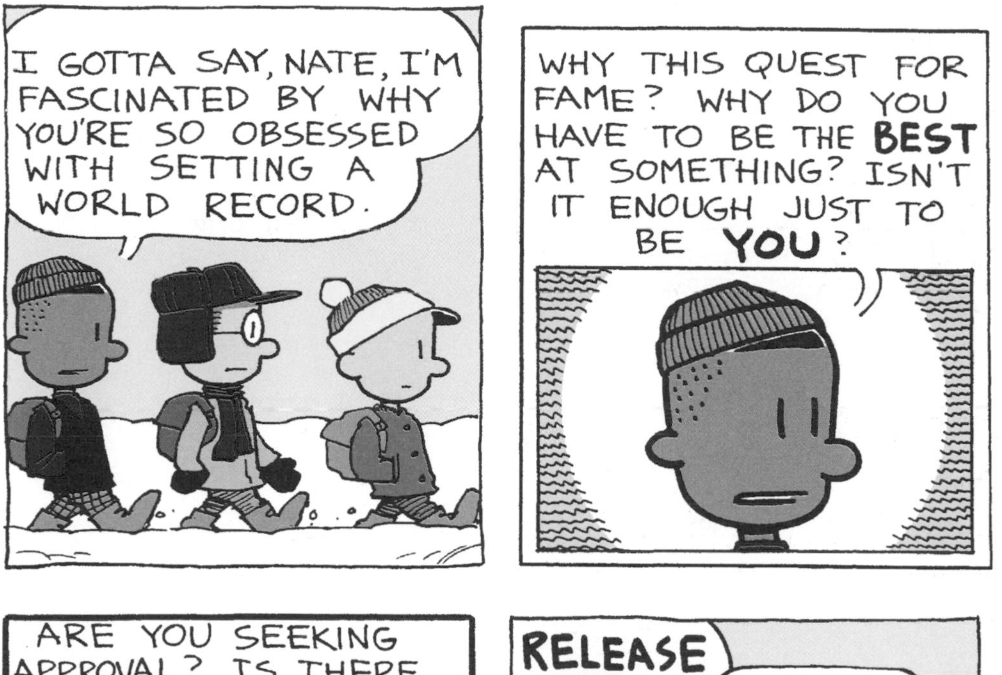
I GOTTA SAY, NATE, I'M FASCINATED BY WHY YOU'RE SO OBSESSED WITH SETTING A WORLD RECORD.
WHY THIS QUEST FOR FAME? WHY DO YOU HAVE TO BE THE **BEST** AT SOMETHING? ISN'T IT ENOUGH JUST TO BE **YOU**?
ARE YOU SEEKING APPROVAL? IS THERE A TRAUMA IN YOUR PAST YOU'RE TRYING TO COMPENSATE FOR? **OPEN UP**, MAN! **TALK** ABOUT IT!
RELEASE THE WOUNDED CHILD WITHIN!
SNORT!
THERE'S GONNA BE A WOUNDED CHILD, BUT IT'S NOT GONNA BE ME.
peirce

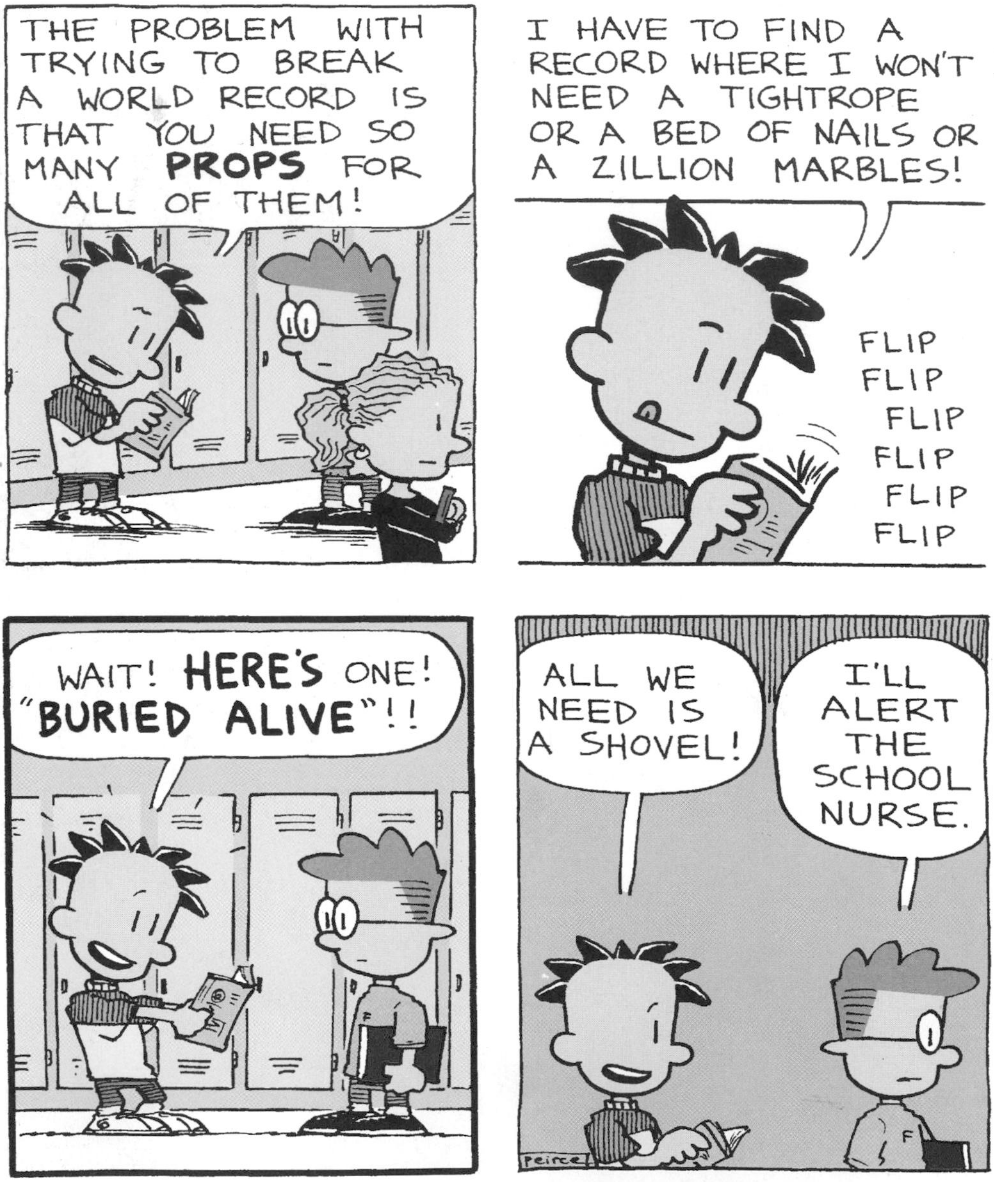
THE PROBLEM WITH TRYING TO BREAK A WORLD RECORD IS THAT YOU NEED SO MANY **PROPS** FOR ALL OF THEM!
I HAVE TO FIND A RECORD WHERE I WON'T NEED A TIGHTROPE OR A BED OF NAILS OR A ZILLION MARBLES!
FLIP FLIP FLIP FLIP FLIP FLIP
WAIT! **HERE'S** ONE! "**BURIED ALIVE**"!!
ALL WE NEED IS A SHOVEL!
I'LL ALERT THE SCHOOL NURSE.
peirce

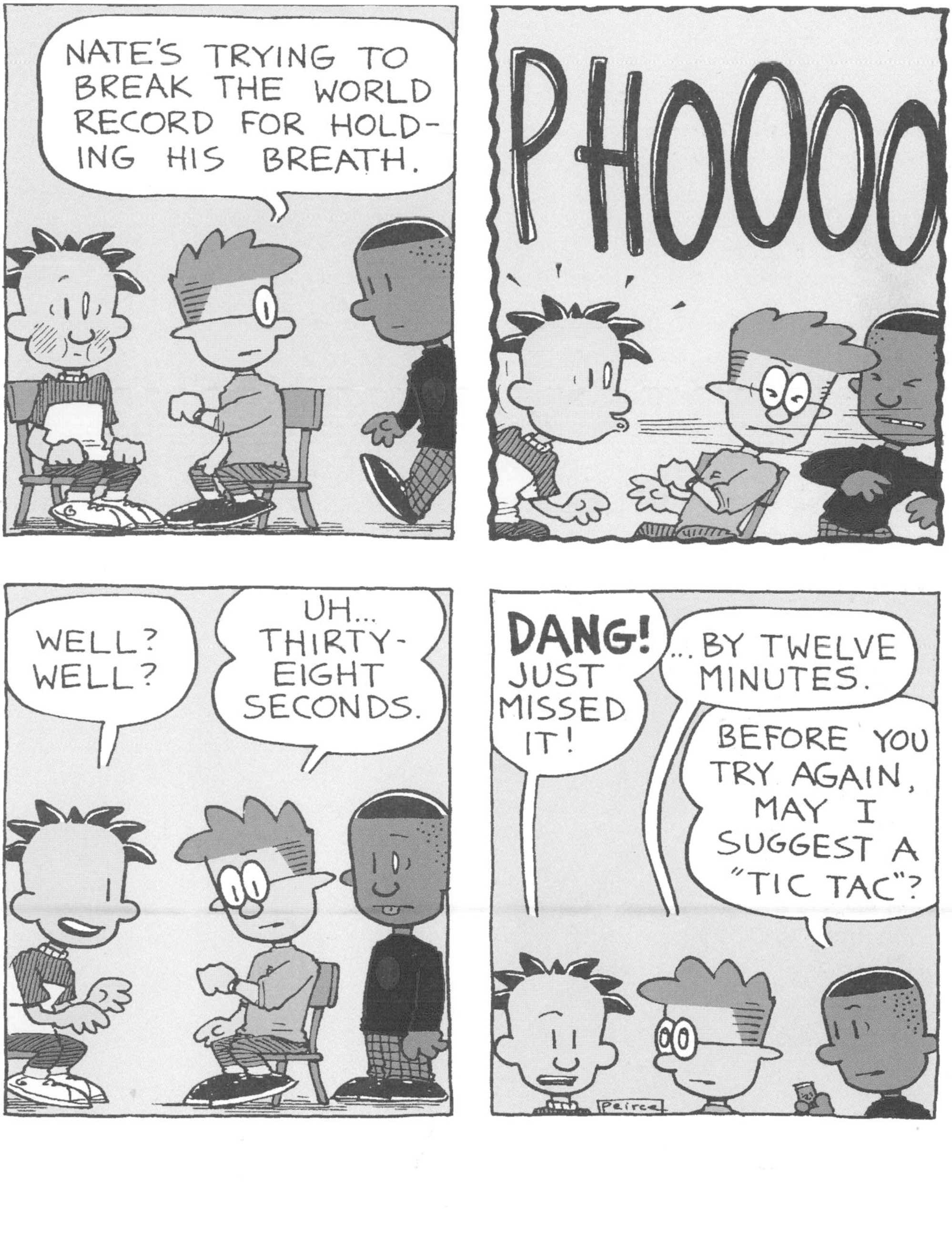
NATE'S TRYING TO BREAK THE WORLD RECORD FOR HOLD-ING HIS BREATH.
PHOOOO
WELL? WELL?
UH... THIRTY-EIGHT SECONDS.
DANG! JUST MISSED IT!
... BY TWELVE MINUTES.
BEFORE YOU TRY AGAIN, MAY I SUGGEST A "TIC TAC"?
PEIRCE

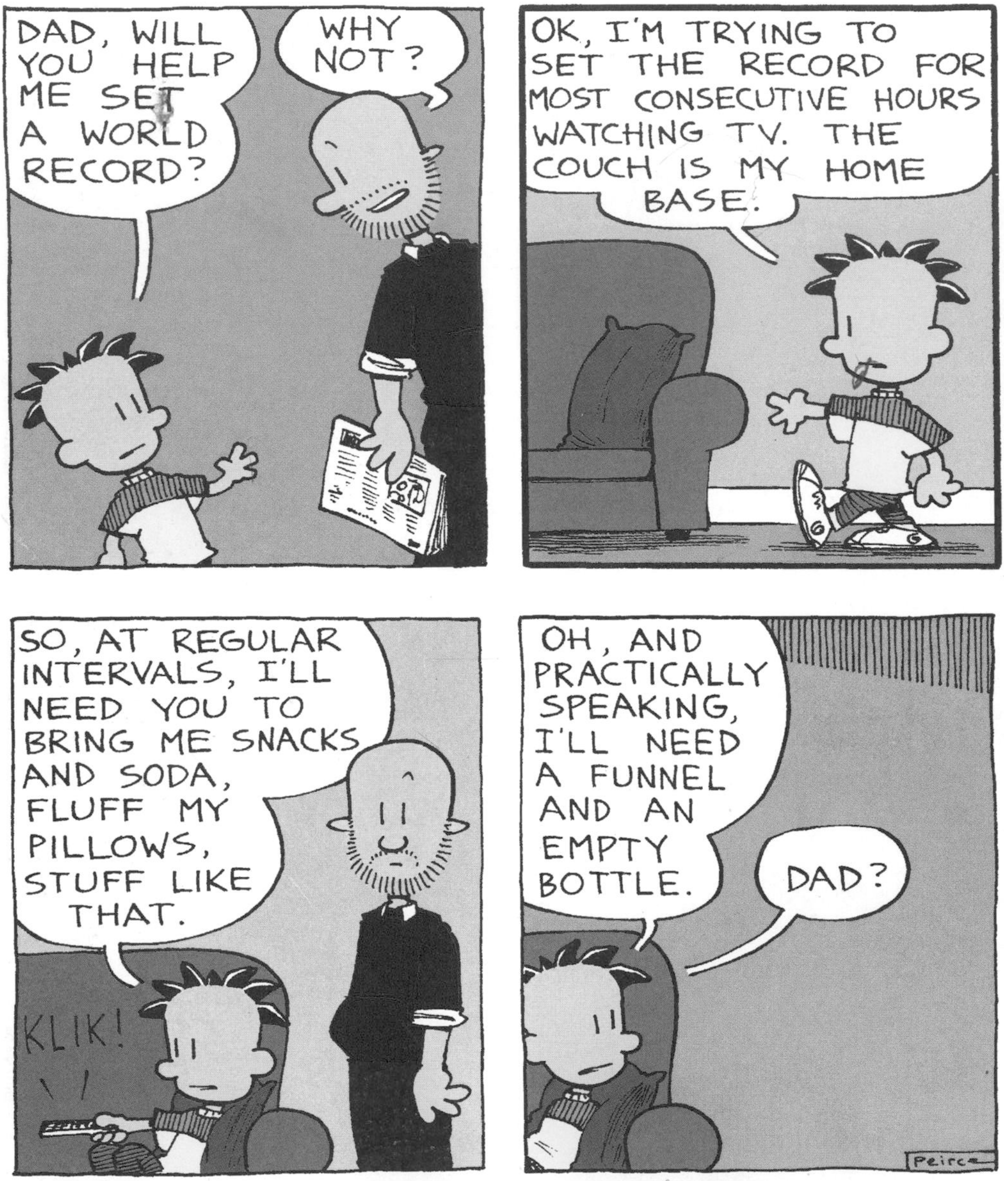
DAD, WILL YOU HELP ME SET A WORLD RECORD?
WHY NOT?
OK, I'M TRYING TO SET THE RECORD FOR MOST CONSECUTIVE HOURS WATCHING TV. THE COUCH IS MY HOME BASE.
SO, AT REGULAR INTERVALS, I'LL NEED YOU TO BRING ME SNACKS AND SODA, FLUFF MY PILLOWS, STUFF LIKE THAT.
KLIK!
OH, AND PRACTICALLY SPEAKING, I'LL NEED A FUNNEL AND AN EMPTY BOTTLE.
DAD?
Peirce

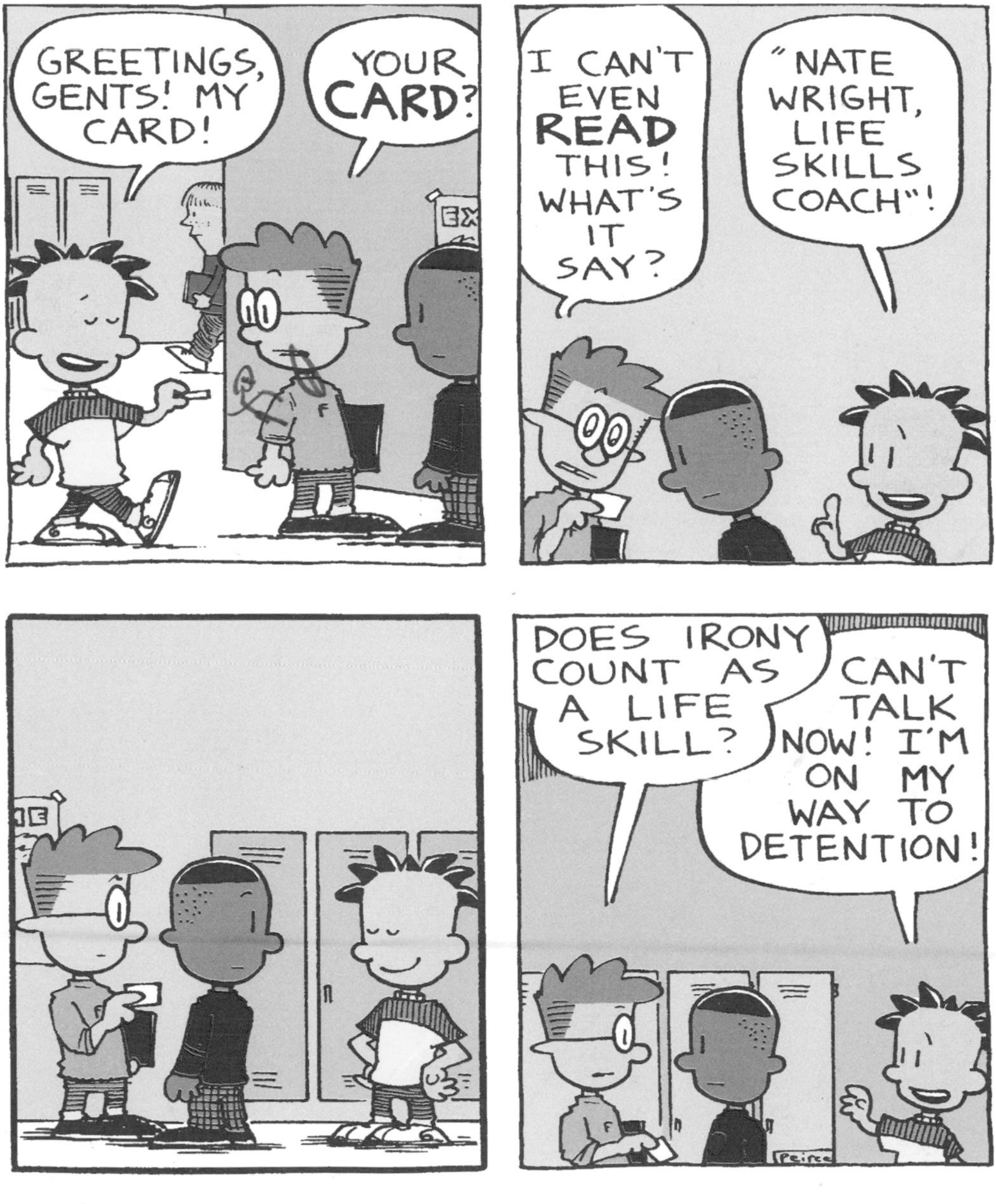
GREETINGS, GENTS! MY CARD!
YOUR CARD?
I CAN'T EVEN READ THIS! WHAT'S IT SAY?
"NATE WRIGHT, LIFE SKILLS COACH"!
DOES IRONY COUNT AS A LIFE SKILL?
CAN'T TALK NOW! I'M ON MY WAY TO DETENTION!
Peirce

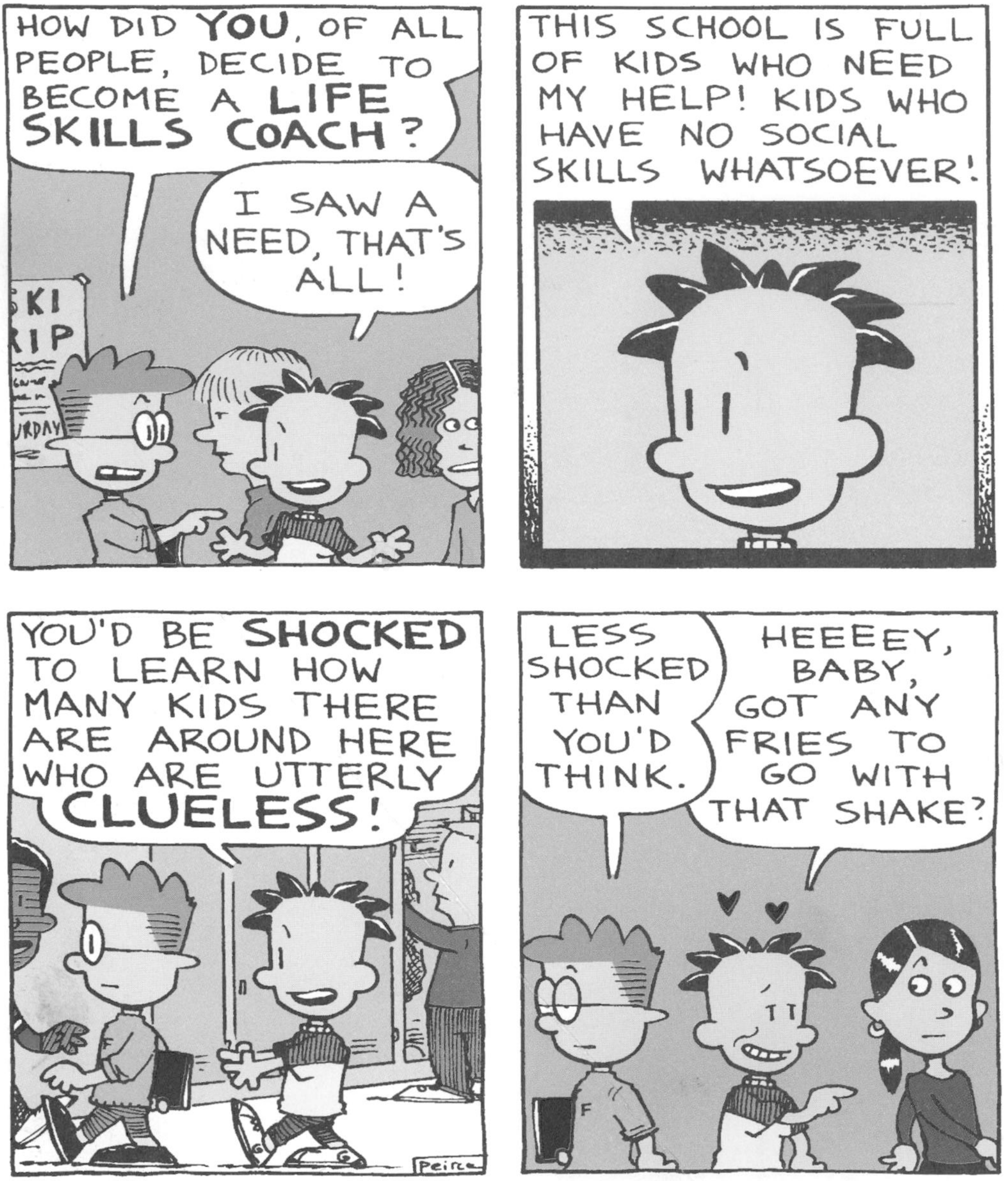
HOW DID **YOU**, OF ALL PEOPLE, DECIDE TO BECOME A **LIFE SKILLS COACH**?
I SAW A NEED, THAT'S ALL!
SKI TRIP
THIS SCHOOL IS FULL OF KIDS WHO NEED MY HELP! KIDS WHO HAVE NO SOCIAL SKILLS WHATSOEVER!
YOU'D BE **SHOCKED** TO LEARN HOW MANY KIDS THERE ARE AROUND HERE WHO ARE UTTERLY **CLUELESS**!
LESS SHOCKED THAN YOU'D THINK.
HEEEEY, BABY, GOT ANY FRIES TO GO WITH THAT SHAKE?

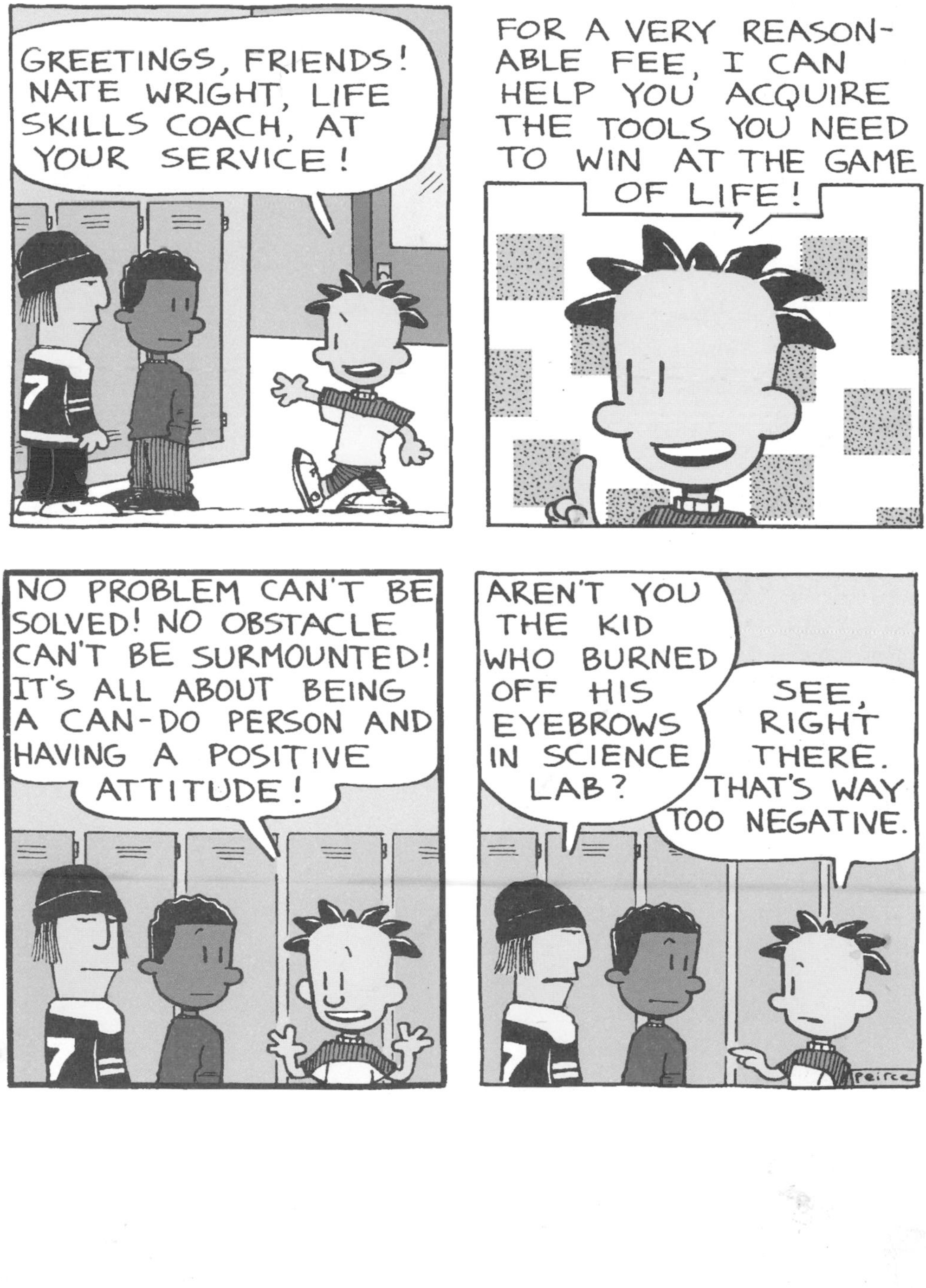
GREETINGS, FRIENDS! NATE WRIGHT, LIFE SKILLS COACH, AT YOUR SERVICE!
FOR A VERY REASON-ABLE FEE, I CAN HELP YOU ACQUIRE THE TOOLS YOU NEED TO WIN AT THE GAME OF LIFE!
NO PROBLEM CAN'T BE SOLVED! NO OBSTACLE CAN'T BE SURMOUNTED! IT'S ALL ABOUT BEING A CAN-DO PERSON AND HAVING A POSITIVE ATTITUDE!
AREN'T YOU THE KID WHO BURNED OFF HIS EYEBROWS IN SCIENCE LAB?
SEE, RIGHT THERE. THAT'S WAY TOO NEGATIVE.
peirce

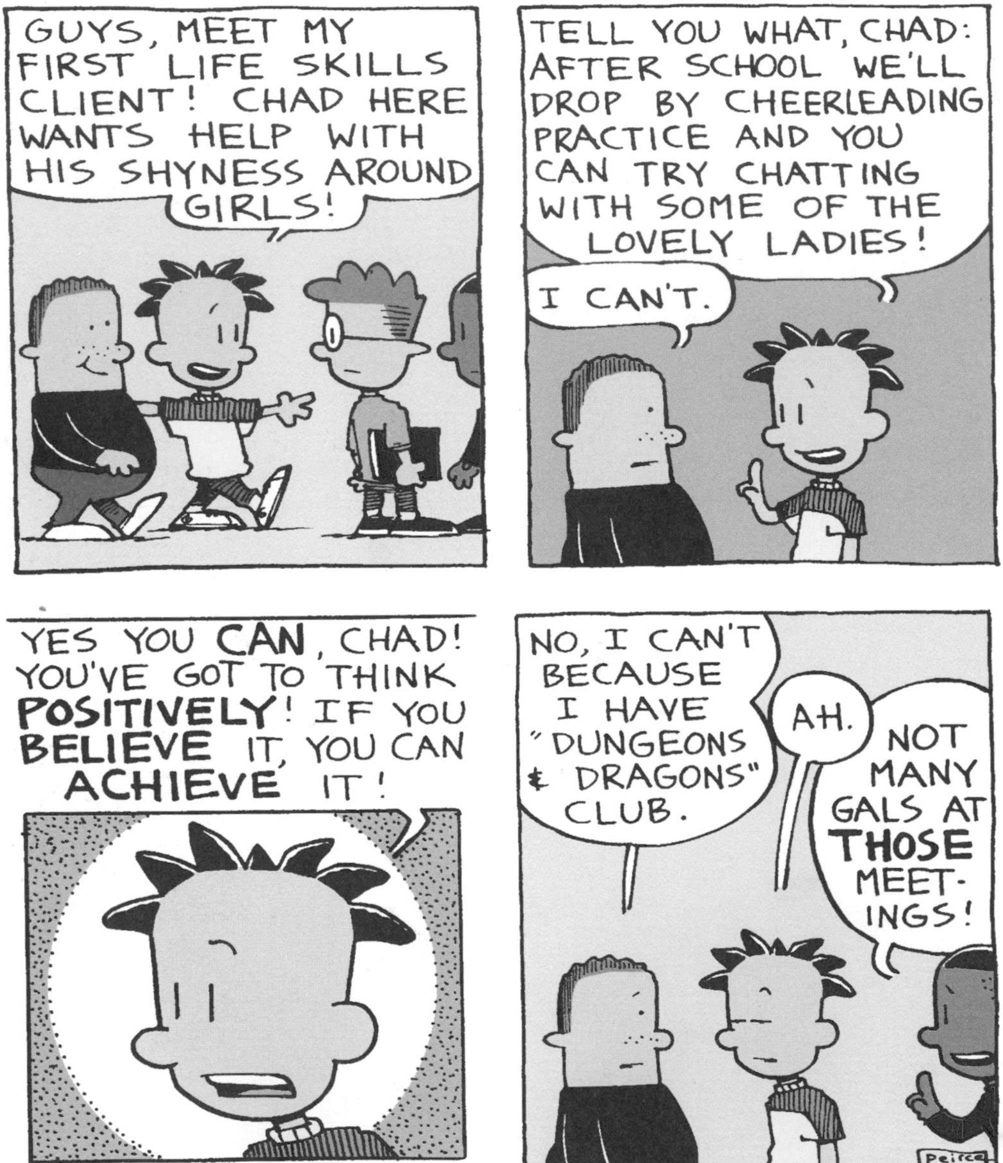
GUYS, MEET MY FIRST LIFE SKILLS CLIENT! CHAD HERE WANTS HELP WITH HIS SHYNESS AROUND GIRLS!
TELL YOU WHAT, CHAD: AFTER SCHOOL WE'LL DROP BY CHEERLEADING PRACTICE AND YOU CAN TRY CHATTING WITH SOME OF THE LOVELY LADIES!
I CAN'T.
YES YOU CAN, CHAD! YOU'VE GOT TO THINK POSITIVELY! IF YOU BELIEVE IT, YOU CAN ACHIEVE IT!
NO, I CAN'T BECAUSE I HAVE "DUNGEONS & DRAGONS" CLUB.
AH.
NOT MANY GALS AT THOSE MEETINGS!
Peirce

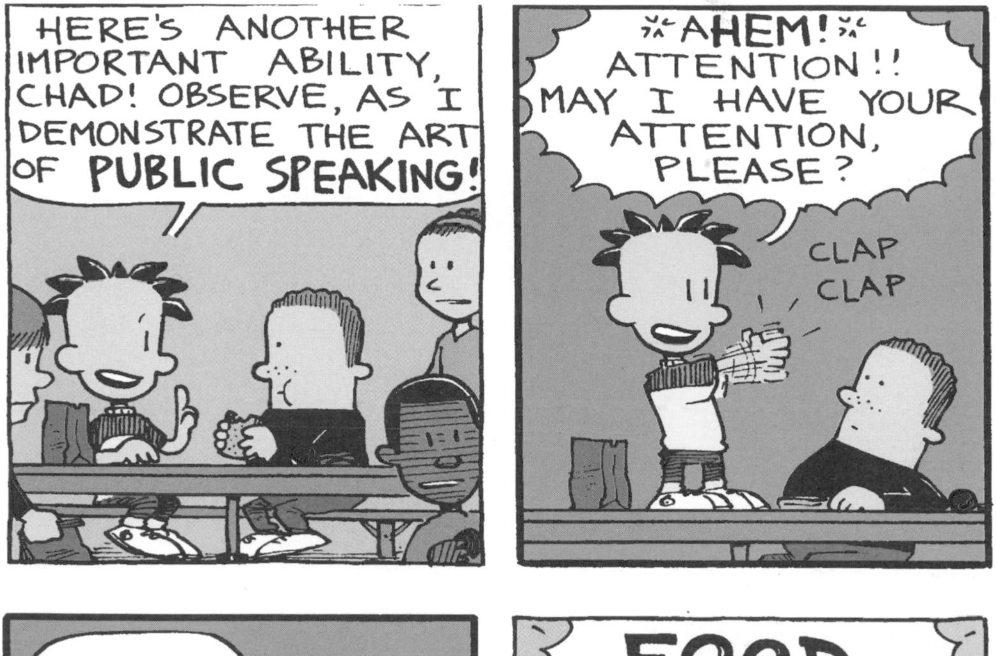
HERE'S ANOTHER IMPORTANT ABILITY, CHAD! OBSERVE, AS I DEMONSTRATE THE ART OF PUBLIC SPEAKING!
AHEM!
ATTENTION!! MAY I HAVE YOUR ATTENTION, PLEASE?
CLAP CLAP
SIDDOWN, SCRUB!
GET HIM!
ZING!
FOOD FIGHT!!
TELL YOU WHAT, CHAD, LET'S MOVE ON TO STUDY SKILLS.
Peirce

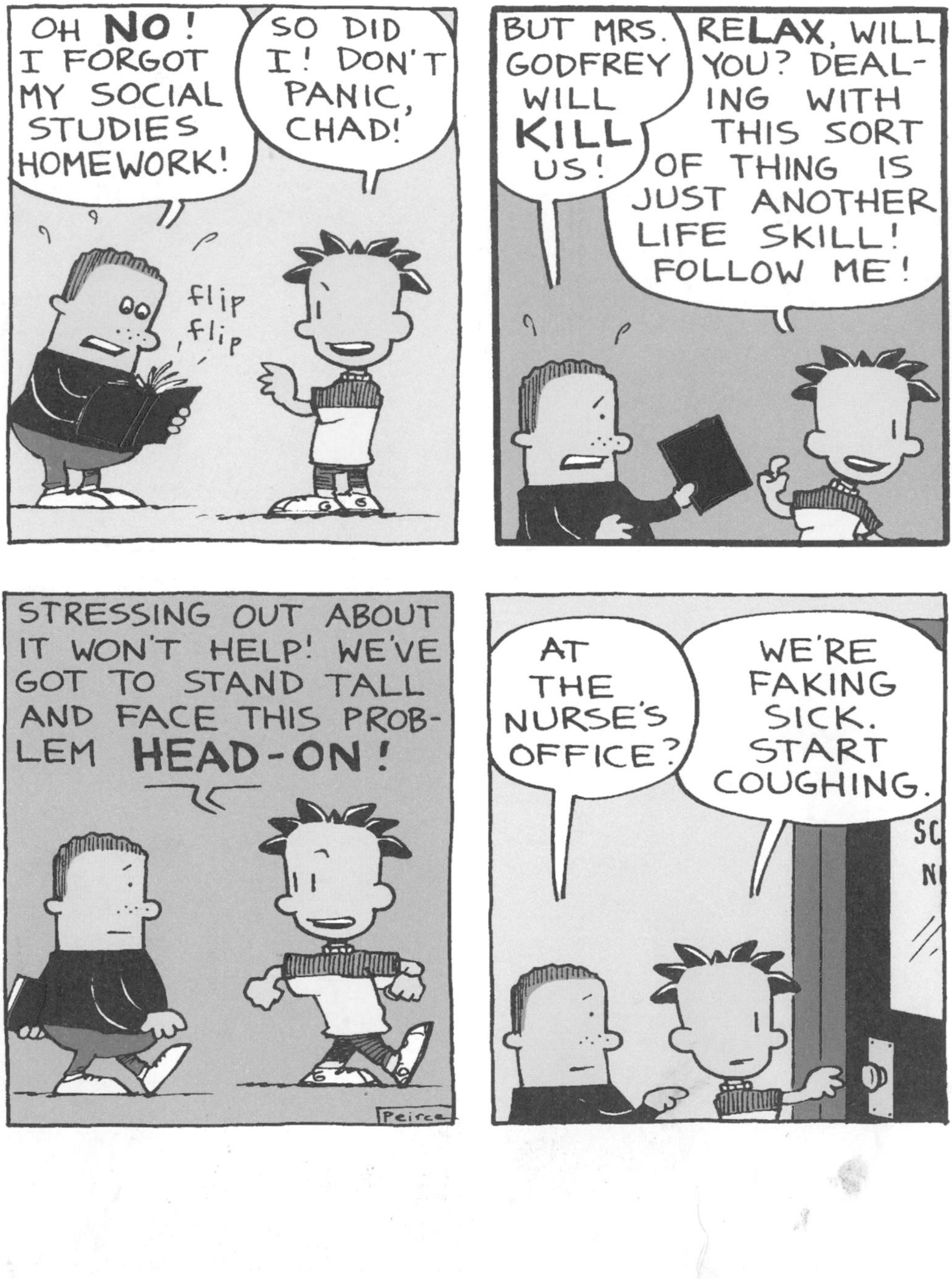
OH NO! I FORGOT MY SOCIAL STUDIES HOMEWORK!
SO DID I! DON'T PANIC, CHAD!
flip flip
BUT MRS. GODFREY WILL KILL US!
RELAX, WILL YOU? DEALING WITH THIS SORT OF THING IS JUST ANOTHER LIFE SKILL! FOLLOW ME!
STRESSING OUT ABOUT IT WON'T HELP! WE'VE GOT TO STAND TALL AND FACE THIS PROBLEM HEAD-ON!
Peirce
AT THE NURSE'S OFFICE?
WE'RE FAKING SICK. START COUGHING.

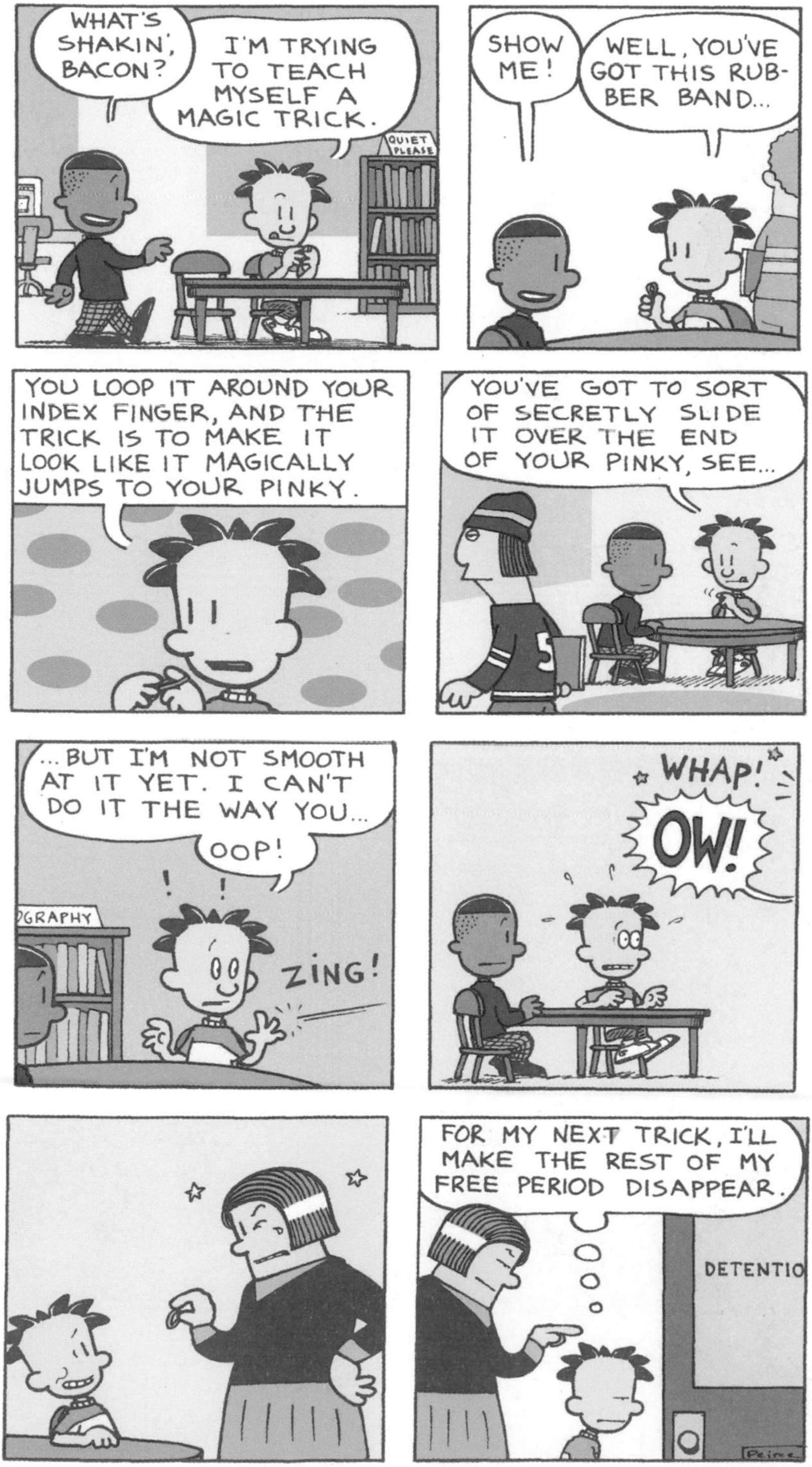
WHAT'S SHAKIN', BACON?
I'M TRYING TO TEACH MYSELF A MAGIC TRICK.
QUIET PLEASE
SHOW ME!
WELL, YOU'VE GOT THIS RUBBER BAND...
YOU LOOP IT AROUND YOUR INDEX FINGER, AND THE TRICK IS TO MAKE IT LOOK LIKE IT MAGICALLY JUMPS TO YOUR PINKY.
YOU'VE GOT TO SORT OF SECRETLY SLIDE IT OVER THE END OF YOUR PINKY, SEE...
...BUT I'M NOT SMOOTH AT IT YET. I CAN'T DO IT THE WAY YOU...
OOP!
GRAPHY
ZING!
WHAP!
OW!
FOR MY NEXT TRICK, I'LL MAKE THE REST OF MY FREE PERIOD DISAPPEAR.
DETENTIO
Peirce

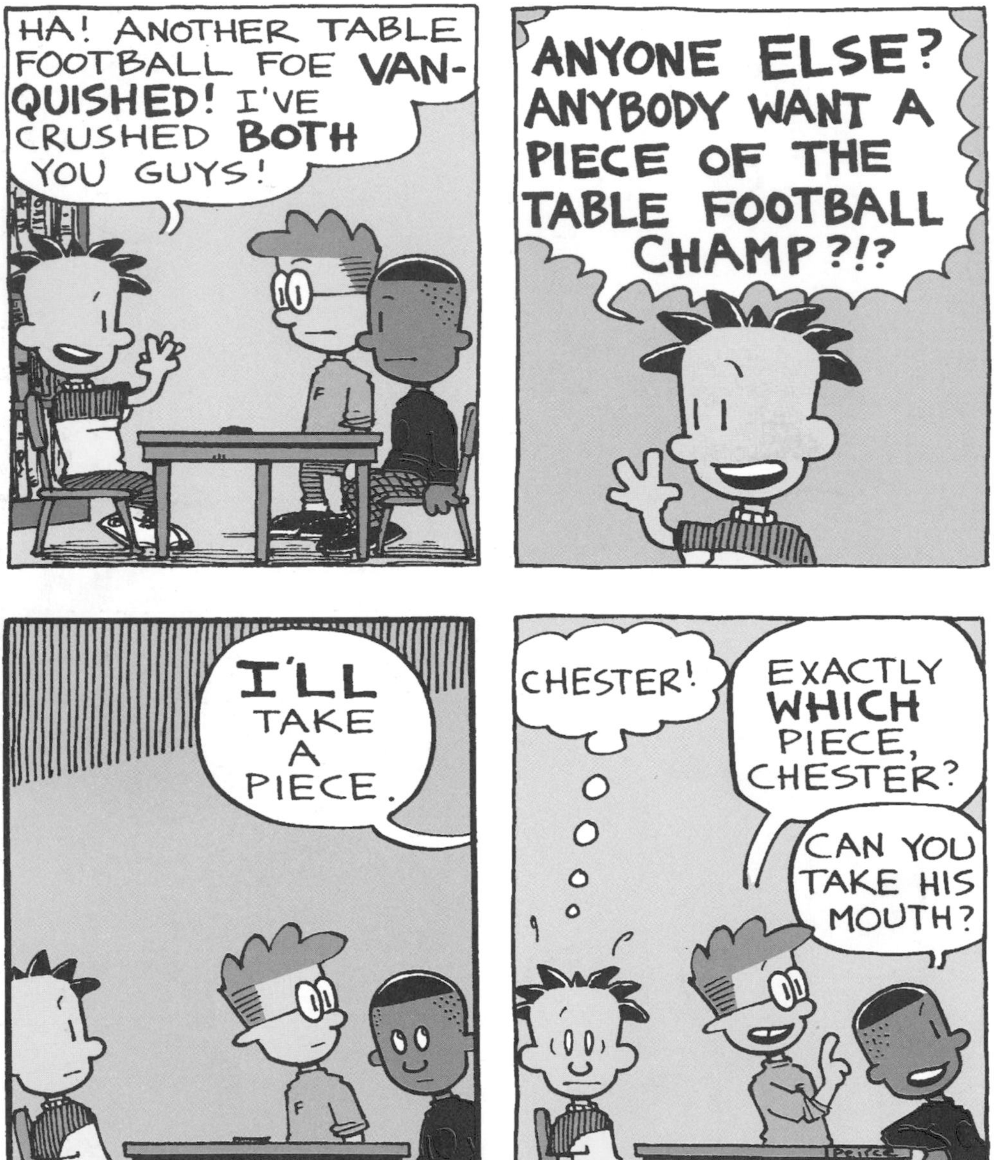
HA! ANOTHER TABLE FOOTBALL FOE VAN-QUISHED! I'VE CRUSHED BOTH YOU GUYS!
ANYONE ELSE? ANYBODY WANT A PIECE OF THE TABLE FOOTBALL CHAMP?!?
I'LL TAKE A PIECE.
CHESTER!
EXACTLY WHICH PIECE, CHESTER?
CAN YOU TAKE HIS MOUTH?
PEIRCE

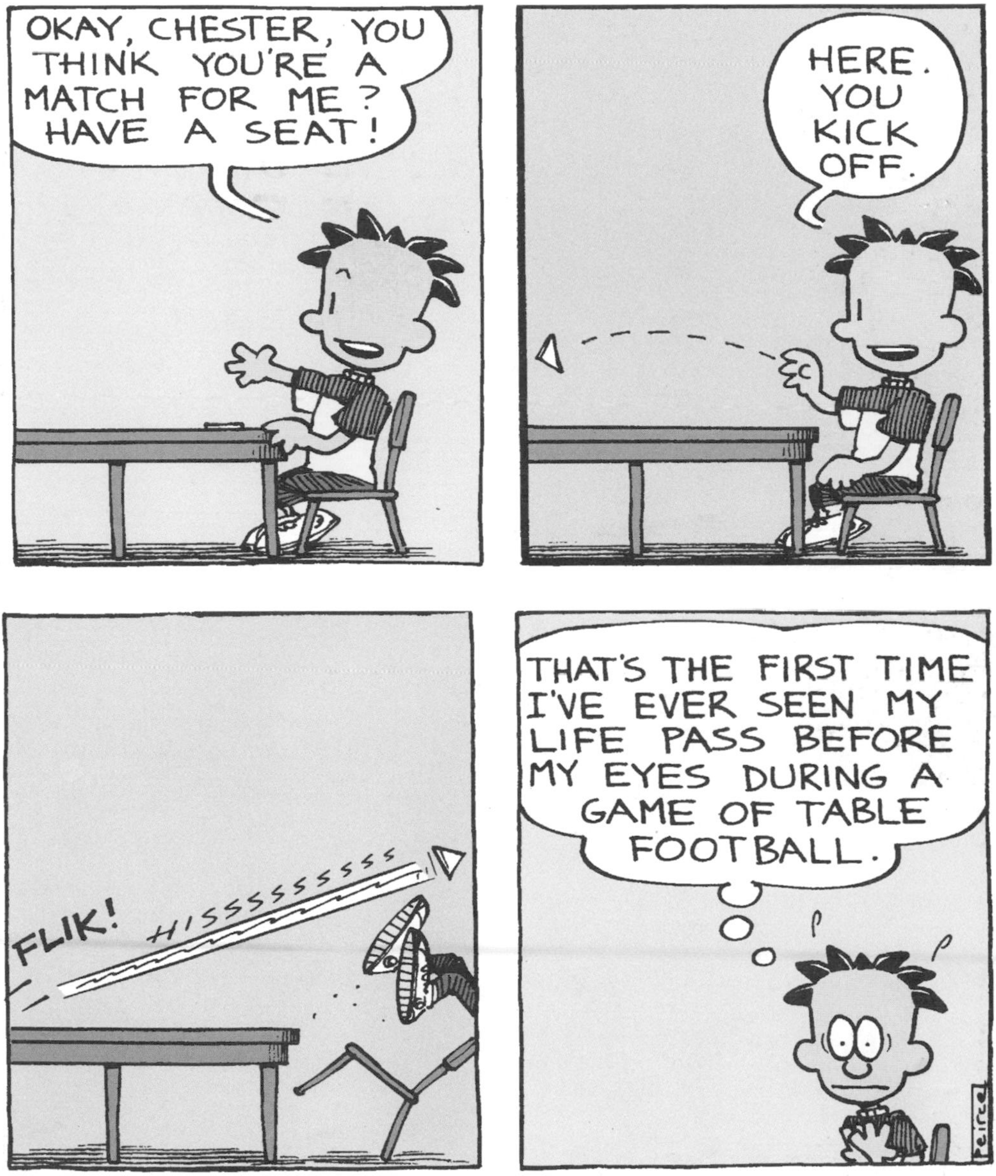
OKAY, CHESTER, YOU THINK YOU'RE A MATCH FOR ME? HAVE A SEAT!
HERE. YOU KICK OFF.
FLIK!
HISSSSSSSSSS
THAT'S THE FIRST TIME I'VE EVER SEEN MY LIFE PASS BEFORE MY EYES DURING A GAME OF TABLE FOOTBALL.
Peirce

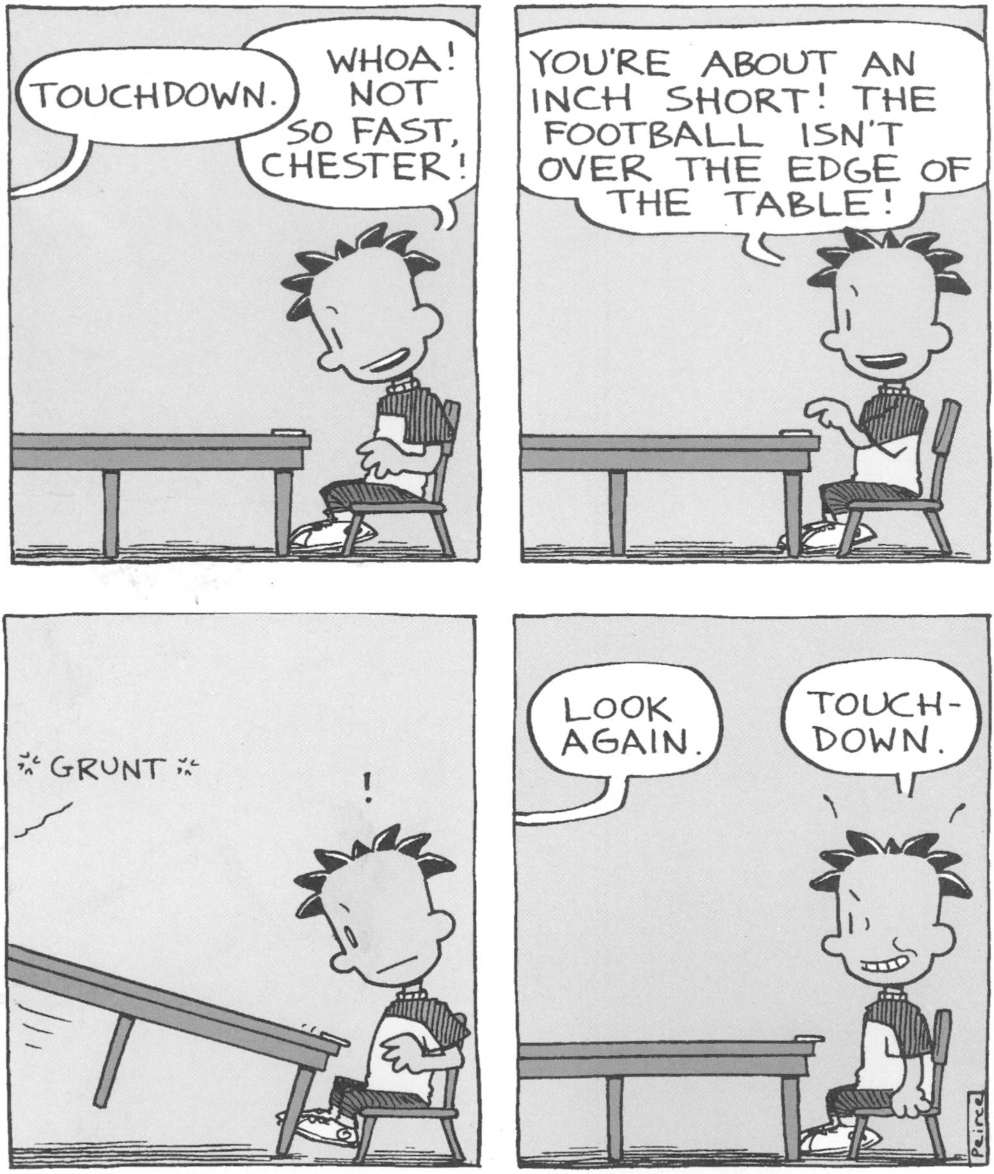
TOUCHDOWN.
WHOA! NOT SO FAST, CHESTER!
YOU'RE ABOUT AN INCH SHORT! THE FOOTBALL ISN'T OVER THE EDGE OF THE TABLE!
GRUNT
!
LOOK AGAIN.
TOUCH-DOWN.
Peirce

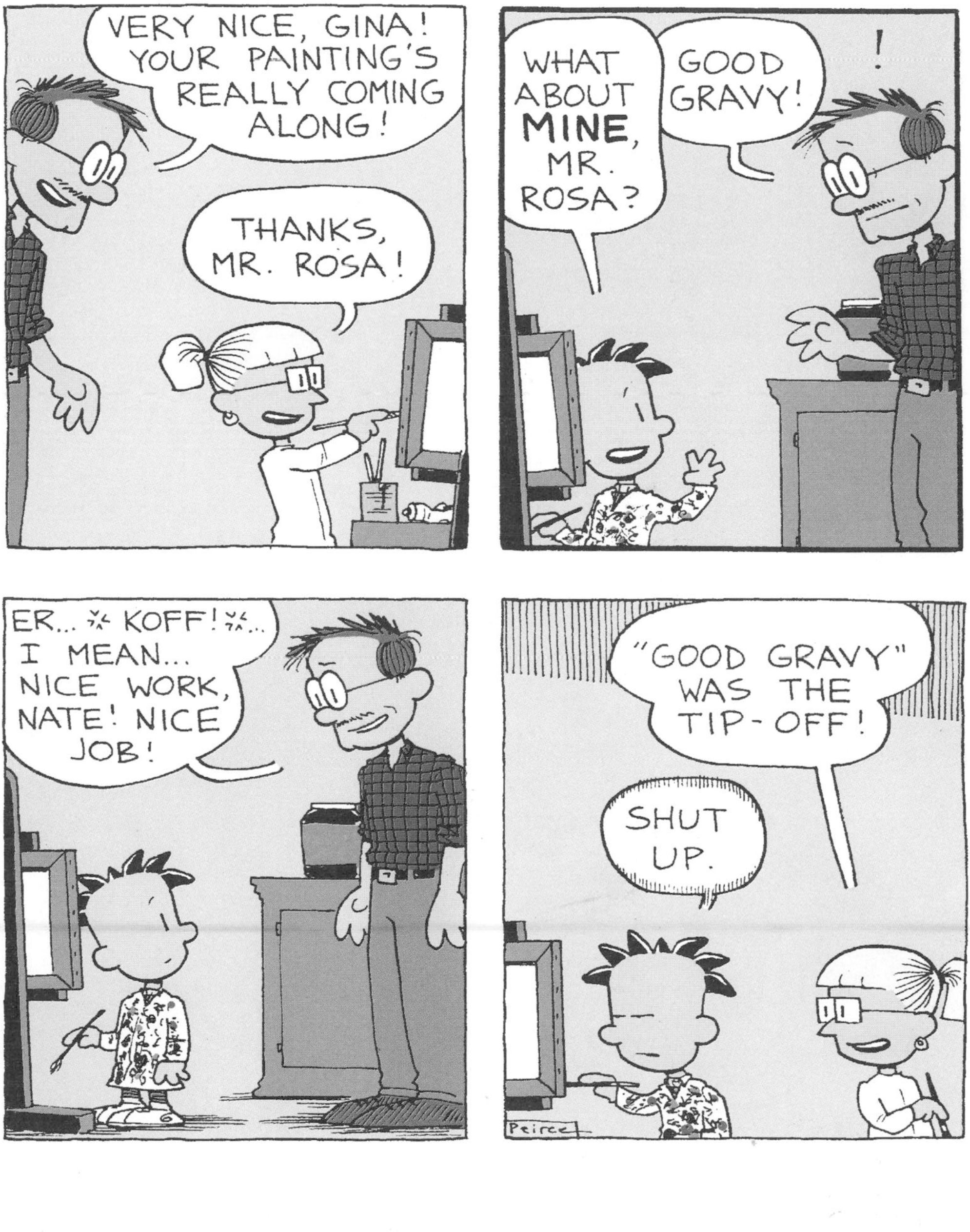
VERY NICE, GINA! YOUR PAINTING'S REALLY COMING ALONG!
THANKS, MR. ROSA!
WHAT ABOUT **MINE**, MR. ROSA?
GOOD GRAVY!
!
ER... KOFF!... I MEAN... NICE WORK, NATE! NICE JOB!
"GOOD GRAVY" WAS THE TIP-OFF!
SHUT UP.
Peirce

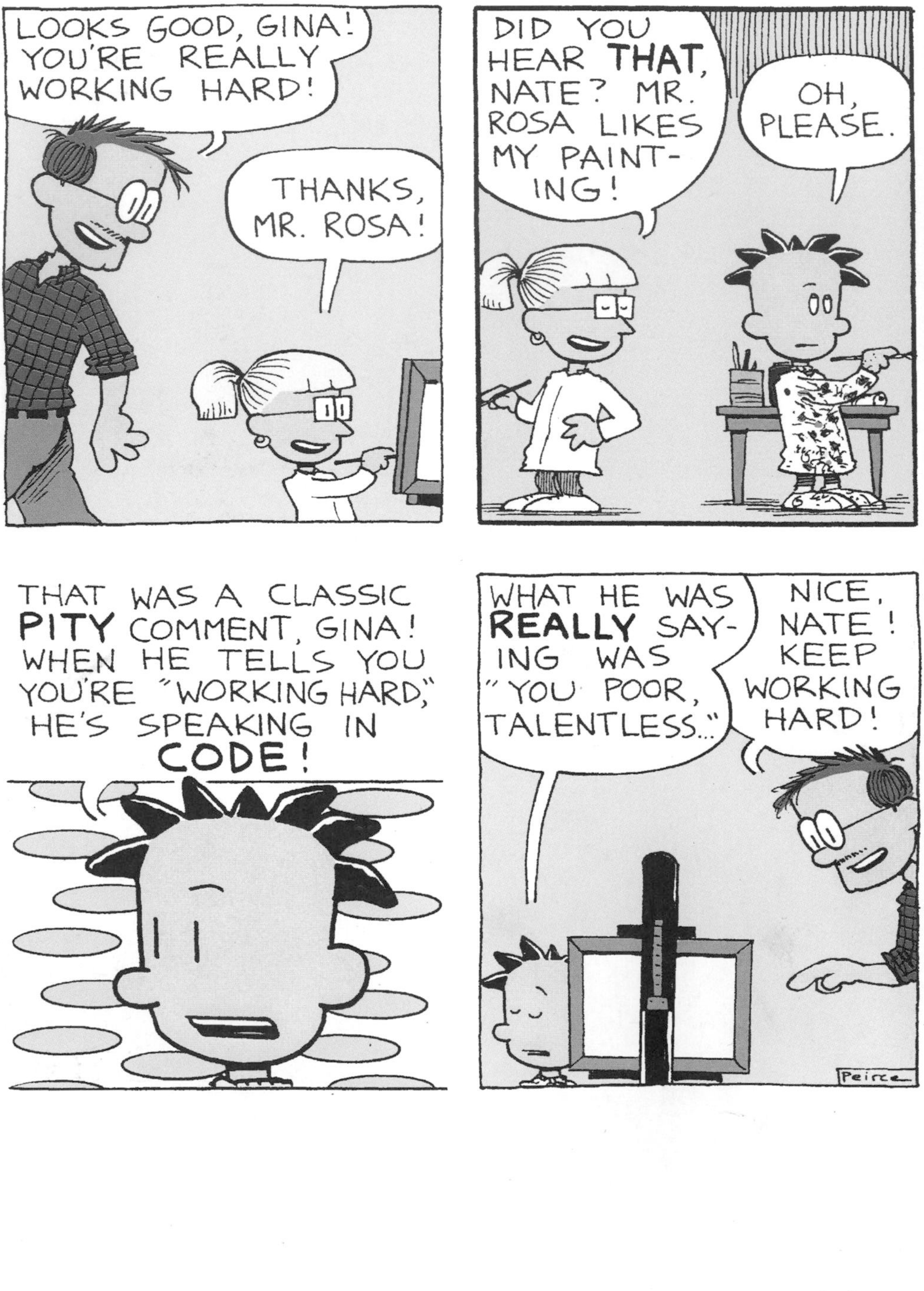
LOOKS GOOD, GINA! YOU'RE REALLY WORKING HARD!
THANKS, MR. ROSA!
DID YOU HEAR THAT, NATE? MR. ROSA LIKES MY PAINT-ING!
OH, PLEASE.
THAT WAS A CLASSIC PITY COMMENT, GINA! WHEN HE TELLS YOU YOU'RE "WORKING HARD," HE'S SPEAKING IN CODE!
WHAT HE WAS REALLY SAY-ING WAS "YOU POOR, TALENTLESS..."
NICE, NATE! KEEP WORKING HARD!
Peirce

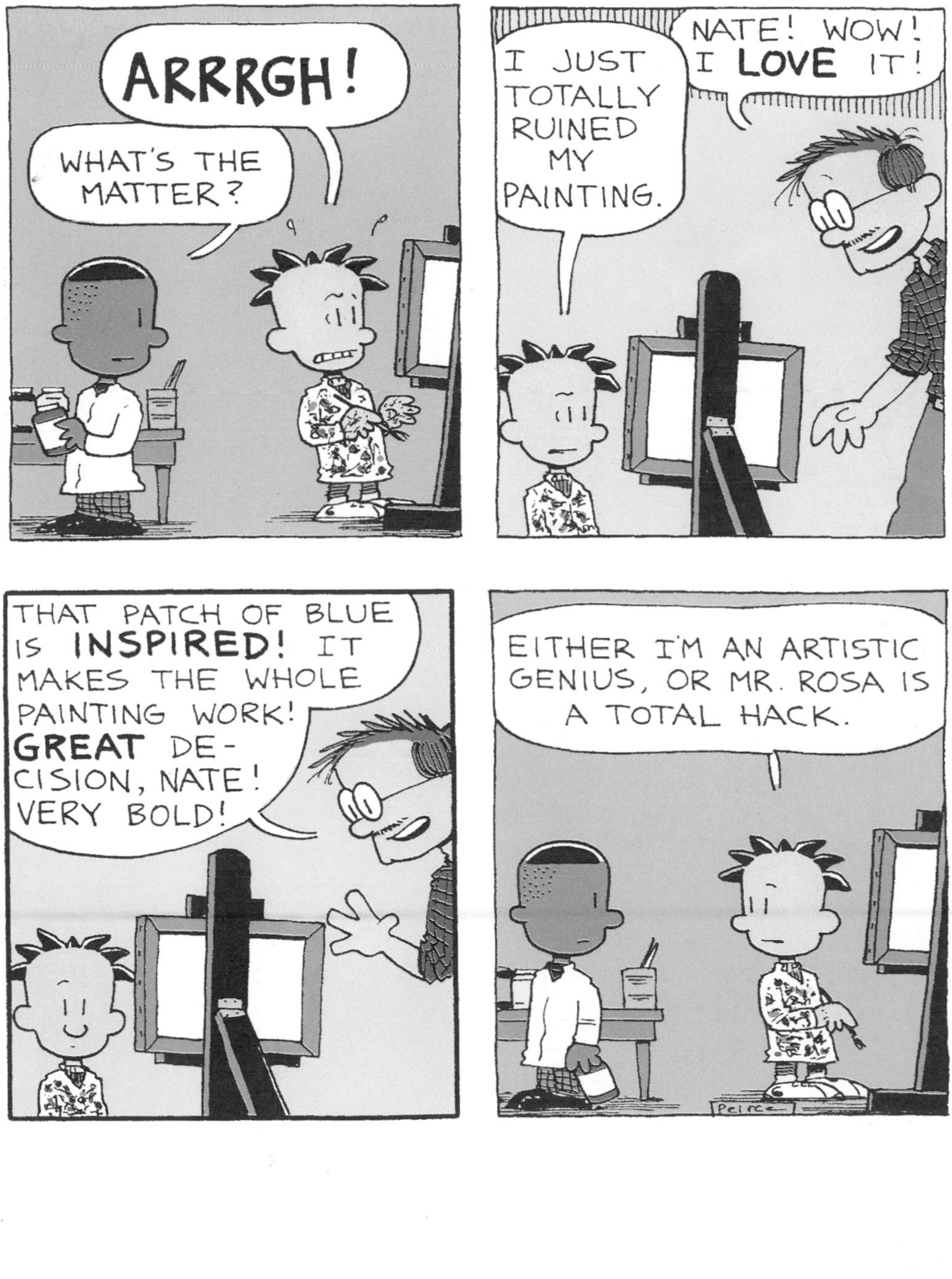
ARRRGH!
WHAT'S THE MATTER?
I JUST TOTALLY RUINED MY PAINTING.
NATE! WOW! I LOVE IT!
THAT PATCH OF BLUE IS INSPIRED! IT MAKES THE WHOLE PAINTING WORK! GREAT DE-CISION, NATE! VERY BOLD!
EITHER I'M AN ARTISTIC GENIUS, OR MR. ROSA IS A TOTAL HACK.
PEIRCE

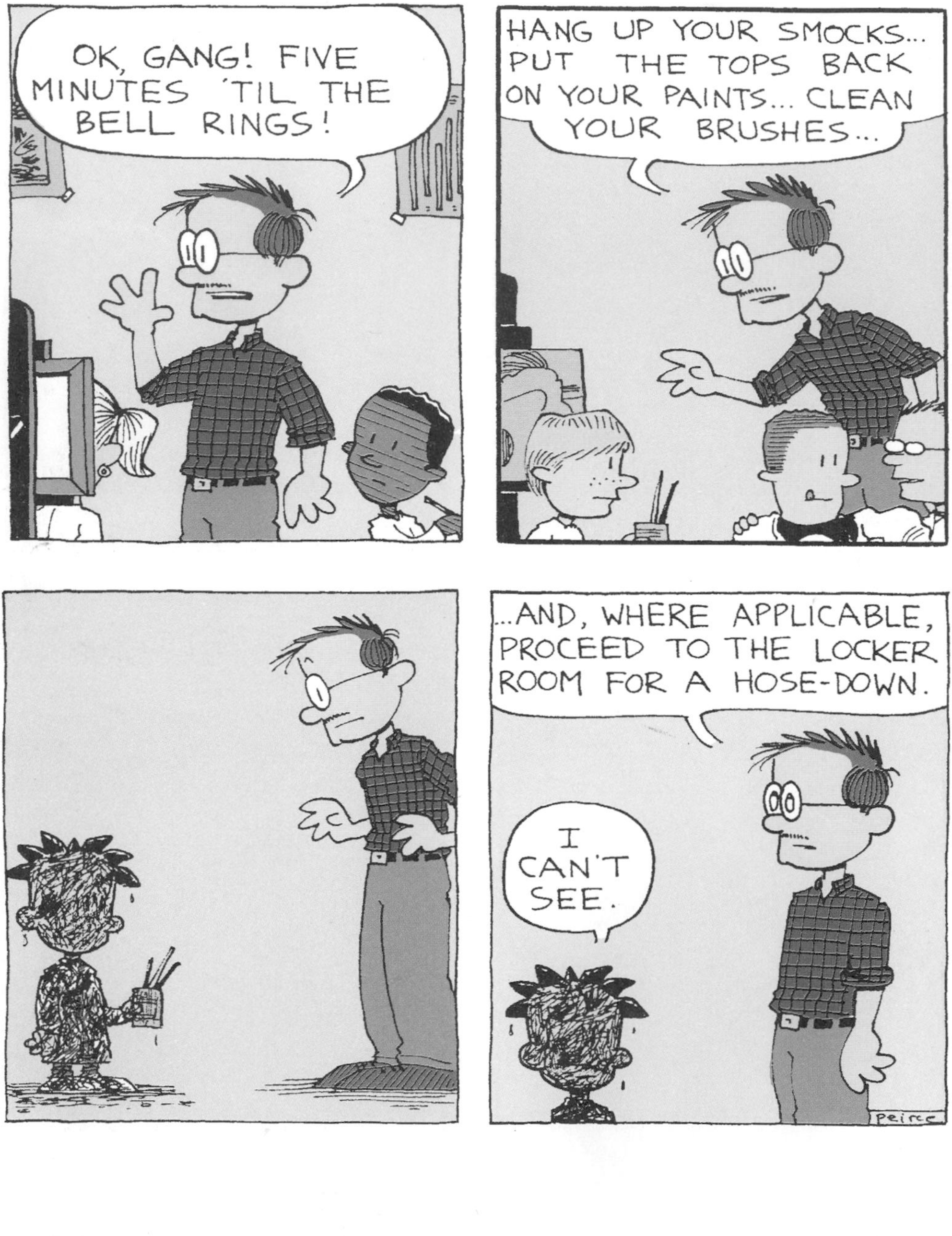
OK, GANG! FIVE MINUTES 'TIL THE BELL RINGS!
HANG UP YOUR SMOCKS... PUT THE TOPS BACK ON YOUR PAINTS... CLEAN YOUR BRUSHES...
...AND, WHERE APPLICABLE, PROCEED TO THE LOCKER ROOM FOR A HOSE-DOWN.
I CAN'T SEE.
peirce

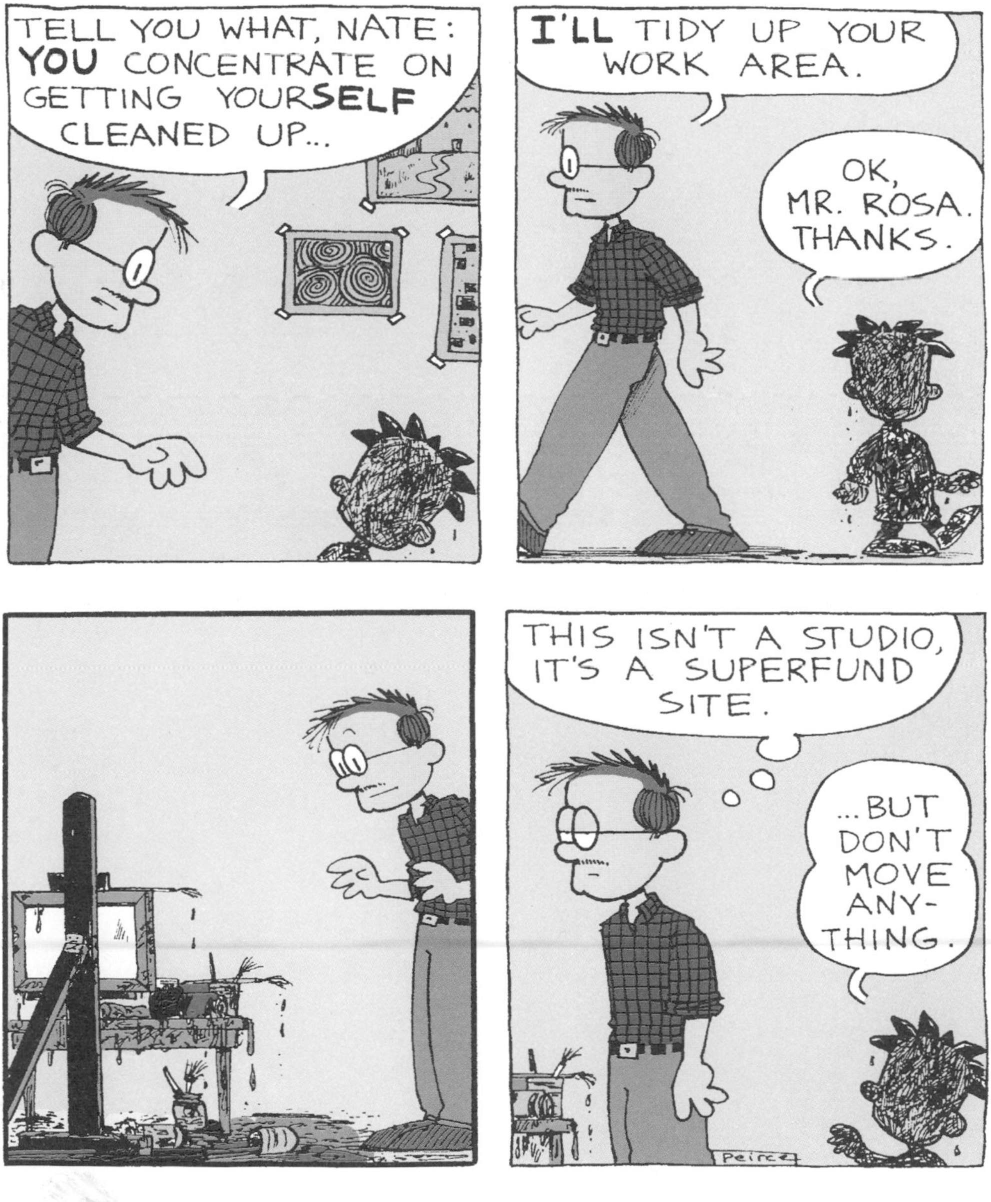
TELL YOU WHAT, NATE: **YOU** CONCENTRATE ON GETTING YOURSELF CLEANED UP...
I'LL TIDY UP YOUR WORK AREA.
OK, MR. ROSA. THANKS.
THIS ISN'T A STUDIO, IT'S A SUPERFUND SITE.
...BUT DON'T MOVE ANY-THING.
peirce

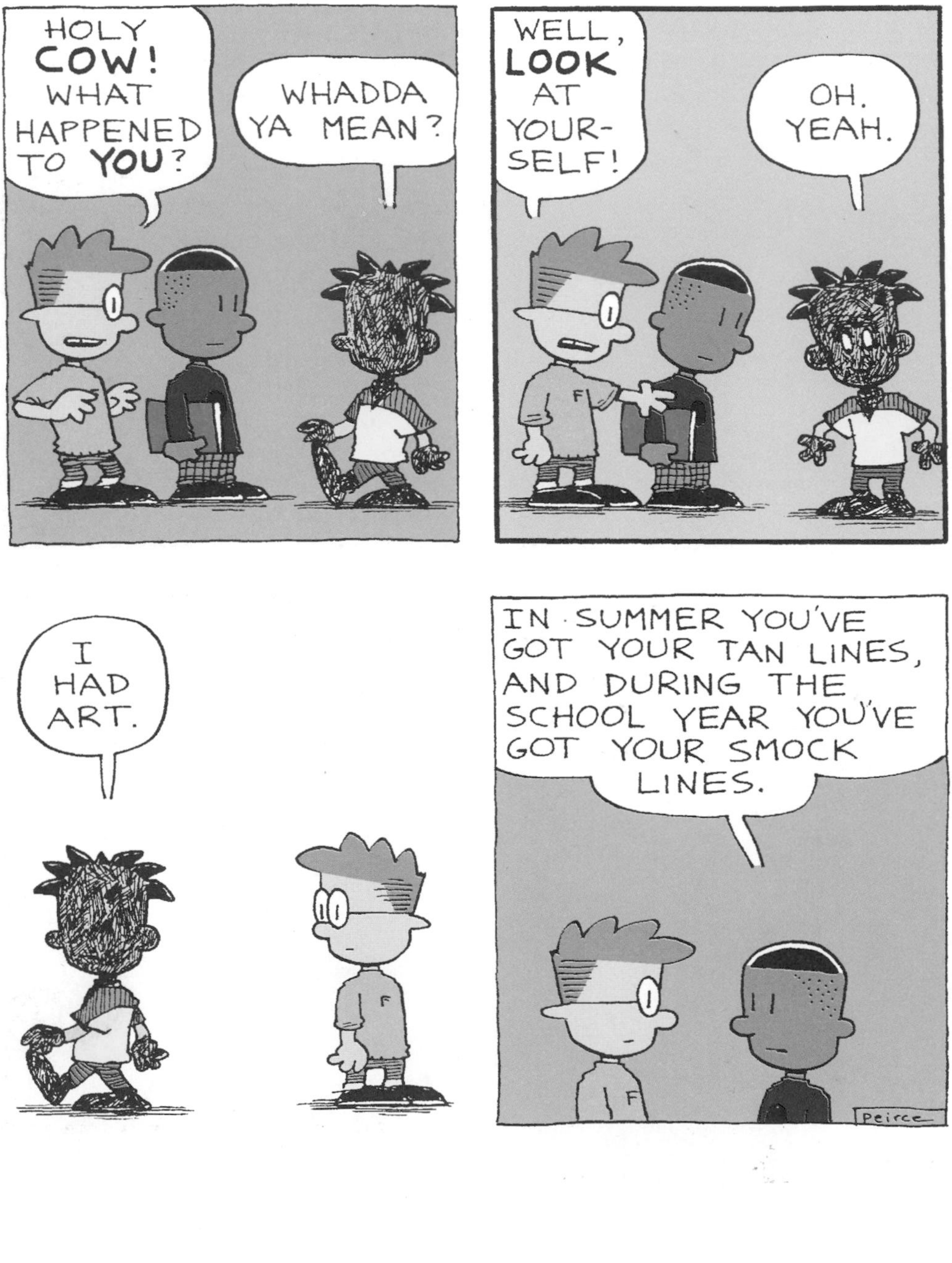
HOLY **COW**! WHAT HAPPENED TO **YOU**?
WHADDA YA MEAN?
WELL, **LOOK** AT YOURSELF!
OH. YEAH.
I HAD ART.
IN SUMMER YOU'VE GOT YOUR TAN LINES, AND DURING THE SCHOOL YEAR YOU'VE GOT YOUR SMOCK LINES.
Peirce

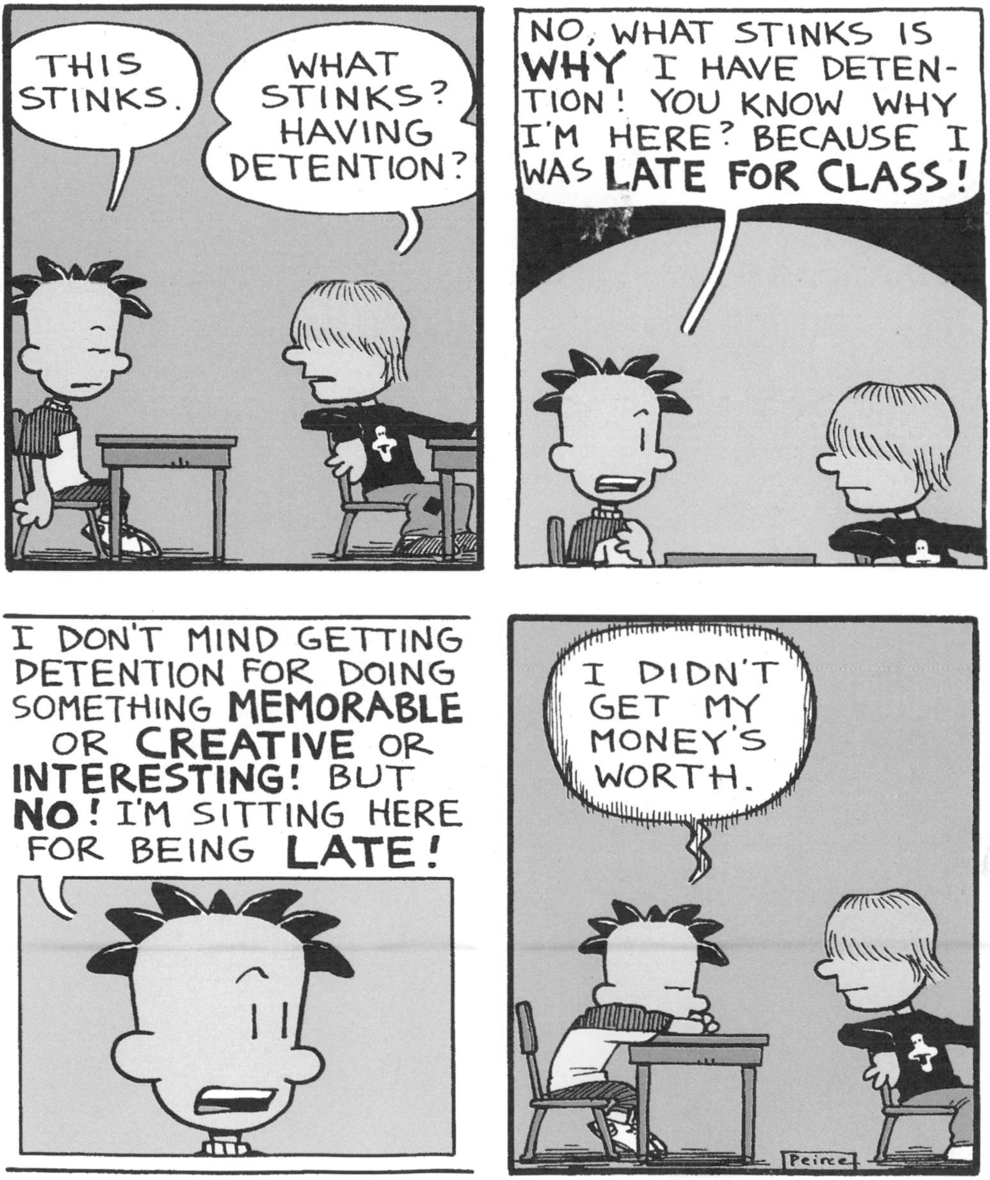
THIS STINKS.
WHAT STINKS? HAVING DETENTION?
NO, WHAT STINKS IS WHY I HAVE DETENTION! YOU KNOW WHY I'M HERE? BECAUSE I WAS LATE FOR CLASS!
I DON'T MIND GETTING DETENTION FOR DOING SOMETHING MEMORABLE OR CREATIVE OR INTERESTING! BUT NO! I'M SITTING HERE FOR BEING LATE!
I DIDN'T GET MY MONEY'S WORTH.
Peirce

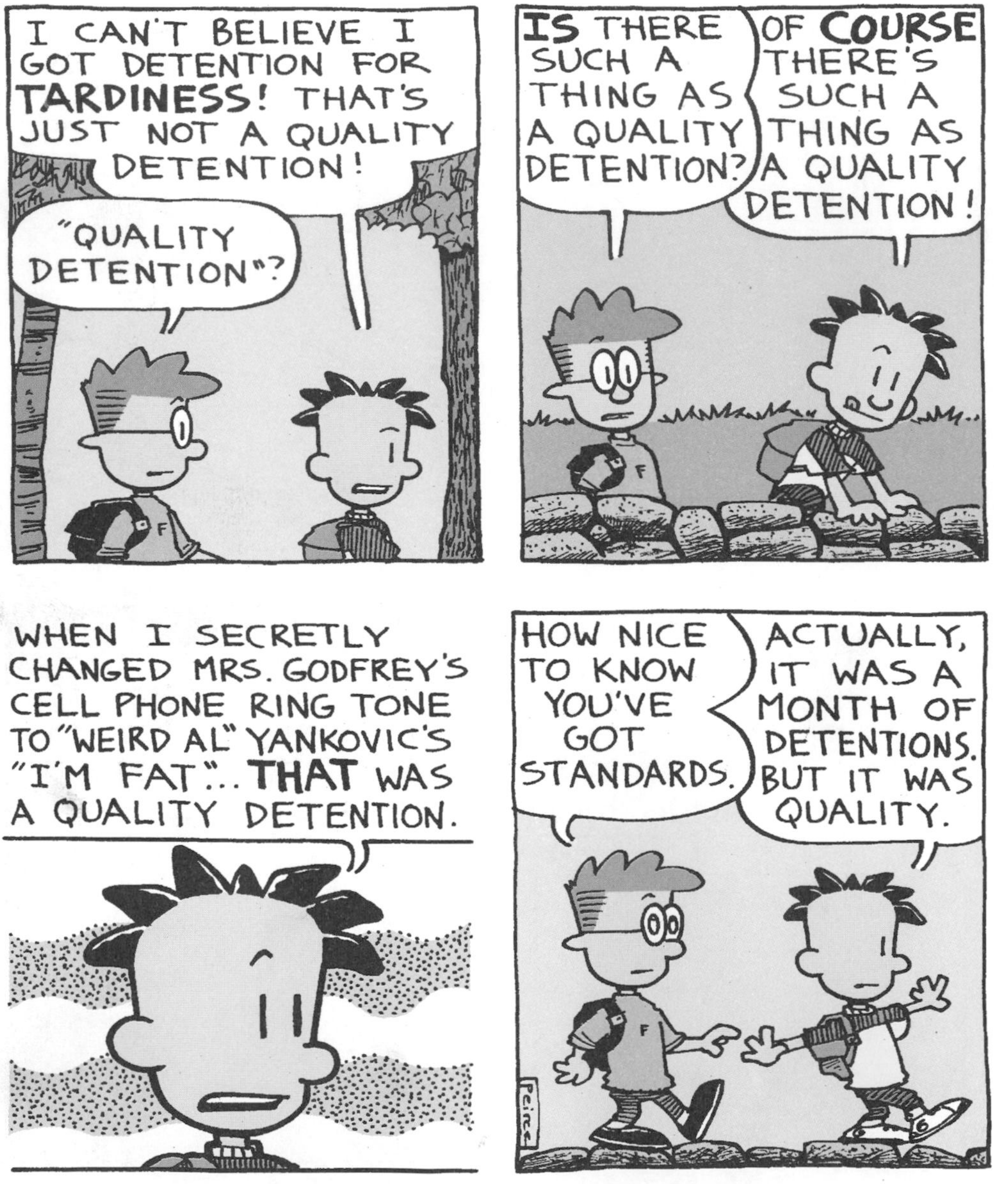
I CAN'T BELIEVE I GOT DETENTION FOR TARDINESS! THAT'S JUST NOT A QUALITY DETENTION!
"QUALITY DETENTION"?
IS THERE SUCH A THING AS A QUALITY DETENTION?
OF COURSE THERE'S SUCH A THING AS A QUALITY DETENTION!
WHEN I SECRETLY CHANGED MRS. GODFREY'S CELL PHONE RING TONE TO "WEIRD AL" YANKOVIC'S "I'M FAT"... THAT WAS A QUALITY DETENTION.
HOW NICE TO KNOW YOU'VE GOT STANDARDS.
ACTUALLY, IT WAS A MONTH OF DETENTIONS. BUT IT WAS QUALITY.
PEIRCE

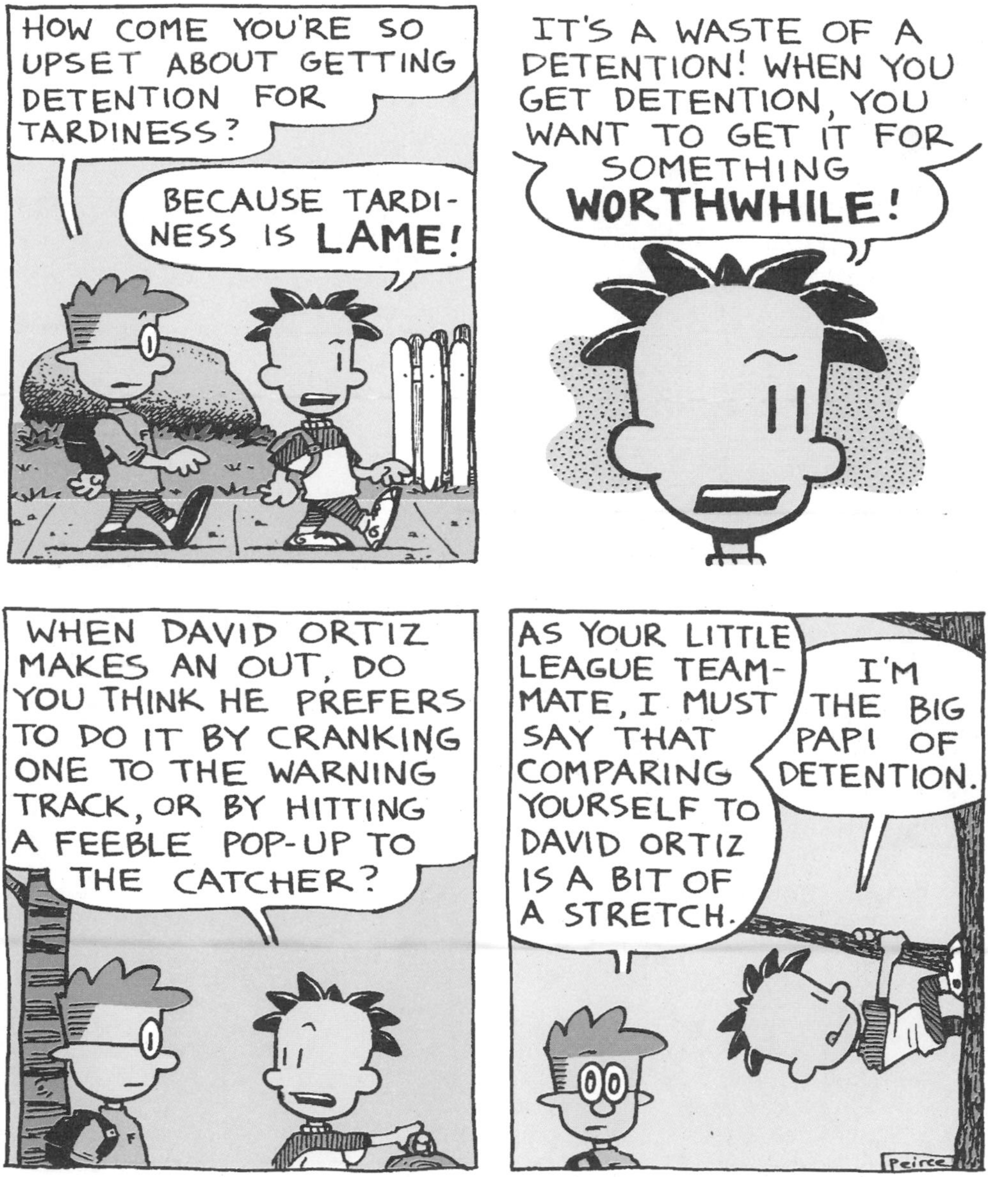
HOW COME YOU'RE SO UPSET ABOUT GETTING DETENTION FOR TARDINESS?
BECAUSE TARDI-NESS IS LAME!
IT'S A WASTE OF A DETENTION! WHEN YOU GET DETENTION, YOU WANT TO GET IT FOR SOMETHING WORTHWHILE!
WHEN DAVID ORTIZ MAKES AN OUT, DO YOU THINK HE PREFERS TO DO IT BY CRANKING ONE TO THE WARNING TRACK, OR BY HITTING A FEEBLE POP-UP TO THE CATCHER?
I'M THE BIG PAPI OF DETENTION.
AS YOUR LITTLE LEAGUE TEAM-MATE, I MUST SAY THAT COMPARING YOURSELF TO DAVID ORTIZ IS A BIT OF A STRETCH.
Peirce

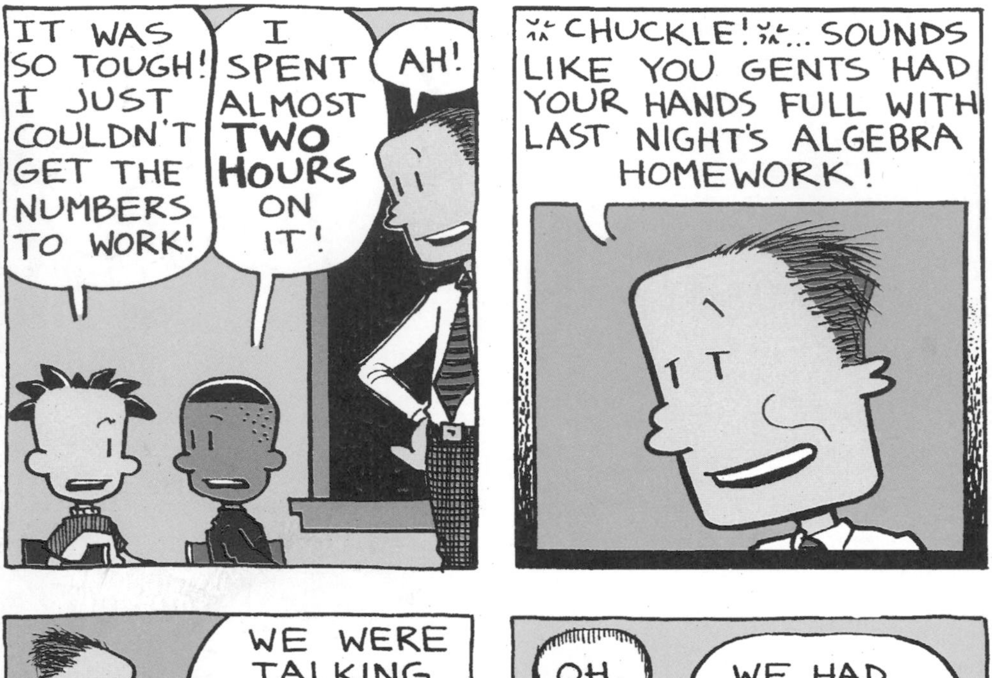
IT WAS SO TOUGH! I JUST COULDN'T GET THE NUMBERS TO WORK!
I SPENT ALMOST **TWO HOURS** ON IT!
AH!
CHUCKLE! ... SOUNDS LIKE YOU GENTS HAD YOUR HANDS FULL WITH LAST NIGHT'S ALGEBRA HOMEWORK!
WE WERE TALKING ABOUT THE SUDOKU IN YES-TERDAY'S NEWSPAPER.
OH.
WE HAD ALGEBRA HOMEWORK?
BEATS ME.
peirce

ARRRRRRRRGH!
RIP! RIP!
RIP! RIP! RI
P! RIP! RIP!
YOU KNOW HOW THEY SAY IT'S A FINE LINE BETWEEN LOVE AND HATE?
I GUESS.
IT'S AN EVEN FINER LINE BETWEEN SUDOKU AND INSANITY.

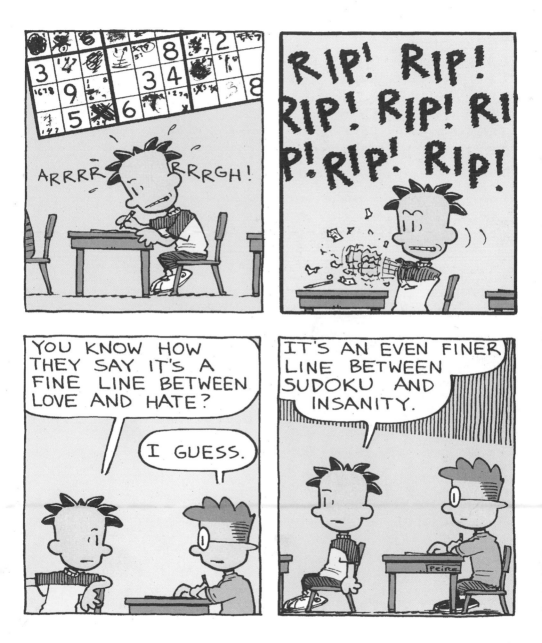

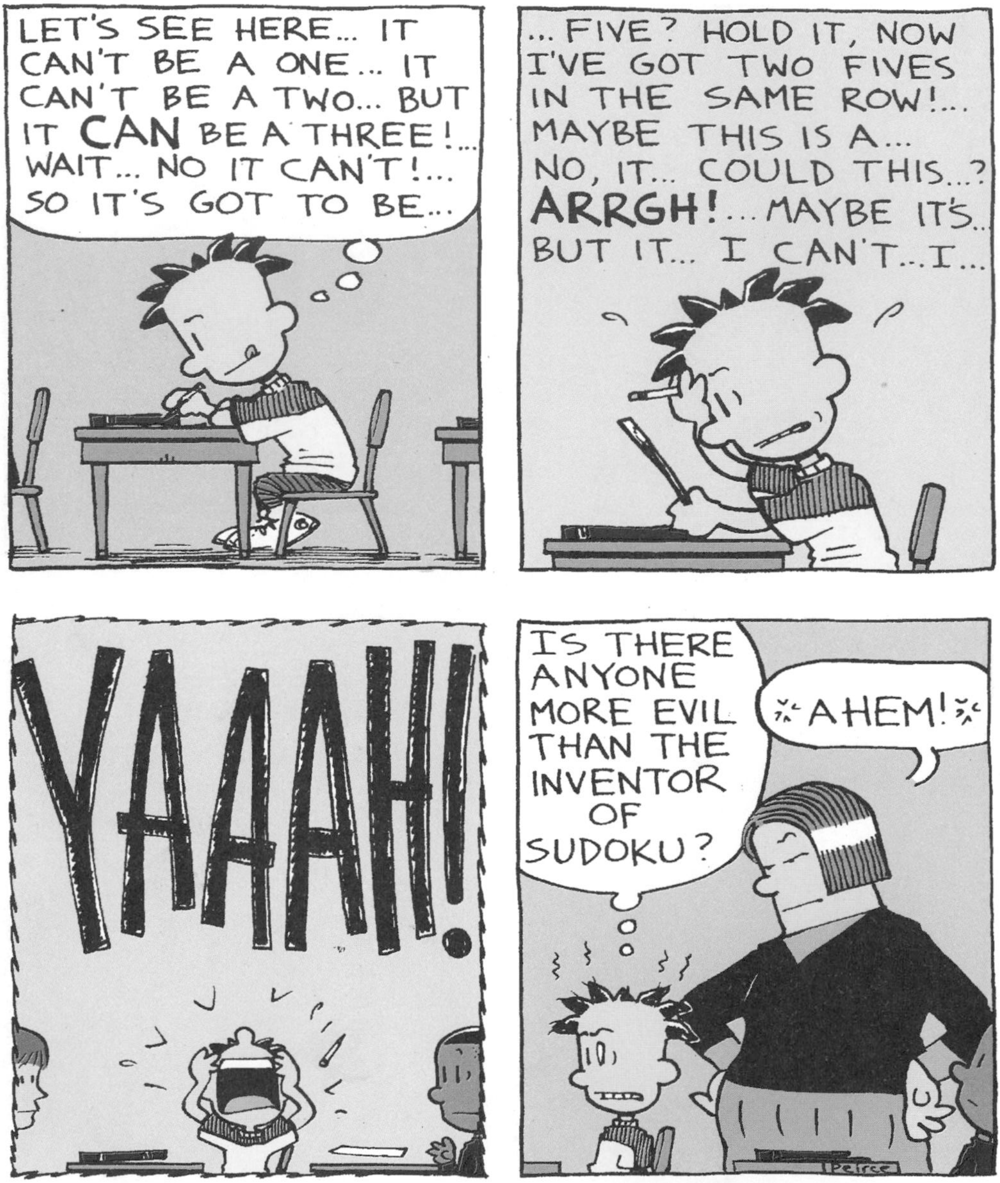
LET'S SEE HERE... IT CAN'T BE A ONE... IT CAN'T BE A TWO... BUT IT CAN BE A THREE!... WAIT... NO IT CAN'T!... SO IT'S GOT TO BE...
...FIVE? HOLD IT, NOW I'VE GOT TWO FIVES IN THE SAME ROW!... MAYBE THIS IS A... NO, IT... COULD THIS...? ARRGH!... MAYBE IT'S... BUT IT... I CAN'T... I...
YAAAH!
IS THERE ANYONE MORE EVIL THAN THE INVENTOR OF SUDOKU?
AHEM!
Peirce

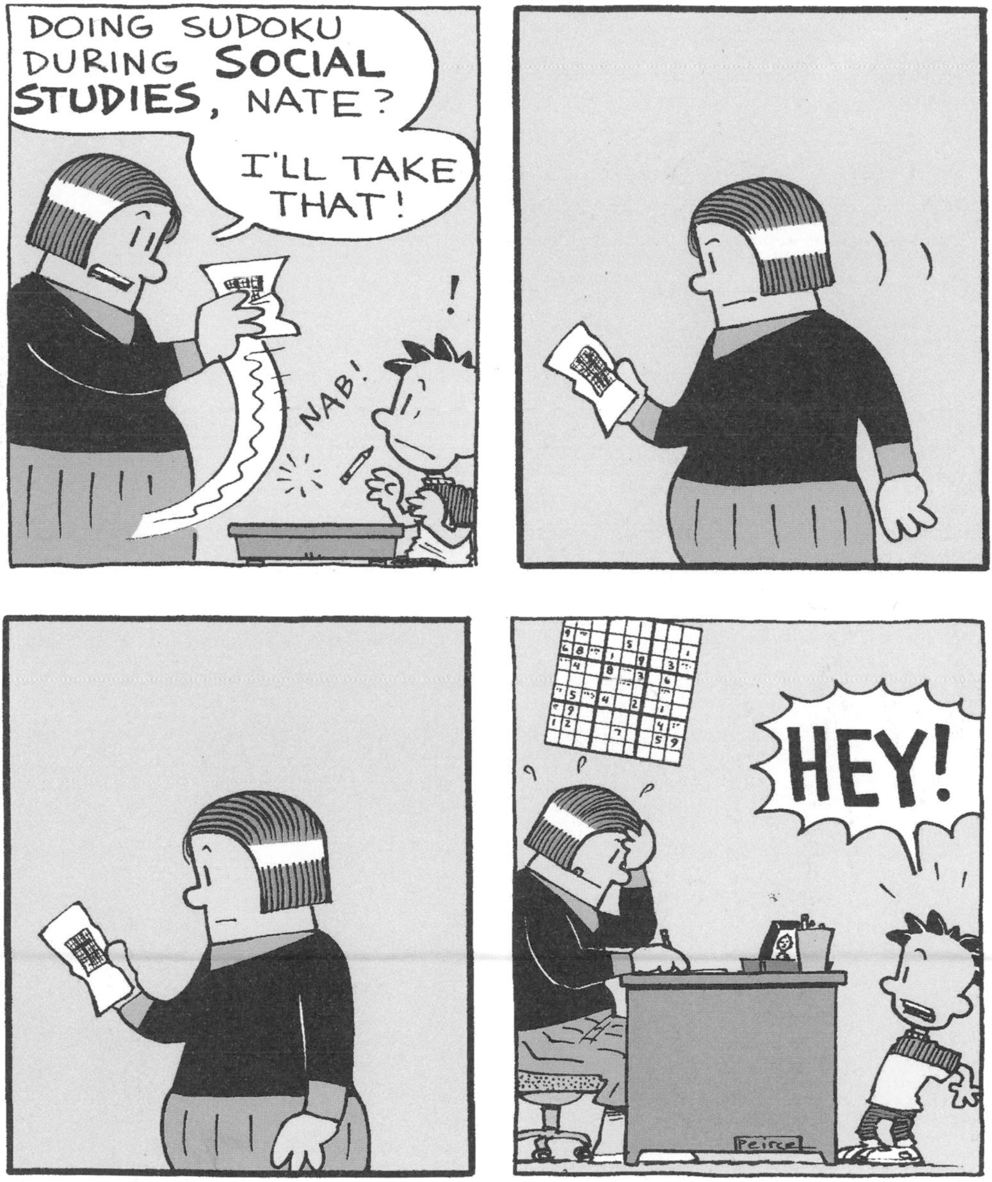
DOING SUDOKU DURING SOCIAL STUDIES, NATE?
I'LL TAKE THAT!
!
NAB!
HEY!
Peirce

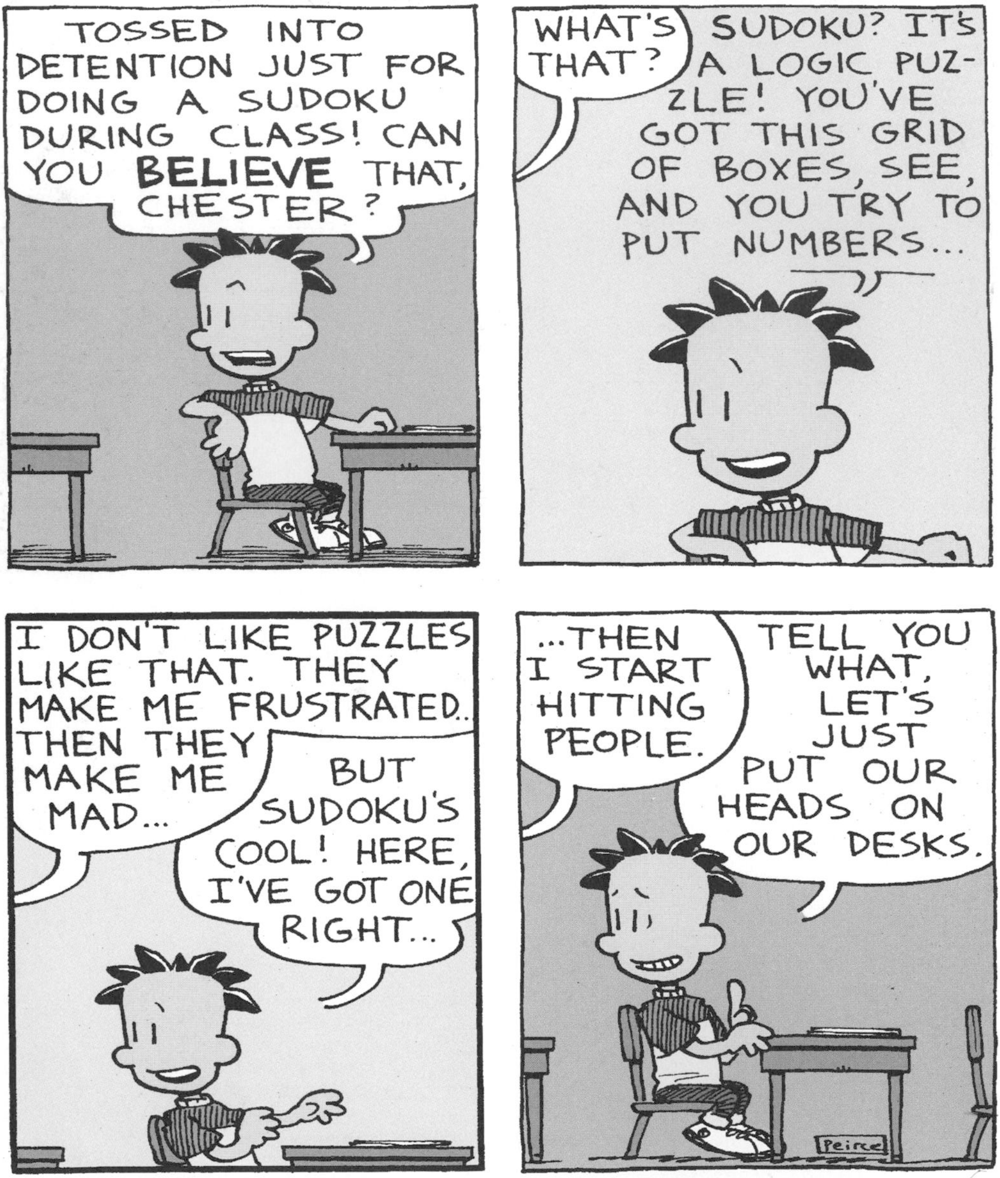
TOSSED INTO DETENTION JUST FOR DOING A SUDOKU DURING CLASS! CAN YOU **BELIEVE** THAT, CHESTER?
WHAT'S THAT?
SUDOKU? IT'S A LOGIC PUZ-ZLE! YOU'VE GOT THIS GRID OF BOXES, SEE, AND YOU TRY TO PUT NUMBERS...
I DON'T LIKE PUZZLES LIKE THAT. THEY MAKE ME FRUSTRATED.. THEN THEY MAKE ME MAD...
BUT SUDOKU'S COOL! HERE, I'VE GOT ONE RIGHT...
...THEN I START HITTING PEOPLE.
TELL YOU WHAT, LET'S JUST PUT OUR HEADS ON OUR DESKS.
Peirce

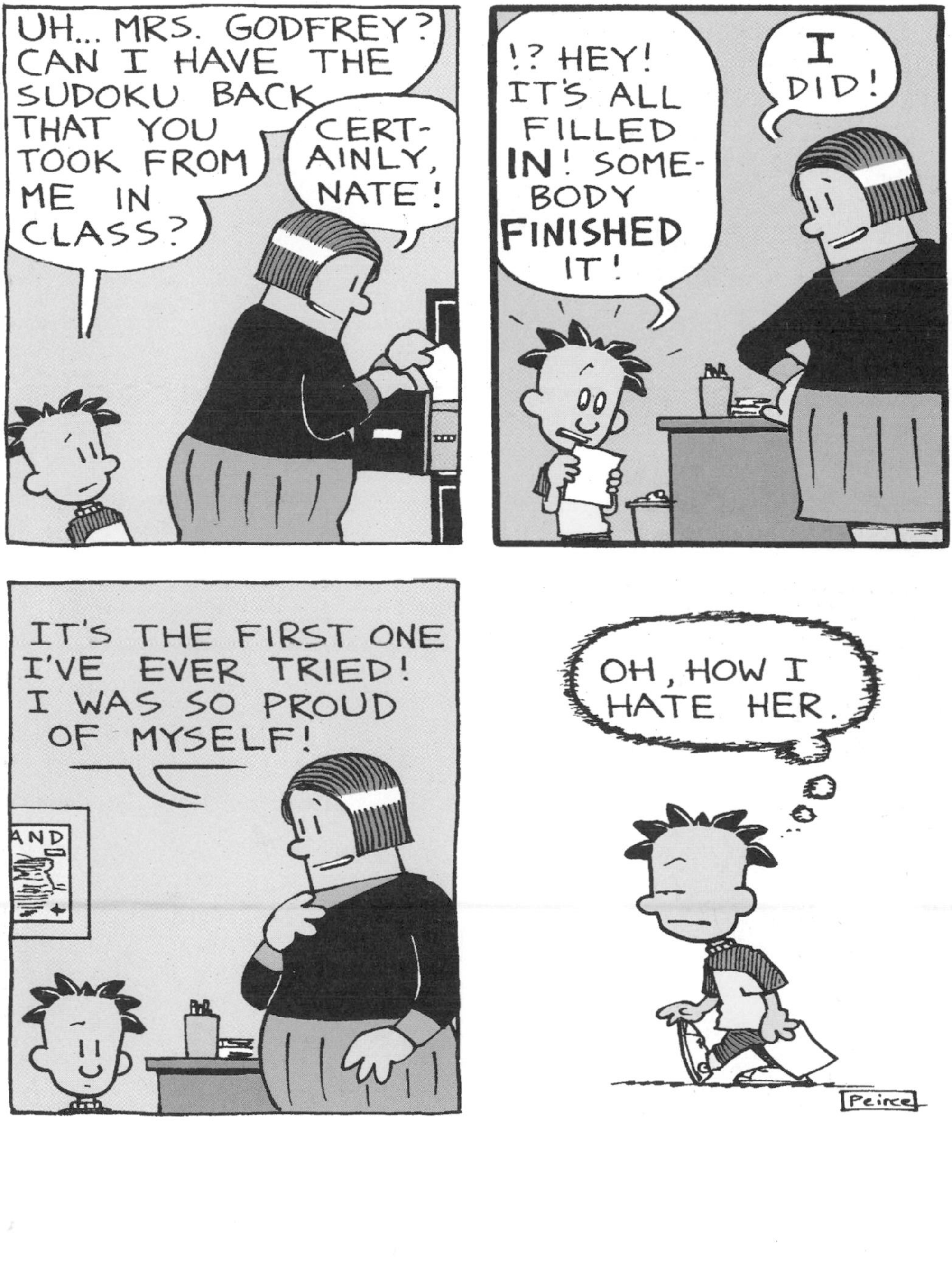
UH... MRS. GODFREY? CAN I HAVE THE SUDOKU BACK THAT YOU TOOK FROM ME IN CLASS?
CERT-AINLY, NATE!
!? HEY! IT'S ALL FILLED IN! SOME-BODY FINISHED IT!
I DID!
IT'S THE FIRST ONE I'VE EVER TRIED! I WAS SO PROUD OF MYSELF!
OH, HOW I HATE HER.
Peirce

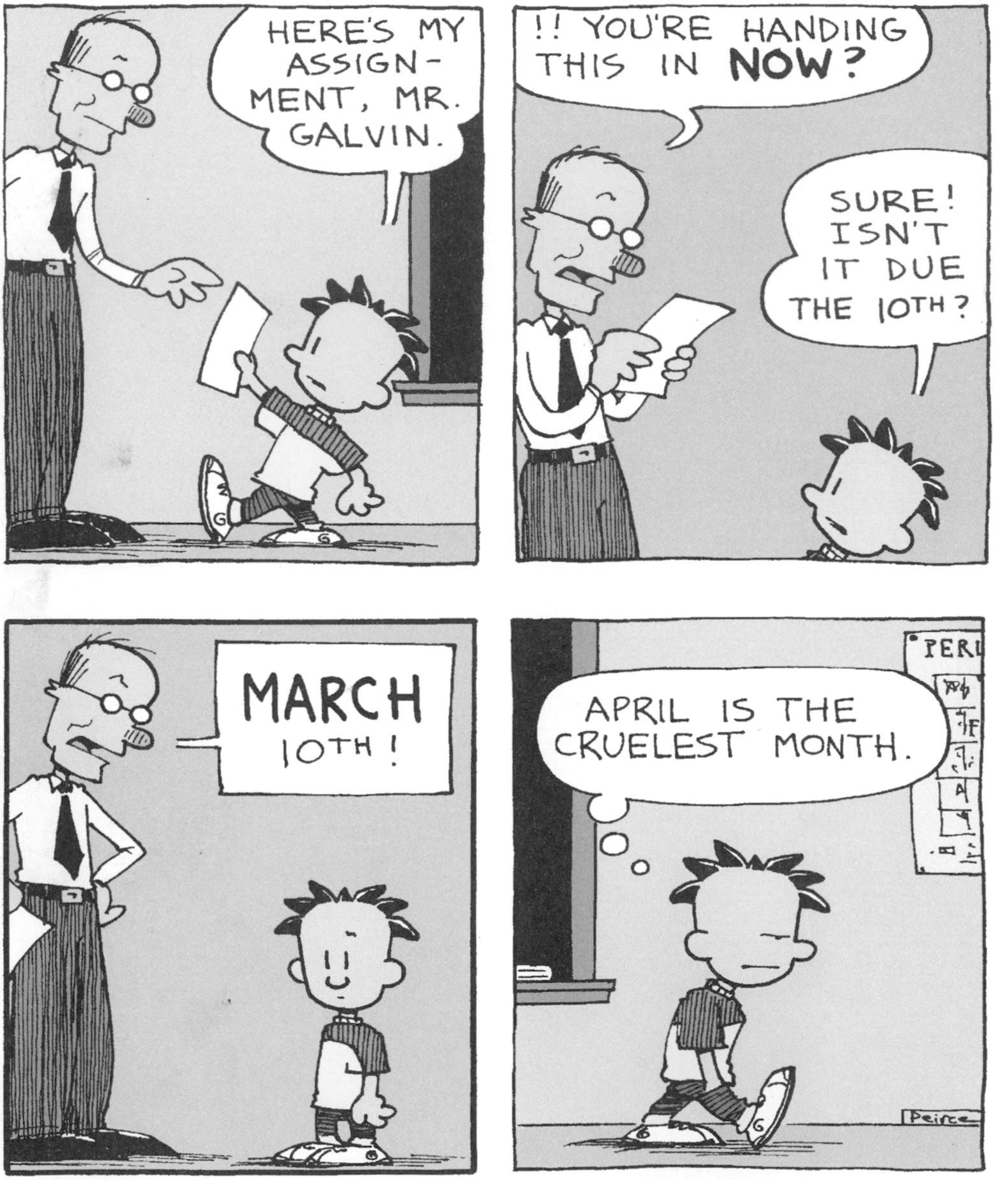
HERE'S MY ASSIGN-MENT, MR. GALVIN.
!! YOU'RE HANDING THIS IN **NOW**?
SURE! ISN'T IT DUE THE 10TH?
MARCH 10TH!
APRIL IS THE CRUELEST MONTH.
Peirce

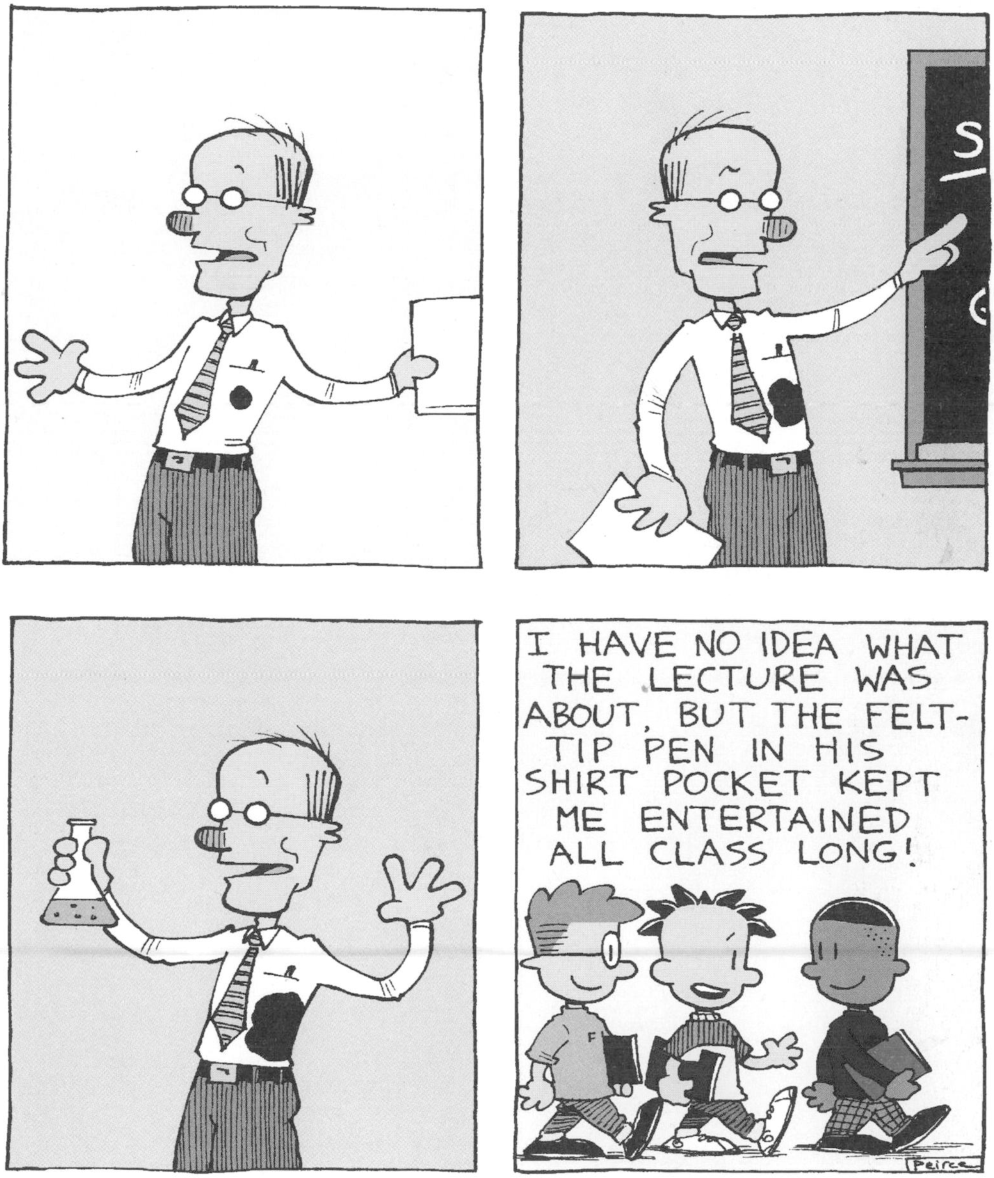
S
I HAVE NO IDEA WHAT THE LECTURE WAS ABOUT, BUT THE FELT-TIP PEN IN HIS SHIRT POCKET KEPT ME ENTERTAINED ALL CLASS LONG!
Peirce

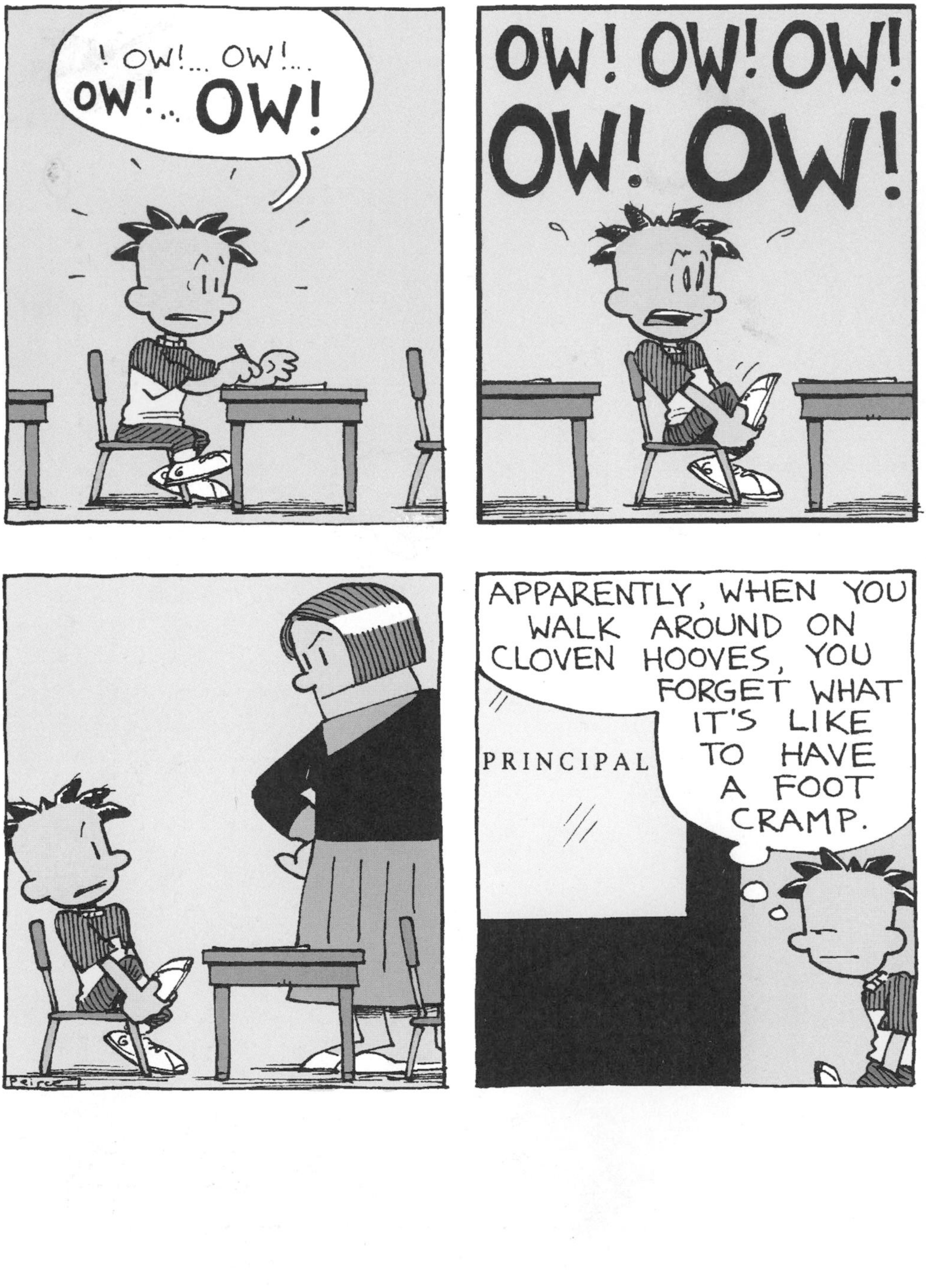

! OW!... OW!... OW!... OW!
OW! OW! OW! OW! OW!
PRINCIPAL
APPARENTLY, WHEN YOU WALK AROUND ON CLOVEN HOOVES, YOU FORGET WHAT IT'S LIKE TO HAVE A FOOT CRAMP.

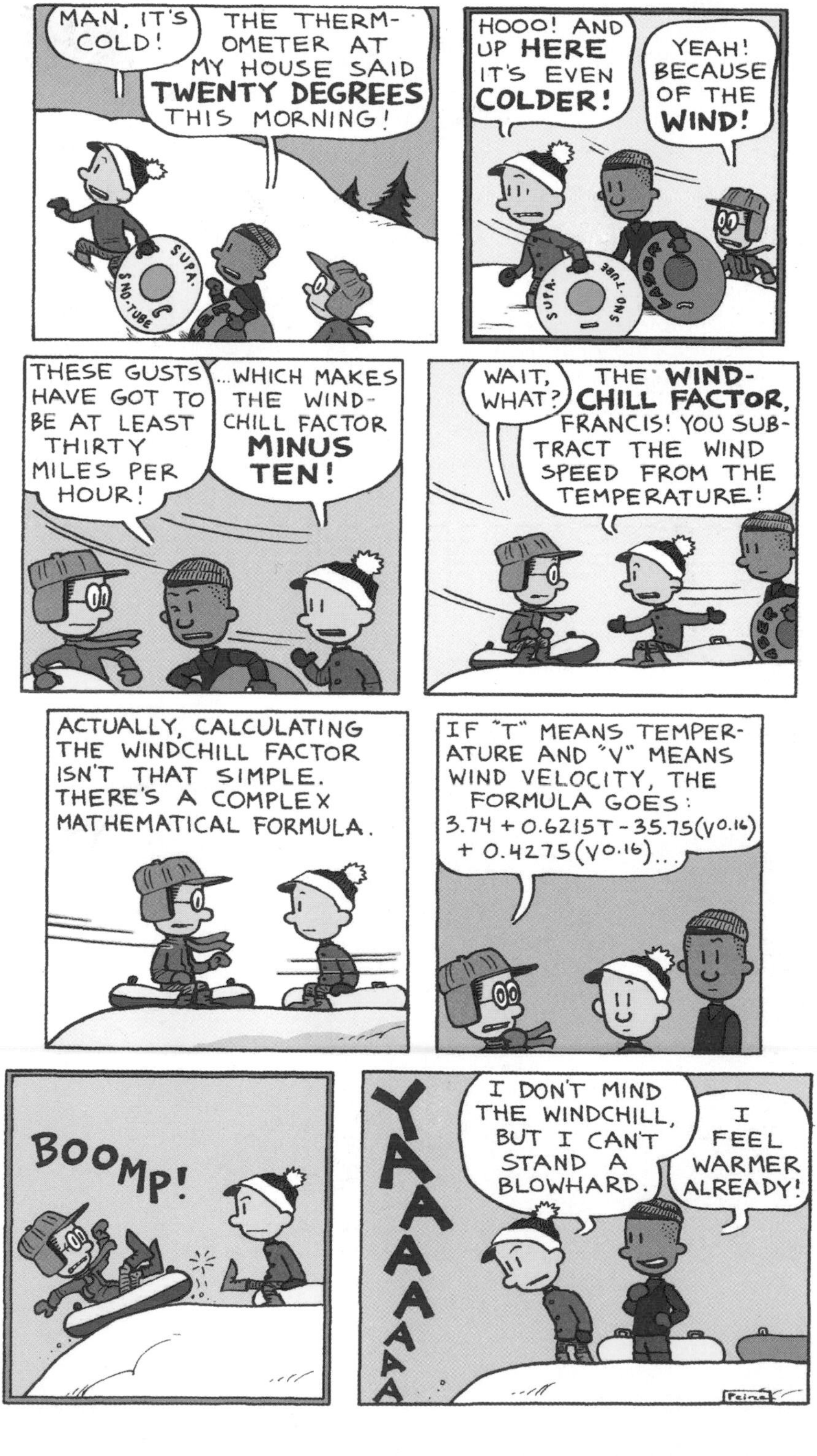
MAN, IT'S COLD!
THE THERMOMETER AT MY HOUSE SAID **TWENTY DEGREES** THIS MORNING!
SUPA. SNO-TUBE
HOOO! AND UP **HERE** IT'S EVEN **COLDER!**
YEAH! BECAUSE OF THE **WIND!**
SUPA. SNO-TUBE
THESE GUSTS HAVE GOT TO BE AT LEAST THIRTY MILES PER HOUR!
...WHICH MAKES THE WIND-CHILL FACTOR **MINUS TEN!**
WAIT, WHAT?
THE **WIND-CHILL FACTOR,** FRANCIS! YOU SUBTRACT THE WIND SPEED FROM THE TEMPERATURE!
ACTUALLY, CALCULATING THE WINDCHILL FACTOR ISN'T THAT SIMPLE. THERE'S A COMPLEX MATHEMATICAL FORMULA.
IF "T" MEANS TEMPERATURE AND "V" MEANS WIND VELOCITY, THE FORMULA GOES: 3.74 + 0.6215T - 35.75(V0.16) + 0.4275(V0.16)...
BOOMP!
YAAAAAA
I DON'T MIND THE WINDCHILL, BUT I CAN'T STAND A BLOWHARD.
I FEEL WARMER ALREADY!
Peirce

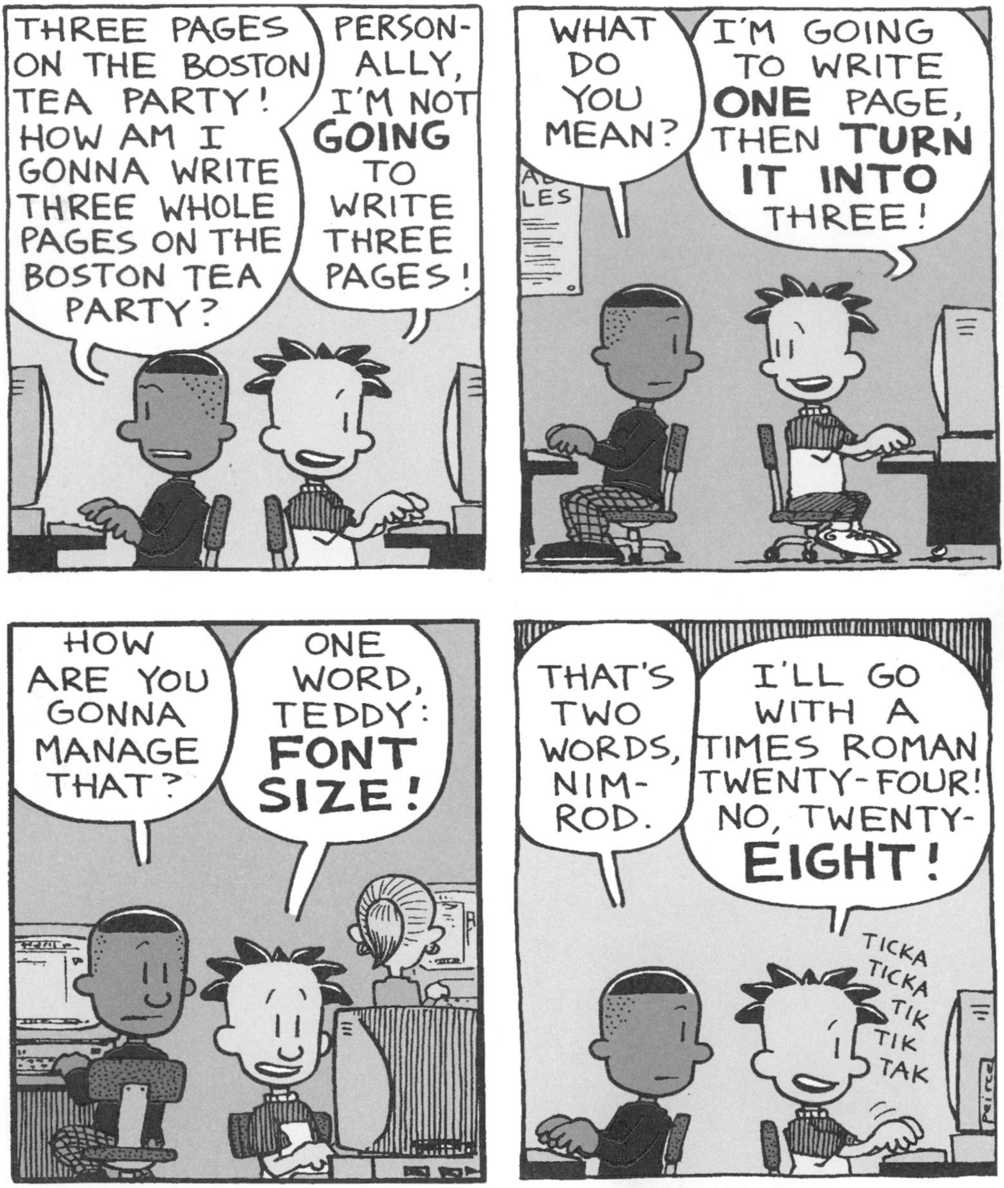
THREE PAGES ON THE BOSTON TEA PARTY! HOW AM I GONNA WRITE THREE WHOLE PAGES ON THE BOSTON TEA PARTY?
PERSON-ALLY, I'M NOT **GOING** TO WRITE THREE PAGES!
WHAT DO YOU MEAN?
I'M GOING TO WRITE **ONE** PAGE, THEN **TURN IT INTO** THREE!
HOW ARE YOU GONNA MANAGE THAT?
ONE WORD, TEDDY: **FONT SIZE!**
THAT'S TWO WORDS, NIM-ROD.
I'LL GO WITH A TIMES ROMAN TWENTY-FOUR! NO, TWENTY-**EIGHT!**
TICKA TICKA TIK TIK TAK
Peirce

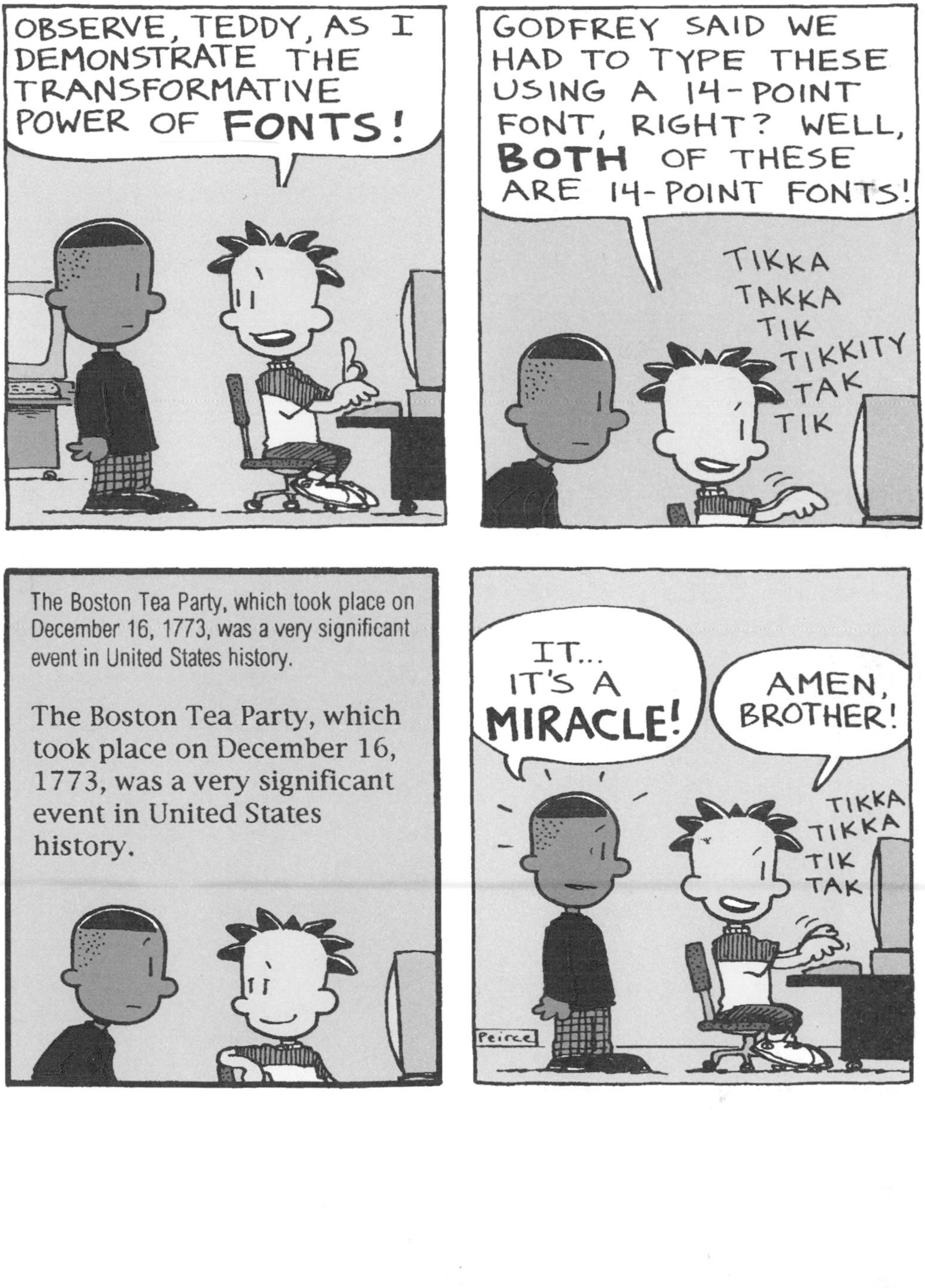
OBSERVE, TEDDY, AS I DEMONSTRATE THE TRANSFORMATIVE POWER OF **FONTS**!
GODFREY SAID WE HAD TO TYPE THESE USING A 14-POINT FONT, RIGHT? WELL, **BOTH** OF THESE ARE 14-POINT FONTS!
TIKKA TAKKA TIK TIKKITY TAK TIK
The Boston Tea Party, which took place on December 16, 1773, was a very significant event in United States history.
The Boston Tea Party, which took place on December 16, 1773, was a very significant event in United States history.
IT... IT'S A **MIRACLE**!
AMEN, BROTHER!
TIKKA TIKKA TIK TAK
Peirce

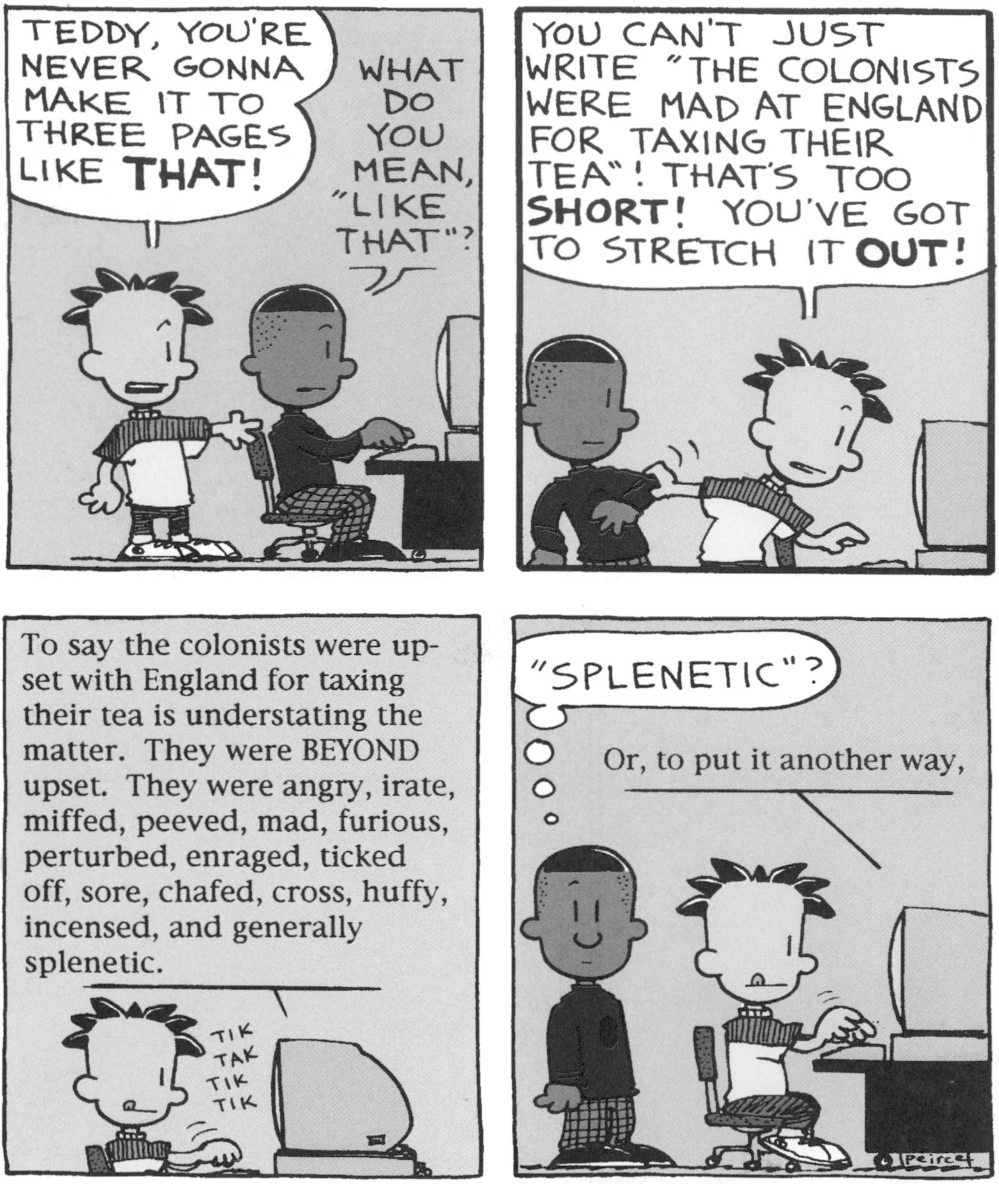
TEDDY, YOU'RE NEVER GONNA MAKE IT TO THREE PAGES LIKE **THAT**!
WHAT DO YOU MEAN, "LIKE THAT"?
YOU CAN'T JUST WRITE "THE COLONISTS WERE MAD AT ENGLAND FOR TAXING THEIR TEA"! THAT'S TOO **SHORT**! YOU'VE GOT TO STRETCH IT **OUT**!
To say the colonists were upset with England for taxing their tea is understating the matter. They were BEYOND upset. They were angry, irate, miffed, peeved, mad, furious, perturbed, enraged, ticked off, sore, chafed, cross, huffy, incensed, and generally splenetic.
TIK TAK TIK TIK
"SPLENETIC"?
Or, to put it another way,
© Peirce

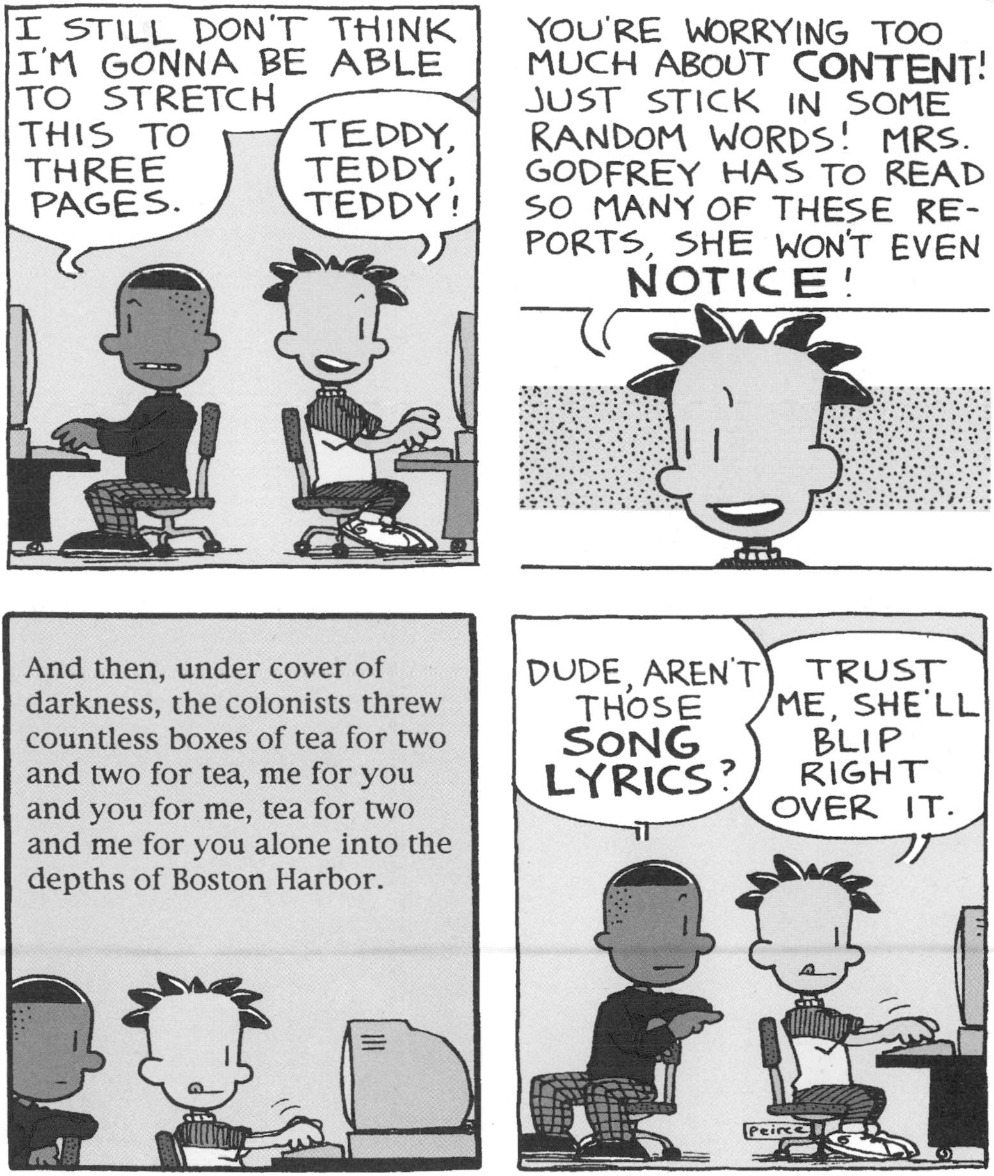
I STILL DON'T THINK I'M GONNA BE ABLE TO STRETCH THIS TO THREE PAGES.
TEDDY, TEDDY, TEDDY!
YOU'RE WORRYING TOO MUCH ABOUT CONTENT! JUST STICK IN SOME RANDOM WORDS! MRS. GODFREY HAS TO READ SO MANY OF THESE REPORTS, SHE WON'T EVEN NOTICE!
And then, under cover of darkness, the colonists threw countless boxes of tea for two and two for tea, me for you and you for me, tea for two and me for you alone into the depths of Boston Harbor.
DUDE, AREN'T THOSE SONG LYRICS?
TRUST ME, SHE'LL BLIP RIGHT OVER IT.
Peirce

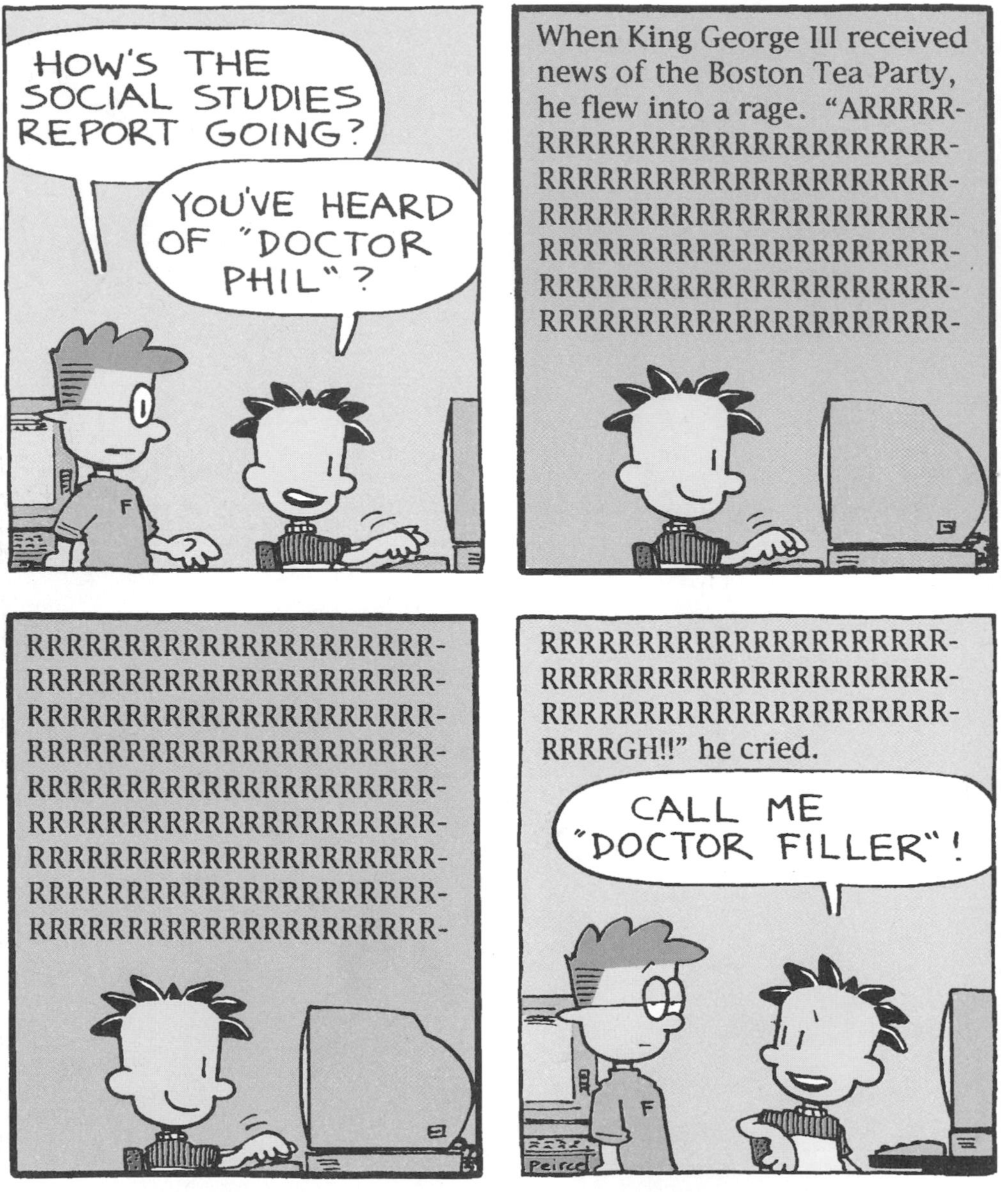

HOW'S THE SOCIAL STUDIES REPORT GOING?
YOU'VE HEARD OF "DOCTOR PHIL"?
When King George III received news of the Boston Tea Party, he flew into a rage. "ARRRRR-
RRRRRRRRRRRRRRRRRRRRR-
RRRRRRRRRRRRRRRRRRRRR-
RRRRRRRRRRRRRRRRRRRRR-
RRRRRRRRRRRRRRRRRRRRR-
RRRRRRRRRRRRRRRRRRRRR-
RRRRRRRRRRRRRRRRRRRRR-
RRRRRRRRRRRRRRRRRRRRR-
RRRRRRRRRRRRRRRRRRRRR-
RRRRRRRRRRRRRRRRRRRRR-
RRRRRRRRRRRRRRRRRRRRR-
RRRRRRRRRRRRRRRRRRRRR-
RRRRRRRRRRRRRRRRRRRRR-
RRRRRRRRRRRRRRRRRRRRR-
RRRRRRRRRRRRRRRRRRRRR-
RRRRRRRRRRRRRRRRRRRRR-
RRRRRRRRRRRRRRRRRRRRR-
RRRRRRRRRRRRRRRRRRRRR-
RRRRRRRRRRRRRRRRRRRRR-
RRRRGH!!" he cried.
CALL ME "DOCTOR FILLER"!
Peirce

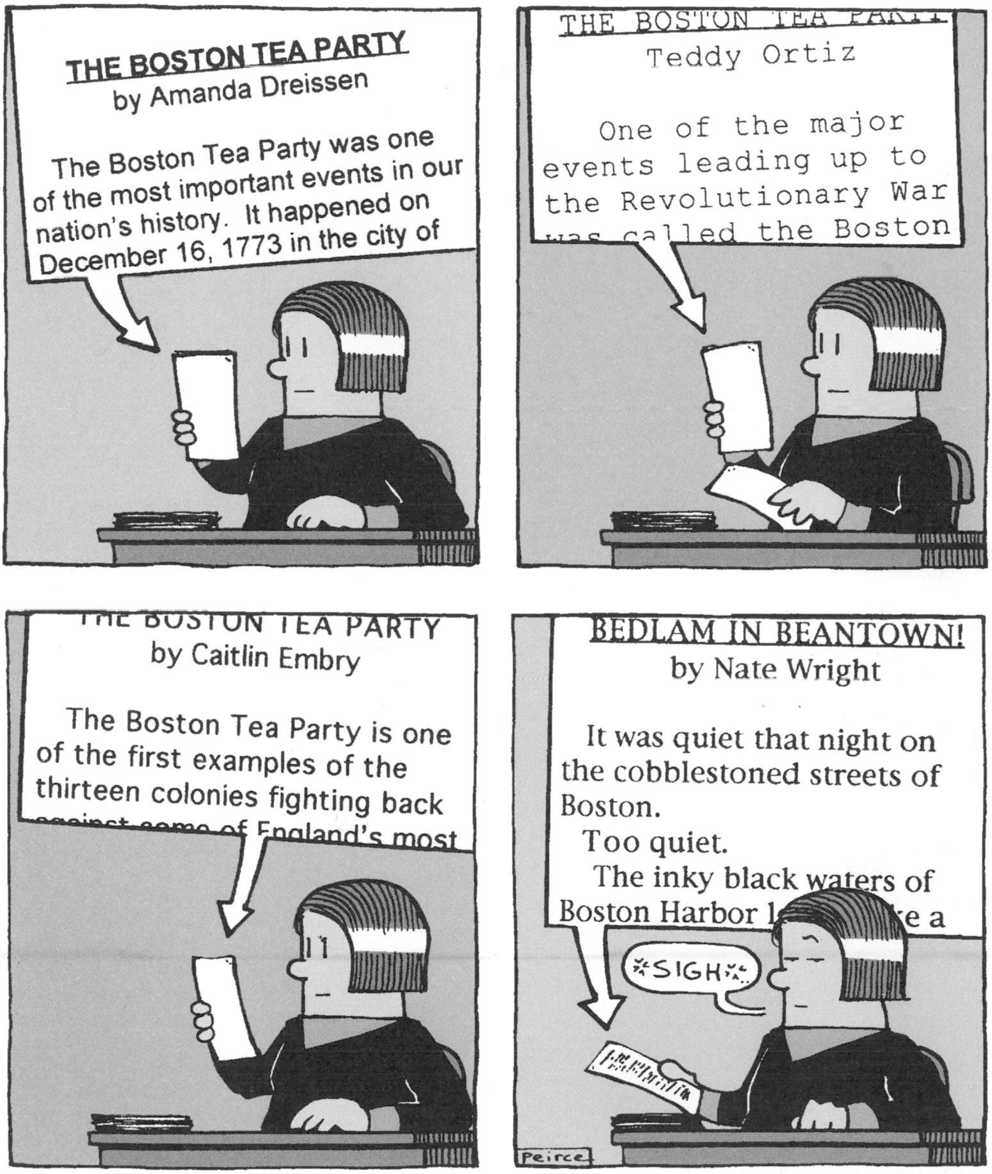
THE BOSTON TEA PARTY
by Amanda Dreissen
The Boston Tea Party was one of the most important events in our nation's history. It happened on December 16, 1773 in the city of
THE BOSTON TEA PARTY
Teddy Ortiz
One of the major events leading up to the Revolutionary War
the Boston
THE BOSTON TEA PARTY
by Caitlin Embry
The Boston Tea Party is one of the first examples of the thirteen colonies fighting back
England's most
BEDLAM IN BEANTOWN!
by Nate Wright
It was quiet that night on the cobblestoned streets of Boston.
Too quiet.
The inky black waters of Boston Harbor
e a
SIGH
Peirce

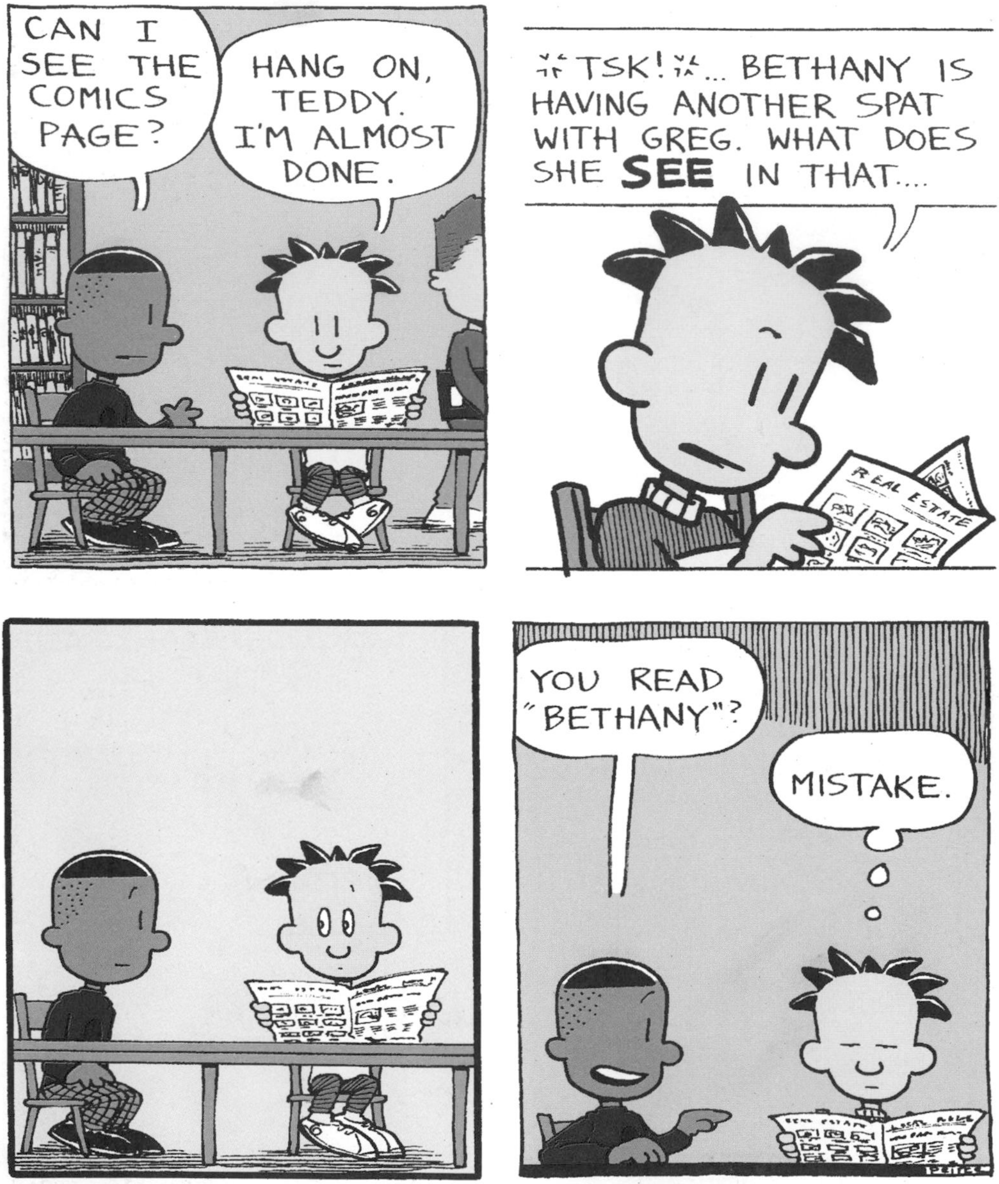
CAN I SEE THE COMICS PAGE?
HANG ON, TEDDY. I'M ALMOST DONE.
TSK! ... BETHANY IS HAVING ANOTHER SPAT WITH GREG. WHAT DOES SHE **SEE** IN THAT...
REAL ESTATE
YOU READ "BETHANY"?
MISTAKE.

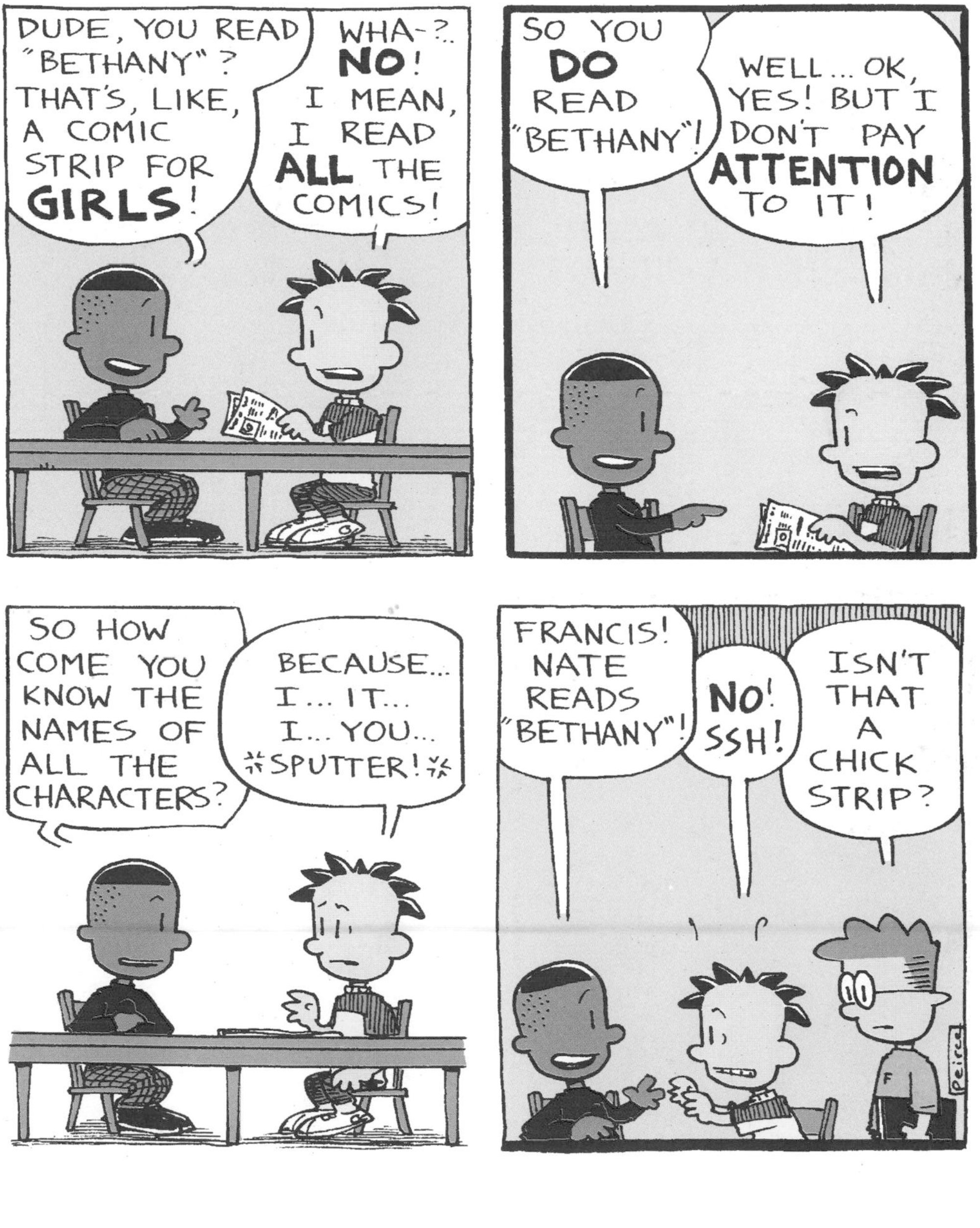
DUDE, YOU READ "BETHANY"? THAT'S, LIKE, A COMIC STRIP FOR GIRLS!
WHA-?.. NO! I MEAN, I READ ALL THE COMICS!
SO YOU DO READ "BETHANY"!
WELL... OK, YES! BUT I DON'T PAY ATTENTION TO IT!
SO HOW COME YOU KNOW THE NAMES OF ALL THE CHARACTERS?
BECAUSE... I... IT... I... YOU... *SPUTTER!*
FRANCIS! NATE READS "BETHANY"!
NO! SSH!
ISN'T THAT A CHICK STRIP?
Peirce

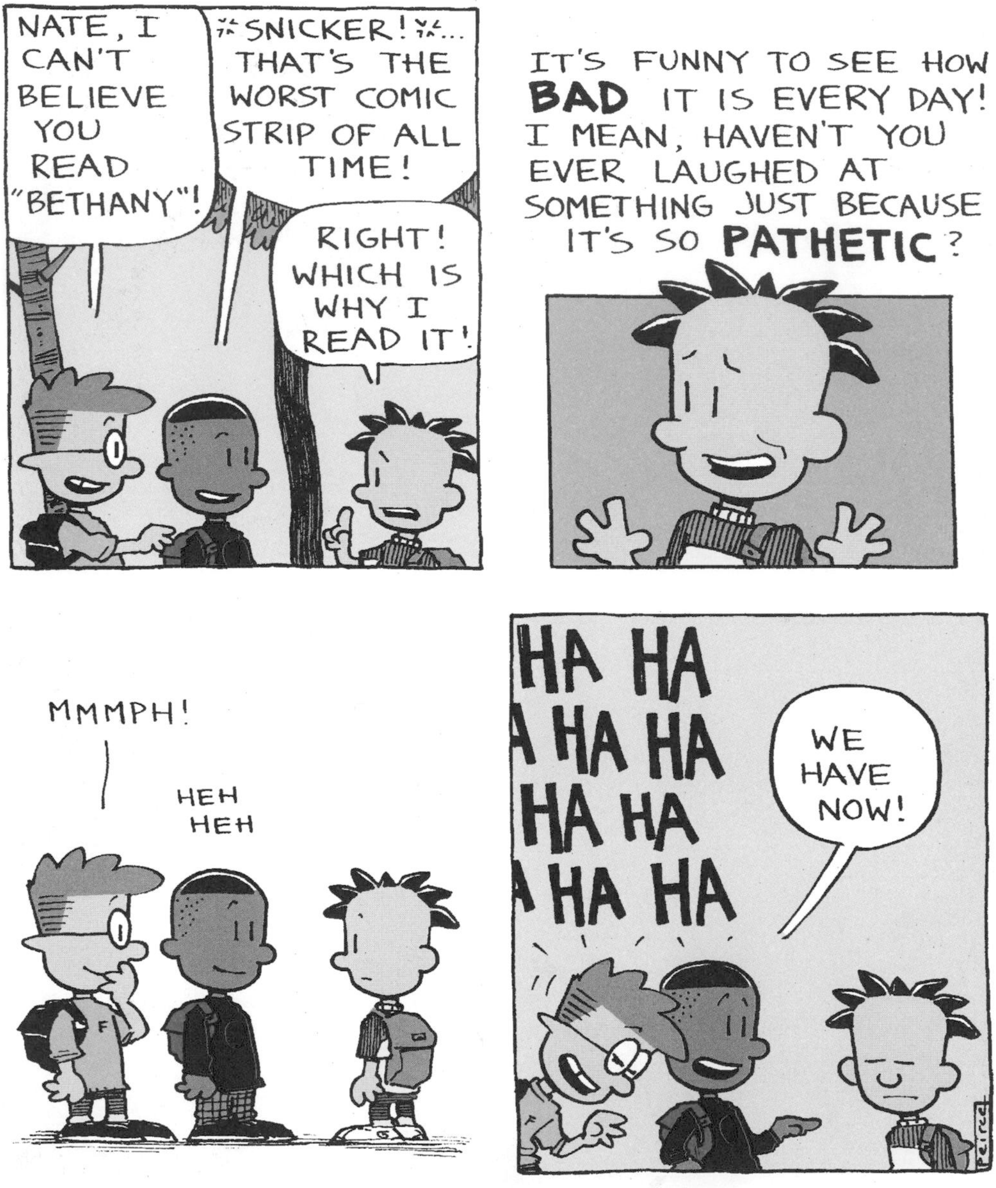
NATE, I CAN'T BELIEVE YOU READ "BETHANY"!
SNICKER!... THAT'S THE WORST COMIC STRIP OF ALL TIME!
RIGHT! WHICH IS WHY I READ IT!
IT'S FUNNY TO SEE HOW BAD IT IS EVERY DAY! I MEAN, HAVEN'T YOU EVER LAUGHED AT SOMETHING JUST BECAUSE IT'S SO PATHETIC?
MMMPH!
HEH HEH
HA HA HA HA HA HA HA HA HA HA HA
WE HAVE NOW!
PEIRCE

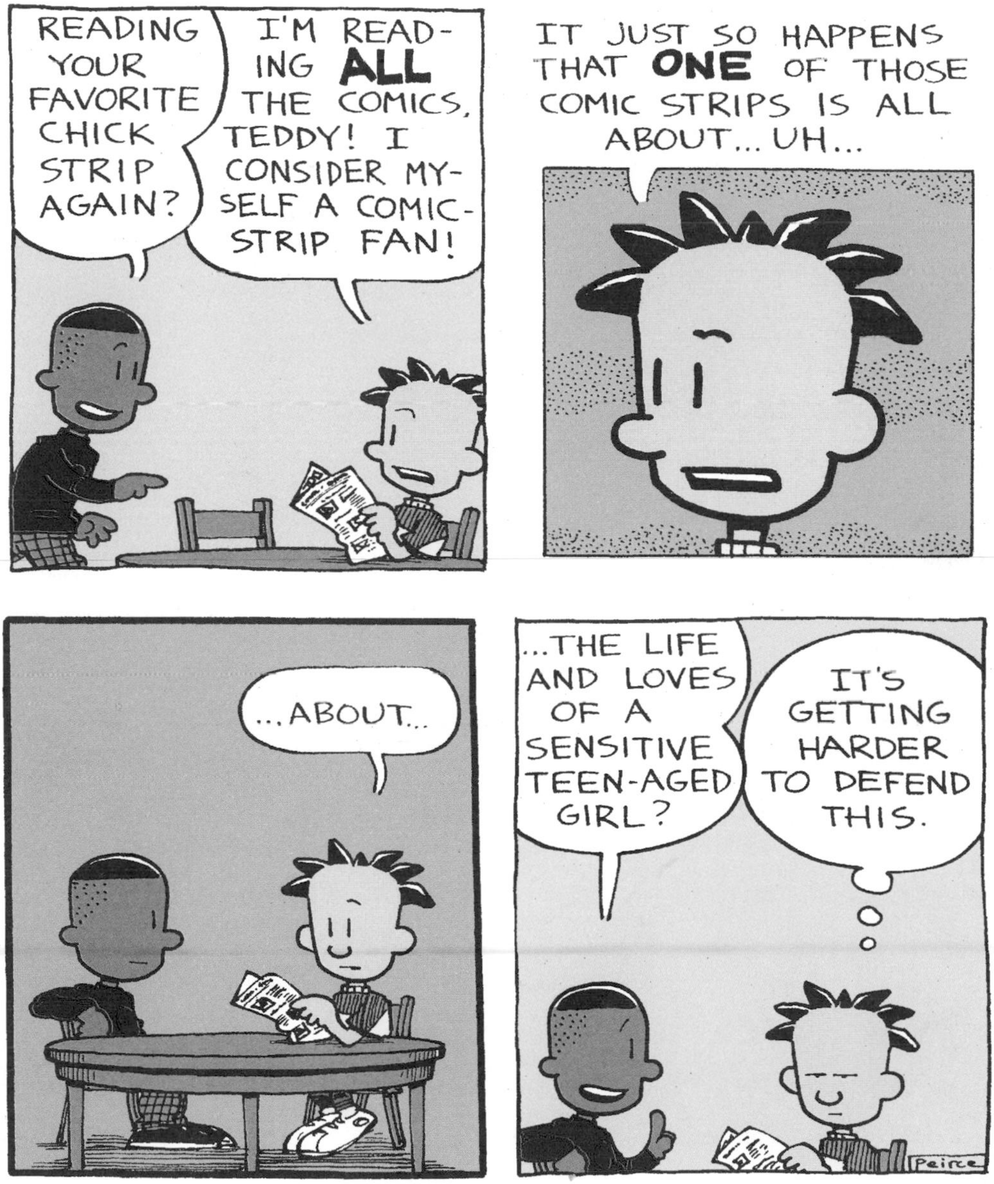
READING YOUR FAVORITE CHICK STRIP AGAIN?
I'M READING ALL THE COMICS, TEDDY! I CONSIDER MYSELF A COMIC-STRIP FAN!
IT JUST SO HAPPENS THAT ONE OF THOSE COMIC STRIPS IS ALL ABOUT... UH...
...ABOUT...
...THE LIFE AND LOVES OF A SENSITIVE TEEN-AGED GIRL?
IT'S GETTING HARDER TO DEFEND THIS.
Peirce

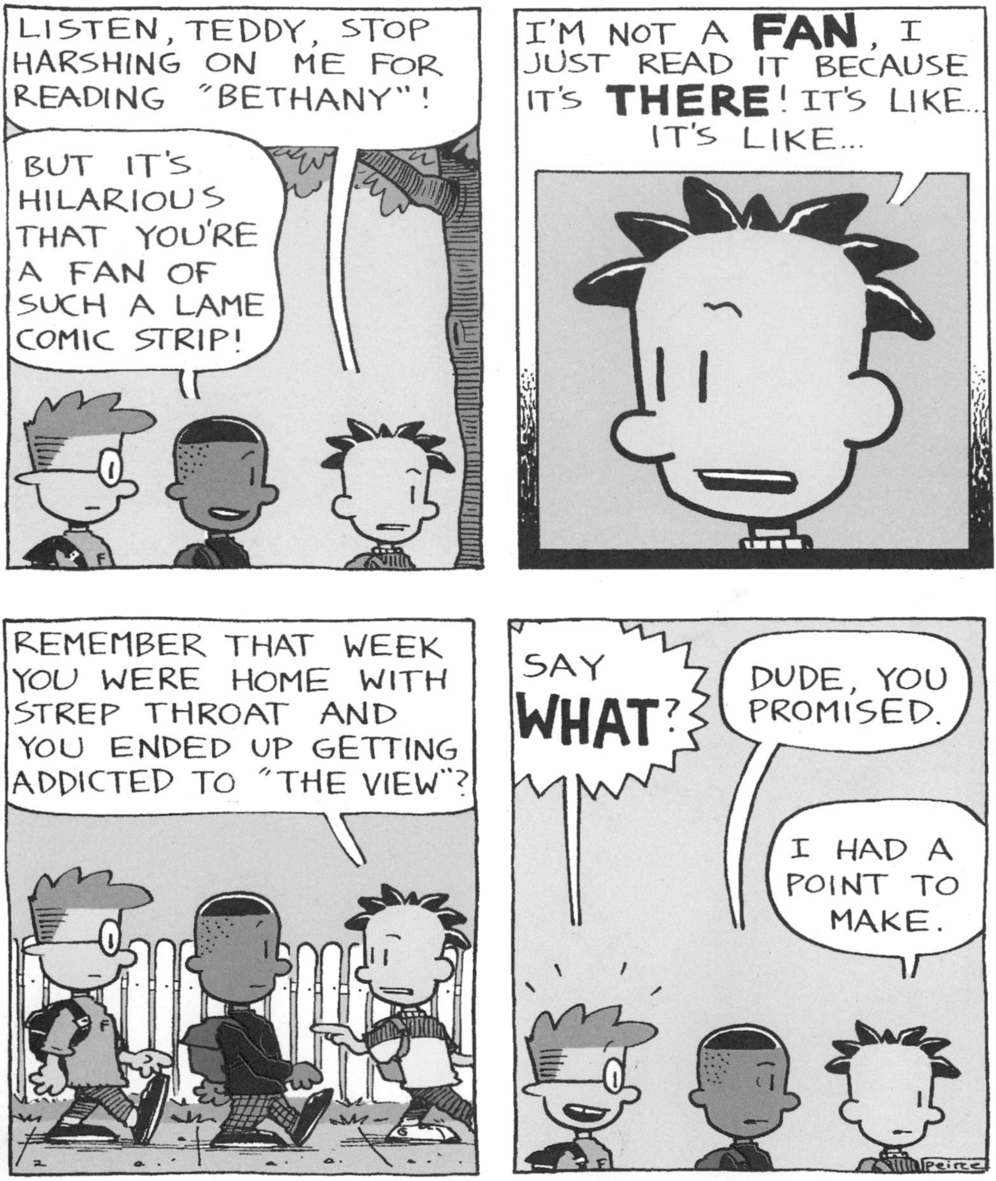
LISTEN, TEDDY, STOP HARSHING ON ME FOR READING "BETHANY"!
BUT IT'S HILARIOUS THAT YOU'RE A FAN OF SUCH A LAME COMIC STRIP!
I'M NOT A FAN, I JUST READ IT BECAUSE IT'S THERE! IT'S LIKE... IT'S LIKE...
REMEMBER THAT WEEK YOU WERE HOME WITH STREP THROAT AND YOU ENDED UP GETTING ADDICTED TO "THE VIEW"?
SAY WHAT?
DUDE, YOU PROMISED.
I HAD A POINT TO MAKE.
peirce

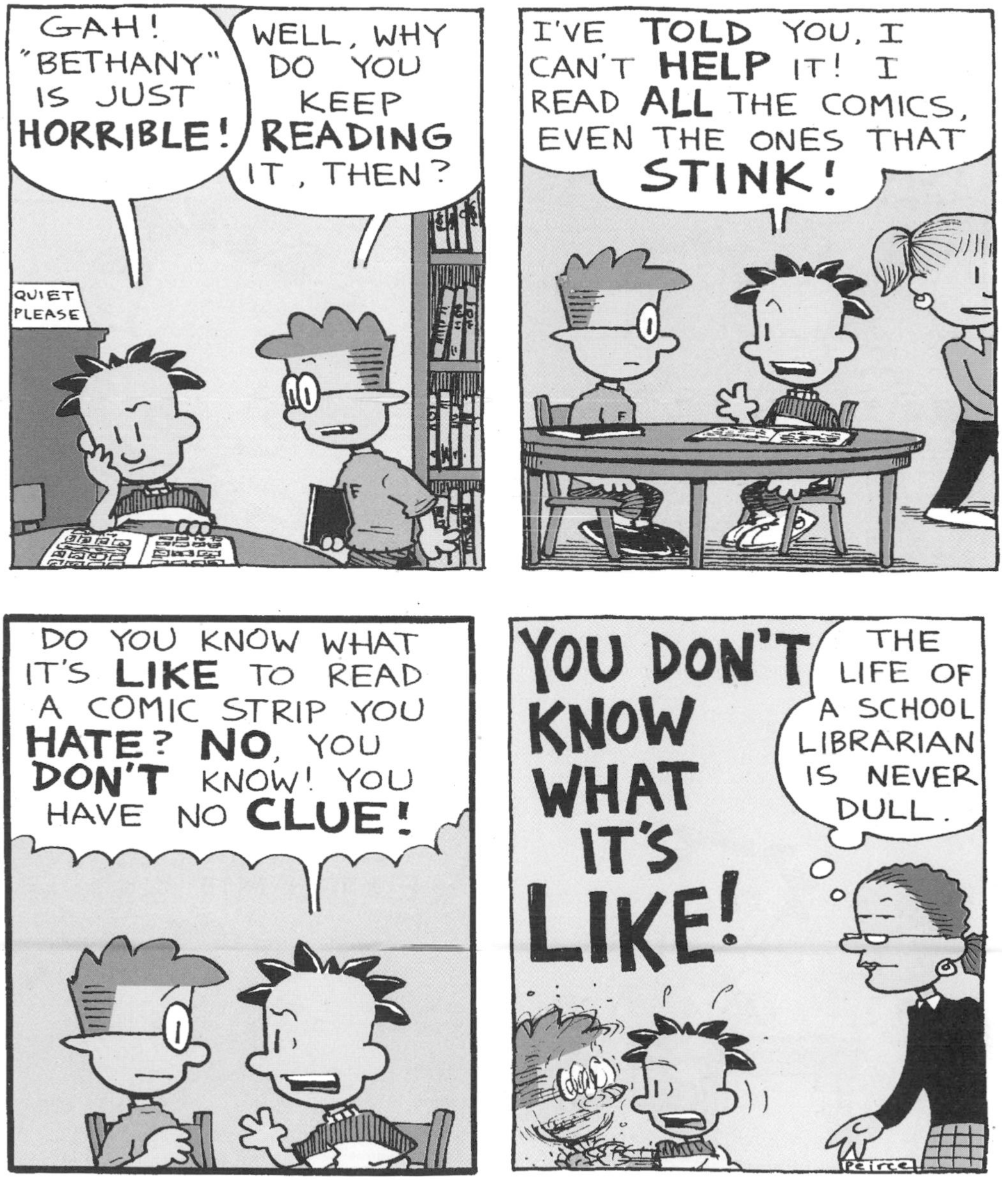
GAH! "BETHANY" IS JUST HORRIBLE!
WELL, WHY DO YOU KEEP READING IT, THEN?
QUIET PLEASE
I'VE TOLD YOU, I CAN'T HELP IT! I READ ALL THE COMICS, EVEN THE ONES THAT STINK!
DO YOU KNOW WHAT IT'S LIKE TO READ A COMIC STRIP YOU HATE? NO, YOU DON'T KNOW! YOU HAVE NO CLUE!
YOU DON'T KNOW WHAT IT'S LIKE!
THE LIFE OF A SCHOOL LIBRARIAN IS NEVER DULL.
Peirce

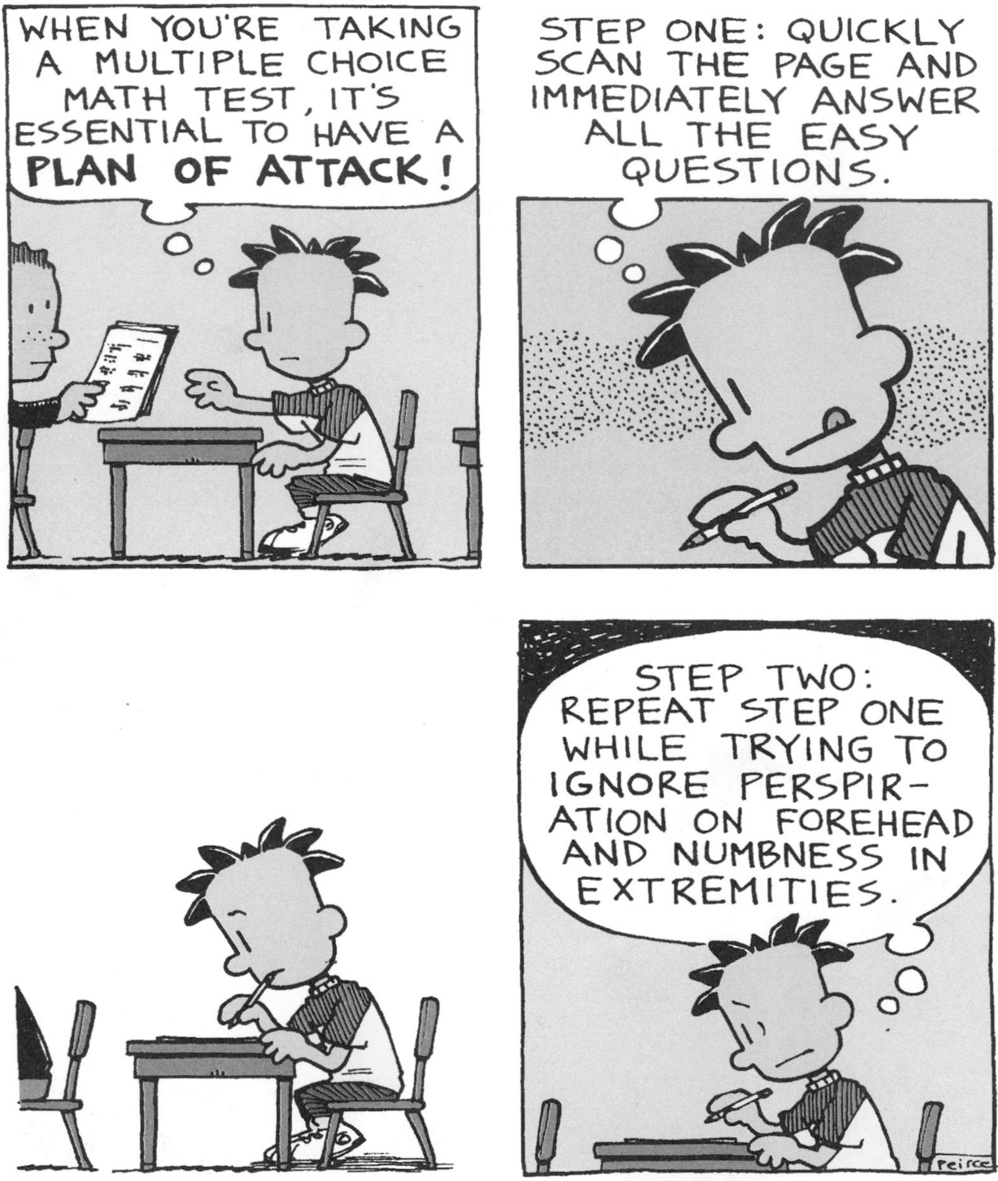
WHEN YOU'RE TAKING A MULTIPLE CHOICE MATH TEST, IT'S ESSENTIAL TO HAVE A **PLAN OF ATTACK!**
STEP ONE: QUICKLY SCAN THE PAGE AND IMMEDIATELY ANSWER ALL THE EASY QUESTIONS.
STEP TWO: REPEAT STEP ONE WHILE TRYING TO IGNORE PERSPIR-ATION ON FOREHEAD AND NUMBNESS IN EXTREMITIES.
Peirce

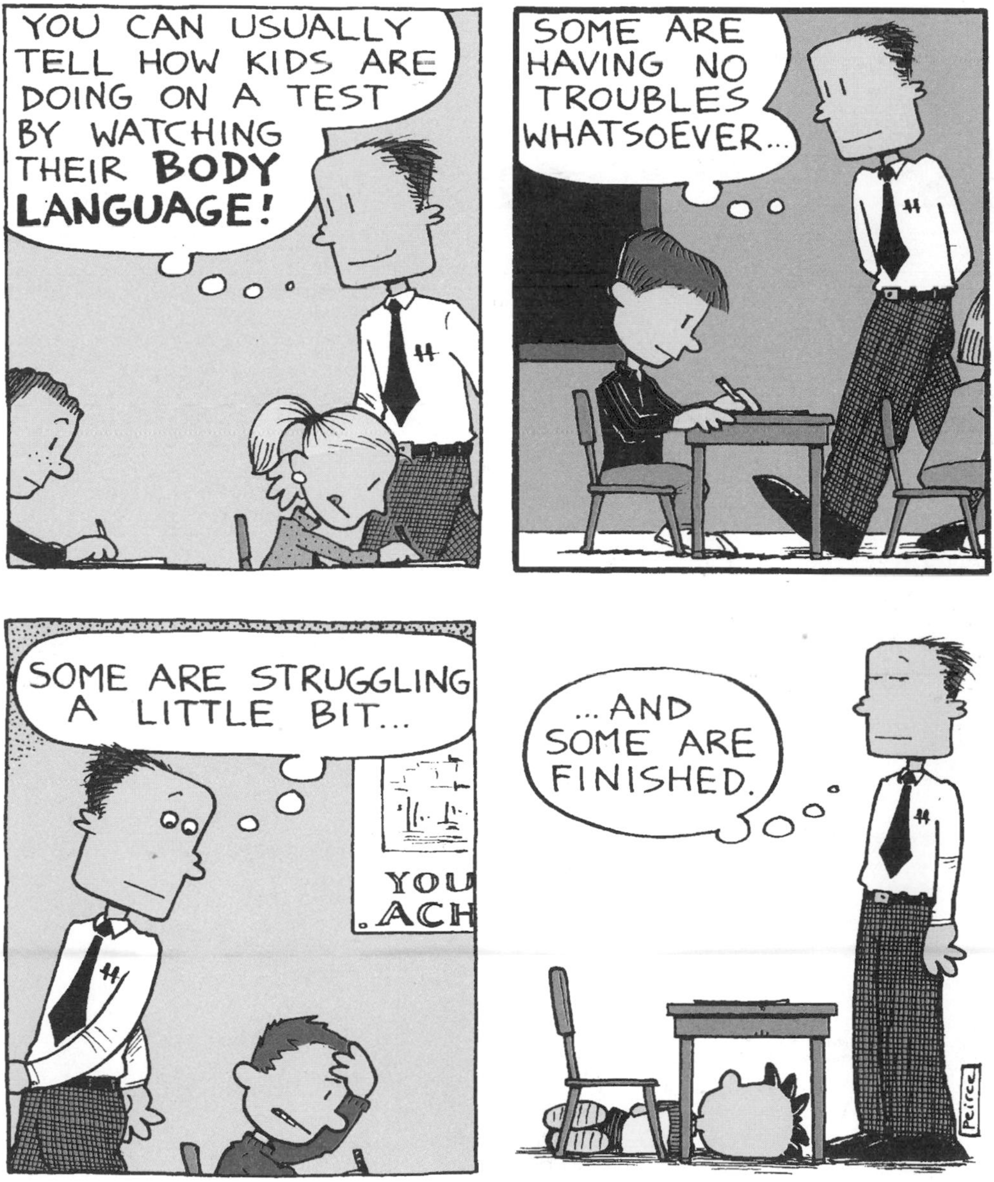
YOU CAN USUALLY TELL HOW KIDS ARE DOING ON A TEST BY WATCHING THEIR **BODY LANGUAGE!**
SOME ARE HAVING NO TROUBLES WHATSOEVER...
SOME ARE STRUGGLING A LITTLE BIT...
YOU
ACH
...AND SOME ARE FINISHED.
Peirce

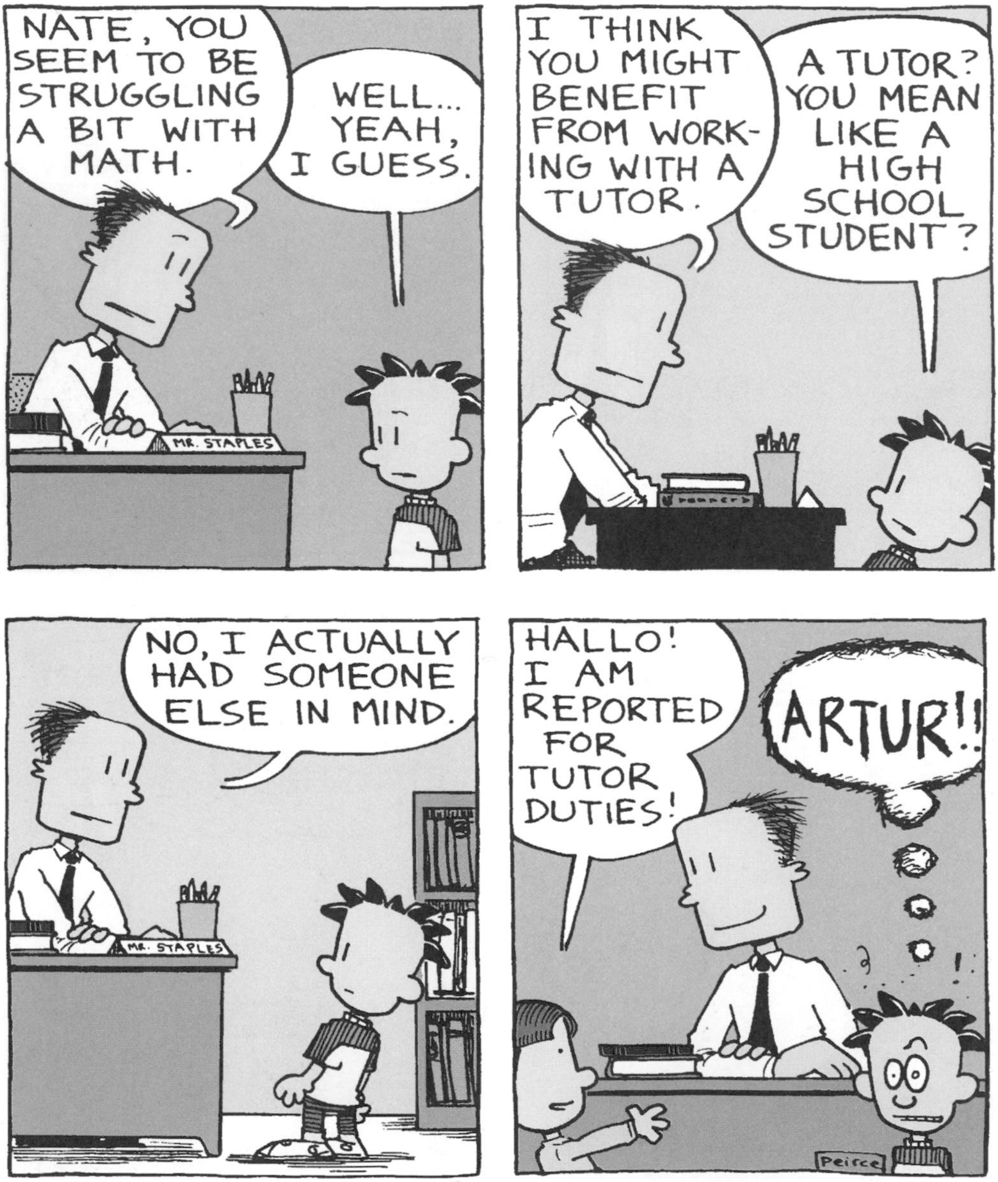
NATE, YOU SEEM TO BE STRUGGLING A BIT WITH MATH.
WELL... YEAH, I GUESS.
MR. STAPLES
I THINK YOU MIGHT BENEFIT FROM WORKING WITH A TUTOR.
A TUTOR? YOU MEAN LIKE A HIGH SCHOOL STUDENT?
NO, I ACTUALLY HAD SOMEONE ELSE IN MIND.
MR. STAPLES
HALLO! I AM REPORTED FOR TUTOR DUTIES!
ARTUR!!
Peirce

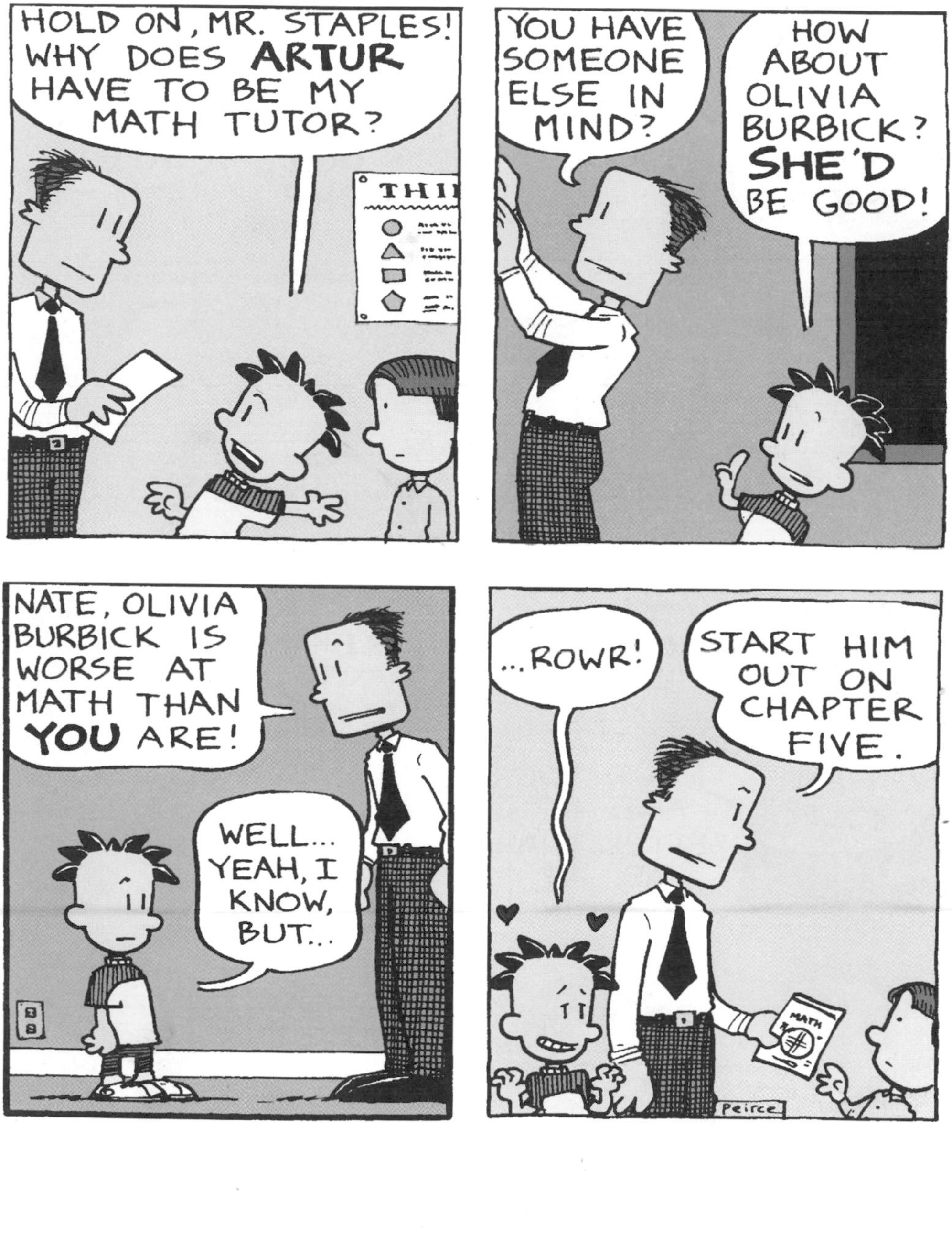
HOLD ON, MR. STAPLES! WHY DOES **ARTUR** HAVE TO BE MY MATH TUTOR?
YOU HAVE SOMEONE ELSE IN MIND?
HOW ABOUT OLIVIA BURBICK? **SHE'D** BE GOOD!
NATE, OLIVIA BURBICK IS WORSE AT MATH THAN **YOU** ARE!
WELL... YEAH, I KNOW, BUT...
...ROWR!
START HIM OUT ON CHAPTER FIVE.
MATH
Peirce

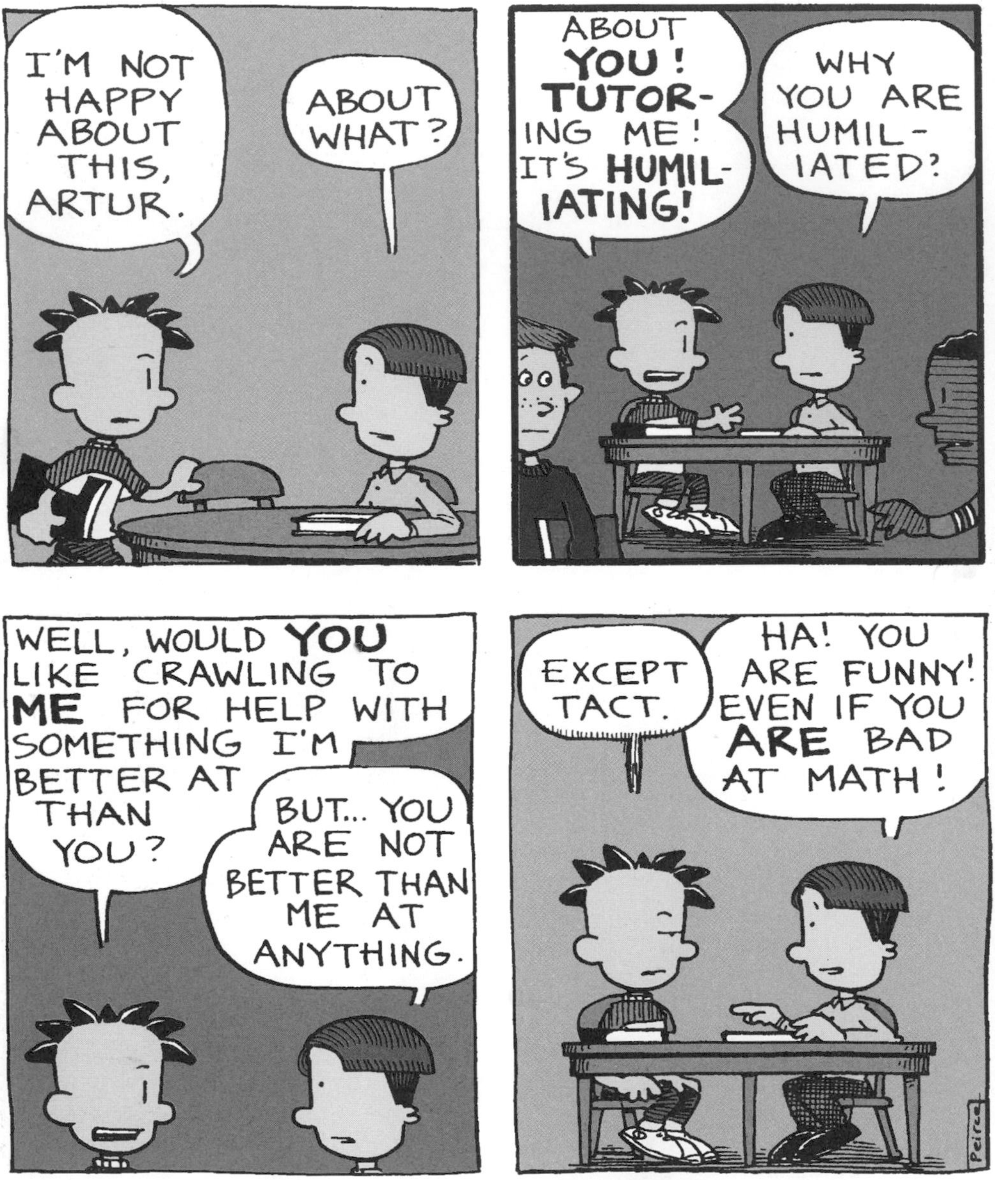
I'M NOT HAPPY ABOUT THIS, ARTUR.
ABOUT WHAT?
ABOUT **YOU**! **TUTOR**-ING ME! IT'S **HUMIL-IATING!**
WHY YOU ARE HUMIL-IATED?
WELL, WOULD **YOU** LIKE CRAWLING TO **ME** FOR HELP WITH SOMETHING I'M BETTER AT THAN YOU?
BUT... YOU ARE NOT BETTER THAN ME AT ANYTHING.
HA! YOU ARE FUNNY! EVEN IF YOU **ARE** BAD AT MATH!
EXCEPT TACT.
Peirce

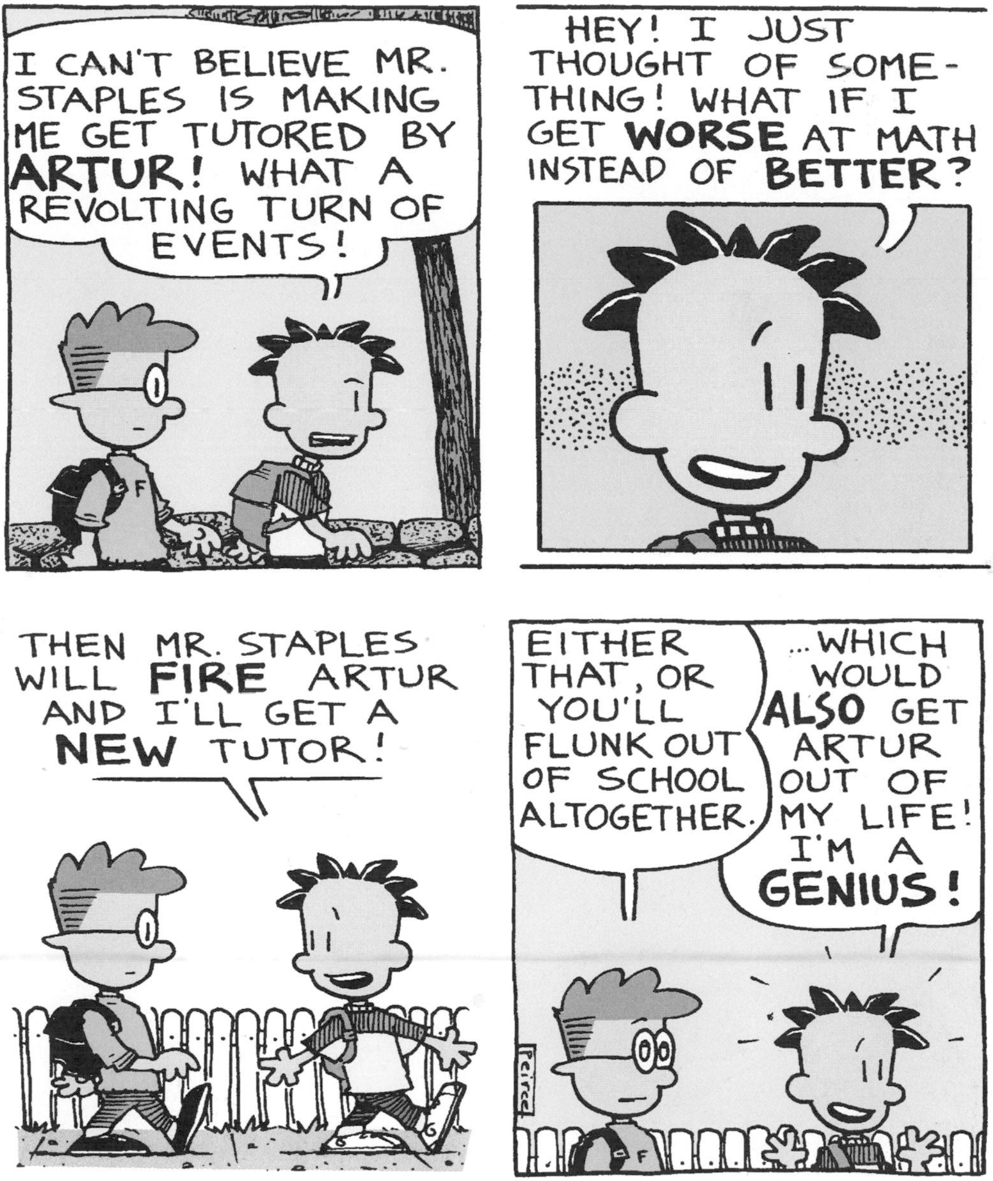
I CAN'T BELIEVE MR. STAPLES IS MAKING ME GET TUTORED BY **ARTUR**! WHAT A REVOLTING TURN OF EVENTS!
HEY! I JUST THOUGHT OF SOMETHING! WHAT IF I GET **WORSE** AT MATH INSTEAD OF **BETTER**?
THEN MR. STAPLES WILL **FIRE** ARTUR AND I'LL GET A **NEW** TUTOR!
EITHER THAT, OR YOU'LL FLUNK OUT OF SCHOOL ALTOGETHER.
...WHICH WOULD **ALSO** GET ARTUR OUT OF MY LIFE! I'M A **GENIUS**!
Peirce

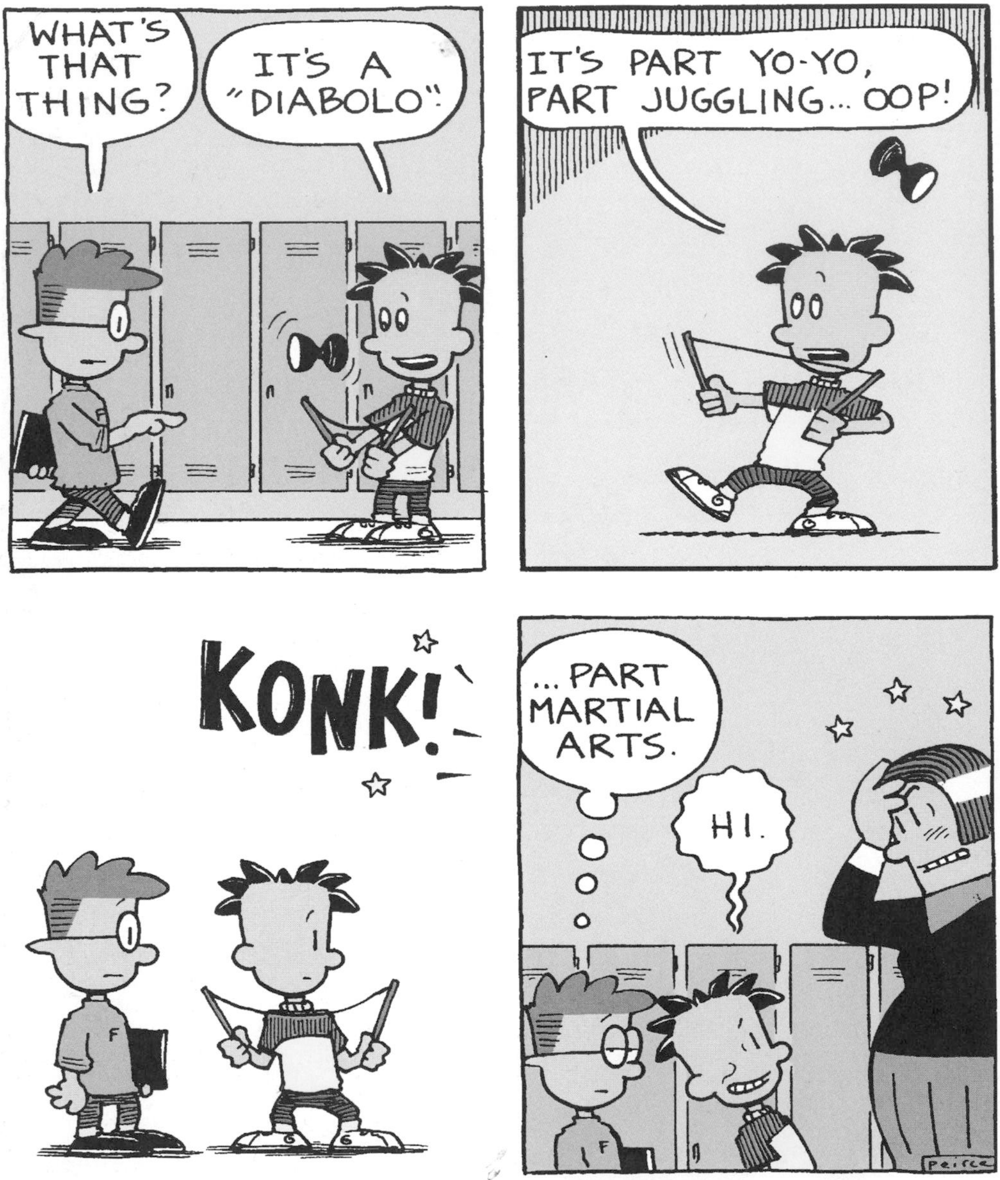
WHAT'S THAT THING?
IT'S A "DIABOLO".
IT'S PART YO-YO, PART JUGGLING... OOP!
KONK!
...PART MARTIAL ARTS.
HI.
Peirce

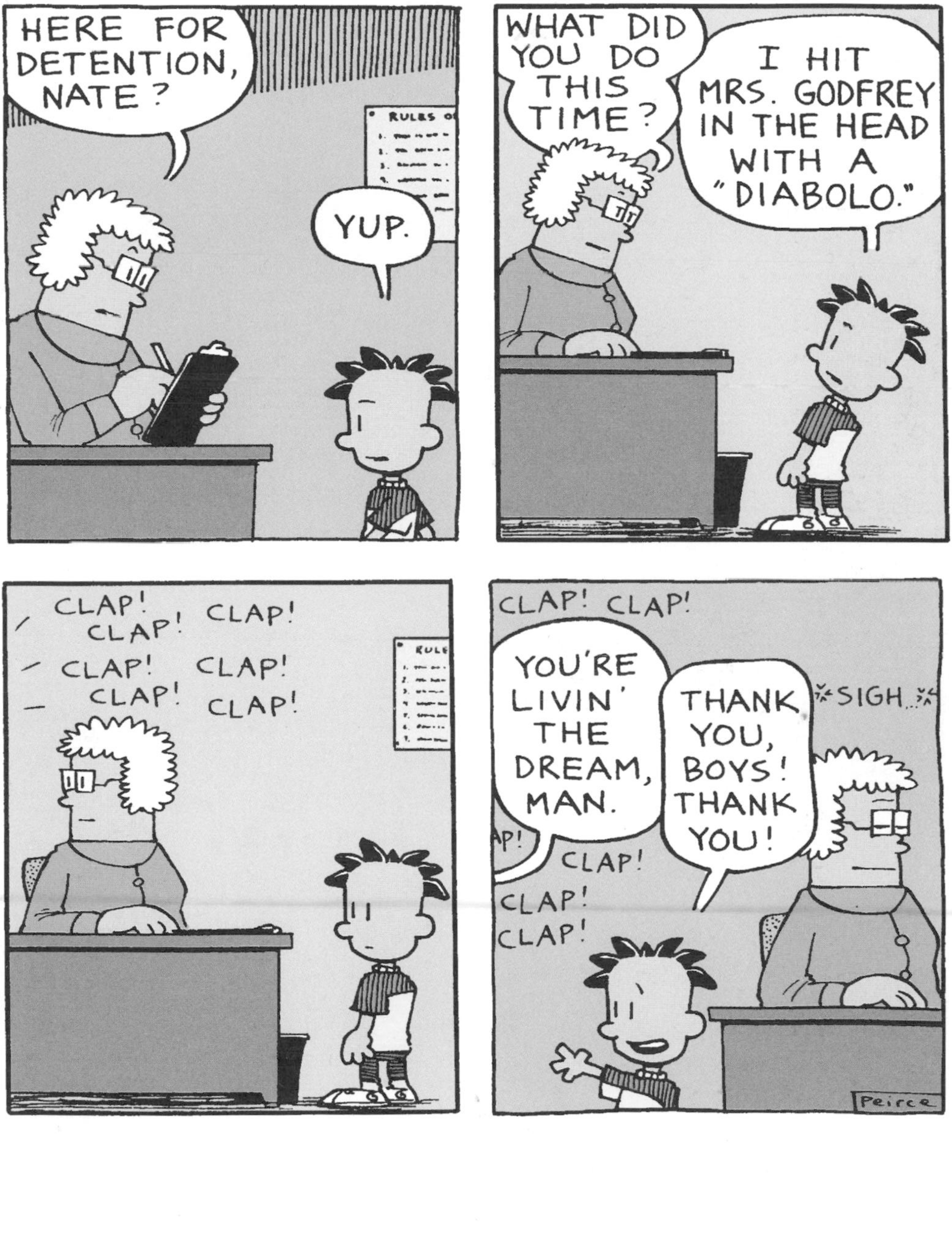
HERE FOR DETENTION, NATE?
YUP.
WHAT DID YOU DO THIS TIME?
I HIT MRS. GODFREY IN THE HEAD WITH A "DIABOLO."
CLAP! CLAP! CLAP!
CLAP! CLAP!
CLAP! CLAP!
CLAP! CLAP!
YOU'RE LIVIN' THE DREAM, MAN.
THANK YOU, BOYS! THANK YOU!
SIGH
CLAP!
CLAP!
CLAP!
Peirce

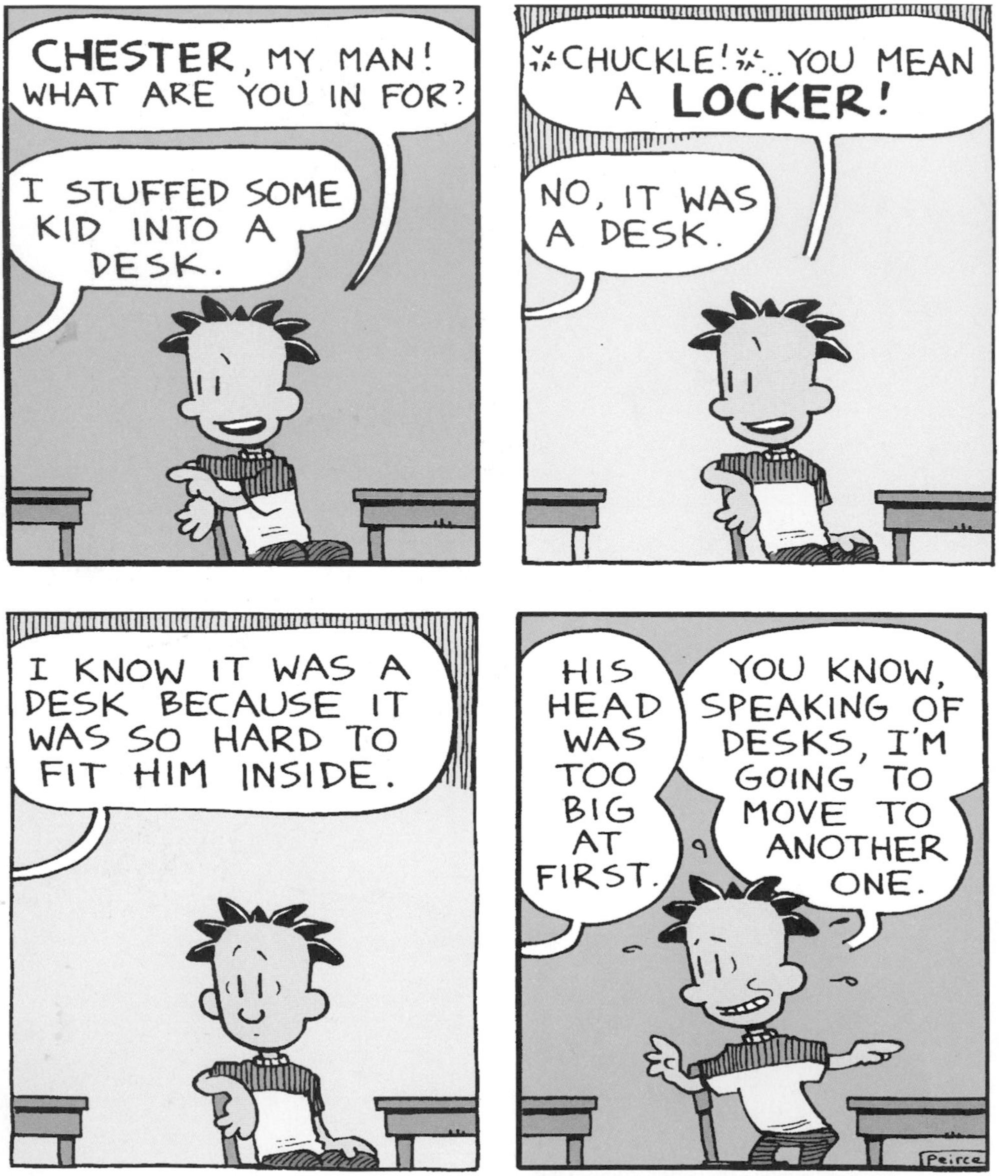
CHESTER, MY MAN! WHAT ARE YOU IN FOR?
I STUFFED SOME KID INTO A DESK.
CHUCKLE!... YOU MEAN A LOCKER!
NO, IT WAS A DESK.
I KNOW IT WAS A DESK BECAUSE IT WAS SO HARD TO FIT HIM INSIDE.
HIS HEAD WAS TOO BIG AT FIRST.
YOU KNOW, SPEAKING OF DESKS, I'M GOING TO MOVE TO ANOTHER ONE.
Peirce

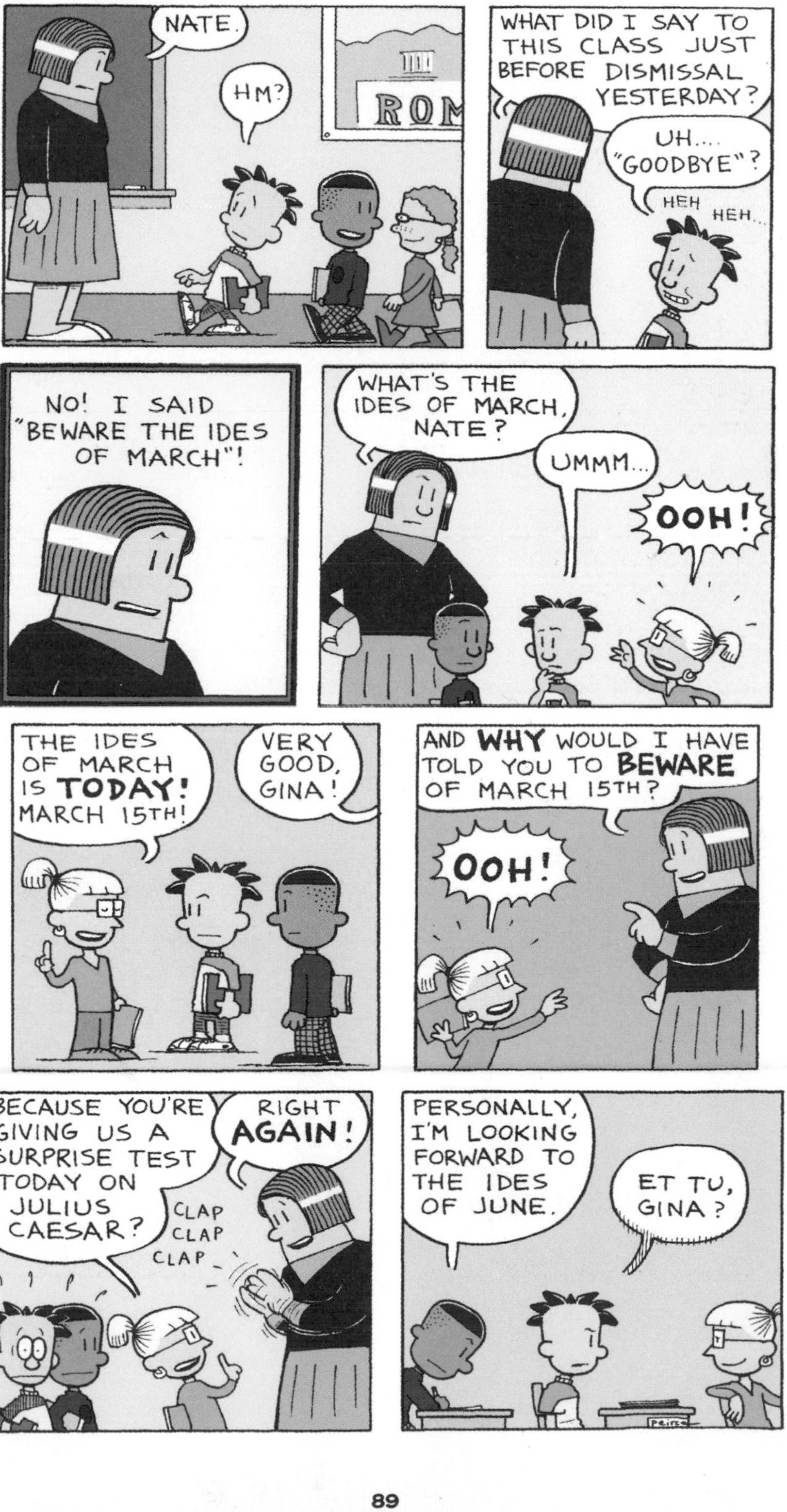
NATE.
HM?
ROM
WHAT DID I SAY TO THIS CLASS JUST BEFORE DISMISSAL YESTERDAY?
UH.... "GOODBYE"?
HEH HEH...
NO! I SAID "BEWARE THE IDES OF MARCH"!
WHAT'S THE IDES OF MARCH, NATE?
UMMM...
OOH!
THE IDES OF MARCH IS TODAY! MARCH 15TH!
VERY GOOD, GINA!
AND WHY WOULD I HAVE TOLD YOU TO BEWARE OF MARCH 15TH?
OOH!
BECAUSE YOU'RE GIVING US A SURPRISE TEST TODAY ON JULIUS CAESAR?
RIGHT AGAIN!
CLAP CLAP CLAP
PERSONALLY, I'M LOOKING FORWARD TO THE IDES OF JUNE.
ET TU, GINA?

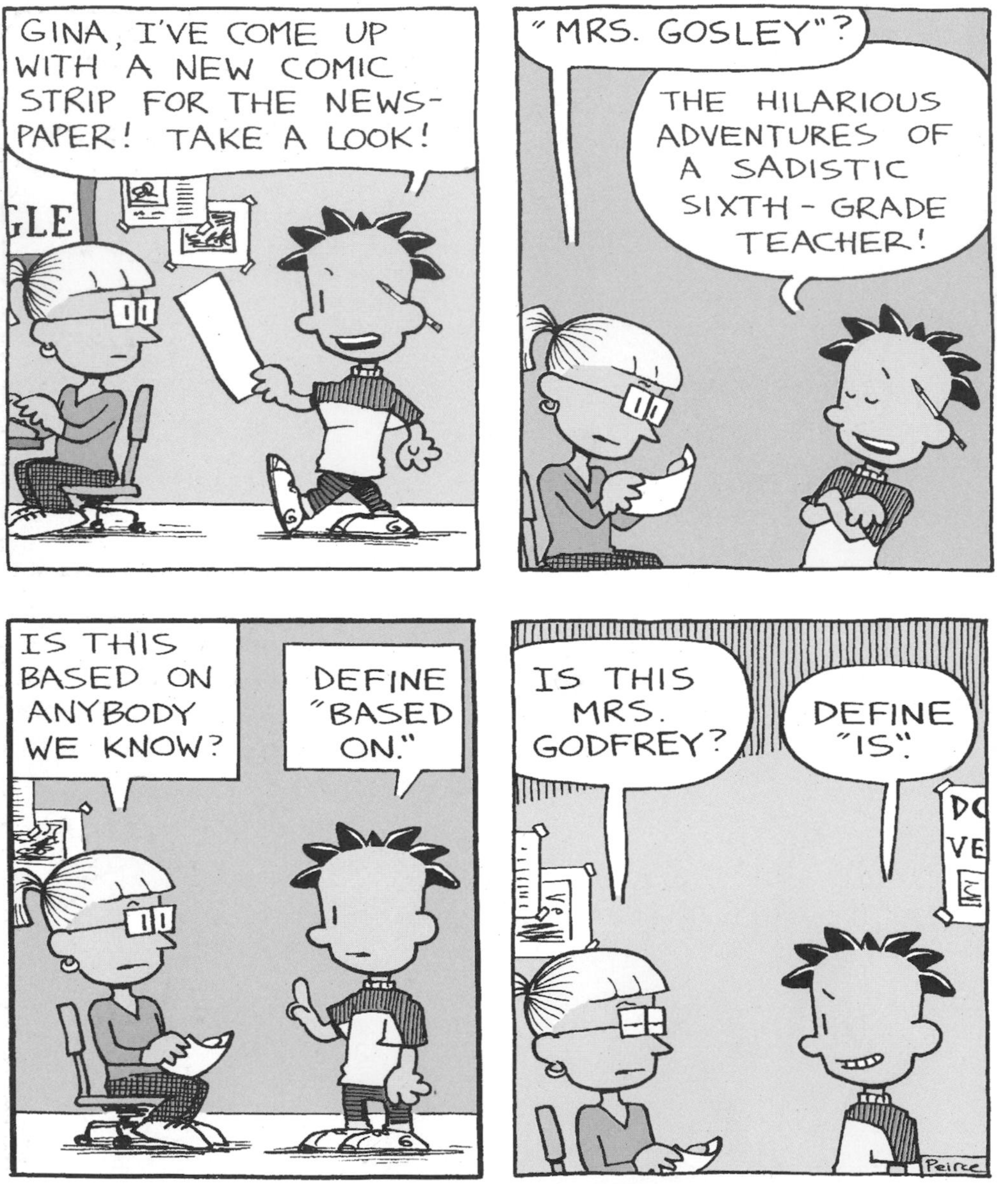
GINA, I'VE COME UP WITH A NEW COMIC STRIP FOR THE NEWSPAPER! TAKE A LOOK!
"MRS. GOSLEY"?
THE HILARIOUS ADVENTURES OF A SADISTIC SIXTH-GRADE TEACHER!
IS THIS BASED ON ANYBODY WE KNOW?
DEFINE "BASED ON."
IS THIS MRS. GODFREY?
DEFINE "IS."
Peirce

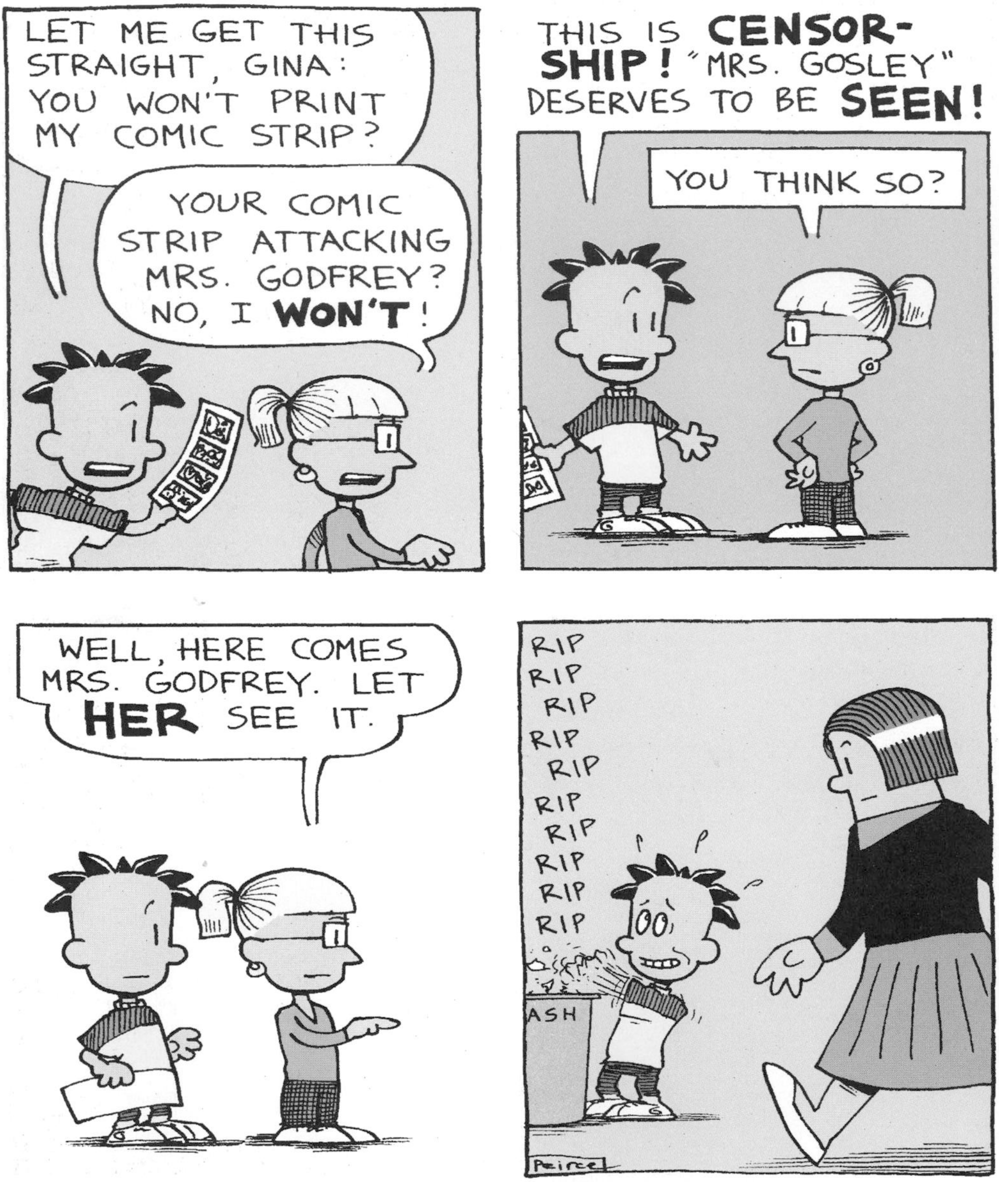
LET ME GET THIS STRAIGHT, GINA: YOU WON'T PRINT MY COMIC STRIP?
YOUR COMIC STRIP ATTACKING MRS. GODFREY? NO, I **WON'T**!
THIS IS **CENSORSHIP!** "MRS. GOSLEY" DESERVES TO BE **SEEN!**
YOU THINK SO?
WELL, HERE COMES MRS. GODFREY. LET **HER** SEE IT.
RIP RIP RIP RIP RIP RIP RIP RIP RIP RIP
ASH
Peirce

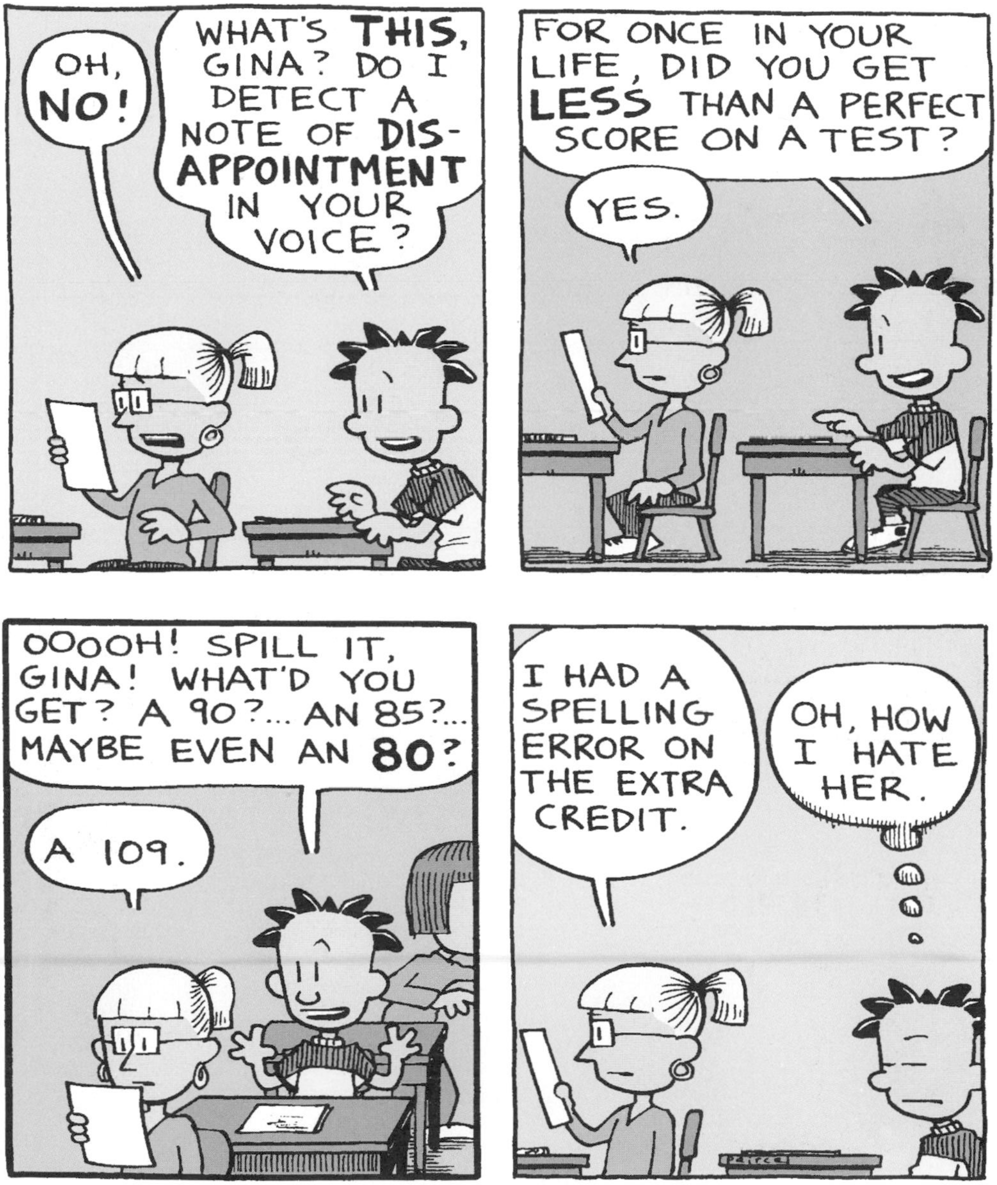
OH, NO!
WHAT'S THIS, GINA? DO I DETECT A NOTE OF DIS-APPOINTMENT IN YOUR VOICE?
FOR ONCE IN YOUR LIFE, DID YOU GET LESS THAN A PERFECT SCORE ON A TEST?
YES.
OOOOH! SPILL IT, GINA! WHAT'D YOU GET? A 90?... AN 85?... MAYBE EVEN AN 80?
A 109.
I HAD A SPELLING ERROR ON THE EXTRA CREDIT.
OH, HOW I HATE HER.

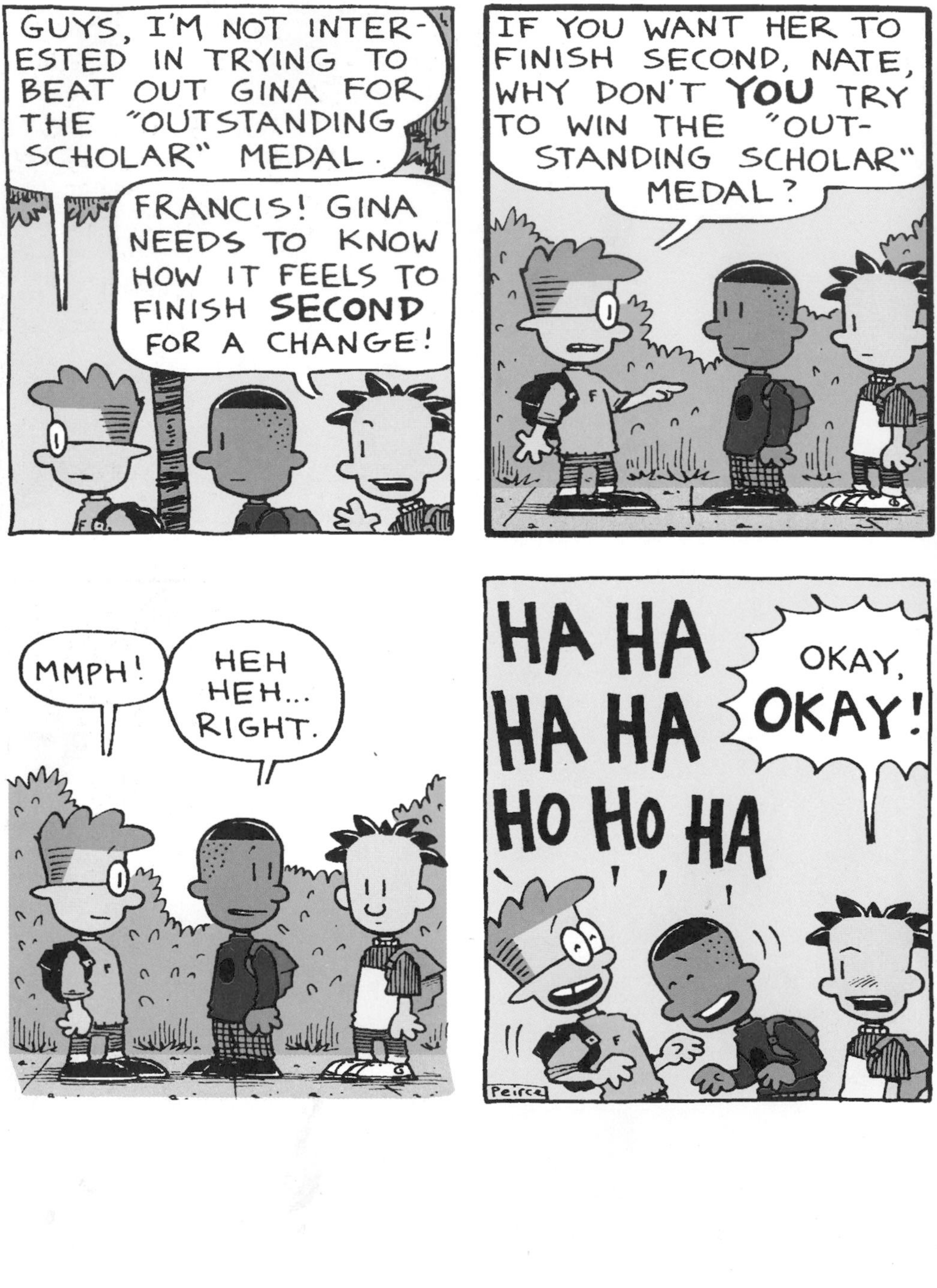
GUYS, I'M NOT INTERESTED IN TRYING TO BEAT OUT GINA FOR THE "OUTSTANDING SCHOLAR" MEDAL.
FRANCIS! GINA NEEDS TO KNOW HOW IT FEELS TO FINISH **SECOND** FOR A CHANGE!
IF YOU WANT HER TO FINISH SECOND, NATE, WHY DON'T **YOU** TRY TO WIN THE "OUTSTANDING SCHOLAR" MEDAL?
MMPH!
HEH HEH... RIGHT.
HA HA HA HA HO HO HA
OKAY, **OKAY!**
Peirce

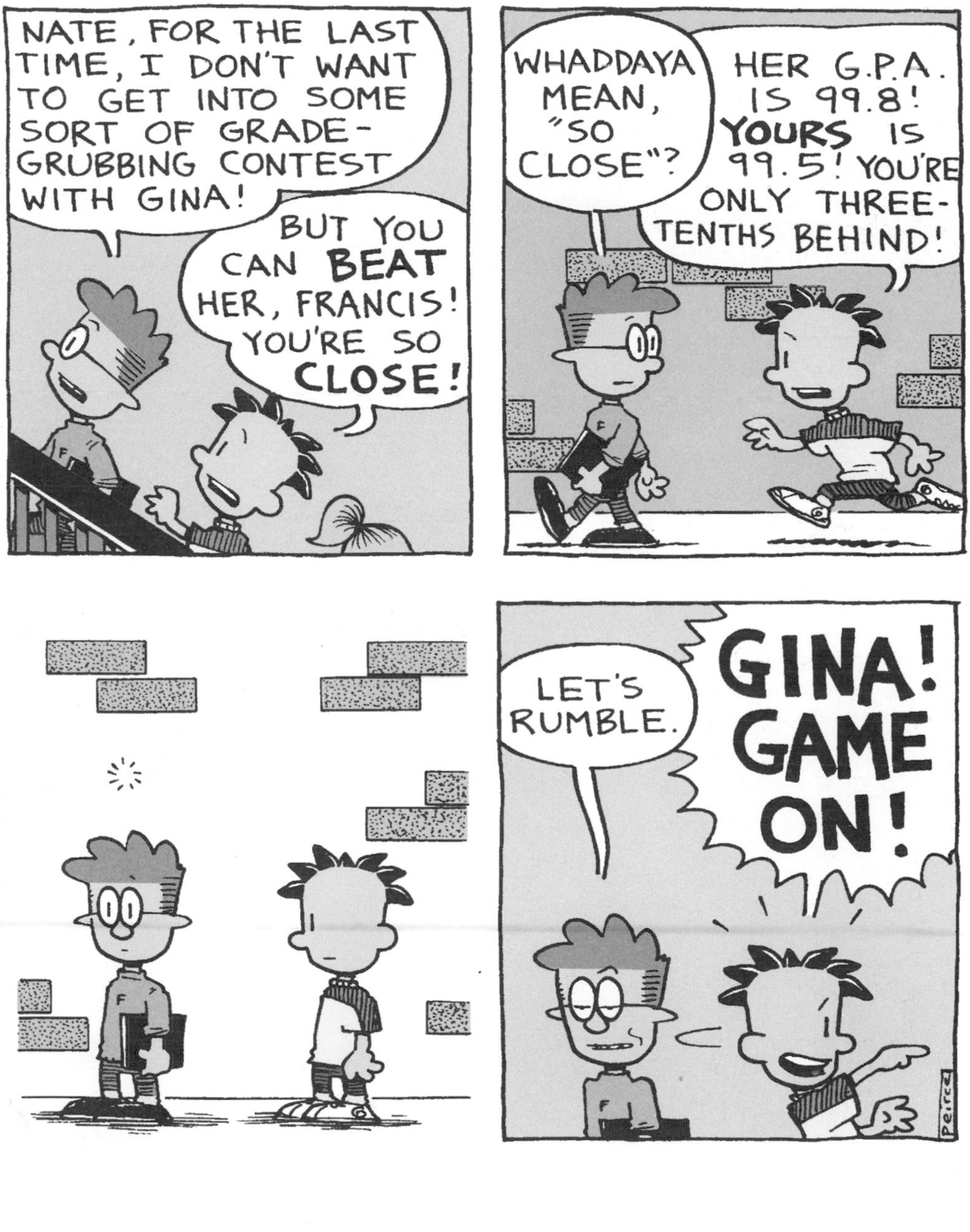
NATE, FOR THE LAST TIME, I DON'T WANT TO GET INTO SOME SORT OF GRADE-GRUBBING CONTEST WITH GINA!
BUT YOU CAN **BEAT** HER, FRANCIS! YOU'RE SO **CLOSE**!
WHADDAYA MEAN, "SO CLOSE"?
HER G.P.A. IS 99.8! **YOURS** IS 99.5! YOU'RE ONLY THREE-TENTHS BEHIND!
LET'S RUMBLE.
GINA! GAME ON!
PEIRCE

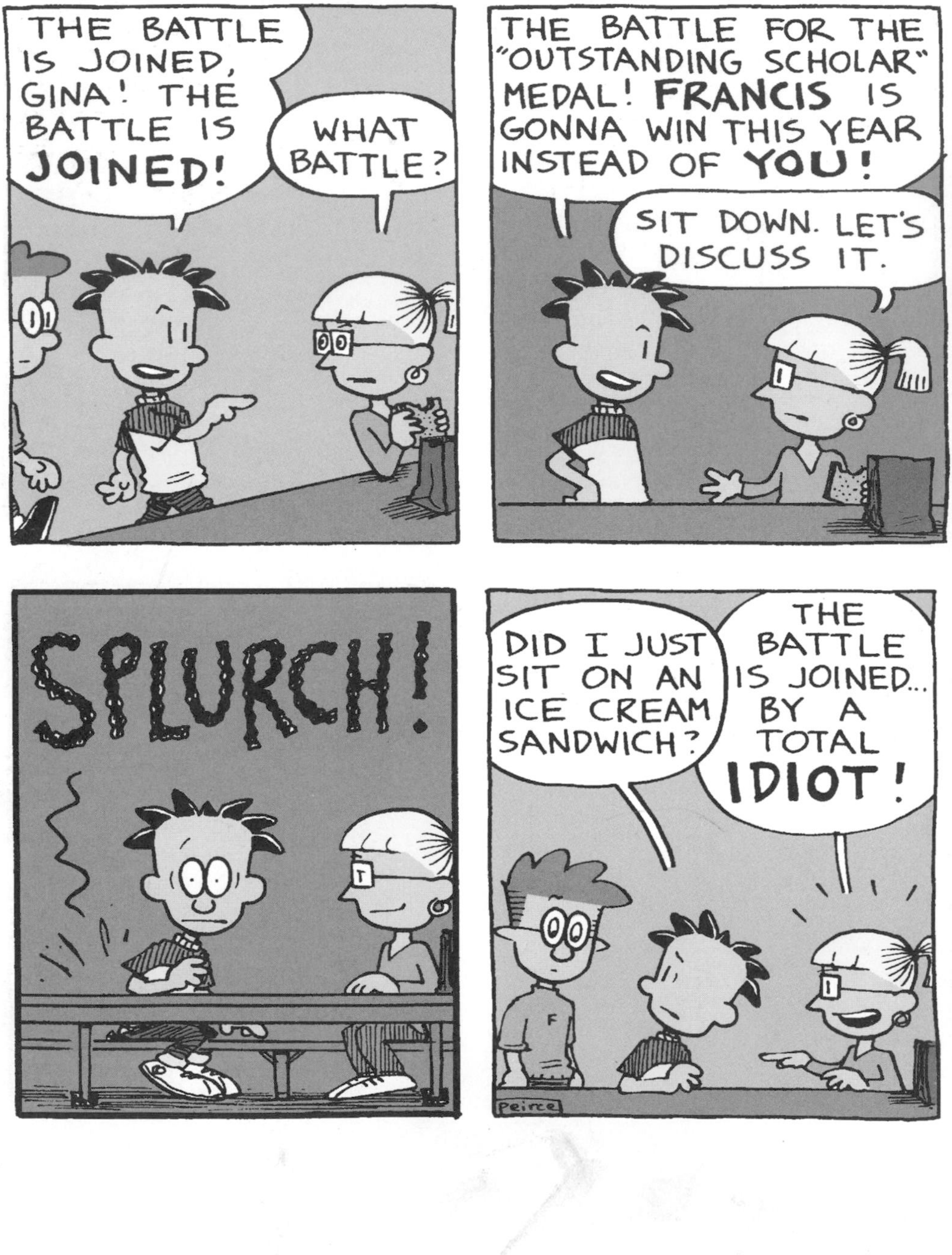
THE BATTLE IS JOINED, GINA! THE BATTLE IS **JOINED**!
WHAT BATTLE?
THE BATTLE FOR THE "OUTSTANDING SCHOLAR" MEDAL! **FRANCIS** IS GONNA WIN THIS YEAR INSTEAD OF **YOU**!
SIT DOWN. LET'S DISCUSS IT.
SPLURCH!
DID I JUST SIT ON AN ICE CREAM SANDWICH?
THE BATTLE IS JOINED... BY A TOTAL **IDIOT**!
Peirce

SO LONG, DAD! I'M GOING OVER TO FRANCIS'S HOUSE FOR A STUDY SESSION!

GREAT!

I'M GLAD TO SEE YOU'RE GETTING READY FOR YOUR FINALS!

OH, WE'LL BE READY, ALL RIGHT!

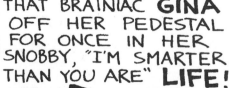
...READY TO KNOCK THAT BRAINIAC **GINA** OFF HER PEDESTAL FOR ONCE IN HER SNOBBY, "I'M SMARTER THAN YOU ARE" **LIFE!**

STUDYING HAS CHANGED A BIT SINCE I WAS A BOY.

BWA HA HA HA HAA!

Peirce

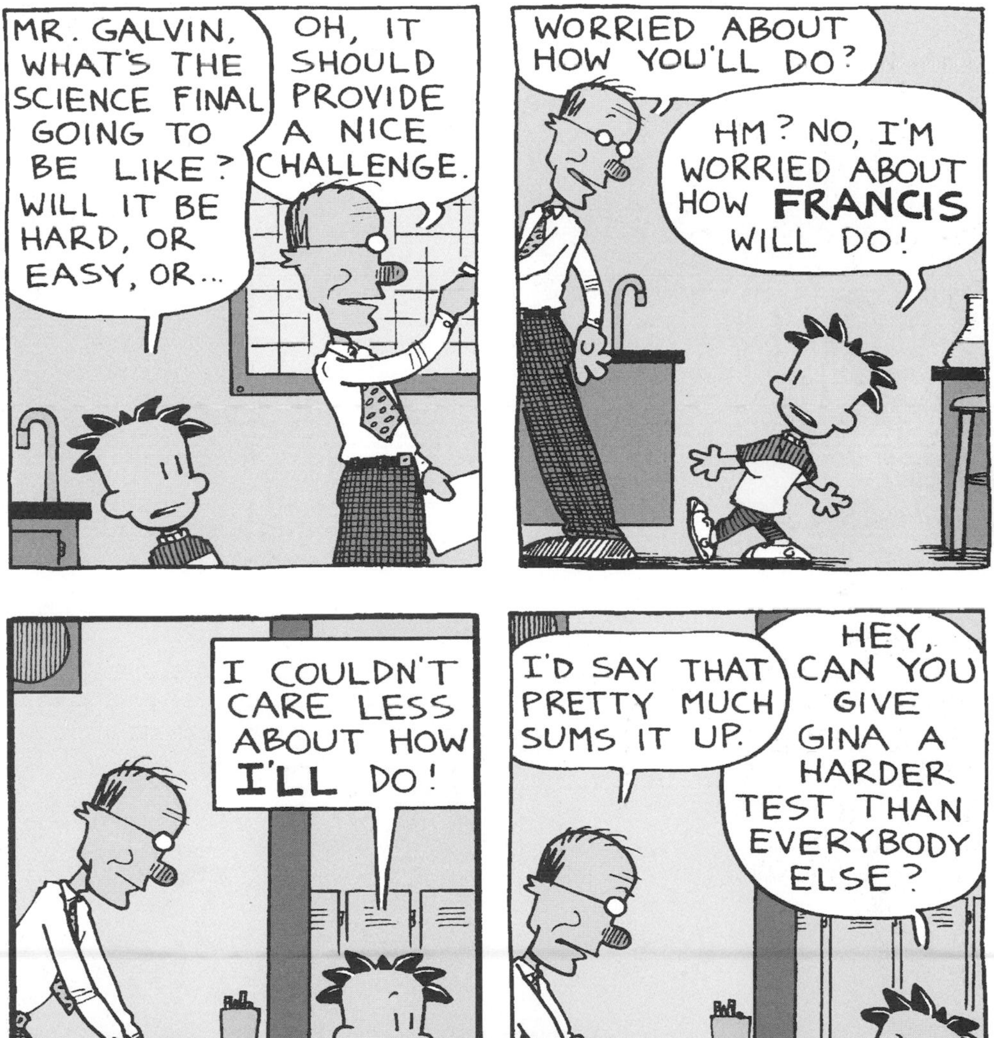
MR. GALVIN, WHAT'S THE SCIENCE FINAL GOING TO BE LIKE? WILL IT BE HARD, OR EASY, OR...
OH, IT SHOULD PROVIDE A NICE CHALLENGE.
WORRIED ABOUT HOW YOU'LL DO?
HM? NO, I'M WORRIED ABOUT HOW **FRANCIS** WILL DO!
I COULDN'T CARE LESS ABOUT HOW **I'LL** DO!
I'D SAY THAT PRETTY MUCH SUMS IT UP.
HEY, CAN YOU GIVE GINA A HARDER TEST THAN EVERYBODY ELSE?
Peirce

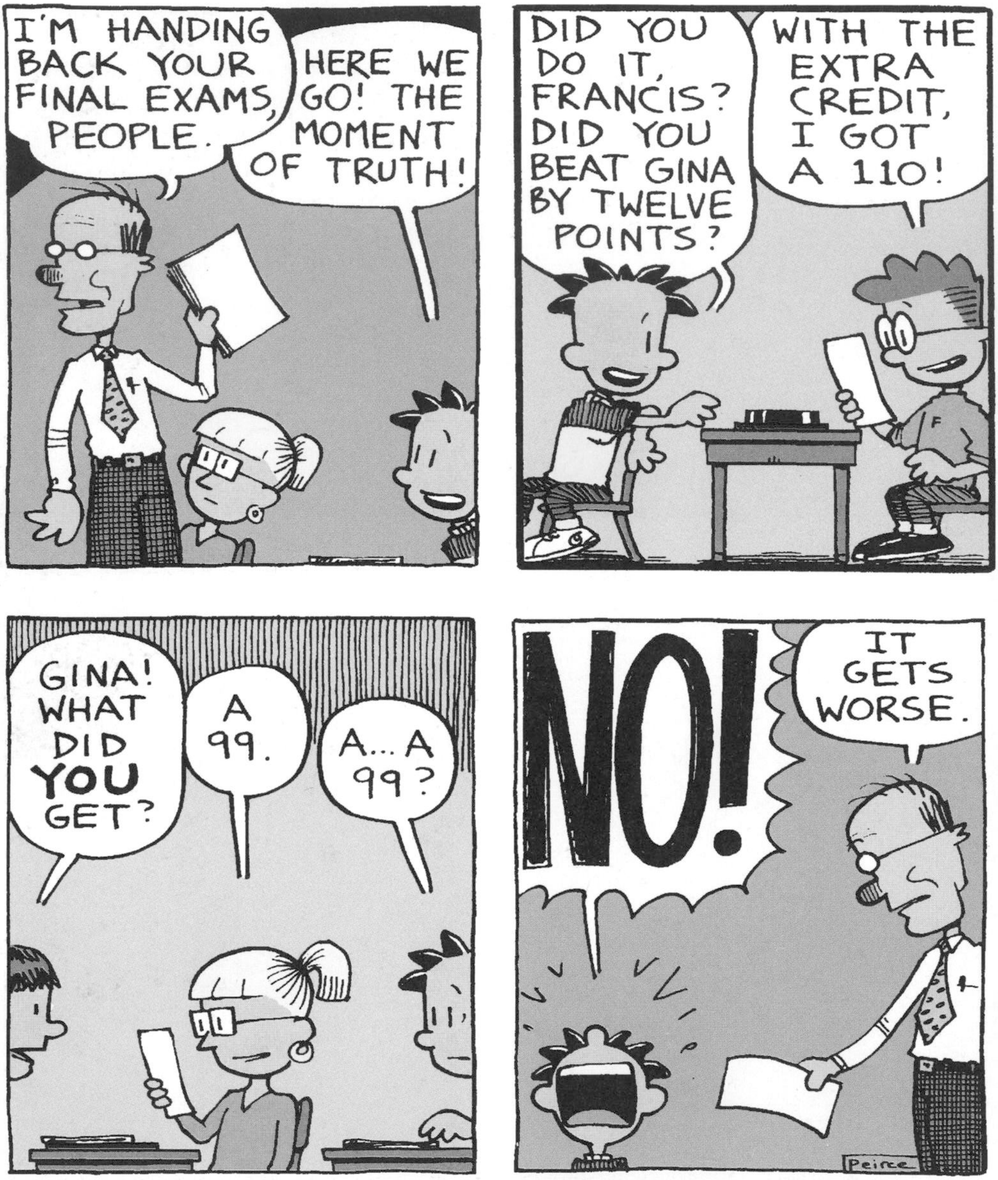
I'M HANDING BACK YOUR FINAL EXAMS, PEOPLE.
HERE WE GO! THE MOMENT OF TRUTH!
DID YOU DO IT, FRANCIS? DID YOU BEAT GINA BY TWELVE POINTS?
WITH THE EXTRA CREDIT, I GOT A 110!
GINA! WHAT DID **YOU** GET?
A 99.
A... A 99?
NO!
IT GETS WORSE.
Peirce

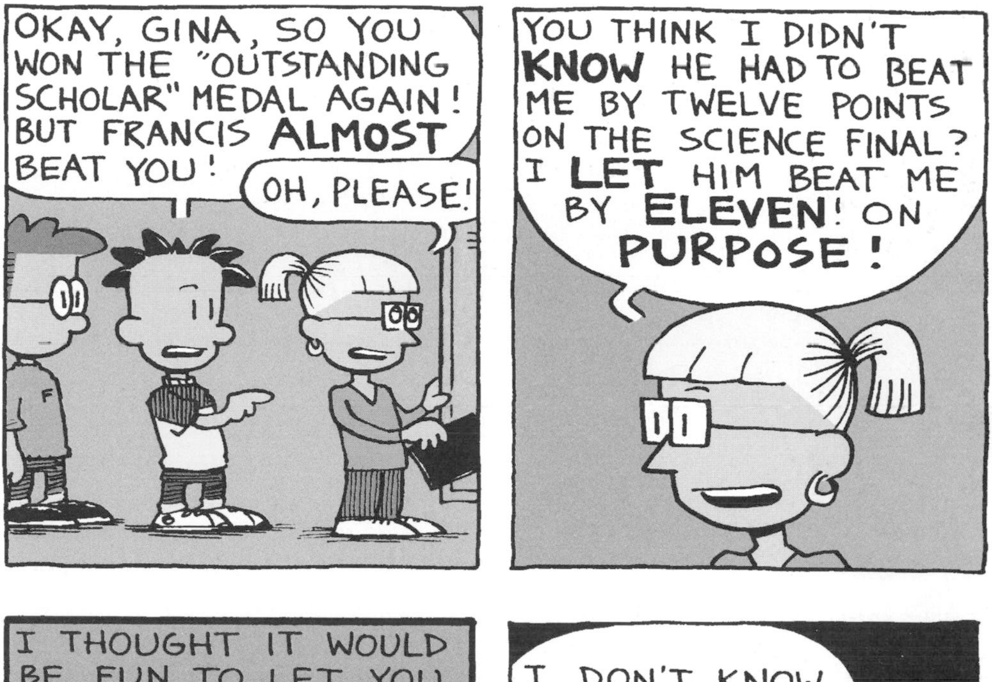
OKAY, GINA, SO YOU WON THE "OUTSTANDING SCHOLAR" MEDAL AGAIN! BUT FRANCIS ALMOST BEAT YOU!
OH, PLEASE!
F
YOU THINK I DIDN'T KNOW HE HAD TO BEAT ME BY TWELVE POINTS ON THE SCIENCE FINAL? I LET HIM BEAT ME BY ELEVEN! ON PURPOSE!
I THOUGHT IT WOULD BE FUN TO LET YOU CLOWNS THINK YOU ACTUALLY HAD A CHANCE TO TAKE MY MEDAL!
F
I DON'T KNOW WHETHER TO BE IMPRESSED OR FRIGHTENED.
OH, IS SHE EVIL.
F
Peirce

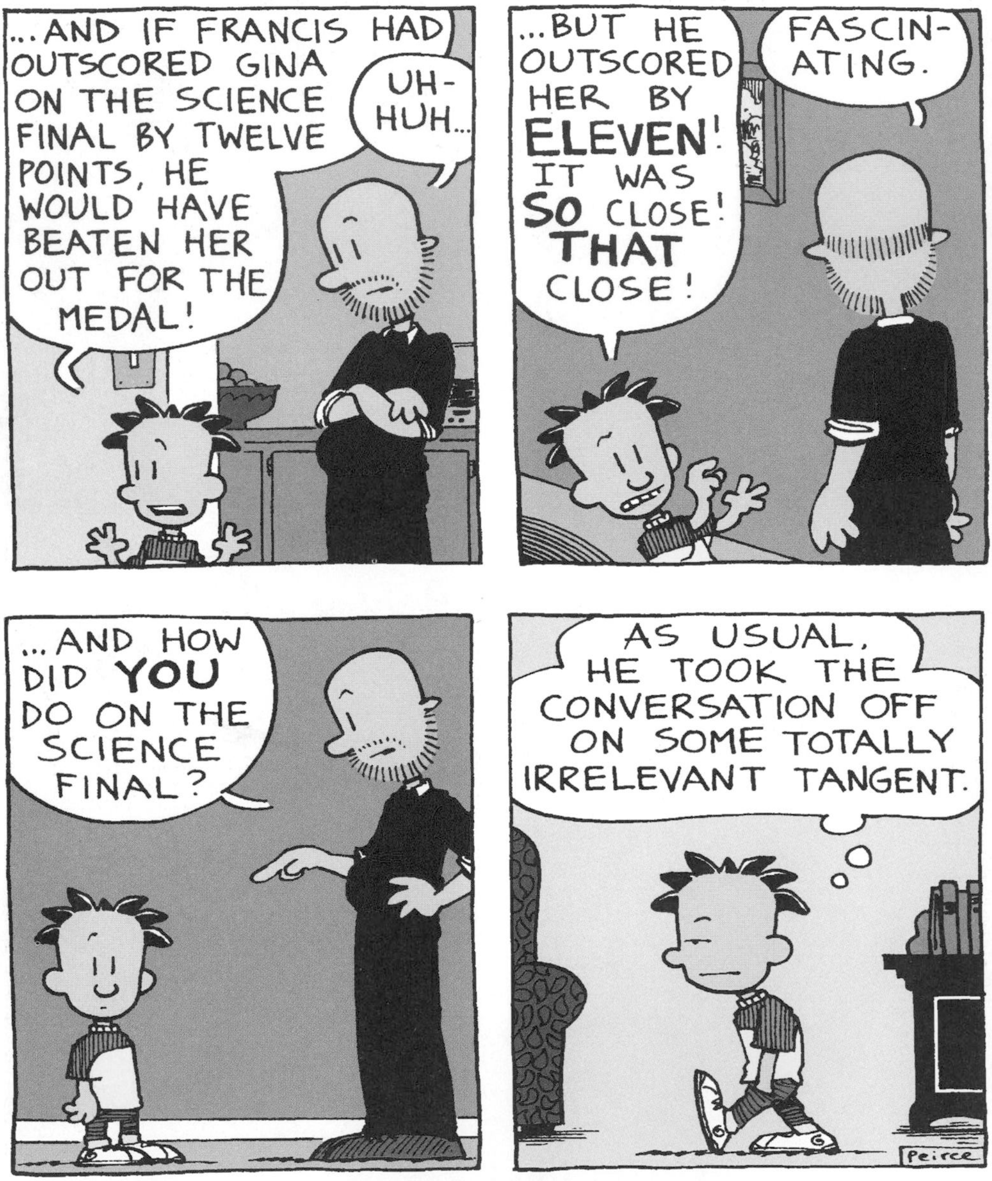
...AND IF FRANCIS HAD OUTSCORED GINA ON THE SCIENCE FINAL BY TWELVE POINTS, HE WOULD HAVE BEATEN HER OUT FOR THE MEDAL!
UH-HUH...
...BUT HE OUTSCORED HER BY ELEVEN! IT WAS SO CLOSE! THAT CLOSE!
FASCIN-ATING.
...AND HOW DID YOU DO ON THE SCIENCE FINAL?
AS USUAL, HE TOOK THE CONVERSATION OFF ON SOME TOTALLY IRRELEVANT TANGENT.
Peirce

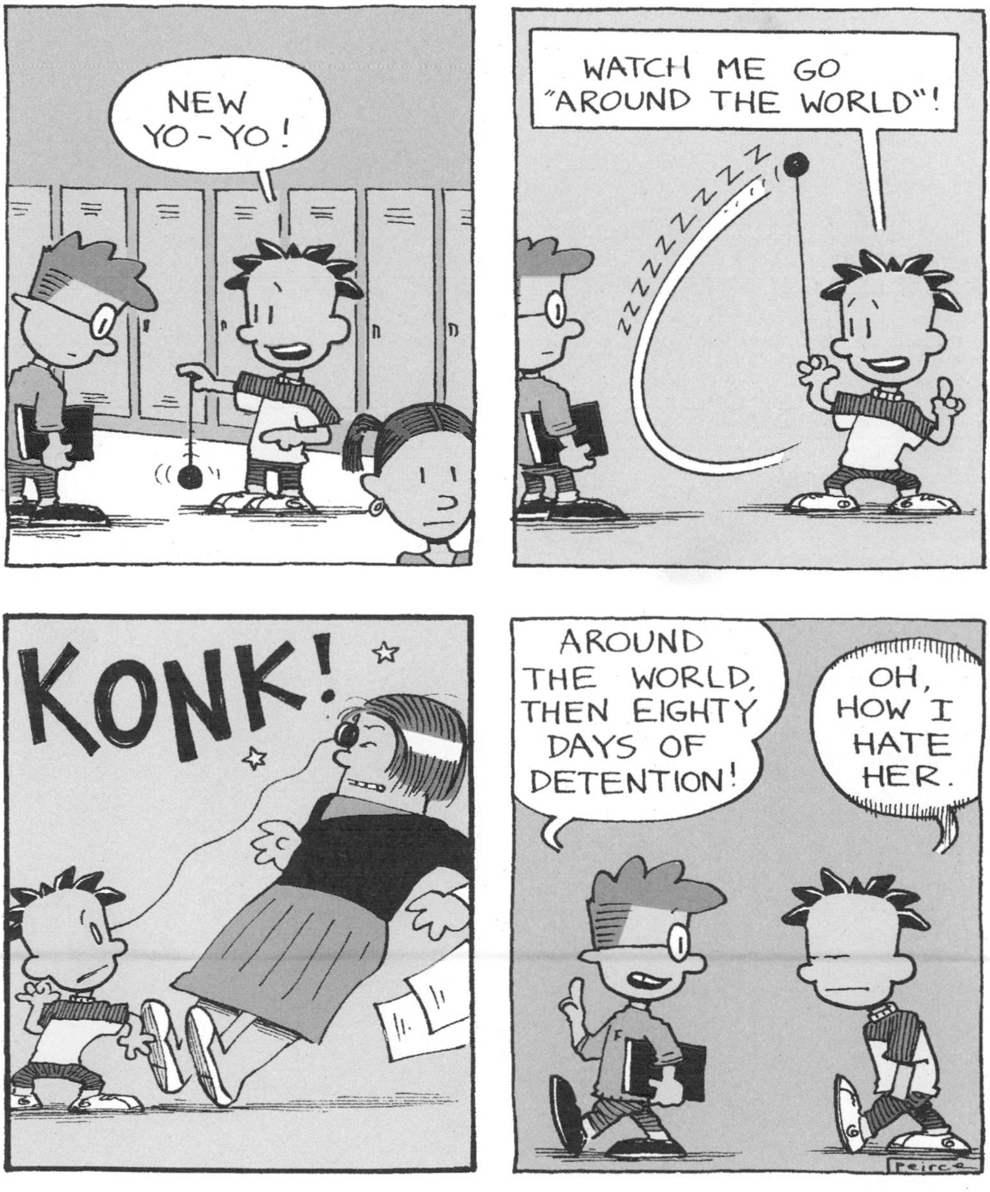
NEW YO-YO!
WATCH ME GO "AROUND THE WORLD"!
ZZZZZZZZZZZ
KONK!
AROUND THE WORLD, THEN EIGHTY DAYS OF DETENTION!
OH, HOW I HATE HER.
Peirce

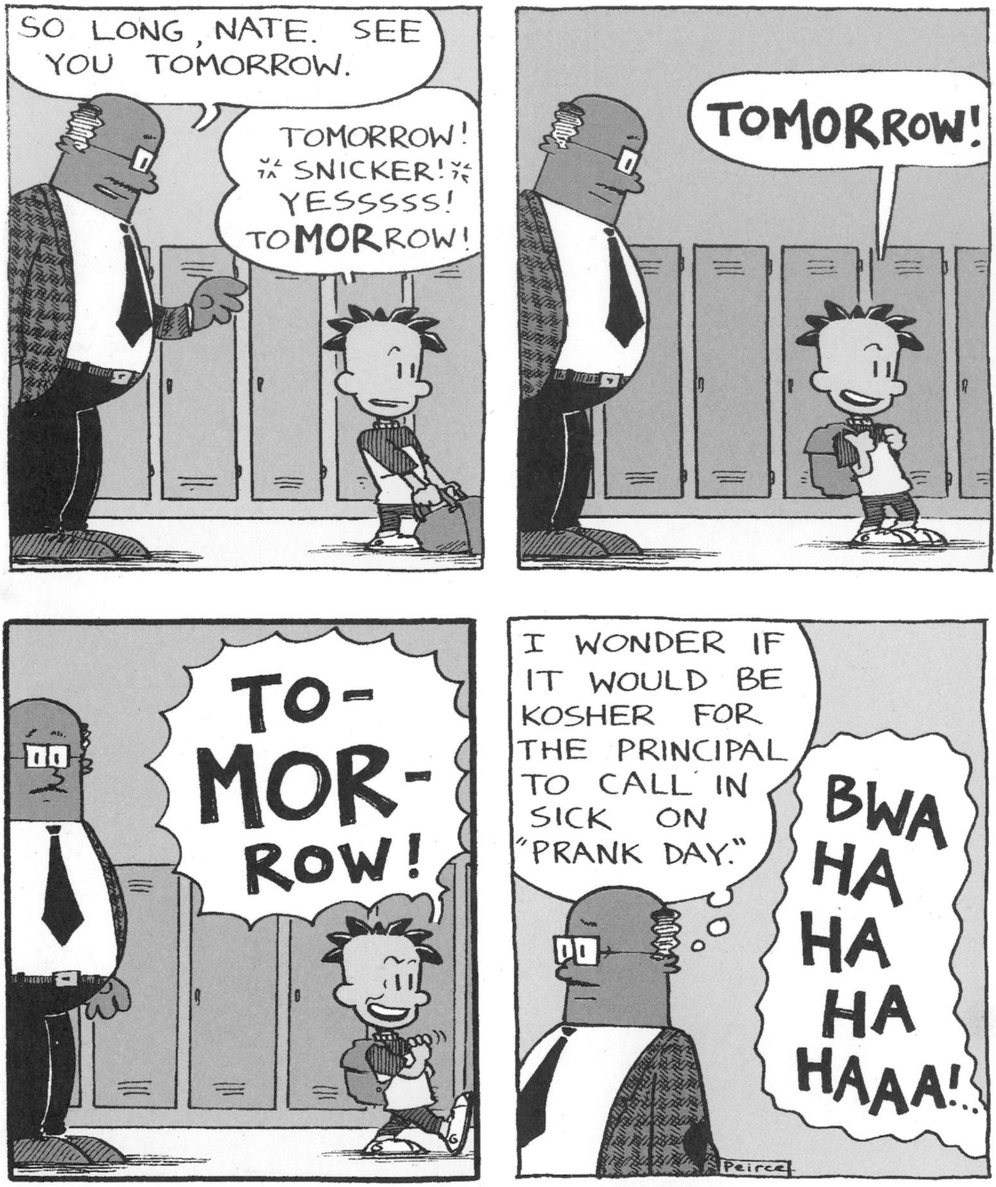
SO LONG, NATE. SEE YOU TOMORROW.
TOMORROW! SNICKER! YESSSSS! TOMORROW!
TOMORROW!
TO-MOR-ROW!
I WONDER IF IT WOULD BE KOSHER FOR THE PRINCIPAL TO CALL IN SICK ON "PRANK DAY."
BWA HA HA HA HA HAAA!...
Peirce

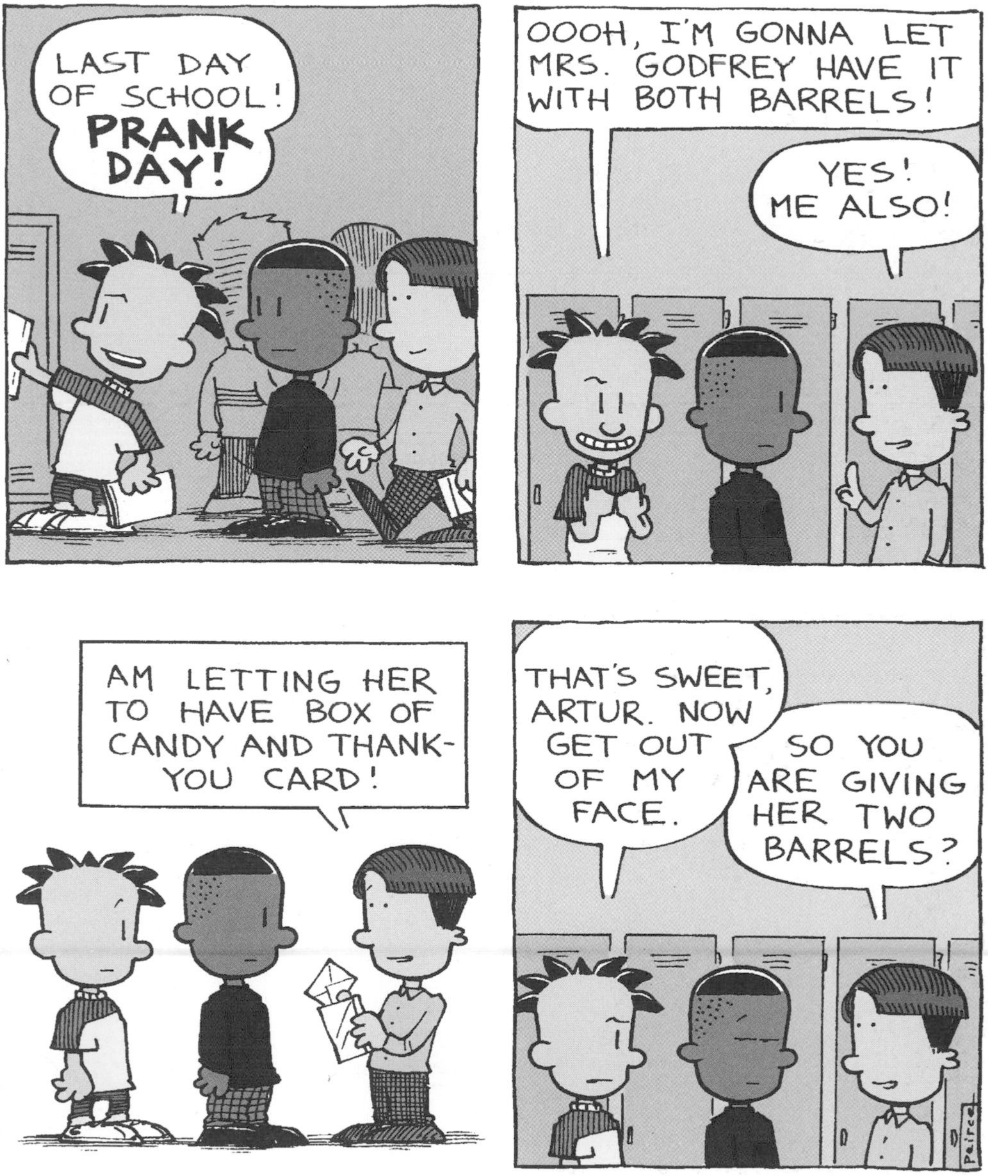

LAST DAY OF SCHOOL! PRANK DAY!
OOOH, I'M GONNA LET MRS. GODFREY HAVE IT WITH BOTH BARRELS!
YES! ME ALSO!
AM LETTING HER TO HAVE BOX OF CANDY AND THANK-YOU CARD!
THAT'S SWEET, ARTUR. NOW GET OUT OF MY FACE.
SO YOU ARE GIVING HER TWO BARRELS?
Peirce

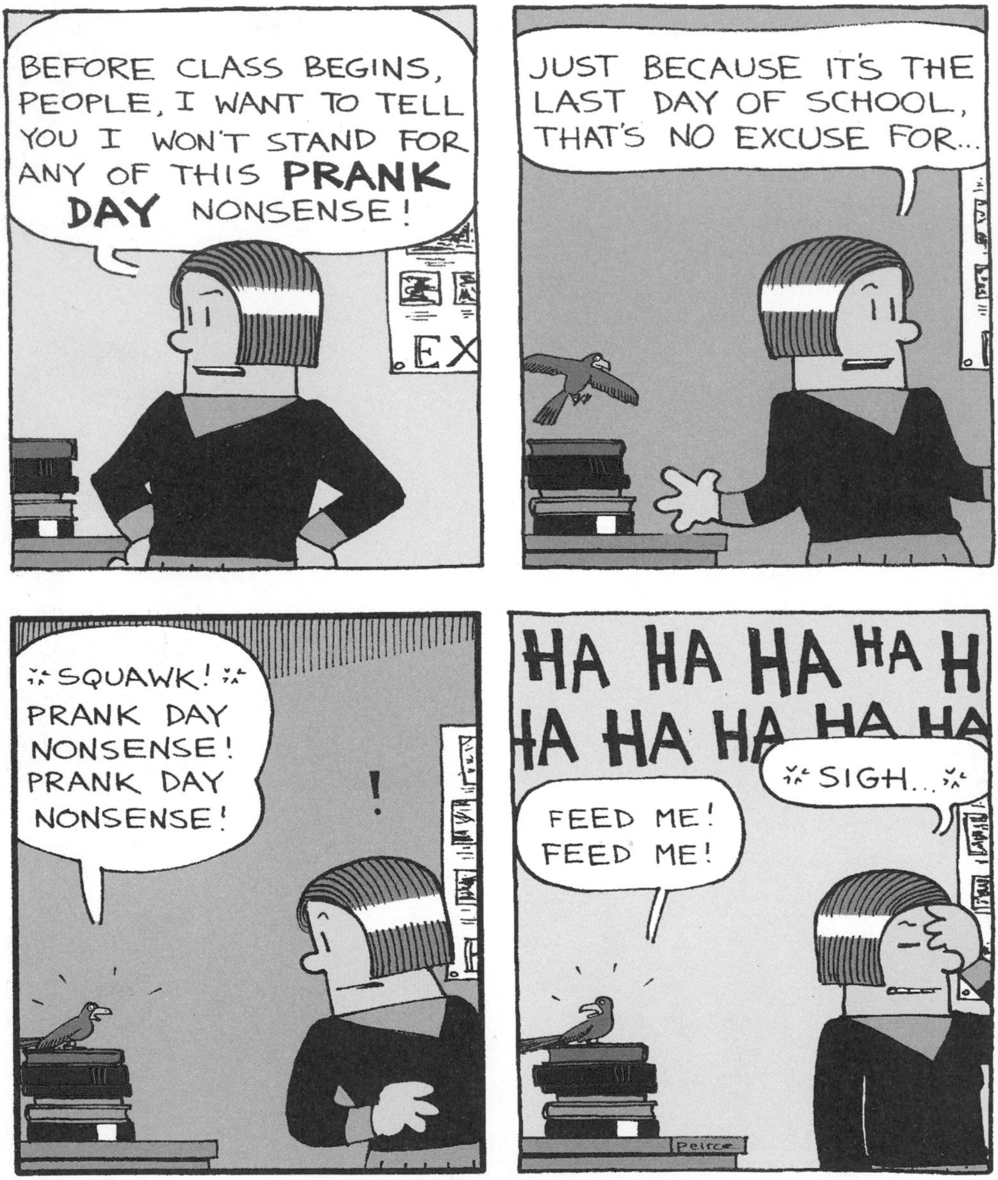
BEFORE CLASS BEGINS, PEOPLE, I WANT TO TELL YOU I WON'T STAND FOR ANY OF THIS **PRANK DAY** NONSENSE!
JUST BECAUSE IT'S THE LAST DAY OF SCHOOL, THAT'S NO EXCUSE FOR...
SQUAWK! PRANK DAY NONSENSE! PRANK DAY NONSENSE!
!
HA HA HA HA H
HA HA HA HA HA
SIGH...
FEED ME! FEED ME!
Peirce

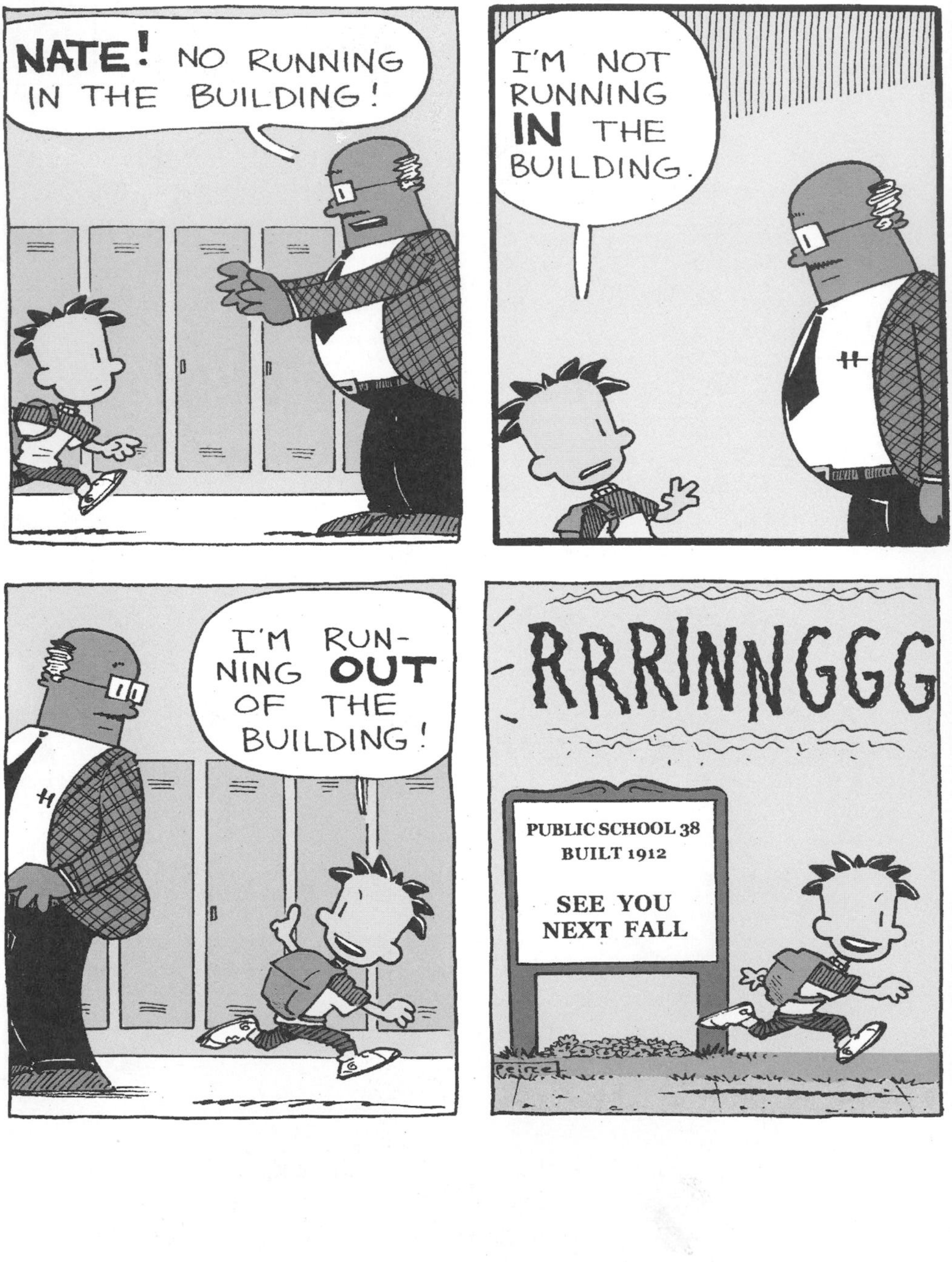
NATE! NO RUNNING IN THE BUILDING!
I'M NOT RUNNING IN THE BUILDING.
I'M RUNNING OUT OF THE BUILDING!
RRRINNGGG
PUBLIC SCHOOL 38
BUILT 1912
SEE YOU NEXT FALL
Peirce

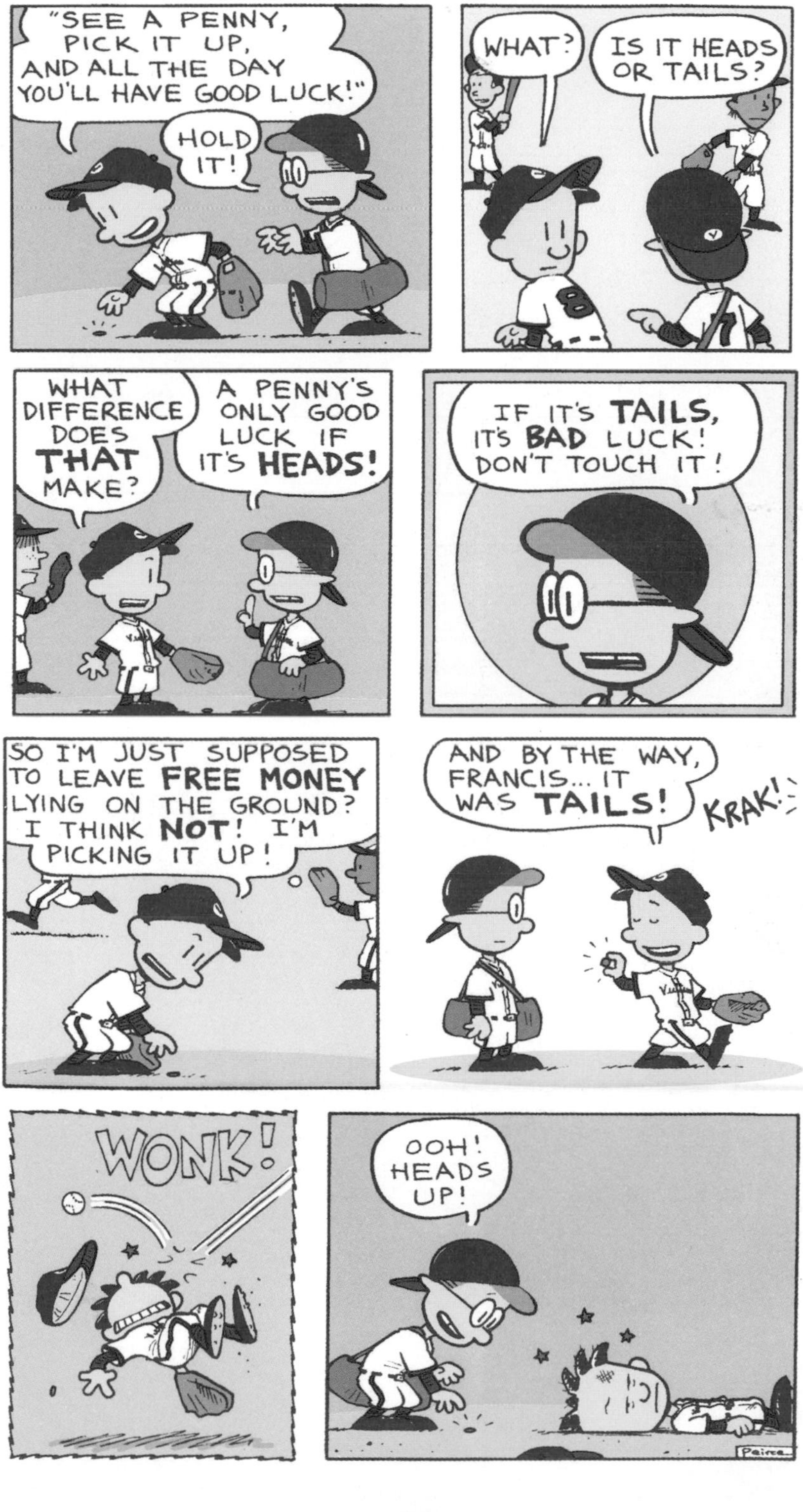
"SEE A PENNY, PICK IT UP, AND ALL THE DAY YOU'LL HAVE GOOD LUCK!"
HOLD IT!
WHAT?
IS IT HEADS OR TAILS?
WHAT DIFFERENCE DOES THAT MAKE?
A PENNY'S ONLY GOOD LUCK IF IT'S HEADS!
IF IT'S TAILS, IT'S BAD LUCK! DON'T TOUCH IT!
SO I'M JUST SUPPOSED TO LEAVE FREE MONEY LYING ON THE GROUND? I THINK NOT! I'M PICKING IT UP!
AND BY THE WAY, FRANCIS... IT WAS TAILS!
KRAK!
WONK!
OOH! HEADS UP!
Peirce

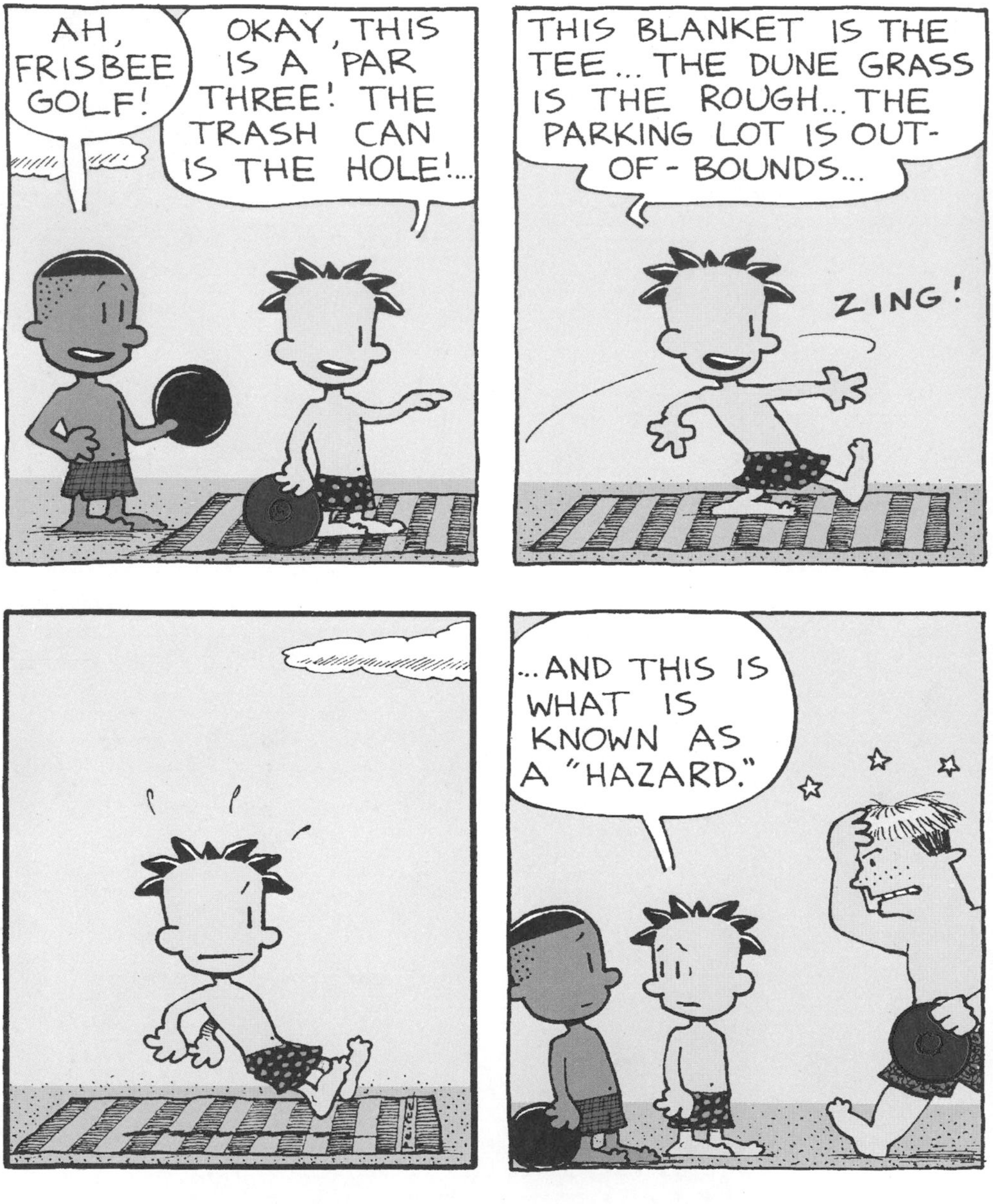
AH, FRISBEE GOLF!
OKAY, THIS IS A PAR THREE! THE TRASH CAN IS THE HOLE!...
THIS BLANKET IS THE TEE... THE DUNE GRASS IS THE ROUGH... THE PARKING LOT IS OUT-OF-BOUNDS...
ZING!
...AND THIS IS WHAT IS KNOWN AS A "HAZARD."

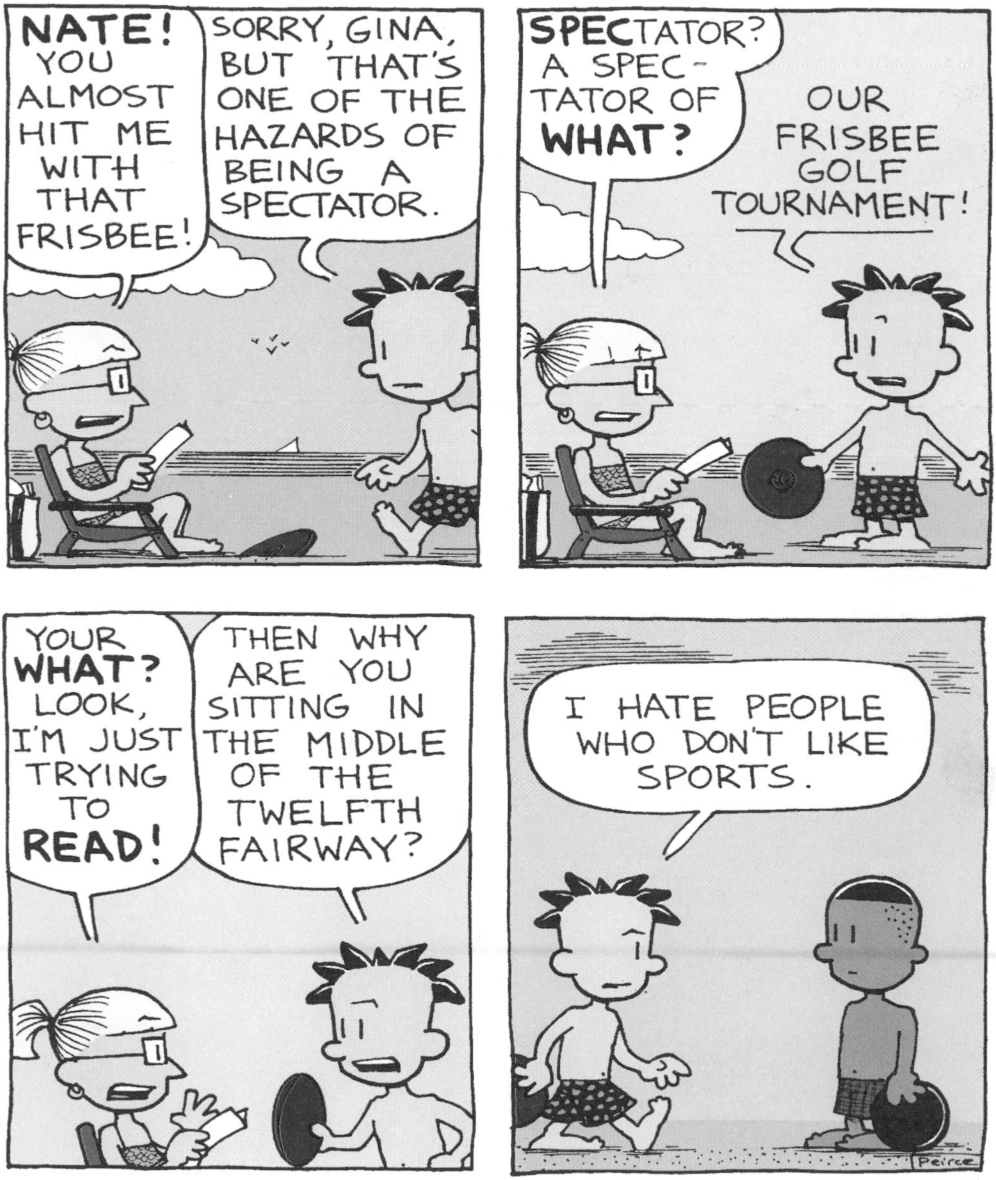
NATE! YOU ALMOST HIT ME WITH THAT FRISBEE!
SORRY, GINA, BUT THAT'S ONE OF THE HAZARDS OF BEING A SPECTATOR.
SPECTATOR? A SPECTATOR OF WHAT?
OUR FRISBEE GOLF TOURNAMENT!
YOUR WHAT? LOOK, I'M JUST TRYING TO READ!
THEN WHY ARE YOU SITTING IN THE MIDDLE OF THE TWELFTH FAIRWAY?
I HATE PEOPLE WHO DON'T LIKE SPORTS.
Peirce

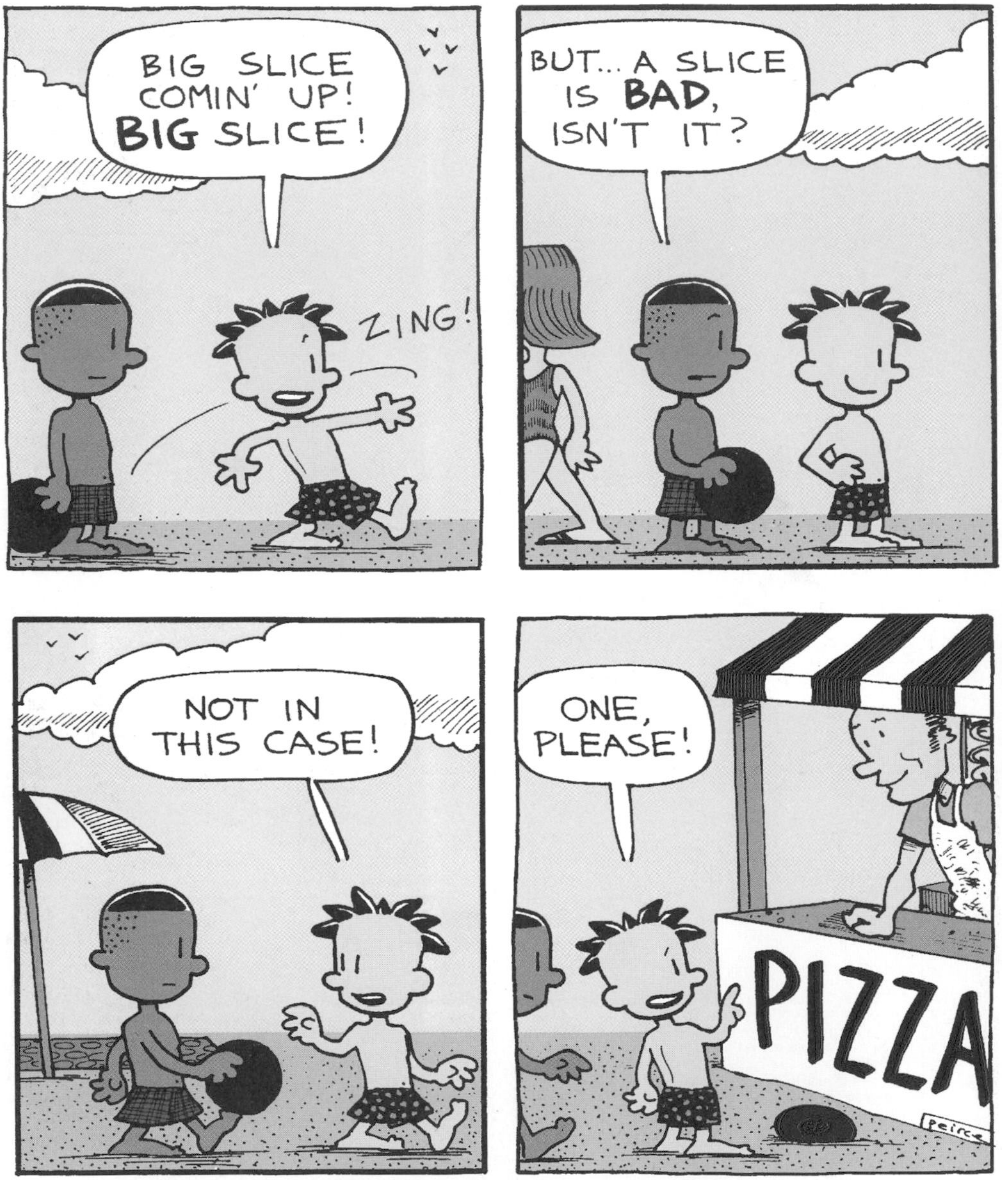
BIG SLICE COMIN' UP! BIG SLICE!
ZING!
BUT... A SLICE IS BAD, ISN'T IT?
NOT IN THIS CASE!
ONE, PLEASE!
PIZZA
peirce

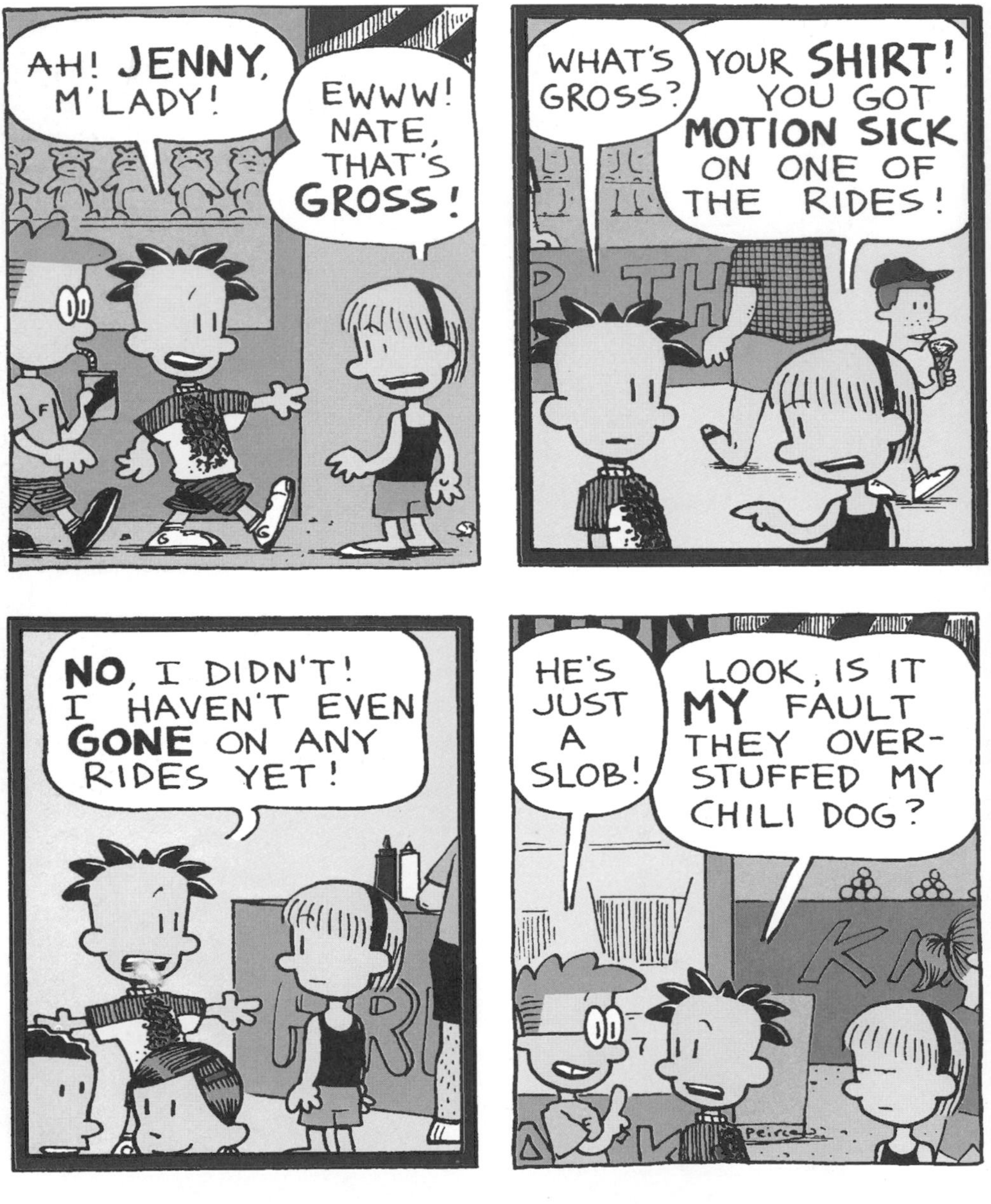
AH! **JENNY**, M'LADY!
EWWW! NATE, THAT'S **GROSS**!
WHAT'S GROSS?
YOUR **SHIRT**! YOU GOT **MOTION SICK** ON ONE OF THE RIDES!
NO, I DIDN'T! I HAVEN'T EVEN **GONE** ON ANY RIDES YET!
HE'S JUST A SLOB!
LOOK, IS IT **MY** FAULT THEY OVER-STUFFED MY CHILI DOG?

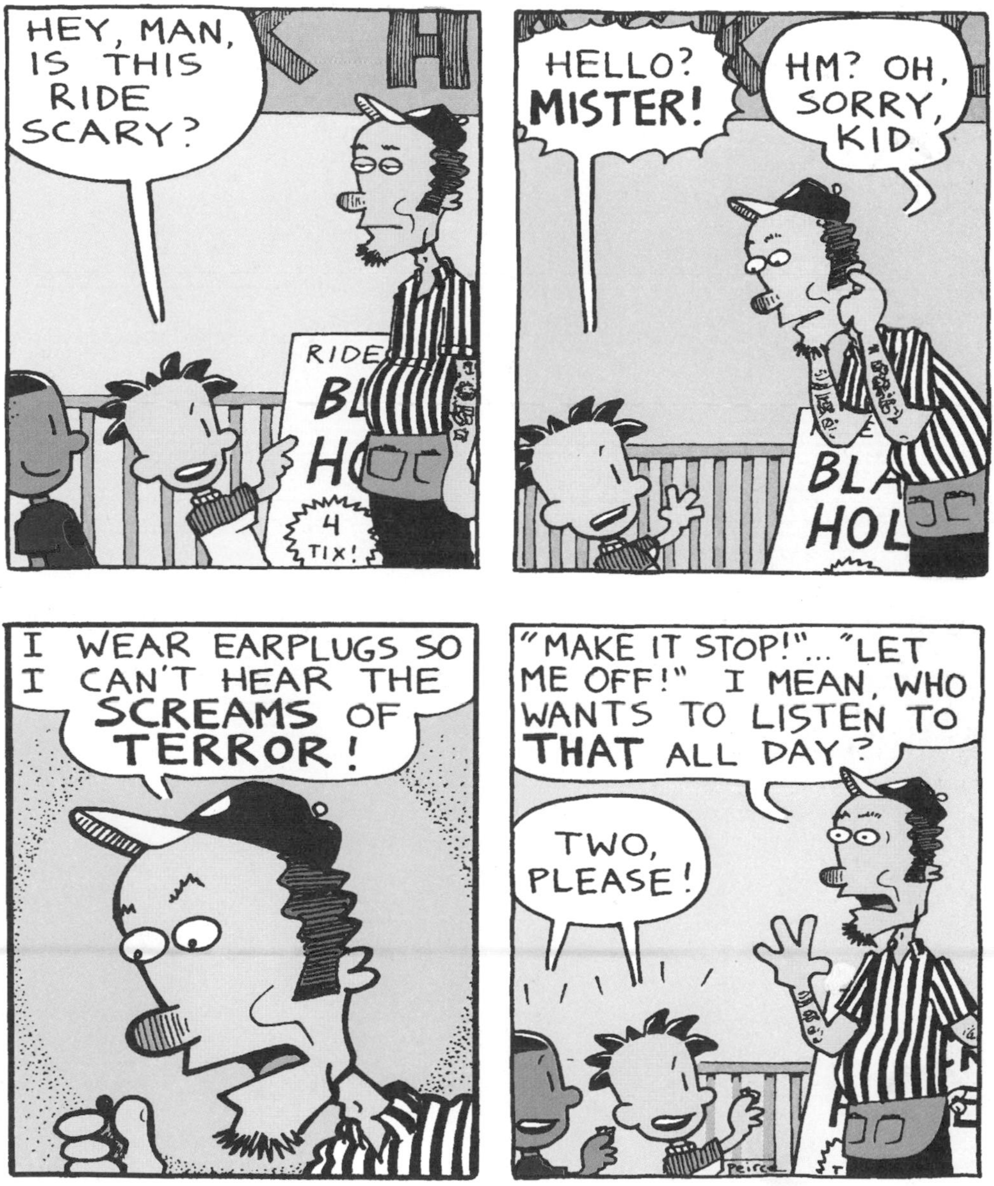
HEY, MAN, IS THIS RIDE SCARY?
RIDE
BL
HO
4 TIX!
HELLO? MISTER!
HM? OH, SORRY, KID.
BLA
HOL
I WEAR EARPLUGS SO I CAN'T HEAR THE SCREAMS OF TERROR!
"MAKE IT STOP!"... "LET ME OFF!" I MEAN, WHO WANTS TO LISTEN TO THAT ALL DAY?
TWO, PLEASE!
Peirce

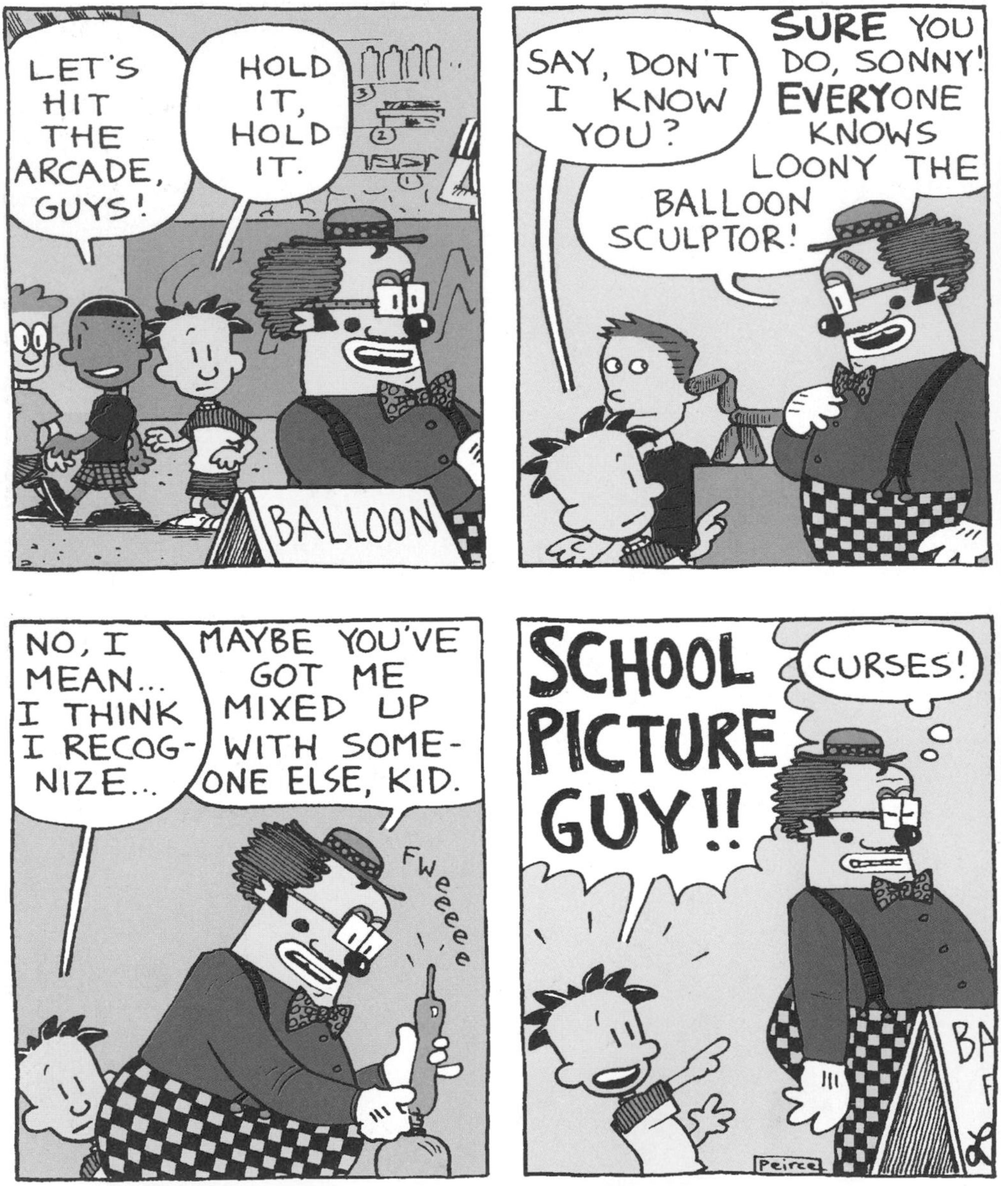
LET'S HIT THE ARCADE, GUYS!
HOLD IT, HOLD IT.
BALLOON
SAY, DON'T I KNOW YOU?
SURE YOU DO, SONNY! EVERYONE KNOWS LOONY THE BALLOON SCULPTOR!
NO, I MEAN... I THINK I RECOGNIZE...
MAYBE YOU'VE GOT ME MIXED UP WITH SOMEONE ELSE, KID.
FWeeeeee
SCHOOL PICTURE GUY!!
CURSES!
Peirce

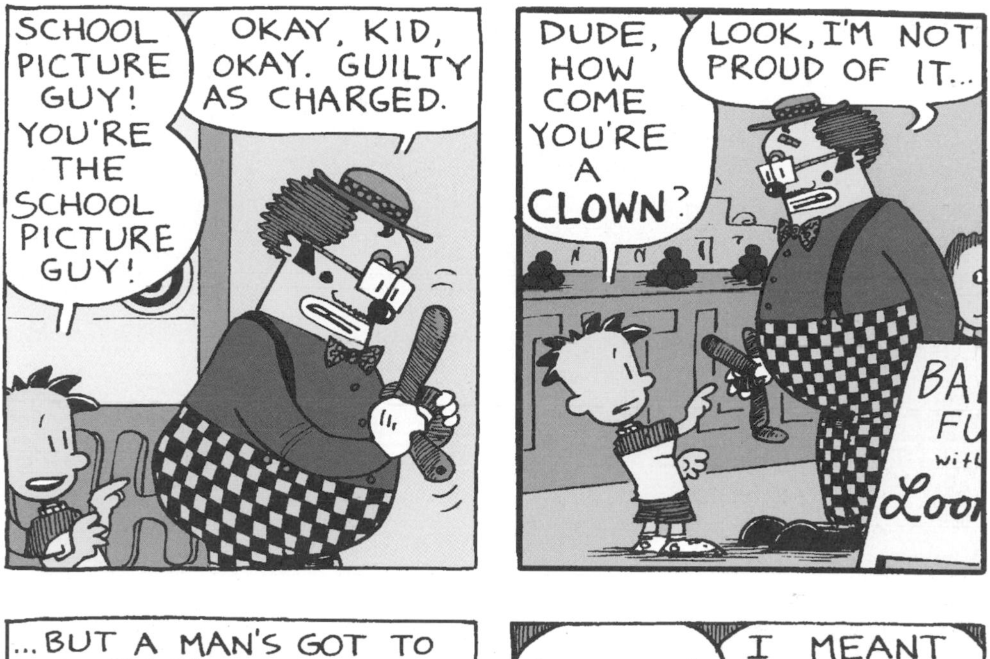
SCHOOL PICTURE GUY! YOU'RE THE SCHOOL PICTURE GUY!
OKAY, KID, OKAY. GUILTY AS CHARGED.
DUDE, HOW COME YOU'RE A **CLOWN**?
LOOK, I'M NOT PROUD OF IT...
...BUT A MAN'S GOT TO PUT **FOOD** ON THE TABLE, AMIGO! A MAN'S GOT TO PAY THE **RENT**!
RENT?
BUT DON'T YOU LIVE IN YOUR MOTHER'S BASEMENT?
I MEANT RENT IN THE METAPHORICAL SENSE, KID. HAVE A GIRAFFE.
Peirce

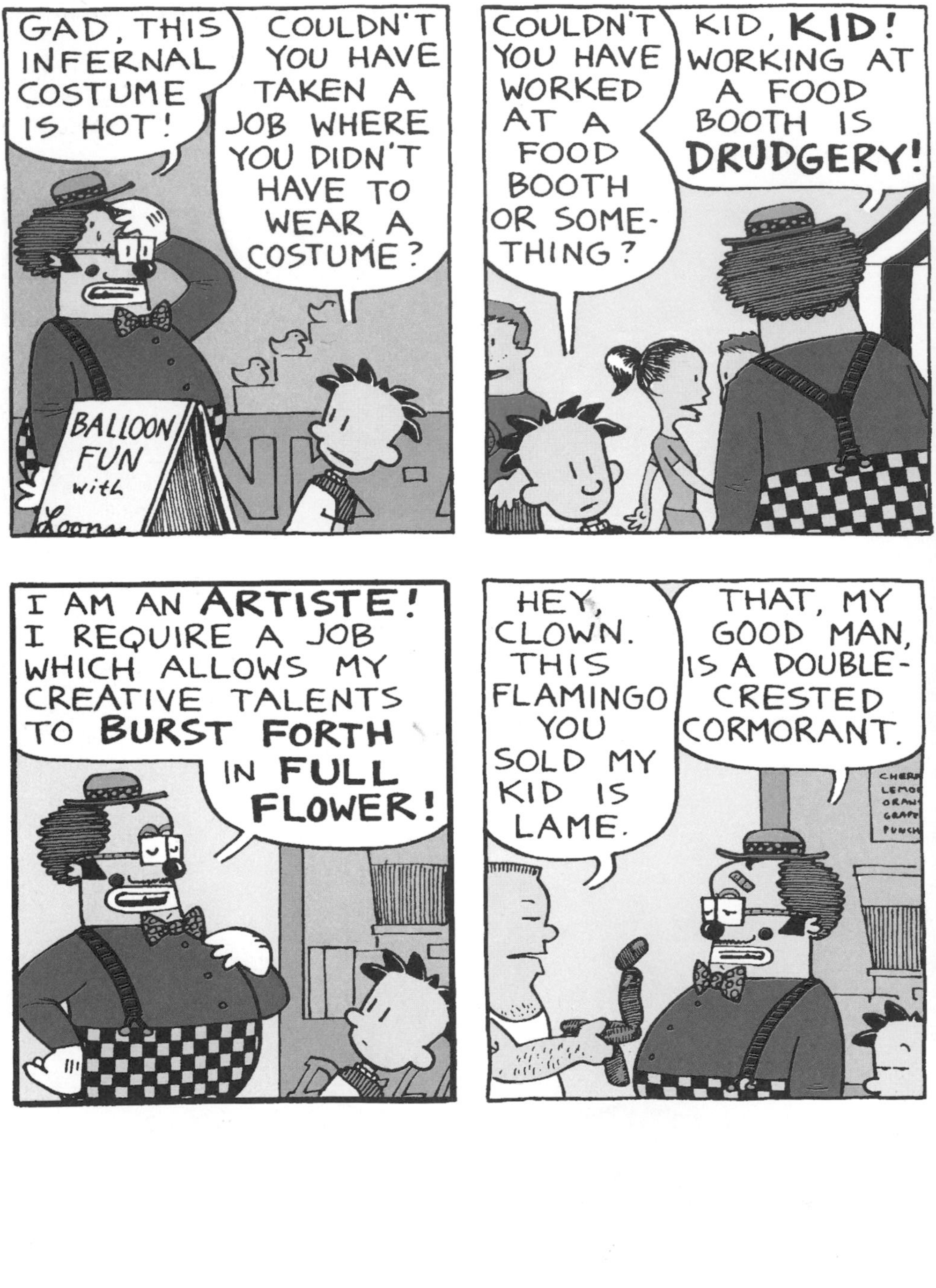
GAD, THIS INFERNAL COSTUME IS HOT!
COULDN'T YOU HAVE TAKEN A JOB WHERE YOU DIDN'T HAVE TO WEAR A COSTUME?
BALLOON FUN with
COULDN'T YOU HAVE WORKED AT A FOOD BOOTH OR SOMETHING?
KID, **KID**! WORKING AT A FOOD BOOTH IS **DRUDGERY**!
I AM AN **ARTISTE**! I REQUIRE A JOB WHICH ALLOWS MY CREATIVE TALENTS TO **BURST FORTH** IN **FULL FLOWER**!
HEY, CLOWN. THIS FLAMINGO YOU SOLD MY KID IS LAME.
THAT, MY GOOD MAN, IS A DOUBLE-CRESTED CORMORANT.
PUNCH

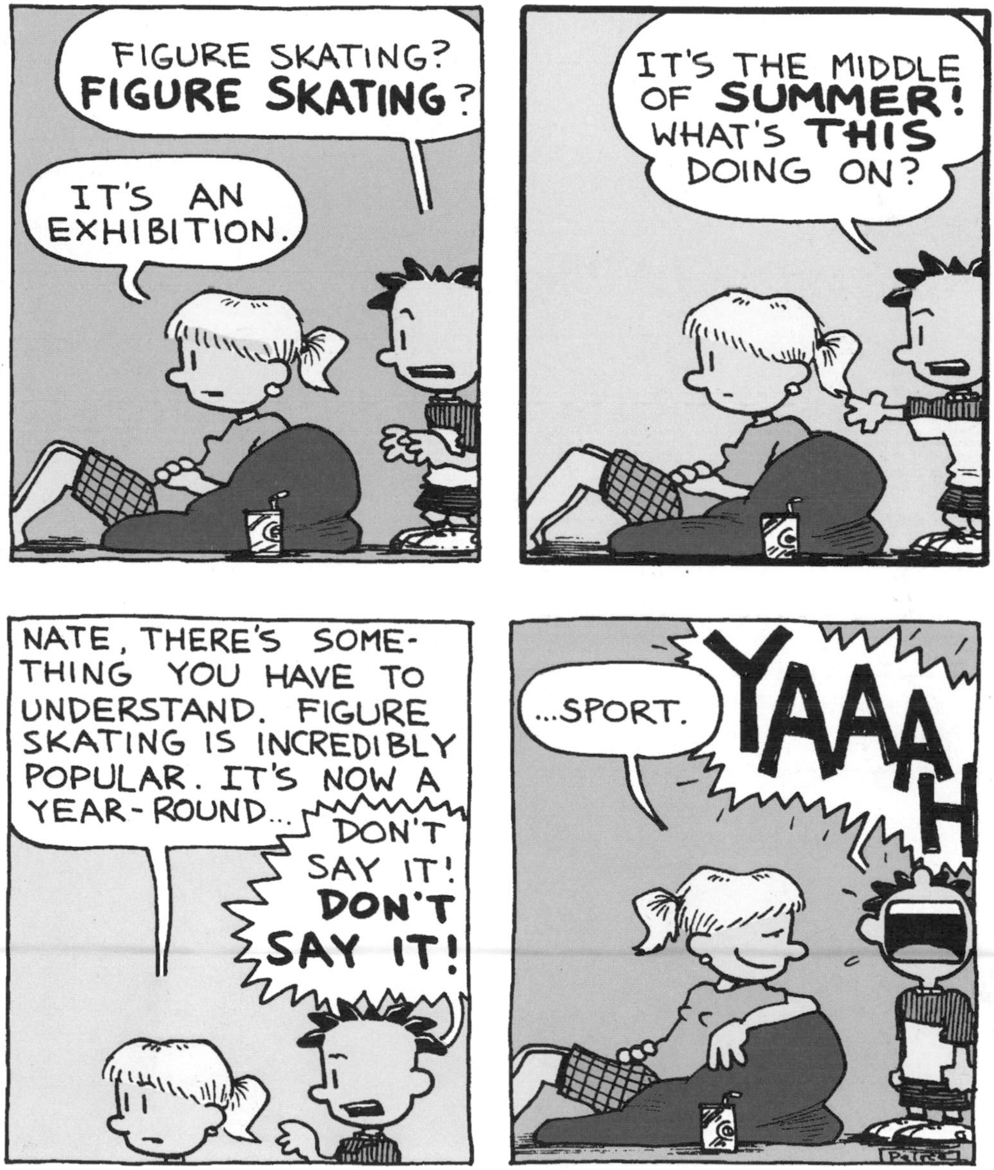
FIGURE SKATING? FIGURE SKATING?
IT'S AN EXHIBITION.
IT'S THE MIDDLE OF SUMMER! WHAT'S THIS DOING ON?
NATE, THERE'S SOMETHING YOU HAVE TO UNDERSTAND. FIGURE SKATING IS INCREDIBLY POPULAR. IT'S NOW A YEAR-ROUND...
DON'T SAY IT! DON'T SAY IT!
...SPORT.
YAAAH
PEIRCE

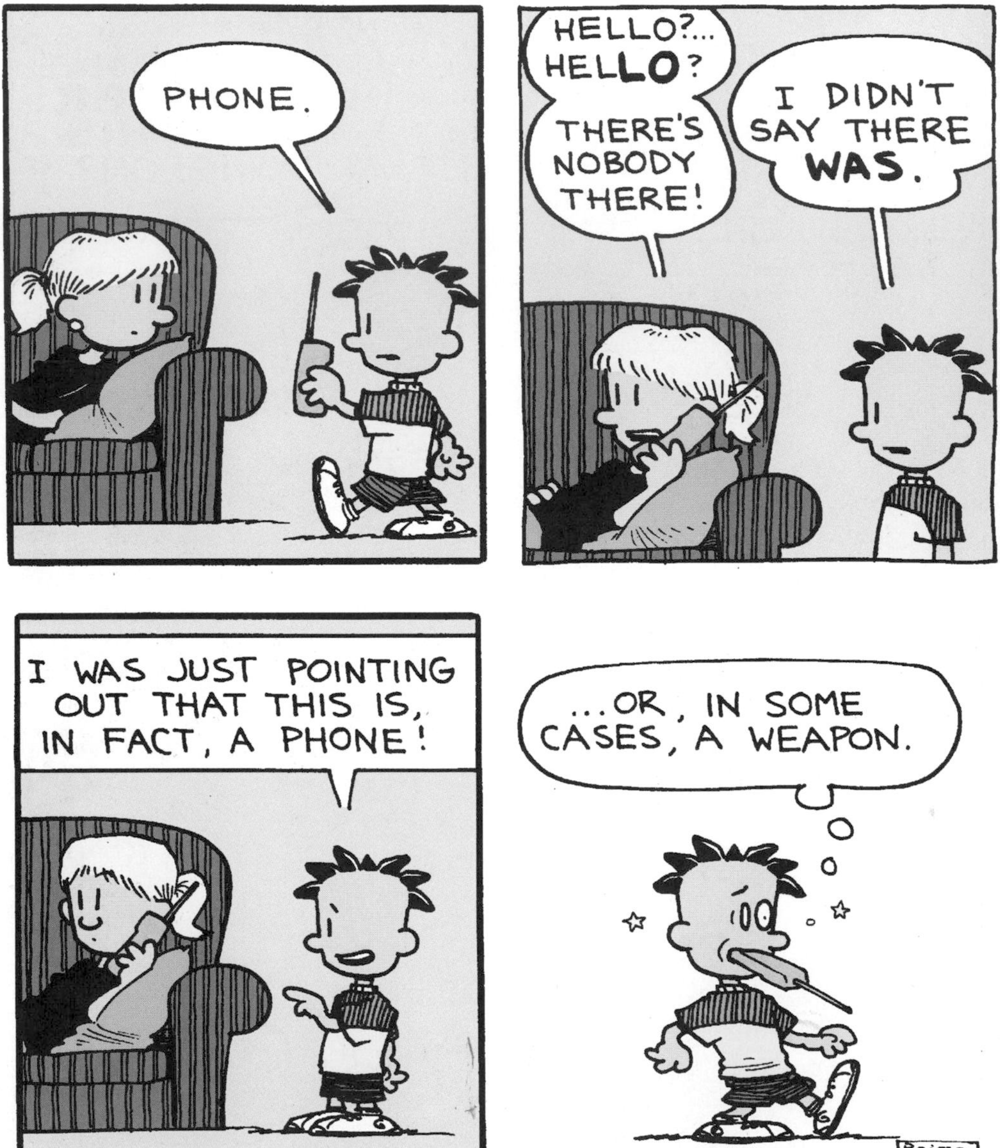
PHONE.
HELLO?... HELLO?
THERE'S NOBODY THERE!
I DIDN'T SAY THERE WAS.
I WAS JUST POINTING OUT THAT THIS IS, IN FACT, A PHONE!
...OR, IN SOME CASES, A WEAPON.
Peirce

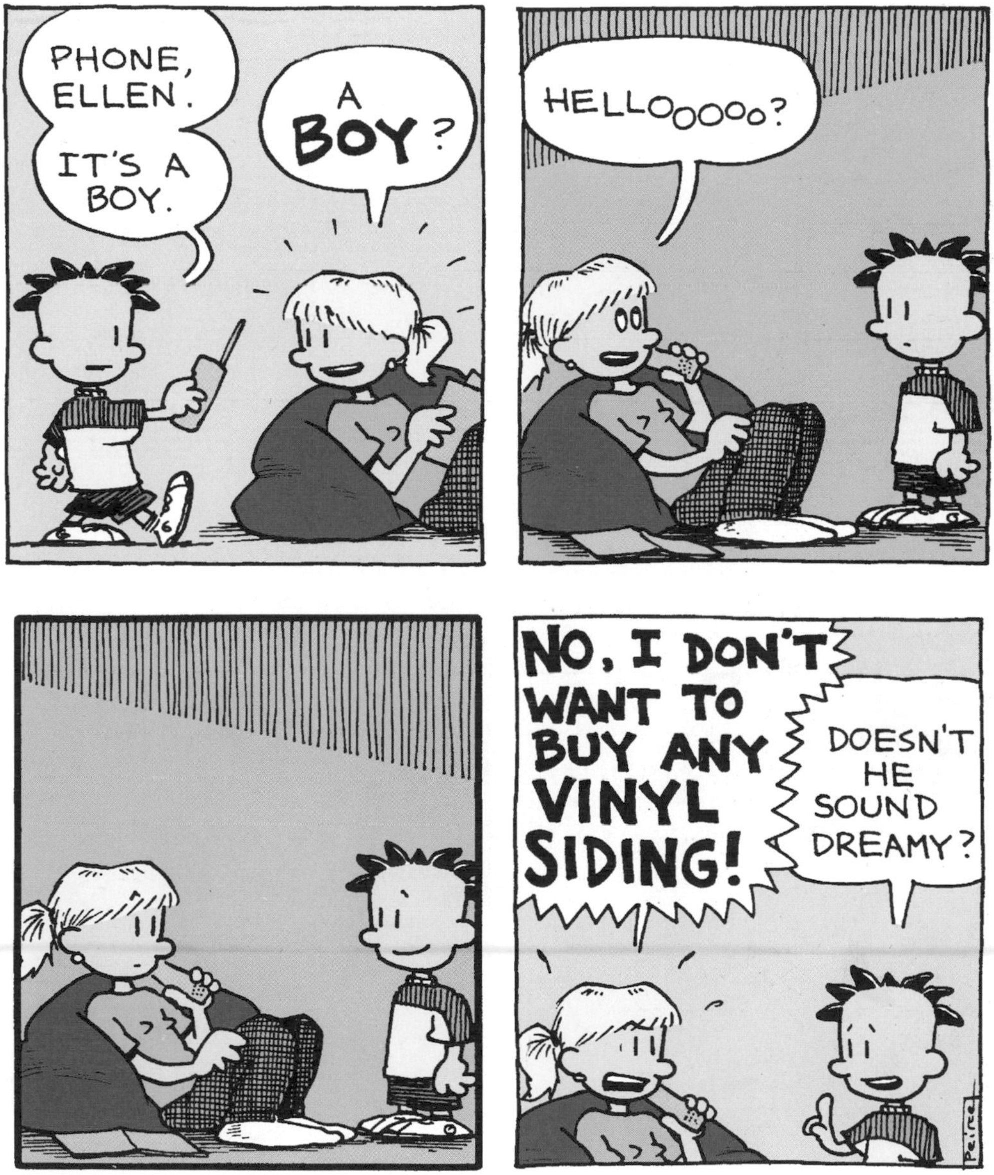
PHONE, ELLEN. IT'S A BOY.
A BOY?
HELLOooooo?
NO, I DON'T WANT TO BUY ANY VINYL SIDING!
DOESN'T HE SOUND DREAMY?
Peirce

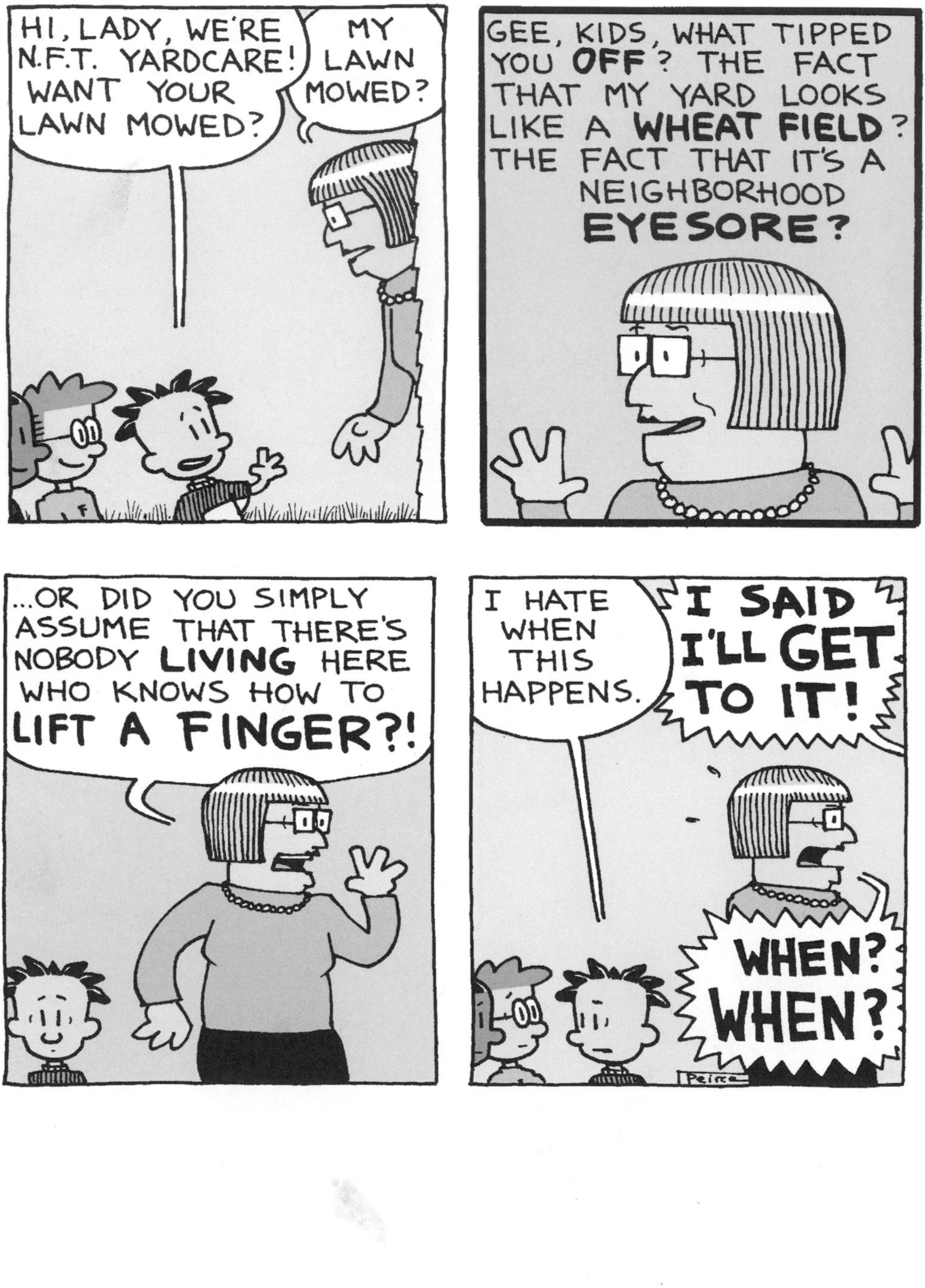
HI, LADY, WE'RE N.F.T. YARDCARE! WANT YOUR LAWN MOWED?
MY LAWN MOWED?
GEE, KIDS, WHAT TIPPED YOU OFF? THE FACT THAT MY YARD LOOKS LIKE A WHEAT FIELD? THE FACT THAT IT'S A NEIGHBORHOOD EYESORE?
...OR DID YOU SIMPLY ASSUME THAT THERE'S NOBODY LIVING HERE WHO KNOWS HOW TO LIFT A FINGER?!
I HATE WHEN THIS HAPPENS.
I SAID I'LL GET TO IT!
WHEN? WHEN?
Peirce

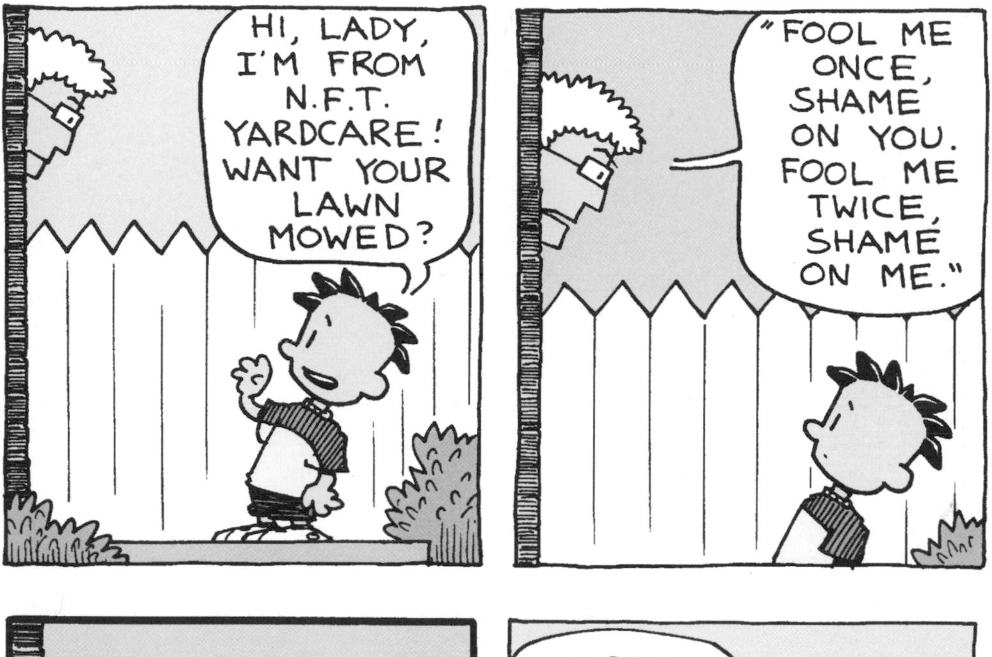
HI, LADY, I'M FROM N.F.T. YARDCARE! WANT YOUR LAWN MOWED?
"FOOL ME ONCE, SHAME ON YOU. FOOL ME TWICE, SHAME ON ME."
SLAM!
NOW I REMEMBER HER.
TOLD YA!
F
Peirce

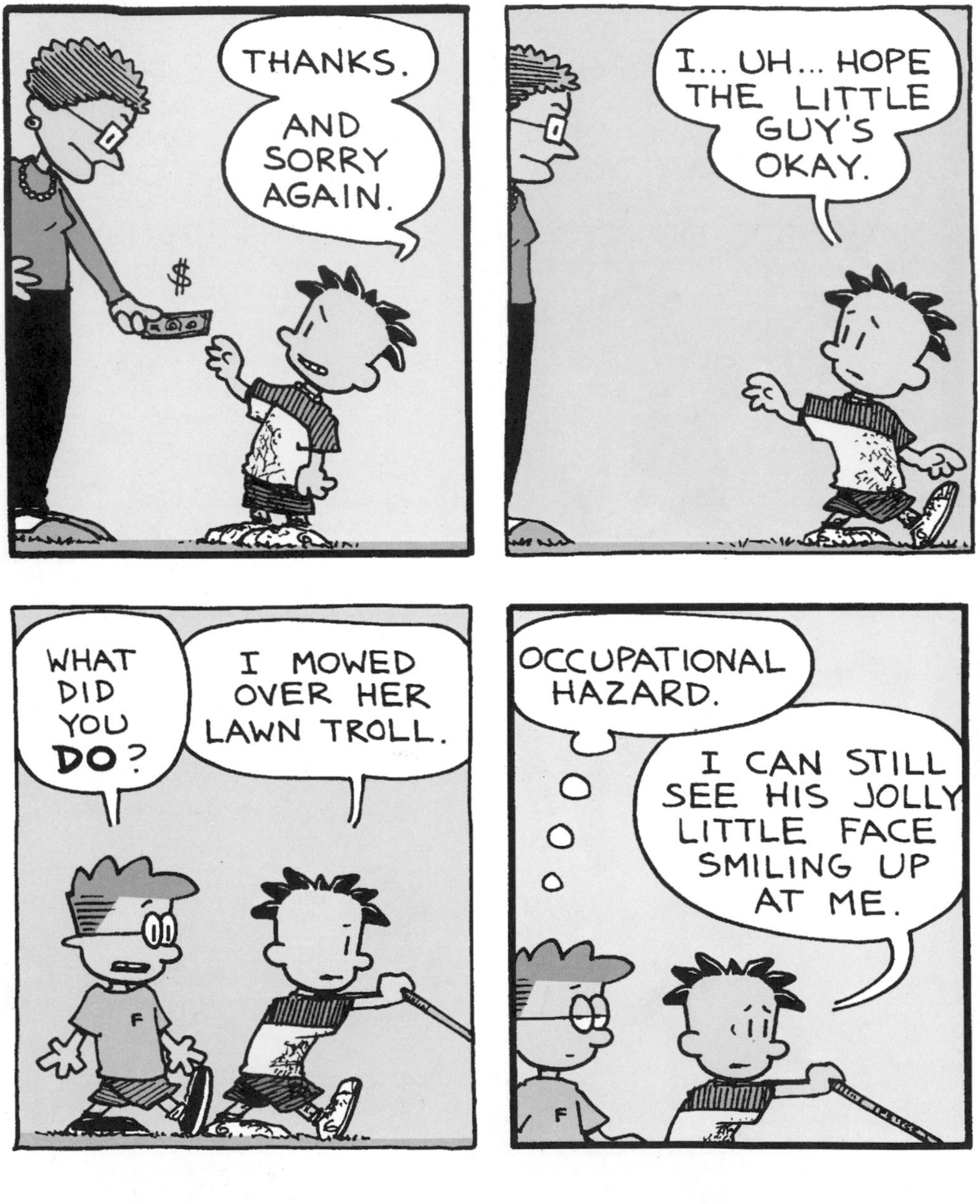
THANKS.
AND SORRY AGAIN.
$
I... UH... HOPE THE LITTLE GUY'S OKAY.
WHAT DID YOU DO?
I MOWED OVER HER LAWN TROLL.
OCCUPATIONAL HAZARD.
I CAN STILL SEE HIS JOLLY LITTLE FACE SMILING UP AT ME.

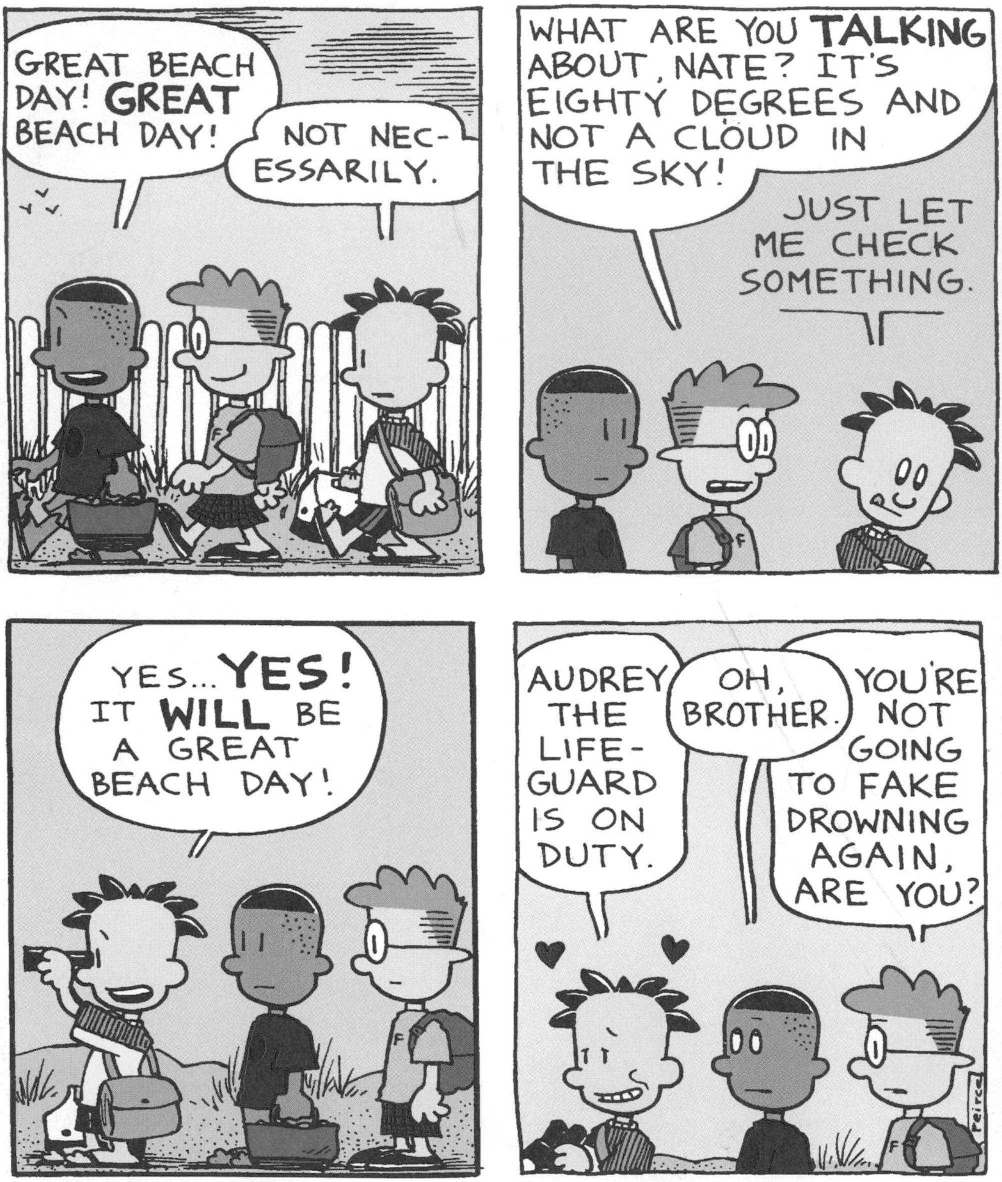
GREAT BEACH DAY! **GREAT** BEACH DAY!
NOT NEC- ESSARILY.
WHAT ARE YOU **TALKING** ABOUT, NATE? IT'S EIGHTY DEGREES AND NOT A CLOUD IN THE SKY!
JUST LET ME CHECK SOMETHING.
YES... **YES!** IT **WILL** BE A GREAT BEACH DAY!
AUDREY THE LIFE- GUARD IS ON DUTY.
OH, BROTHER.
YOU'RE NOT GOING TO FAKE DROWNING AGAIN, ARE YOU?
Peirce

HEL-LOOO, AUDREY!
HI, NATE.
LIFEGU
ON DU
SAY, DO YOU HAVE ANY SCUBA GEAR?
SCUBA GEAR?
LIFEGU
ON DU
YEAH, I WAS JUST WON-DERING IF I COULD BORROW AN OXYGEN TANK.
LIFEGU
ON DU
...'CAUSE YOU TAKE MY BREATH AWAY.
CRIPES.
LIFEGU
ON DU
Peirce

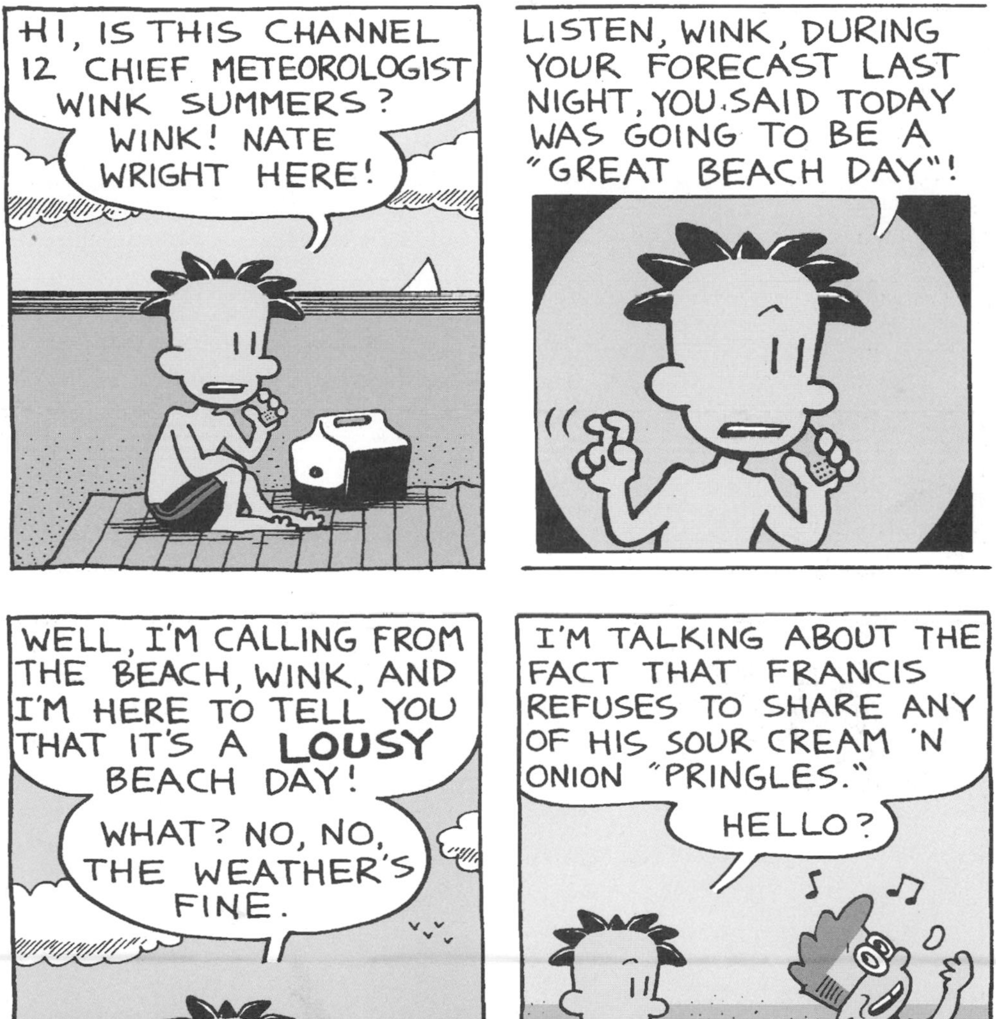
HI, IS THIS CHANNEL 12 CHIEF METEOROLOGIST WINK SUMMERS?
WINK! NATE WRIGHT HERE!
LISTEN, WINK, DURING YOUR FORECAST LAST NIGHT, YOU SAID TODAY WAS GOING TO BE A "GREAT BEACH DAY"!
WELL, I'M CALLING FROM THE BEACH, WINK, AND I'M HERE TO TELL YOU THAT IT'S A **LOUSY** BEACH DAY!
WHAT? NO, NO, THE WEATHER'S FINE.
I'M TALKING ABOUT THE FACT THAT FRANCIS REFUSES TO SHARE ANY OF HIS SOUR CREAM 'N ONION "PRINGLES."
HELLO?
peirce

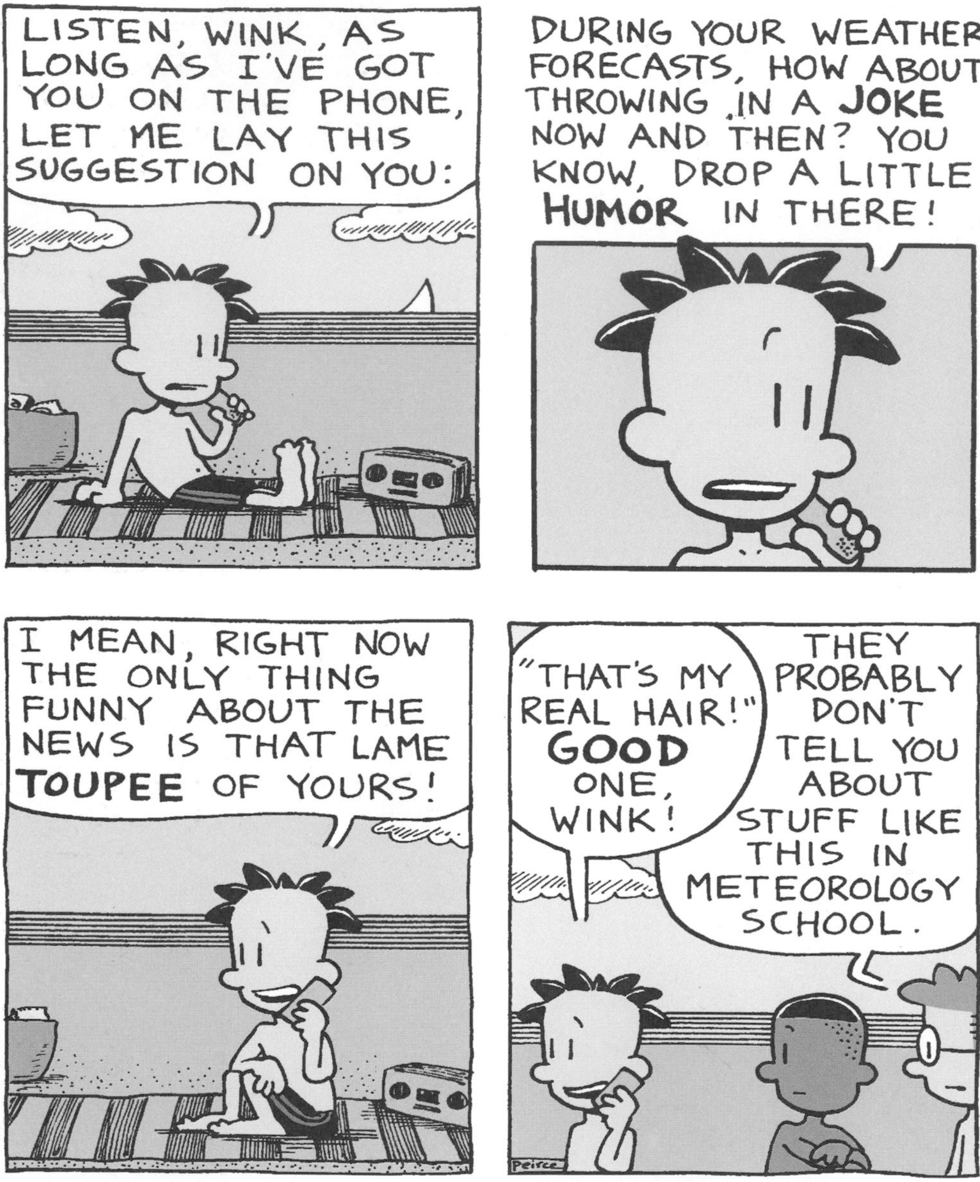
LISTEN, WINK, AS LONG AS I'VE GOT YOU ON THE PHONE, LET ME LAY THIS SUGGESTION ON YOU:
DURING YOUR WEATHER FORECASTS, HOW ABOUT THROWING IN A **JOKE** NOW AND THEN? YOU KNOW, DROP A LITTLE **HUMOR** IN THERE!
I MEAN, RIGHT NOW THE ONLY THING FUNNY ABOUT THE NEWS IS THAT LAME **TOUPEE** OF YOURS!
"THAT'S MY REAL HAIR!" **GOOD** ONE, WINK!
THEY PROBABLY DON'T TELL YOU ABOUT STUFF LIKE THIS IN METEOROLOGY SCHOOL.
Peirce

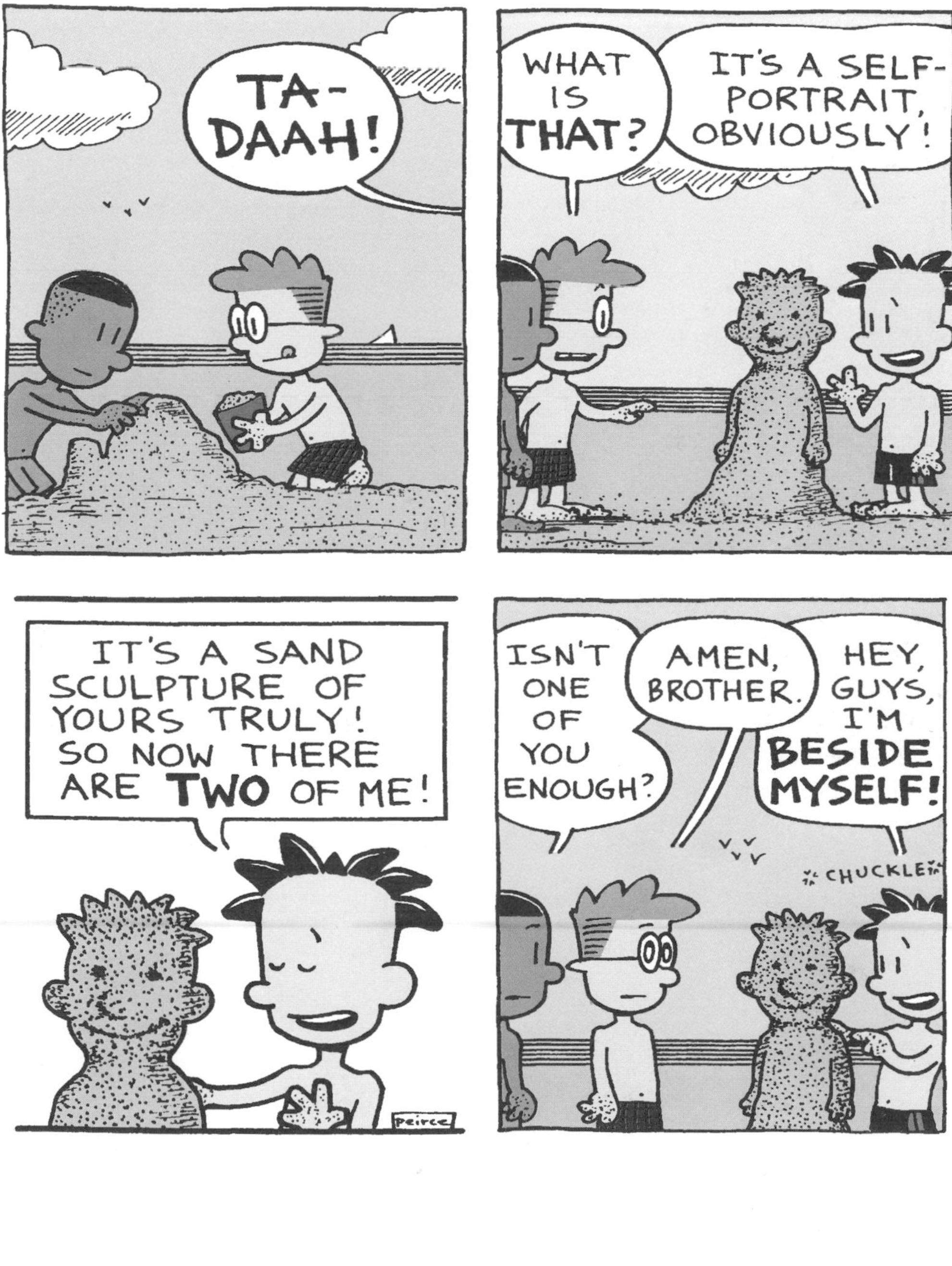
TA-DAAH!
WHAT IS THAT?
IT'S A SELF-PORTRAIT, OBVIOUSLY!
IT'S A SAND SCULPTURE OF YOURS TRULY! SO NOW THERE ARE TWO OF ME!
Peirce
ISN'T ONE OF YOU ENOUGH?
AMEN, BROTHER.
HEY, GUYS, I'M BESIDE MYSELF!
CHUCKLE

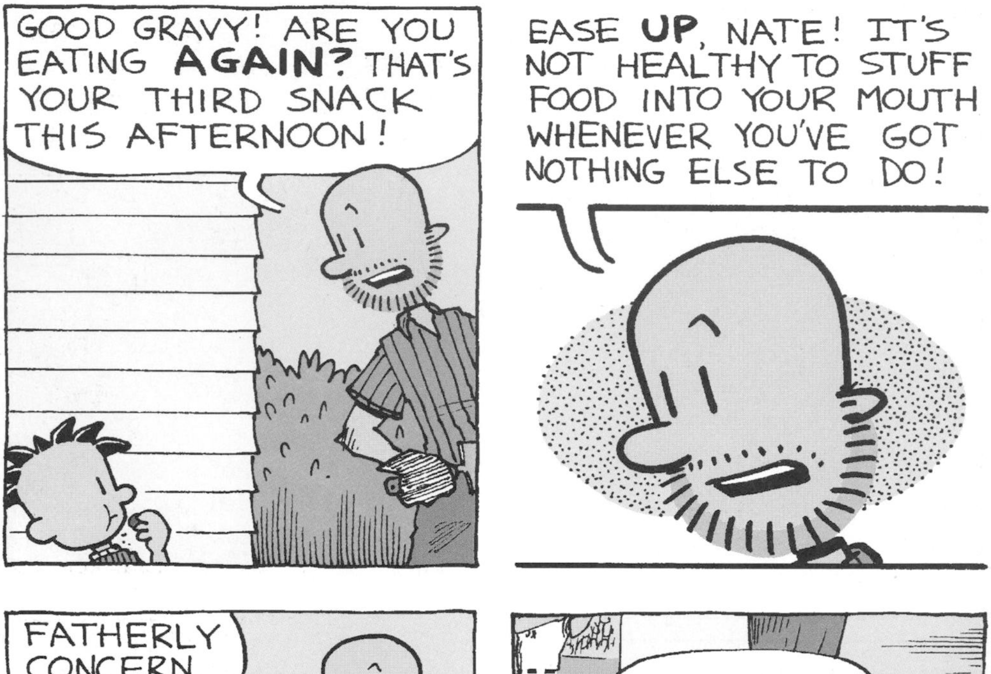
GOOD GRAVY! ARE YOU EATING **AGAIN?** THAT'S YOUR THIRD SNACK THIS AFTERNOON!
EASE **UP**, NATE! IT'S NOT HEALTHY TO STUFF FOOD INTO YOUR MOUTH WHENEVER YOU'VE GOT NOTHING ELSE TO DO!
FATHERLY CONCERN, DAD? OR... **JEALOUSY?**
PAT PAT
JEALOUSY.
PARRA
peirce

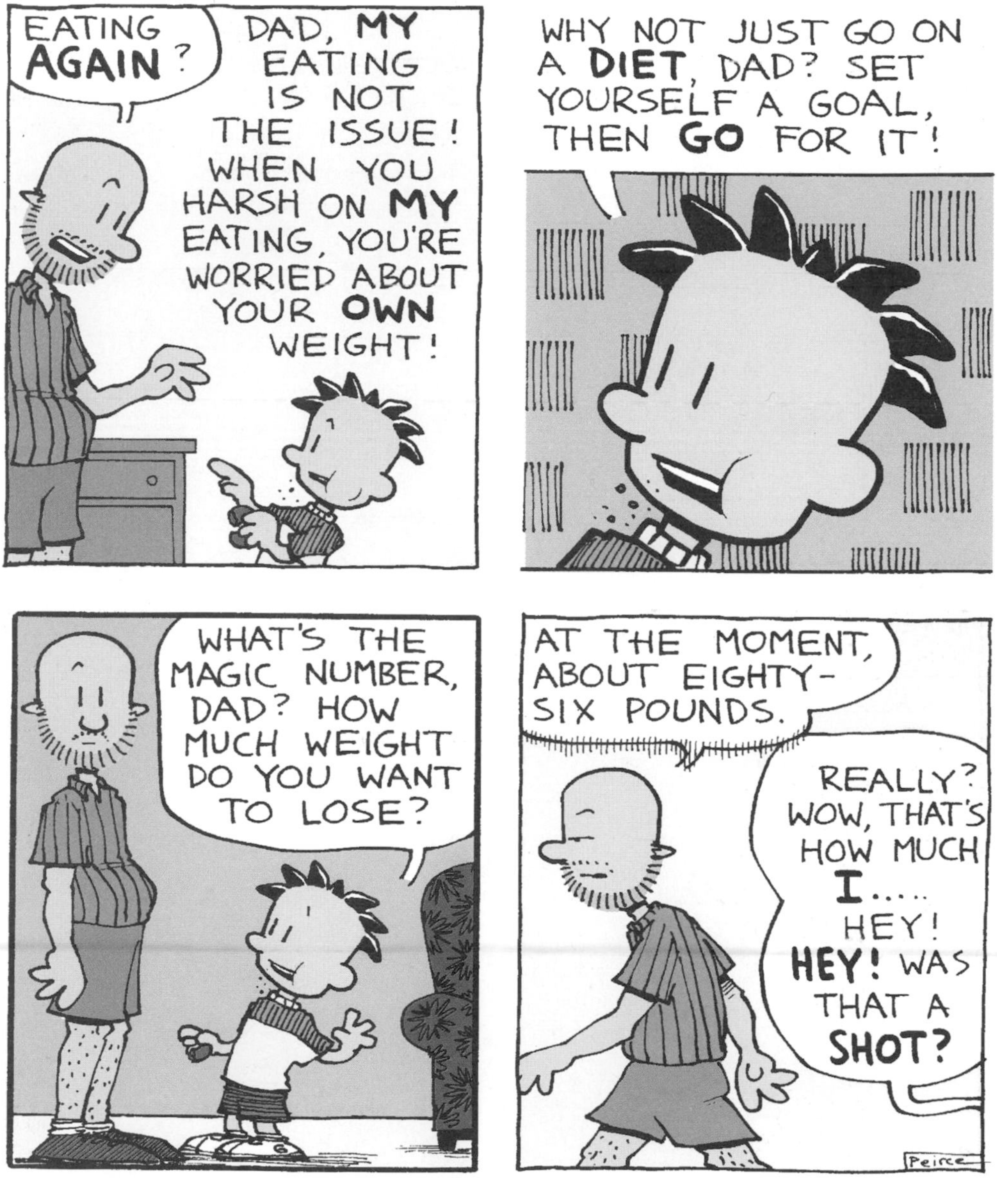
EATING AGAIN?
DAD, MY EATING IS NOT THE ISSUE! WHEN YOU HARSH ON MY EATING, YOU'RE WORRIED ABOUT YOUR OWN WEIGHT!
WHY NOT JUST GO ON A DIET, DAD? SET YOURSELF A GOAL, THEN GO FOR IT!
WHAT'S THE MAGIC NUMBER, DAD? HOW MUCH WEIGHT DO YOU WANT TO LOSE?
AT THE MOMENT, ABOUT EIGHTY-SIX POUNDS.
REALLY? WOW, THAT'S HOW MUCH I..... HEY! HEY! WAS THAT A SHOT?
Peirce

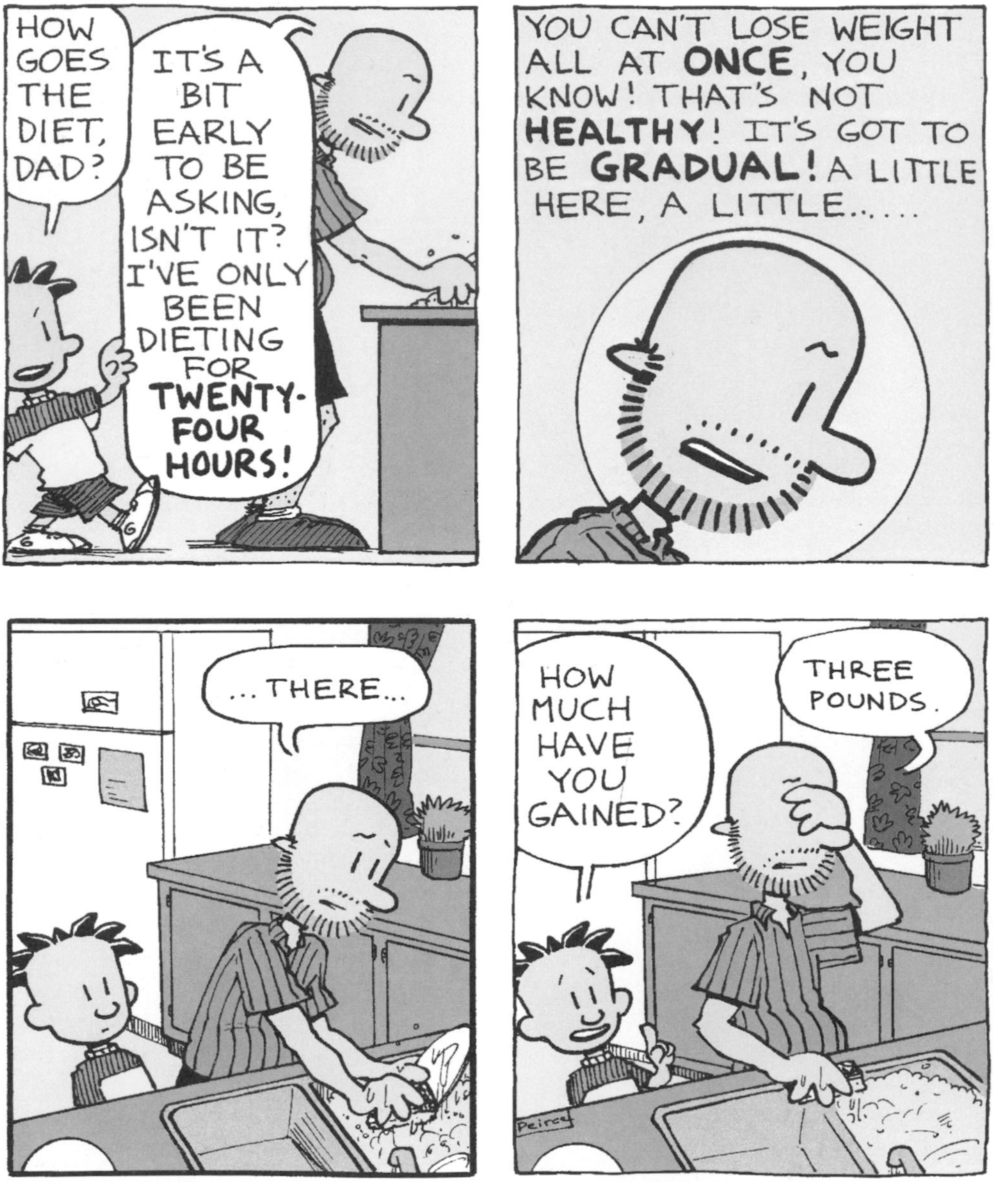
HOW GOES THE DIET, DAD?
IT'S A BIT EARLY TO BE ASKING, ISN'T IT? I'VE ONLY BEEN DIETING FOR TWENTY-FOUR HOURS!
YOU CAN'T LOSE WEIGHT ALL AT ONCE, YOU KNOW! THAT'S NOT HEALTHY! IT'S GOT TO BE GRADUAL! A LITTLE HERE, A LITTLE.....
...THERE...
HOW MUCH HAVE YOU GAINED?
THREE POUNDS.
Peirce

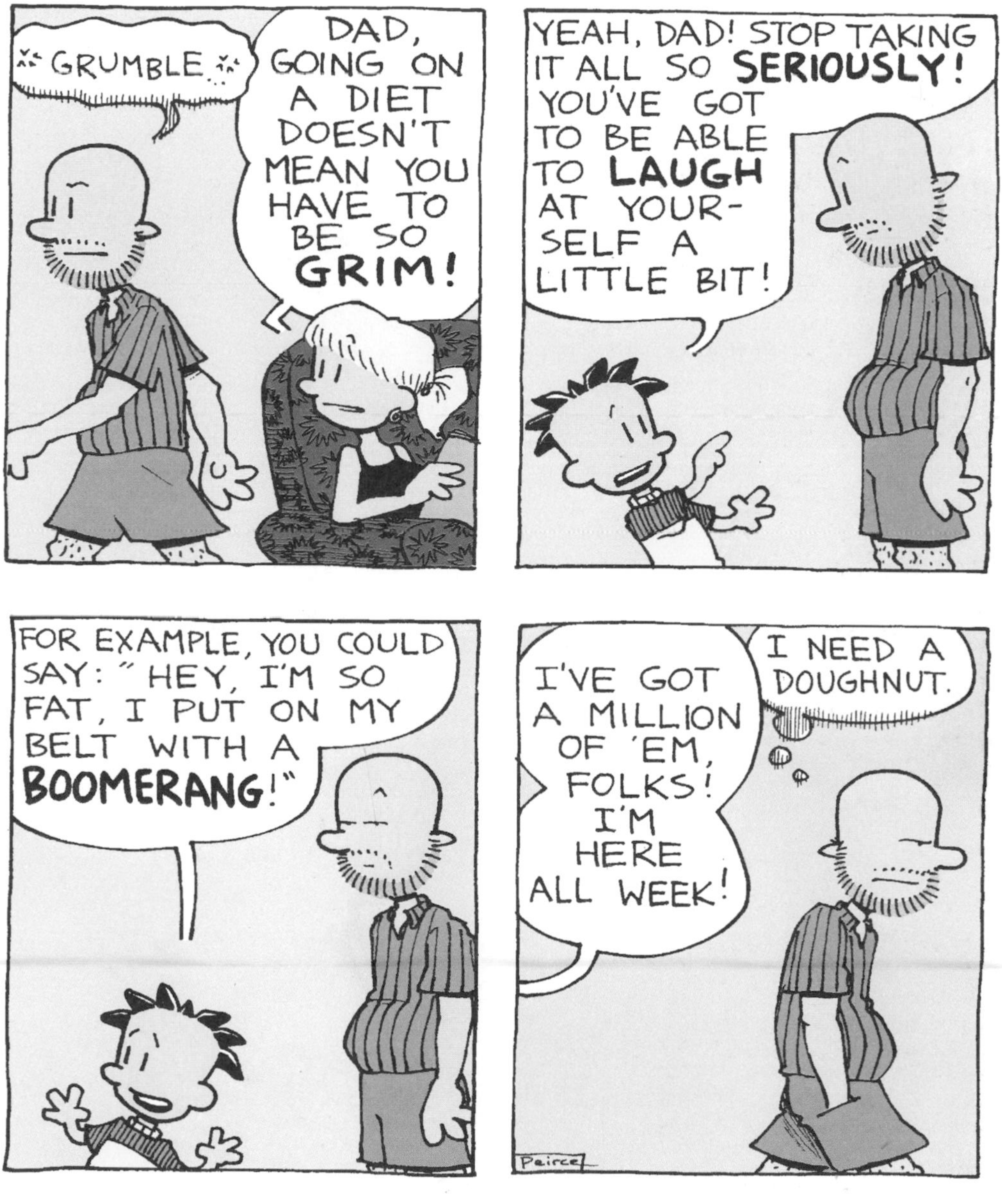
GRUMBLE
DAD, GOING ON A DIET DOESN'T MEAN YOU HAVE TO BE SO GRIM!
YEAH, DAD! STOP TAKING IT ALL SO SERIOUSLY! YOU'VE GOT TO BE ABLE TO LAUGH AT YOURSELF A LITTLE BIT!
FOR EXAMPLE, YOU COULD SAY: "HEY, I'M SO FAT, I PUT ON MY BELT WITH A BOOMERANG!"
I'VE GOT A MILLION OF 'EM, FOLKS! I'M HERE ALL WEEK!
I NEED A DOUGHNUT.
Peirce

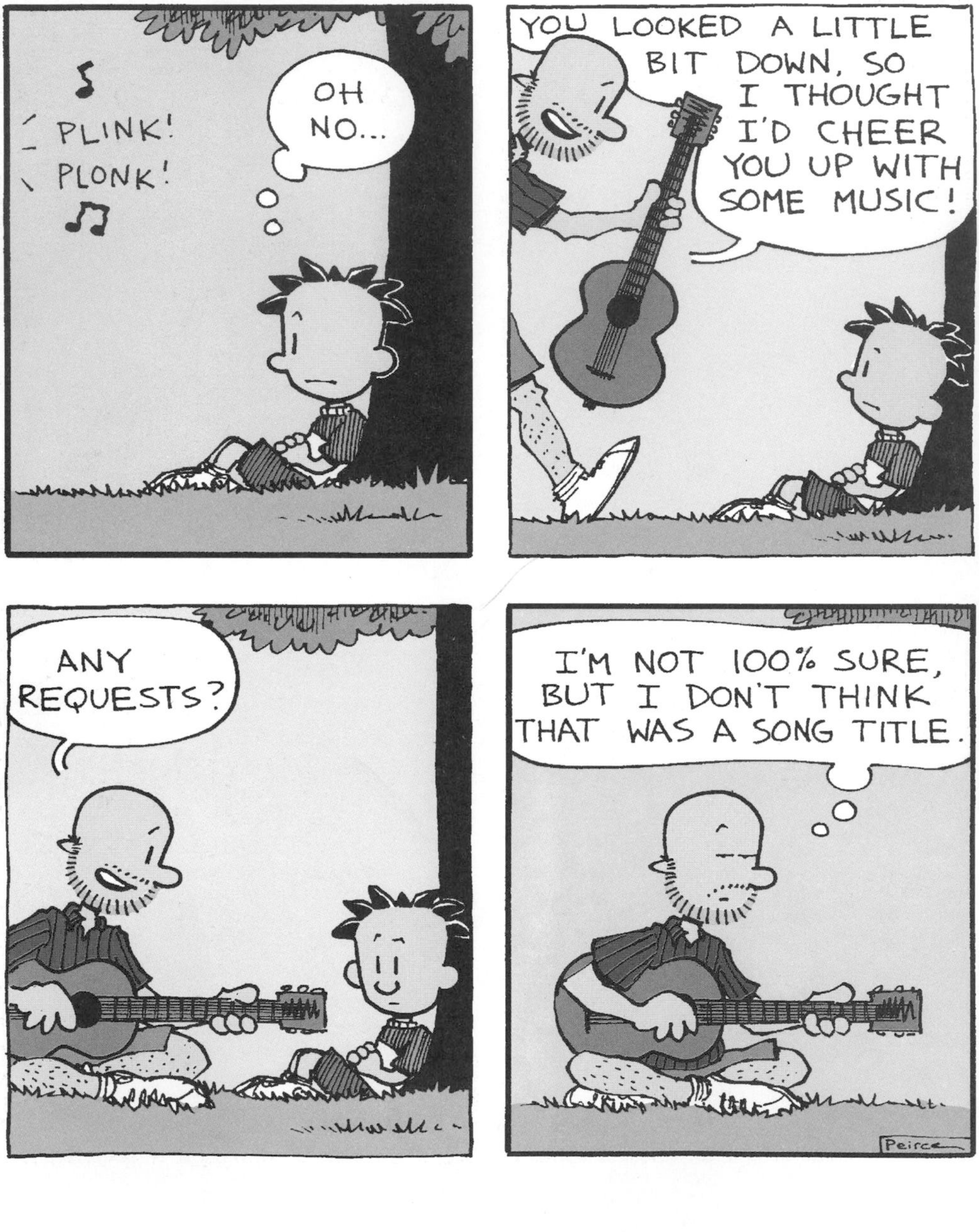
PLINK!
PLONK!
OH NO...
YOU LOOKED A LITTLE BIT DOWN, SO I THOUGHT I'D CHEER YOU UP WITH SOME MUSIC!
ANY REQUESTS?
I'M NOT 100% SURE, BUT I DON'T THINK THAT WAS A SONG TITLE.
Peirce

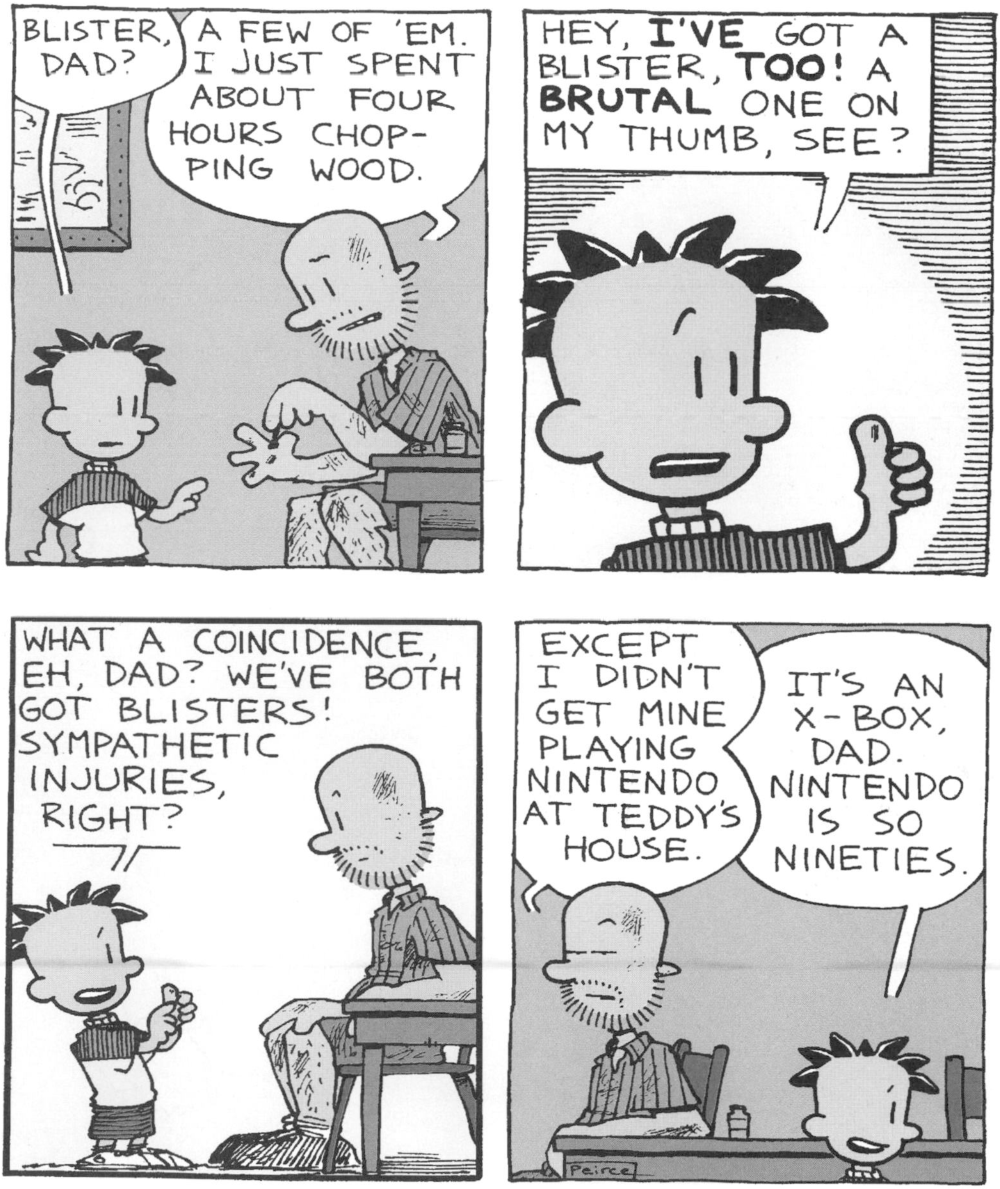
BLISTER, DAD?
A FEW OF 'EM. I JUST SPENT ABOUT FOUR HOURS CHOP-PING WOOD.
HEY, **I'VE** GOT A BLISTER, **TOO**! A **BRUTAL** ONE ON MY THUMB, SEE?
WHAT A COINCIDENCE, EH, DAD? WE'VE BOTH GOT BLISTERS! SYMPATHETIC INJURIES, RIGHT?
EXCEPT I DIDN'T GET MINE PLAYING NINTENDO AT TEDDY'S HOUSE.
IT'S AN X-BOX, DAD. NINTENDO IS SO NINETIES.
Peirce

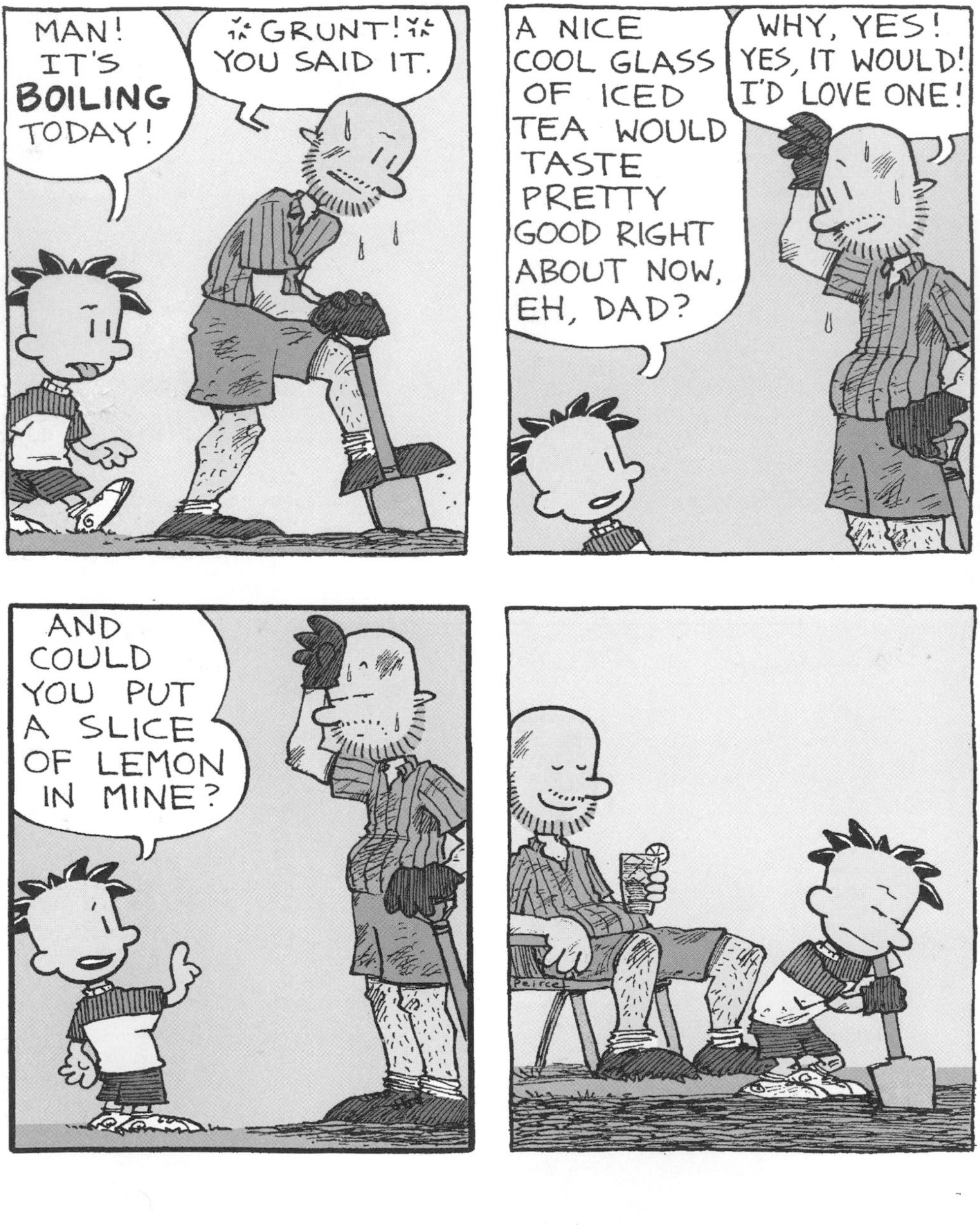
MAN! IT'S **BOILING** TODAY!
GRUNT! YOU SAID IT.
A NICE COOL GLASS OF ICED TEA WOULD TASTE PRETTY GOOD RIGHT ABOUT NOW, EH, DAD?
WHY, YES! YES, IT WOULD! I'D LOVE ONE!
AND COULD YOU PUT A SLICE OF LEMON IN MINE?
Peirce

HERE'S THE REALITY, MR. EUSTIS: I CAN'T KEEP MOWING LAWNS IF MY **HEART'S** NOT IN IT!

THE GREAT ONES KNOW WHEN IT'S TIME TO SAY GOODBYE, AND **THIS** IS **MY** TIME!

I MEAN, IF **NOLAN RYAN** HAD KNOWN WHEN TO HANG UP HIS SPIKES, MAYBE HE'D BE IN THE **HALL OF FAME!**

NOLAN RYAN **IS** IN THE HALL OF FAME.

OKAY, WHATEVER. THE POINT IS, I'M SICK OF MOWING LAWNS.

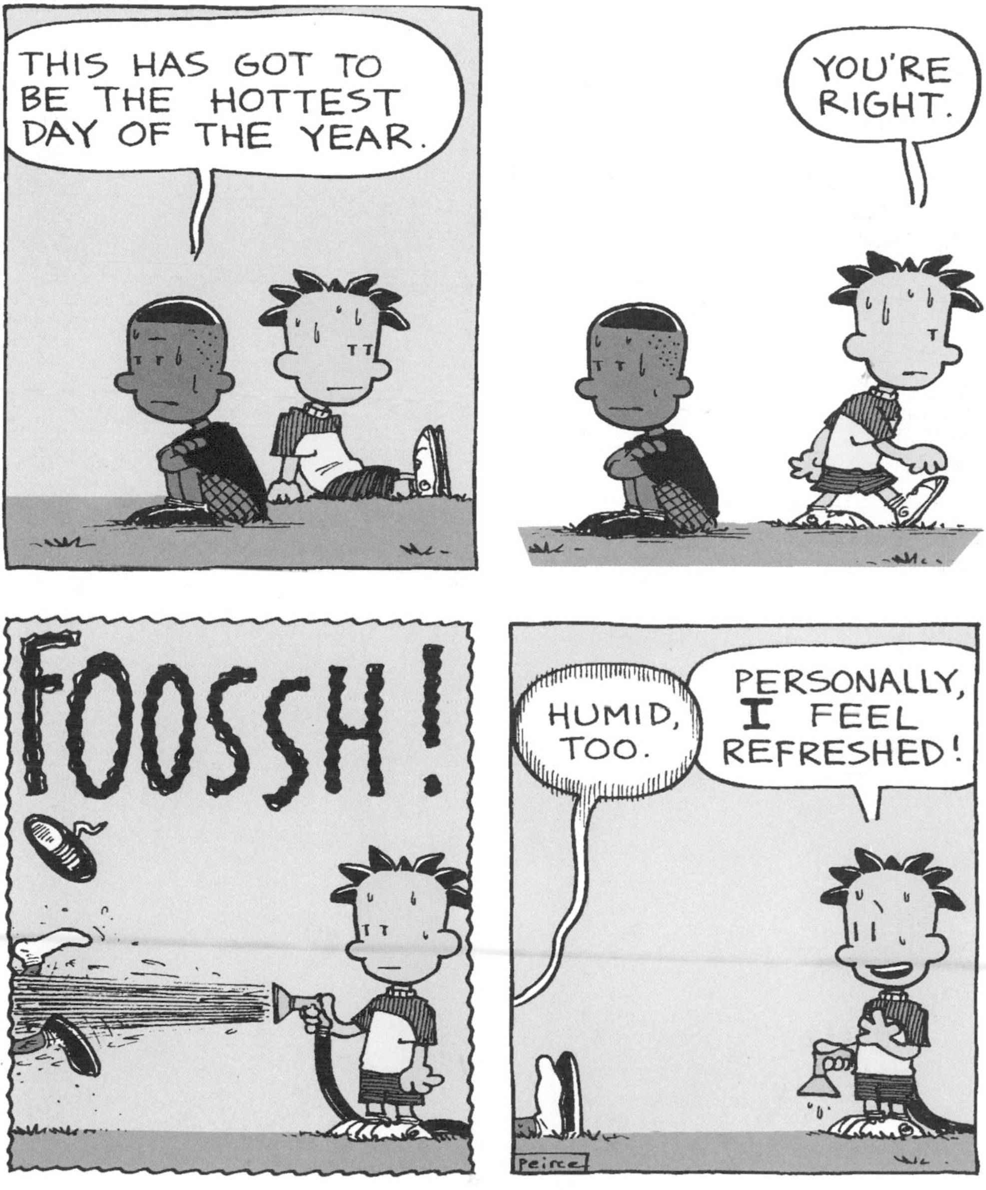
THIS HAS GOT TO BE THE HOTTEST DAY OF THE YEAR.
YOU'RE RIGHT.
FOOSSH!
HUMID, TOO.
PERSONALLY, I FEEL REFRESHED!
Peirce

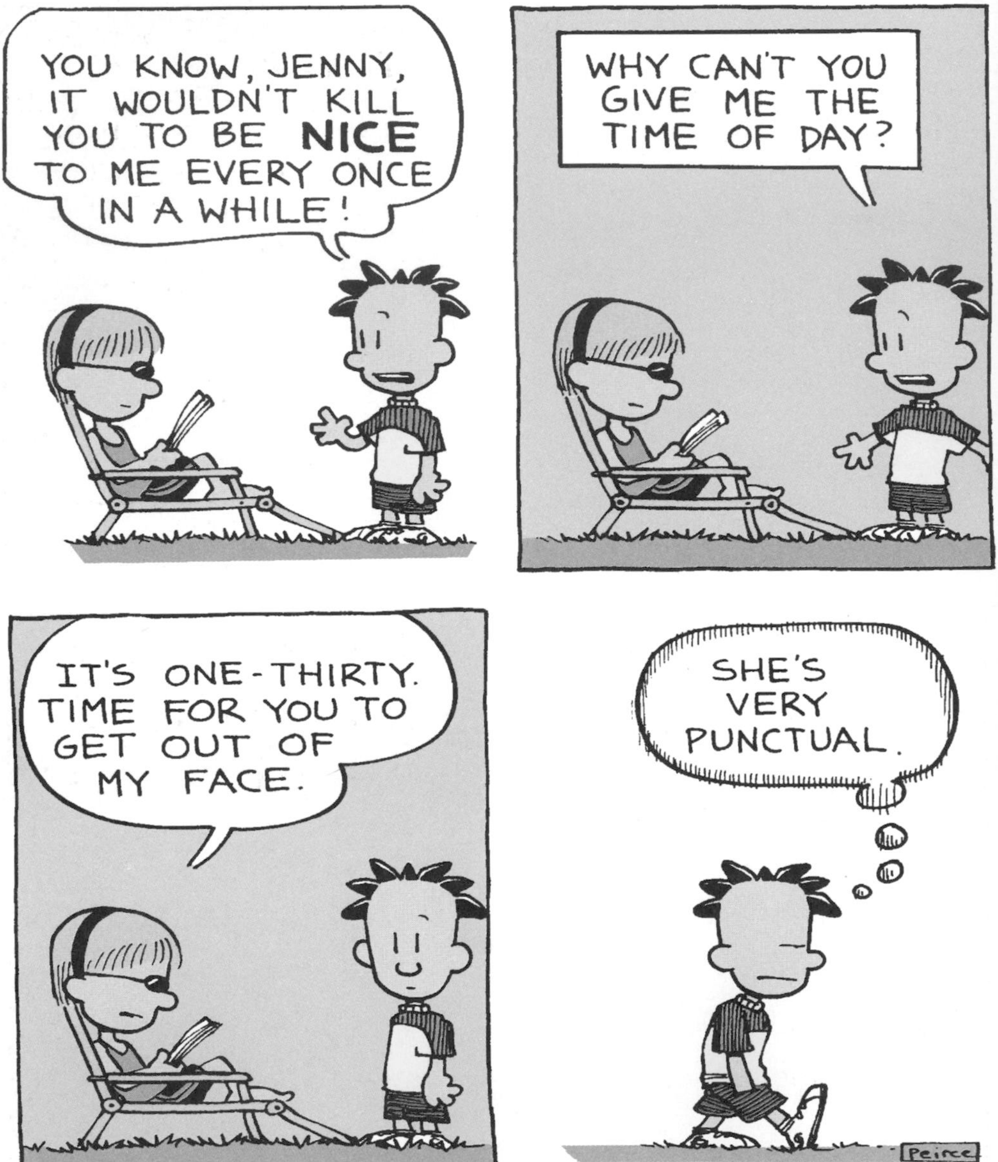
YOU KNOW, JENNY, IT WOULDN'T KILL YOU TO BE **NICE** TO ME EVERY ONCE IN A WHILE!
WHY CAN'T YOU GIVE ME THE TIME OF DAY?
IT'S ONE-THIRTY. TIME FOR YOU TO GET OUT OF MY FACE.
SHE'S VERY PUNCTUAL.
Peirce

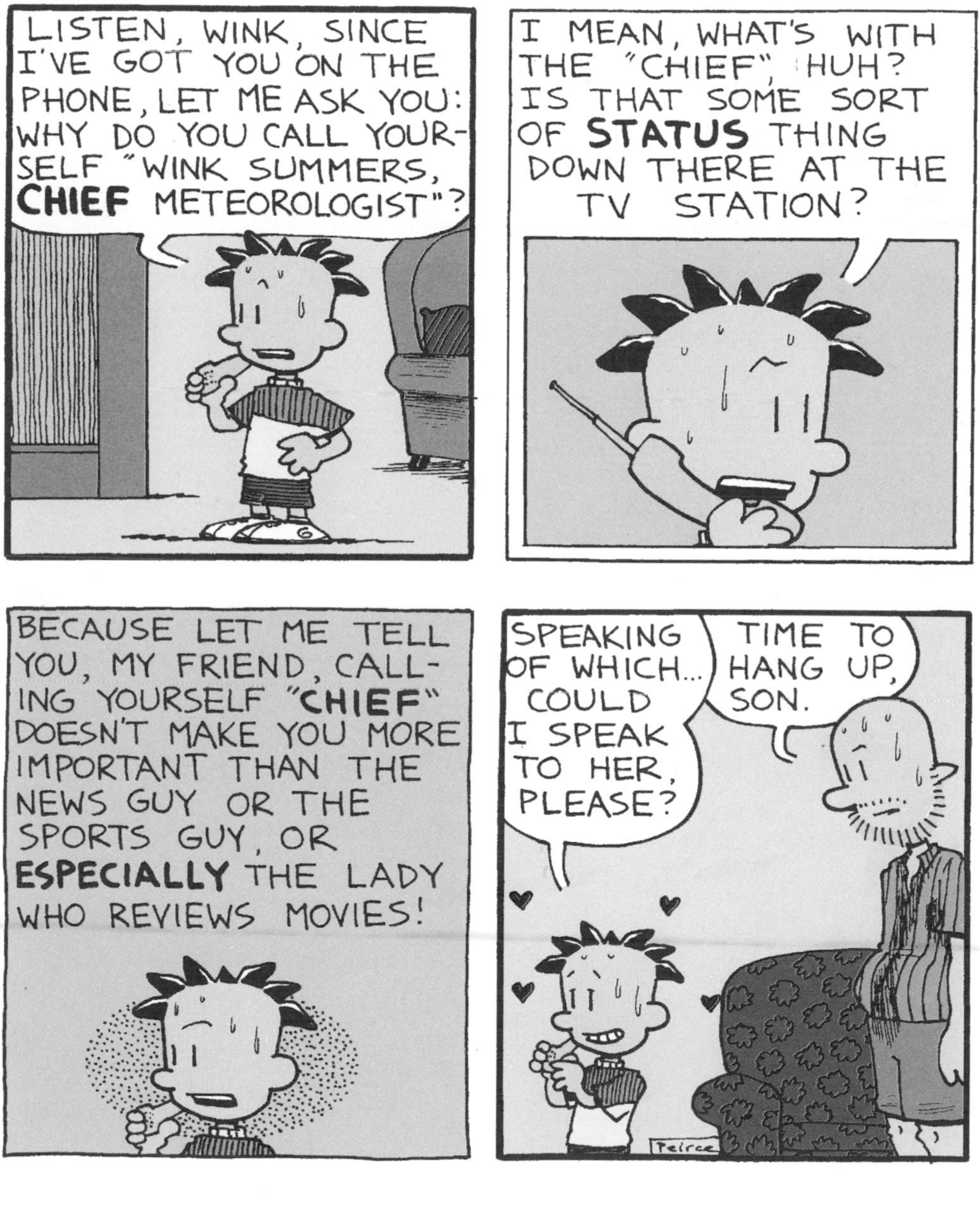
LISTEN, WINK, SINCE I'VE GOT YOU ON THE PHONE, LET ME ASK YOU: WHY DO YOU CALL YOURSELF "WINK SUMMERS, **CHIEF** METEOROLOGIST"?
I MEAN, WHAT'S WITH THE "CHIEF", HUH? IS THAT SOME SORT OF **STATUS** THING DOWN THERE AT THE TV STATION?
BECAUSE LET ME TELL YOU, MY FRIEND, CALLING YOURSELF "**CHIEF**" DOESN'T MAKE YOU MORE IMPORTANT THAN THE NEWS GUY OR THE SPORTS GUY, OR **ESPECIALLY** THE LADY WHO REVIEWS MOVIES!
SPEAKING OF WHICH... COULD I SPEAK TO HER, PLEASE?
TIME TO HANG UP, SON.
Peirce

RRUMMBLE!...

DON'T TRICK-OR-TREAT AT **MY** HOUSE TOMORROW! MY DAD HAS STRUCK AGAIN!

HUH?

HE'S HANDING OUT **SOY NUTS** FOR HALLOWEEN! IT SOUNDS LIKE A **BAD JOKE**, EXCEPT GUESS WHAT: **NOBODY'S** LAUGHING!

HA HA HA HA WA HA HA HA HA HA HA HA

MY FAMILY SHAME CONTINUES.

REMEMBER THAT YEAR HE HANDED OUT **RICE CAKES?**

DO I? MY MOM STILL USES MINE AS A **COASTER!**

HA HA HA

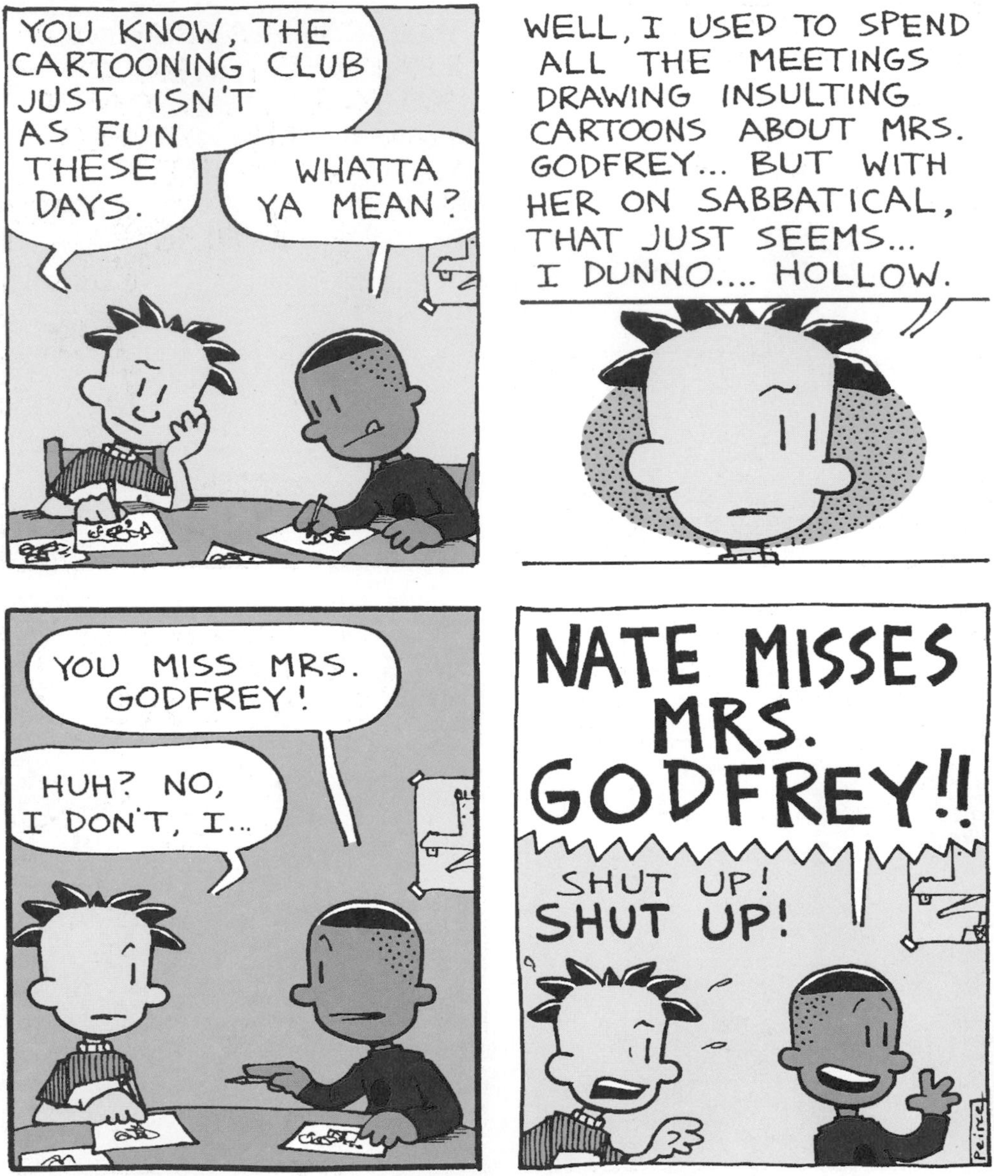
YOU KNOW, THE CARTOONING CLUB JUST ISN'T AS FUN THESE DAYS.
WHATTA YA MEAN?
WELL, I USED TO SPEND ALL THE MEETINGS DRAWING INSULTING CARTOONS ABOUT MRS. GODFREY... BUT WITH HER ON SABBATICAL, THAT JUST SEEMS... I DUNNO.... HOLLOW.
YOU MISS MRS. GODFREY!
HUH? NO, I DON'T, I...
NATE MISSES MRS. GODFREY!!
SHUT UP! SHUT UP!
Peirce

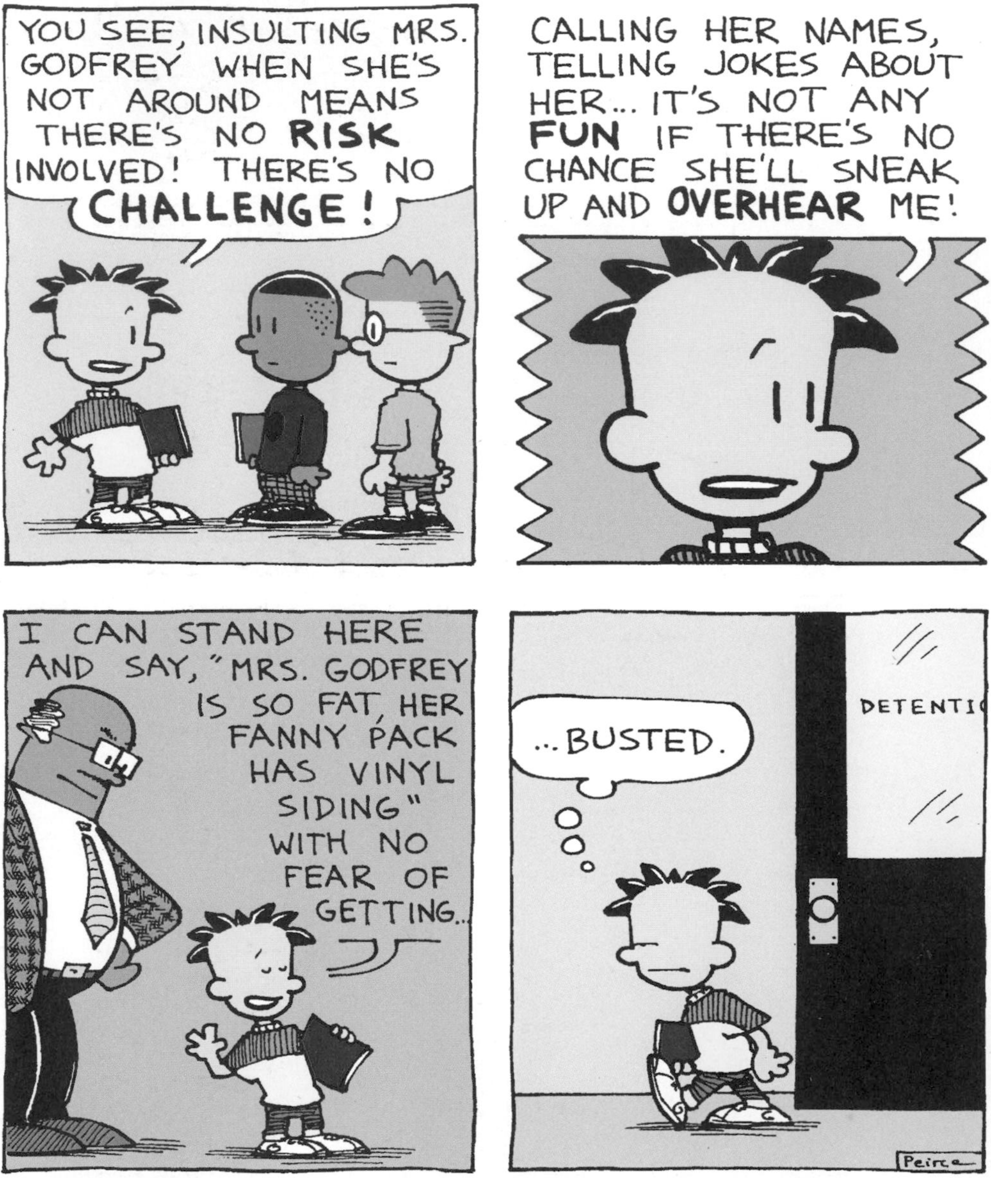
YOU SEE, INSULTING MRS. GODFREY WHEN SHE'S NOT AROUND MEANS THERE'S NO RISK INVOLVED! THERE'S NO CHALLENGE!
CALLING HER NAMES, TELLING JOKES ABOUT HER... IT'S NOT ANY FUN IF THERE'S NO CHANCE SHE'LL SNEAK UP AND OVERHEAR ME!
I CAN STAND HERE AND SAY, "MRS. GODFREY IS SO FAT, HER FANNY PACK HAS VINYL SIDING" WITH NO FEAR OF GETTING...
DETENTI
...BUSTED.
Peirce

Mmmm!... Gravy!!
THANKSGIVING
with the PILGRIMS!
Plymouth, 1627...
hot in here... so take off all your clothes...
Heavens to Betsy!
Howdy, Mayor!
So this is your idea of a Thanksgiving celebration, is it? Cavorting to music? Eating and drinking to excess!? Shaming your families and...
EGAD!
Are those FLAMES I see over there?
That's our bonfire!
Yeah, we found a bunch of logs piled up in the town square!
Those were SUPPOSED to be for Tuesday's WITCH BURNING!
Oopsy.
Have a s'more!

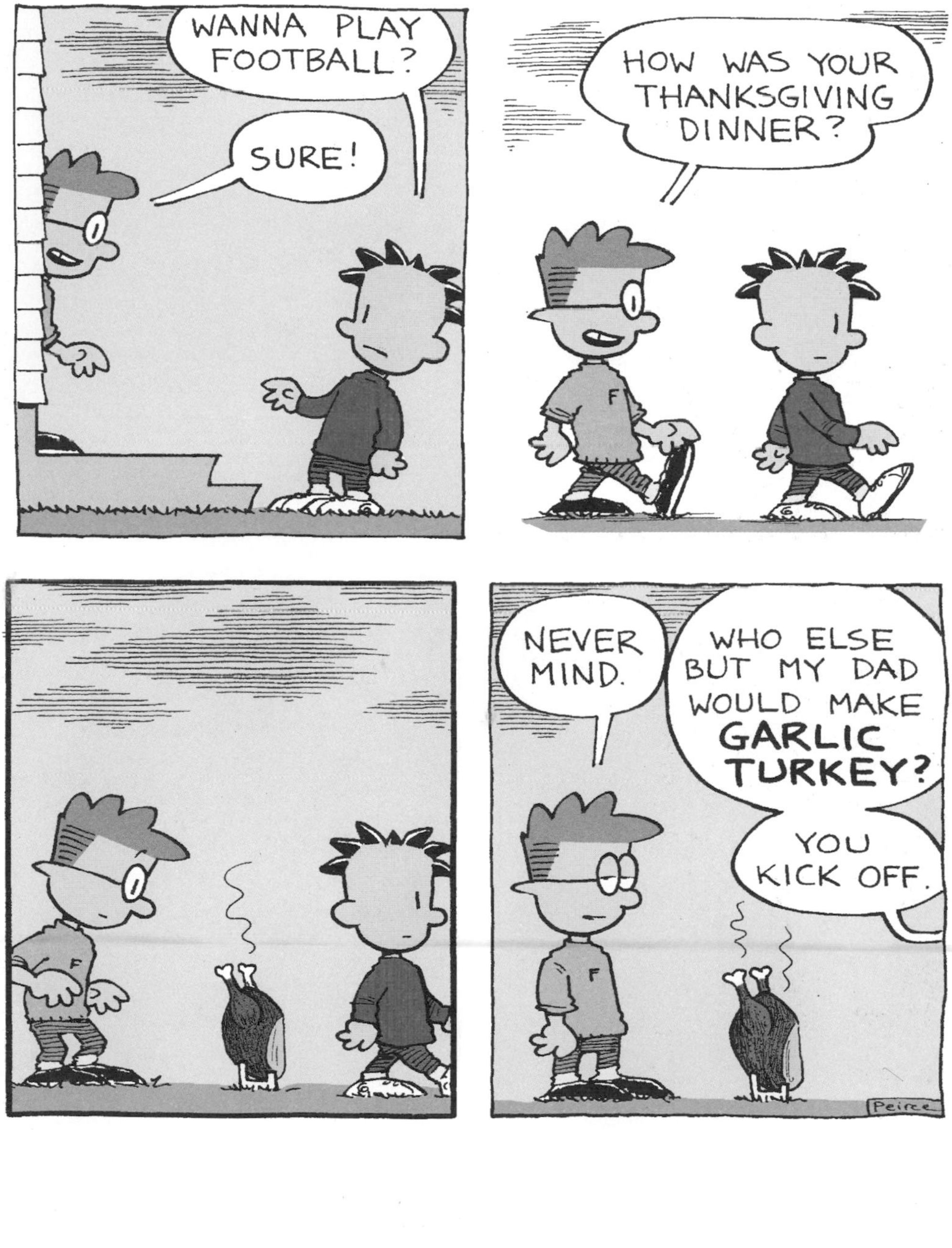
WANNA PLAY FOOTBALL?
SURE!
HOW WAS YOUR THANKSGIVING DINNER?
NEVER MIND.
WHO ELSE BUT MY DAD WOULD MAKE **GARLIC TURKEY?**
YOU KICK OFF.
Peirce

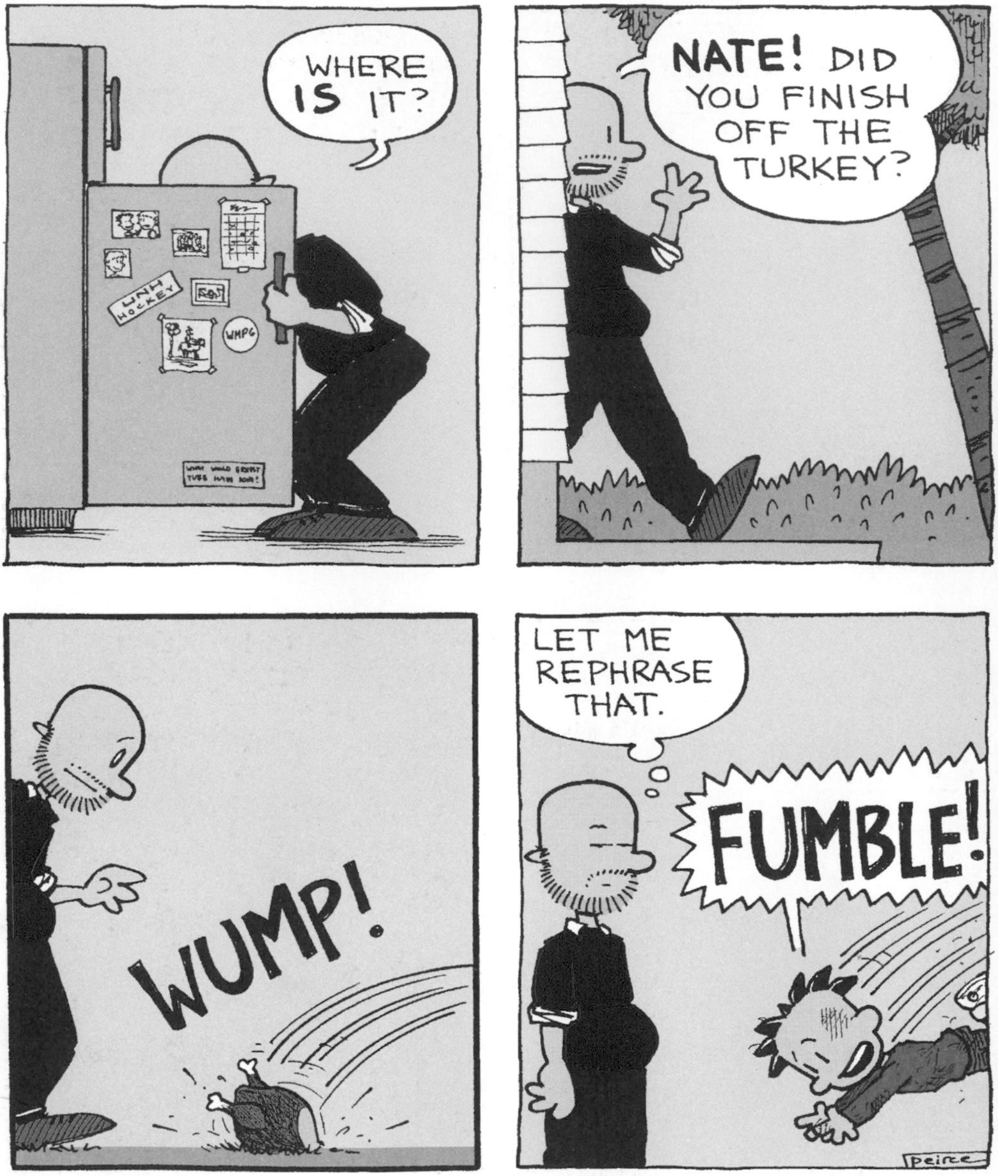
WHERE IS IT?
UNH HOCKEY
WMPG
NATE! DID YOU FINISH OFF THE TURKEY?
WUMP!
LET ME REPHRASE THAT.
FUMBLE!
peirce

YOU SEE, MR. GAFFNEY, THE FACT THAT THE STUDENTS HAVE GIVEN YOU A NICKNAME MEANS YOU'VE **MADE** IT!

MADE IT?

YOU'RE NO LONGER THOUGHT OF AS A **SUB**! SUBS DON'T **GET** NICKNAMES! BUT **REAL** TEACHERS **DO**!

ACCORDING TO WHOM?

ACCORDING TO **ME**! I'M THE COMMISSIONER OF NICKNAMES!

A SELF-APPOINTED POST, I'M GUESSING.

HEEEEY! **Q**-TIP!

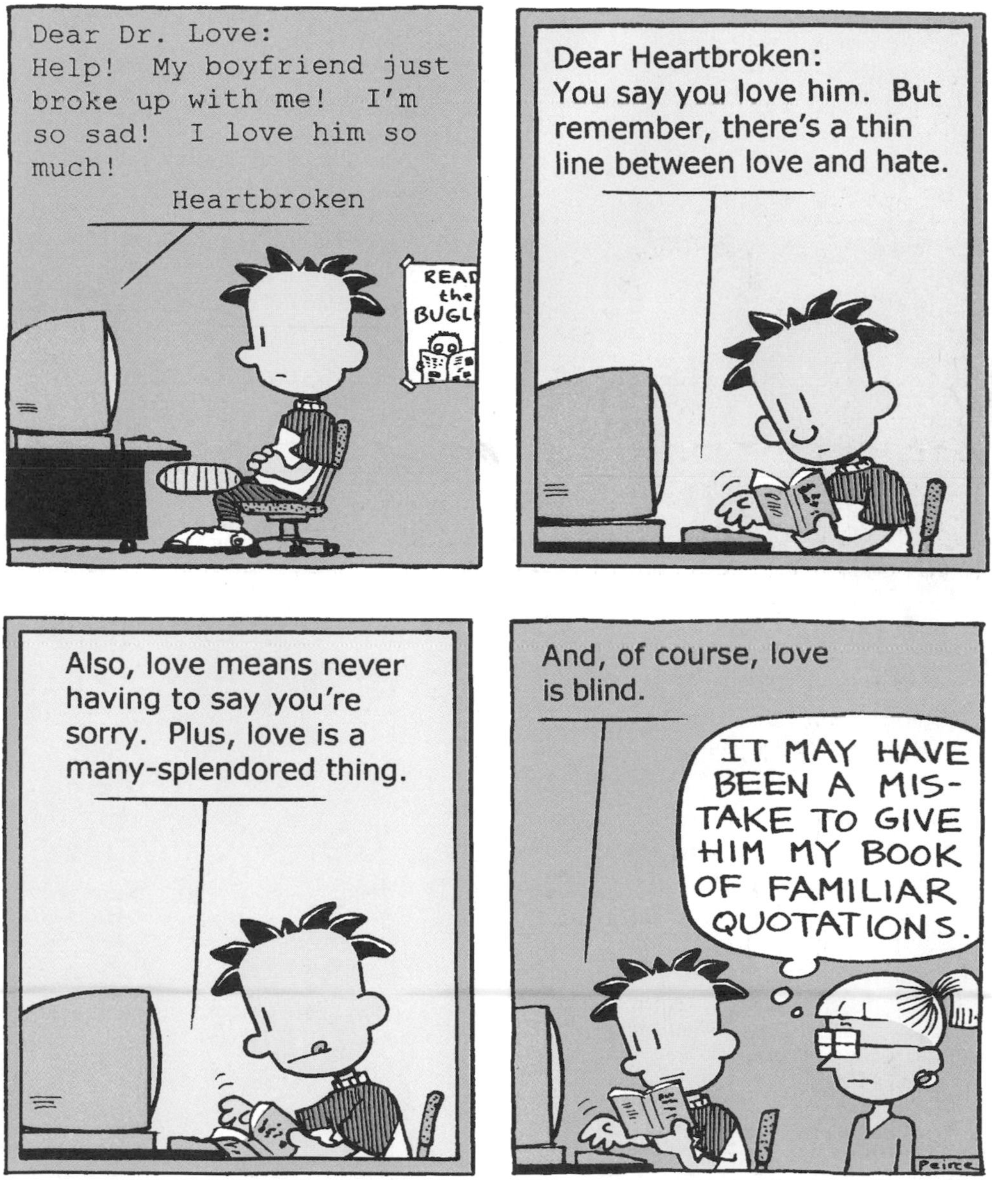
Dear Dr. Love:
Help! My boyfriend just broke up with me! I'm so sad! I love him so much!
Heartbroken
READ the BUGLE
Dear Heartbroken:
You say you love him. But remember, there's a thin line between love and hate.
Also, love means never having to say you're sorry. Plus, love is a many-splendored thing.
And, of course, love is blind.
IT MAY HAVE BEEN A MISTAKE TO GIVE HIM MY BOOK OF FAMILIAR QUOTATIONS.
Peirce

Be sure to check out these other books from

Snoopy: Cowabunga!
ISBN: 978-1-4494-5079-3
$9.99 USA ($11.99 CAN)

AAAA! A FoxTrot Kids Edition
ISBN: 978-1-4494-2305-6
$9.99 USA ($11.99 CAN)

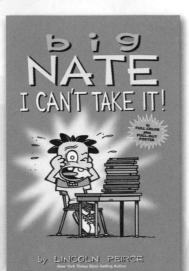

Big Nate: I Can't Take It!
ISBN: 978-1-4494-2937-9
$9.99 USA ($11.99 CAN)

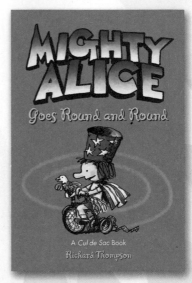

Mighty Alice Goes Round and Round
ISBN: 978-1-4494-3721-3
$9.99 USA ($11.99 CAN)